"What if I give you what you wish?" He lowered his voice to silky softness. "Will you give me a gift in turn?"

"I've given you a gift. Your friend is alive. Isn't that enough for you?"

"I don't know the meaning of enough. The prize just over the horizon is always the sweetest."

"So you reach out and take it," she said flatly.

"Or barter for it. I prefer the latter. It suits my merchant's soul. I suppose you've been told that I'm more trader than knight?"

"No, I've heard you were the son of a king and capable of being anything you want to be."

"Which obviously did not impress you."

"Why should it? It does not matter their station, men are all the same."

He smiled. "Certainly in some aspects. You didn't answer. Will you barter with me?"

"I have nothing with which to barter."

"You're a woman. A woman always has great bartering power."

BOOKS BY IRIS JOHANSEN

Midnight Warrior

Iris Johansen

Bantam Books

New York   Toronto
London   Sydney   Auckland

MIDNIGHT WARRIOR
A Bantam Book

PUBLISHING HISTORY
Bantam mass market edition published August 1994
Bantam reissue / July 2008

Published by Bantam Dell
A Division of Random House, Inc.
New York, New York

This is a work of fiction. Names, characters, places, and incidents
either are the product of the author's imagination or are used
fictitiously. Any resemblance to actual persons, living or dead, events,
or locales is entirely coincidental.

Bantam Books and the rooster colophon are registered
trademarks of Random House, Inc.

ISBN 978-0-553-59216-0

Printed in the United States of America
www.bantamdell.com

OPM   10 9 8 7 6 5 4 3 2 1

Librarians are the unsung partners of all writers. This book is dedicated to librarians everywhere but most particularly to that wonderful research maven, Mary Wallace Day.

One

THE LIGHT BLAZED across the dark heavens like a banner unfurled for battle.

Brynn stared up at the midnight sky in fascination and delight. It was like watching a mysterious flower blossom in the shadowy depths of the forest. She had prayed it would still be there tonight.

"Did you do it?"

She stiffened but did not turn around. She had come to this tiny room in the back of the stable hoping to steal this time for herself, but she should have known she would not be permitted to enjoy this wonder alone. At least, it was only Delmas. Perhaps she could rid herself of him quickly. "Did I do what? I don't know what you mean."

She heard his steps behind her and then felt his heavy hand on her shoulder. She felt a surge of revulsion but didn't move.

"Look at me."

She reluctantly turned her back on the glory in the heavens and gazed boldly at him.

He immediately looked away as he usually did when she directly confronted him. "Be quick, I'm weary and would seek my bed," she said.

"Not too weary to do *that*," he snarled as he gestured at the sky. "I want it stopped. Do you hear? I want it gone."

She stared at him in astonishment. "I beg your pardon?"

"Don't pretend innocence." His eyes glittered wildly in the moonlight. "It's your doing. I know it. You brought it to destroy me so that you could return to your precious Gwynthal."

She wanted to laugh She had not dreamed even Delmas could believe something so outrageous. "I waved my hand and a comet streaked through the sky? Don't be foolish."

Pain streaked through her jaw as his palm made contact.

"Send it away!"

She shook her head to clear it of pain and darkness. It had been a long time since Delmas had struck her, and she cursed herself for miscalculating the depth of his fear and panic. She could not afford to make such mistakes. He might offer her little protection, but it was all she had in this foreign land. "I didn't bring the comet."

"I watched your face when you saw it last night. Everyone else in the manor was filled with fear but you . . . you were triumphant."

He had mistaken her wonder for triumph. She supposed she should have pretended to share their fear, but it had not occurred to her. In truth, she had been amazed at their terror. Miracles occurred every day and this was only another. Wasn't a rainbow a miracle? Why did they not marvel at the changing seasons? And surely the birth of a child was the most glorious of mysteries. "You were mistaken. I only—"

He struck her again, harder. "I want it gone from here."

She reached out and grasped the wall to keep herself upright as the room swam around her. She had given up trying to convince Delmas she had no magical powers and now used his fear and superstition to protect herself. The ploy had worked very well for the past three years, but now his belief was a danger in itself. She must find a way to soothe his fear. "All right. I did it."

Satisfaction lit his face. "I knew it. Now send it away."

"I cannot send it away." She took a hurried step back to avoid the blow she knew would come. "Not at once. The magic is too great and must run its course, but I will make sure it harms no one."

He frowned uncertainly.

"It is all I can do," she said firmly.

"It will go away?"

"Yes." She breathed a prayer she was not lying.

"When?"

"Soon." She added quickly, "It takes time to break a spell as strong as this one." She closed the shutters of the window to block out the sky from him. "Now may I go to my bed?"

"No." He gazed at the shutters and then evidently decided to accept the partial victory. "Lady Adwen needs you. She woke in great distress and sent her servant to rouse me. It was then I discovered you had left your bed."

"Why did you not tell me at once?" She moved quickly toward the door. "Have you summoned Lord Richard?"

"He knows. He was occupied." Delmas followed her into the hall. "He said to call you and he would be there shortly."

Occupied with his latest leman, Joan of Danworth, no doubt, Brynn thought bitterly. Adwen could die and he would not care. Indeed, she was sure he would prefer it. He had not been pleased when Lord Kells, Adwen's father, had sent Brynn to Redfern to care for his daughter. A wife unable to bear children was an intolerable inconvenience to a man as hungry for power as Lord Richard. To be free of that wife and retain her fat dowry would be very tempting. God knows, it would not take much to rid himself of such a frail burden: a little neglect, a window left open to induce a chill . . .

Well, she would not let him do it, she thought fiercely. Adwen would live. Brynn would not let her die.

"You wouldn't have to create such havoc if you'd be sensible," Delmas said as he hurried after her. "Give me your promise to lead me to the treasure, and I'll return you to Gwynthal."

She did not look at him. "There is no treasure."

"You lie. I *want* it, Brynn. Give it to me."

Demand and avarice. Dear heaven, how sickened she was of it all. At times she had been tempted to tell him what he wanted to know just to gain peace. But he would have wanted more and then more until he had it all, and she would never let anyone have Gwynthal. "There is no treasure."

"I could buy my freedom. I could buy all of England. You hate it here. Why won't you—"

"There is no treasure."

His hand reached out and closed on her upper arm, biting into the flesh. "Bitch." His voice was laden with frustration and anger. "Someday I'll choke it out of you."

The threat didn't frighten her. He had tried torture in those first few weeks after they were wed, before she had learned how to protect herself. "I cannot tell you what I don't know. Be satisfied with what I do bring you." She paused outside Adwen's chamber door. "It's more than what you had when you married me."

"But not enough. Not nearly enough." He released her and gazed at the door with uneasiness. "Do you need me?"

He was hoping she would say no, she realized contemptuously. He had witnessed his parents perish from a fever within a few days of each other and was deathly afraid of sickness. At these times he was almost as much afraid of Brynn's healing skills as he was of losing his chance to become a free man. He was sure she used not her herbs or the knowledge her mother had taught her, but some magical way of banishing the demons who stole life. She should be grateful, she thought wearily; because of his belief she had been able to retain possession of her soul, if not her body. "I don't know. Stay close. I'll summon you if I need anything."

Adwen's servant, Alice, was standing by the large, curtained bed and looked up with a sigh of relief as she saw Brynn. "She's very bad."

"Her stomach?" The day before, Adwen had been violently ill and unable to keep anything down. Brynn strode over to the bed. Adwen's eyes were closed and she appeared asleep.

Alice shook her head. "I don't think so. She just suddenly woke and started to shake and weep."

Adwen opened her eyes. "Brynn?" she whispered. She groped wildly for Brynn's hand. "Midnight . . . he's coming."

"Shh . . ." She quickly took Adwen's hand in both of hers and pressed it reassuringly. "What's wrong? Do you have pain?"

Adwen shook her head. "I saw him. He's coming."

Brynn felt a chill. Who was coming? Death? She had cared for others trembling on the verge of the other side who had claimed to see visions that foretold their time. It was almost impossible to bring them back after they had gone through that experience. "You've been dreaming."

"No."

"Yes," she said firmly. "And it's no wonder you're shaking. It's cold in this room. Why is the window open, Alice?"

Alice's blue eyes widened in alarm, but she did not answer.

"Richard was here earlier and said the room was overheated and I should have more air," Adwen said wearily. "He's always so warm."

A *window left open* . . .

Brynn hid the flare of anger that exploded through her as she recalled that only moments before she had thought how easy it would be to destroy Adwen. "Well, Lord Richard isn't here now." She strode over to the window and closed the shutters. "And I'm sure he didn't realize it would turn this chill."

"Perhaps not," Adwen said. "But he doesn't like to be disobeyed. Perhaps you should—"

"They stay closed," Brynn said flatly. She took the candlestick from the table beside the window and brought it closer to the bed. Adwen's face appeared pale and streaked with tears, but that was not unusual. Brynn would have been more worried if she had been flushed with fever.

She was struck anew by the youthful fragility of the woman. Slight and fine-boned with long black hair, Adwen looked a mere child. She was scarcely more than that, Brynn thought angrily. Richard of Redfern had taken her to wife when she was only thirteen and had promptly set about trying to take from her what he most desired. Adwen had lost four children before she came to term and had spent almost the entire past five years in this room guarding the little health she had remaining so that it could be expended in giving her husband a child.

"Why are you frowning?" Adwen whispered. "Are you angry with me?"

Brynn smiled. "Of course not." Gentle Adwen always feared disapproval. "Why should I be angry with you?"

"It was not I who sent for you. I know you are tired

from tending me for the past two nights. You know I would not have disturbed you—"

"It is no disturbance. Have you forgotten my husband was slave to Lord Kells before he was given to your husband? Your father sent us to Redfern to serve you, my lady."

"You know I do not look upon you as a servant. You *are* angry with me."

She tried to restrain her impatience. "I told you I was not angry. I want to be here. Now, what is wrong?"

Adwen smiled wistfully. "You're so strong. You're never afraid, are you? You must think me very foolish."

"No." She nodded for Alice to leave. She wasn't sure she trusted the woman and was never comfortable in her presence. Alice appeared fond of Adwen, but it was common knowledge at the manor that the maid occupied Lord Richard's bed on occasion. Brynn knew she should not fault her for this, when it was entirely possible the woman had no choice. Lord Richard was master here and he slept with any servant who took his fancy. Thank God, his fear of Lord Kells's displeasure had kept him from looking in her own direction. Adwen's father would not have been pleased if his healer had been used for a purpose other than the one she had been sent to perform.

When the door closed behind Alice, Brynn sat down on the bed. "It's not foolish to be afraid, only to hold it close and let it smother you. Tell me and it will go away."

"It is—you're hurt!" Adwen's concerned gaze was on Brynn's cheek. "You have a bruise."

"It is nothing."

"Someone struck you," Adwen whispered. "Your husband?"

Brynn shrugged. "I displeased him."

"You should be more careful. A woman is so helpless . . ."

"She does not have to be."

"Please, do not be so bold," Adwen pleaded earnestly. "I hate to be selfish, but I do not think I could bear life without you." She forced a smile. "I suppose I am very fortunate. Richard has never struck me, even though I have failed him."

Anger flared again. Oh, no, Lord Richard had never struck Adwen. He had only used her frail body as a vessel for his lust and barely let her rise from the childbed before trying to get her with child again. He had broken her health and her spirit and robbed her of all joy. "You have not failed him. There's time yet for you to bear children."

Adwen shook her head. "I am too tired. Sometimes I think I'm too tired to draw another breath." She was silent a moment and then said, "Will you blow out the candle? I want to tell you about my dream, but I don't want to see you laugh at my foolishness."

Brynn blew out the candle and then took Adwen's hands again. "Are you warm enough? Should I get you another cover?"

"No." Adwen nestled deeper under the blanket. "Did you see the shooting star tonight?"

"It's not a shooting star. The good monks call it a comet."

"Alice helped me to the window and I saw it. Was it not wondrous?"

"Yes."

"Alice was frightened. She said it was an omen of bad fortune."

"Alice is very stupid."

"I don't think it is bad fortune. I believe it means that my wish for a child will come true. Is it terribly vain of me to believe that God could be so concerned with my needs?"

Brynn swallowed to ease the aching tightness in her throat. "No, you are not vain." She paused. "But did you ever consider that perhaps God did not mean you to have a babe?"

"Of course not, it is my duty to give my lord an heir."

She would very likely die trying to perform her duty, Brynn thought with exasperation. There was something very wrong with this world that valued one life over another.

"Perhaps if you gave Delmas a child he would not treat you so cruelly," Adwen said.

"A child is not what my husband wishes of me."

"It is what all men want of women."

It was true. Even Delmas would be puffed up with pride if he got her with child. She shuddered at the thought. A child would tie her to Delmas as those forced vows had never done. After that first hideous week in his bed she had concocted a scheme to fool him into believing her healing powers would be lessened by copulation, but there was always the possibility Delmas might overcome this fear.

No, she would not think of it. She would have no child and someday she would escape Delmas and go back to Gwynthal, where she belonged. She would lose herself in the forest and he would never, never find her.

"What else does he want of you?"

"What?" She had lost track of the conversation. She wrenched herself back from those memories of the cool, green forests of home.

"You said Delmas wants something else of you."

"Oh. Lord Kells has promised Delmas he will make him a free man if you are made well again."

"And what of you?"

"I am his wife. There is no freedom for me." Unless she took it. Unless she ran away from this hated place.

"It does not seem just. You are only one and twenty and he is old and ugly."

"Not so old." She did not know Delmas's exact age.

His beard was streaked with gray but his powerful body was still firm. She supposed he would appear old and ugly to Adwen. Lord Richard was a young man, golden of hair and fair and virile as a god from Olympus. In Brynn's eyes it seemed terrible for evil to be so winsomely cloaked. Delmas and Lord Richard were both ambitious, ruthless men, but she would far more deal with Delmas, who had no pleasant mask to hide his inner ugliness.

"Could your father not find a younger man for you?"

"You don't understand." She had no intention of explaining. Adwen had enough troubles of her own and needed none of Brynn's burdens.

"Brynn?"

Her hand tightened around Adwen's. "Go to sleep, my lady."

"I've told you not to call me that. We are friends."

"Lord Richard would not approve of such a friendship."

She was silent a moment. "He need not know. We could keep it a secret, couldn't we? Say we are friends."

Brynn was silent. She knew Adwen must need her friendship desperately to disobey her husband even in secret, but she did not want to say the words Adwen desired of her. She had tried to push Adwen away, to keep her at a distance. Friendship with the girl would keep her as much a prisoner at Redfern as Adwen.

"I ask too much," Adwen whispered. "Why should you wish to be friends with me? I am only a burden to you."

Pity rushed over Brynn in an inevitable tide. "Nonsense. We are friends . . . Adwen. Now will you go to sleep?"

"What if the dream comes again?"

She reached out and stroked Adwen's hair. "Did it frighten you so?"

"Not at first. I was happy to see him."

"Who?"

"The warrior. He was on horseback riding up the hill. It was very dark and close to midnight."

"How could you know the hour?"

"I just . . . knew. I could see the magic star behind him."

"Comet."

"He was in mail armor that glittered in the moonlight. I could not see his face, but I was sure he wouldn't hurt me. But I was wrong, I saw Redfern burning. . . ."

Brynn breathed a sign of relief as she realized this was no death dream. "It's all this talk about William of Normandy. No wonder you're unsettled."

"It wasn't about that Norman. He wasn't—it wasn't him."

"Of course it is." She tucked the cover around Adwen. "I overheard Lord Richard talking just last night in the dining hall about the danger of invasion by the Duke of Normandy."

"I remember. He was very angry. He said he had better things to do than follow King Harold into battle." She sighed. "You don't think it was a vision, then?"

"It was a dream."

"He was so real . . . I could even see the glint of red in his hair from the fires behind him."

"A dream."

"I'm glad." Adwen was silent for a long time, and Brynn thought she had drifted off to sleep. "I feel so alone. Will you lie beside me?"

Brynn lay down on the bed and gathered Adwen's delicate form close. She had grown thinner since she had lost the last child. Childbed fever had sapped her strength and Brynn was not sure another bout would not carry her away.

"I like this. I feel safe," Adwen whispered. "You

held me like this the night I almost died. I was drifting away . . . and you pulled me back."

Brynn stiffened. "It was the herbal broth I gave you."

"I don't think so."

"Then it was God," she said quickly. "I'm a healer, not a sorceress."

"Have I offended?" Adwen asked anxiously. "I would never accuse you of such a thing. I only—"

"Hush. All is well. Rest."

"And will you stay here until I go to sleep?"

"I'll stay."

Despair and desperation rushed through Brynn. It was happening again as it had happened time after time during the past three years. Adwen was asking for only this moment, but Gwynthal appeared farther away than ever. She was a healer. How could she run away from this sick child who begged for her friendship and would die without her care? She could escape Delmas, but Adwen's need bound her to Redfern with chains of iron.

"The star . . ." Adwen murmured drowsily. "I think you're wrong, Brynn. He's coming . . ."

April 20, 1066
Normandy

"It's a sign from God." William of Normandy gestured to the brilliant comet and then turned to Gage Dumont with a smile. "Who could want more proof that my claim on the English throne is just?"

"Who, indeed?" Gage Dumont said impassively. "But, of course, Harold of England is quite probably telling his barons the comet is a sign that his cause is just and that God is on his side."

William's smile faded. "Are you saying that I am using God to further my claim for power?"

"I'm only a humble merchant. Would I dare to accuse your grace of such blasphemy?"

The impudent rascal would dare to tweak the beard of the Pope if it suited him, William thought with annoyance. He was tempted to give him a sharp set-down but restrained himself. "Hardly humble. It's rumored you possess more wealth than I do. Is it true you have a grand palace in Byzantium?"

"Rumors are often in error," Dumont said in evasion.

"And your castle at Bellerieve is said to be full of wondrous treasures from the East."

"I'm a merchant and a trader. As your grace knows, I often journey to the Byzantine to acquire goods. Do you begrudge me a few comforts to ease my days?" He raised a brow. "Perhaps you sent for me to ask to share my baubles?"

William gestured impatiently. It was not Dumont's riches he needed. "Bellerieve is also said to possess the finest soldiers and archers in Normandy."

Gage Dumont's expression hardened. "Your knights think a lowly merchant is fair game. It was necessary to make sure I had the means to discourage them."

"I realize my knights can be a little . . . boisterous."

"Acts of rape and pillage are considered by some to be a trifle more than boisterous."

"Knights are trained only for warfare. It is understandable that they grow restless in times of peace."

"So restless, they ravage the helpless countryside. That is why I hired mercenaries to make sure I was not equally helpless."

William decided it time to abandon a defensive

position and attack. "You killed Jean of Brestain last year."

Wariness flickered in Gage's expression. "True."

"It caused a great uproar among my barons. They do not like commoners interfering with their sport. They wanted me to raze your castle to the ground and take your head. Do you know why I did not?"

"Kindness?"

William ignored the sarcasm. "Because your Bellerieve guards my coast well and I knew you would no more permit an invader to breach your walls than you did my knights."

"I'm very grateful."

"You are not." William met his gaze. "You are as arrogant and without respect as your father."

A flicker of expression crossed Dumont's face. "I have no father. I'm a bastard." He bowed slightly. "Like your grace."

"Your mother claimed that you were Hardraada's son."

"And Hardraada refused her claim. The King of Norway has issue enough for his taste and needs no bastard to lay claim to his land. Particularly the son born of the daughter of a Norman merchant."

"He must have some fondness for you. He trained you in warfare and took you on several voyages with him."

Gage's eyes narrowed on William's face. "I find it curious that you know such a great deal about me."

"Why? Surely you expected me to keep an eye on you. Being a bastard myself, I know the hunger illegitimacy brings for power, the desire to take what's yours by any means possible. Since Hardraada would not give you the position you deserved, there was the chance you might decide to take mine." He smiled. "I was grateful that instead you chose to gain power by amassing the wealth of Solomon." He raised his brows. "But wealth is not enough for you, is it?"

He shrugged. "Gold can buy almost anything."

"Almost," William said softly. "But not what Hardraada could have given you. Not what I can give you. Gold cannot let you take your place as a noble. It cannot clean the common dirt from your shoes."

Gage looked down at his shoes. "I see no dirt. I'm shocked you would think I'd enter your august presence besmirched."

"You know what I mean."

"You must be more clear. As a merchant, I'm used to firm language when bargaining. I take it, this is a bargain?" He leaned back against the balustrade and said bluntly, "You want my archers and my soldiers when you invade England. You probably also will want a goodly sum to feed and clothe them during the invasion. Is that correct?"

"That is quite correct."

"And what do you offer me in return?"

"I don't have to offer you anything," William said testily. "My army could sweep over Bellerieve on the way to England and take what I need."

"And come out of the siege weaker than you can afford to be. What do you offer me?"

"To knight you for services rendered."

"Not enough."

"A barony," he said reluctantly. He had been hoping the damned merchant would be content without being lifted to the ranks of the elite of the land. "But not here. England. There will be land and honors aplenty when we defeat the Saxons."

"My choice of property?"

"You ask a great deal."

"So do you. According to what I've heard, you've offered these Saxons' lands to every mercenary and noble in Normandy. There may not be sufficient to go around, and I will not wait to be given my reward at your discretion."

"I'm not sure you would be entirely comfortable with knighthood," William said coldly. "You clearly have been taught to whine and barter like your trades-man grandfather."

"You're only half mistaken. My grandfather never whined but he was magnificent at the art of bartering." He paused. "A quality necessary in a ruler as well as a merchant."

William grimaced as he realized his thrust had been turned aside. He was extremely sensitive about his own tanner grandfather and had hoped to spark a resentment that might enable him to get the upper hand over this rogue. He studied him, seeking another weakness.

He saw none. The giant before him had the confidence of a royal combined with a brilliant mind that had allowed him to amass the fortune that had won him a unique place in Norman society. William had heard that while Dumont was with Hardraada's raiding parties he was reputed to have been as ruthless in war as he later became in the trade. William might be able to break him but he would not bend. "Very well. Your choice of property."

Dumont straightened away from the balustrade. "I'll consider it." He bowed. "Good night, your grace."

"You'll *consider* it?" William said, outraged. "I want an answer now."

"I'll send you word in two days' time." Dumont moved toward the door. "My 'tradesman' grandfather also taught me never to accept a bargain without first examining it from all sides."

William smothered his anger. He would need every possible advantage when he launched his invasion, and Dumont's fighting force was truly formidable. "I will wait two days and no more. Don't think to play games with me."

"I don't play games. I leave that to the lords and ladies of your illustrious court."

"Oh, one more thing," William said. "If you decide to accept my offer, you must leave the Saracen here in France."

Gage's expression did not change. "You are speaking of Malik Kalar?"

"If that is his name. The Saracen who travels with you. I'm hoping to get the Pope's approval on this invasion and I will not have him offended by a Saracen in my ranks."

"*If* I choose to join you, Malik will most certainly accompany me. Resign yourself to that fact." He turned on his heel and left the chamber.

Stubborn, arrogant whoreson. The rest of the world might wonder, but William had no doubt the man who had just departed was that Viking devil's son. When he had summoned Dumont he had expected to be able to manipulate and control him, but now he was not sure who had been triumphant during this interview.

"Matilda!"

His wife opened the door of the antechamber, where William had stationed her with the door slightly ajar. He valued her judgment more than any of his nobles and often had her listen and watch when he had a meeting. "Well?"

"An interesting man." She came forward—tiny, sturdy, indomitable. "And every bit as comely as I'd heard from Lady Genevieve." She smiled slyly. "She says he's as vigorous in bed as a stallion and knows many exotic ways to please a lady. Now I can believe she spoke truly. He certainly appears to have a certain . . . power."

Comely? The man was big as a mountain, rough-featured, and had no claim to any comeliness that he could see. Matilda must be trying to spark his jealousy again. She knew it was an easy task and constantly stirred it as a way to keep his interest strong. She succeeded admirably; even after these many years of marriage their union was as ardent as the day they had wed. "*Merde*, I didn't ask you to assess his virility but his character."

She shrugged. "Clever, hard, guarded . . . hungry."

"Hungry? You mean ambitious?"

"Perhaps . . ." Her brow wrinkled as she tried to define that vague quality she had sensed in Dumont. Then she shrugged. "Hungry."

"Did he take the bait? He must know Hardraada also wants the English throne. Will he take his forces to Norway and offer them to his father?"

"I think not." She frowned thoughtfully. "I sensed a certain bitterness. . . . There is little affection there. However, he may decide to stay here in Normandy and gobble up the fiefs that are left behind instead of chancing defeat in England. As I said, I judge him to be a very clever man."

William shook his head. "If he stays, he remains a wealthy merchant who can only pull the strings behind the scenes. He has no liking for being scorned by my nobles. I'd wager he'll pay my price to stand on equal ground with them."

"Then why did you ask my opinion, if you'd already made up your mind?" Matilda asked tartly. "I have better things to do with my time than listen at doors in the dead of night."

He moved at once to soothe her. No one could make life more unpleasant than Matilda in a fury. "You know I always value your opinion." He changed the subject as he slipped his arms about her. "Except as regards the man's capability as a stallion. Admit it, you merely said that to annoy me. The man has no attraction for you."

Matilda opened her lips to reply and then thought

better of it as she caught the slight frown on his face. She reached up and gently stroked her husband's cheek. "How very wise you are, my love. I was but teasing you a trifle. Of course I do not find this Gage Dumont in the least attractive."

"You've been a long time." Malik didn't turn around from his position at the open window as Gage strode into his chamber at Bellerieve. "Did he offer you the entire world, or just a part of it?"

"Knighthood, a barony, the property of my choice in England." Gage moved to stand beside him. "He seemed to think he was being very generous."

"But you do not." Malik still didn't look away from the comet. "Do you not trust him?"

"He summons me to his presence near midnight so that his barons will not know he's dealing with me. He threatens to take Bellerieve if I don't give him what he wants. Should I trust him?"

Malik did not answer.

"And why should I take the chance? I have everything I could want or need here." His gaze went around the chamber, taking in an exquisitely crafted golden elephant on the table, the magnificent tapestry portraying a lion hunt in the desert gracing the far wall. He had made sure every corner of the castle brimmed with finely carved furniture and ornaments of gold and silver and ivory. When he had furnished Bellerieve he had tried to emulate the luxury and beauty of the palaces he had visited in Byzantium rather than the sparse comforts of the manors of Normandy or his father's hall in Norway.

"Not everything," Malik said. "Here you must fight for respect and to keep what is yours."

"England would probably be the same. Only I would have to fight the Saxons as well as my Norman brothers. Yes, I should stay here."

"But you will not." Malik smiled. "You are a man

who was born to rule, and England is a step in that
direction."

"A barony is not a kingdom." He raised his brows.
"Or do you believe I intend to overthrow William?"

"It is a possibility."

Gage did not deny the thought had occurred to
him. At times the slights and rejections he received
goaded him to the point where he was tempted to ride
roughshod straight to the throne. "I'm a rich man, but it
would take the wealth of Solomon to gain support
enough to oust William."

"True. Ah, but you will still go. You've grown too
restless in the past year. You're a man who must always
have a new mountain to conquer and William's knights
are not enough to challenge you. If it was not England,
it would be Byzantium." Malik gave a mock shudder.
"Or that cold land to the north again."

"You need not worry. It will not be Norway." His
lips suddenly twitched. "And it cannot be Byzantium if
I'm to continue to be honored with your company. I
believe the sentence was to be castration and then beheading?"

"Do not remind me of that idiocy. As if castration
were not enough indignity, they would take away my
power of reasoning. They truly wished to destroy me."
He sighed resignedly. "But such is the fate of those
granted the gifts of the Almighty. A man with my brilliance and hunger for knowledge always has enemies
seeking to bring him down."

"I believe it was the hunger of your nether parts
that brought you down. The beheading was just an af-
terthought. I've never understood why you chose the
wife of the head of the Imperial Guard to seduce."

"She needed me," he said simply. "Her brute of a
husband was cruel to her."

Gage shook his head. Malik's words did not surprise
him. A woman need not be young or even comely to

earn a place in the rascal's bed; he loved them all. He appeared to enjoy every woman with equal passionate enthusiasm, and they certainly enjoyed Malik.

"I wonder how she is." Malik frowned. "Perhaps we should return to Karza and—"

"No," Gage said firmly. Though they had barely escaped from Byzantium with skin intact, Malik had insisted on taking the woman with them and escorting her safely back to her village. "She's fine. I left enough gold to give her a chance to make a fine life for herself. She does not need you."

"You are probably right. I must give her a chance to find a lesser man to satisfy her." He waved his hand at the comet. "I am like that comet that dims everything else in the heavens with its splendor."

Gage snorted. "It would make my life easier if you would shine a little less brightly and with far less frequency."

Malik turned, a grin lighting his bearded face. "But you do not need an easier life. I provide you with both entertainment and challenge. That is why you chose me for a friend."

"I was wondering why I burdened myself with such a scalawag."

"Why did you not ask me? You know how wise I am."

"I know how arrogant you are."

"Like to like. I have not heard you described as being either shy or modest. So, do we go to this England?"

"I've not decided."

"I think you have."

"If I go, William says I must leave you here. He's afraid that your heathen soul may corrupt his holy expedition and bring down the wrath of heaven."

"Did you tell him I'm a warrior without equal and could vanquish these Saxons even without his army?"

He struck his chest with his fist. "That they would run like sheep from my mighty sword? That they would cover their eyes with terror when they saw me draw aim with my bow? That they would cower and tremble when I rode over them on my giant steed?"

"No, but I told him you would have no problem blowing them off their feet with boastful words."

Malik shook his head mournfully. "You strike me to the heart. To know me so long and not realize my true worth."

"How could I help but realize it when you keep me apprised of your infinite value every minute of the day?"

"Well, it keeps growing. I would not have you ill informed." He looked away from Gage and said quietly, "If it will save trouble, I will stay at Bellerieve."

"And let William dictate to me?"

"He rules Normandy."

"He needs me. I do not need him. If I go, you will go with me." He grimaced. "There's no telling what mischief you'll bestir if I leave you here alone."

"And you will miss my company. How could you help it?" Malik's expression suddenly sobered as he glanced back up at the sky. "Perhaps I should stay here," he murmured. "I have a feeling that a bad thing awaits me across that sea."

"You see it written on the heavens?" Gage asked caustically. "Good God, are you also robbed of reason by the appearance of that infernal comet?"

"If reason does not explain, then we must rely on what we feel is true."

"Or imagine." He smiled sardonically. "Or twist to suit ourselves."

"What a cynic you are," Malik said. "You believe in nothing."

"Not on this earth. No, that's not true. I believe in what I am and what you are. I believe in what I can see and hear and touch." His gaze followed Malik's to the comet. "And I believe you're seeing what you want to see just as William did. If you don't wish to go with me, say it. I will not quarrel with you."

Malik was silent a moment. "I will go. What will be, will be." A sudden grin lit his face. "But you must promise I will not die by the hands of those barbarians. It would not be a fitting end to such a glorious career."

Gage smiled. "I promise."

"Good." Malik moved across the room toward the door. "And now that you have decided to cast us upon the bloody shores of war, I feel I must indulge in the joys of life. I have a lovely damsel who has been waiting in my chamber for the past three hours."

"She may not still be there. Ladies do not like to wait."

"She will be there. She is curious. She wants to see if a Saracen is truly heathen in the physical as well as the spirit." He paused at the door. "It is Lady Genevieve. You said you did not mind?"

Gage shrugged. "Why do you ask? We've shared women before. You're right, she is curious." He and Malik had encountered many noblewomen both there and in Byzantium who had sought to liven their boredom by daring to secretly venture into the forbidden fringes where outcasts dwelled. Genevieve had been more entertaining than most, but Gage did not fool himself into thinking she had any more affection for him than he did for her. "And very inventive. You'll enjoy her."

"If you need a woman, she hinted she would not be averse to both of us in her bed."

"Not tonight."

Malik still hesitated, studying him. "Are you troubled? Do you need to talk? I will stay."

"And keep her waiting even longer?"

"I will keep her waiting forever if you have need of

me. Friendship is far more rewarding than the joys of the flesh."

"Not on an immediate basis." He smiled affectionately and said gruffly, "Go on. I will see you in the morning."

Malik nodded and left the chamber.

Gage looked up at the comet, beginning to feel a faint stirring of excitement.

England. He had memories of Hardraada talking in the twilight dimness of his hall of the rich plum that was England. His father had wanted England, still wanted it. Gage would be pitting himself against Norway and Hardraada if he allied himself with William. He would be casting away the last chance of getting his father to acknowledge him.

There was no chance. He had not even realized a particle of hope remained until that moment. Why should he not recognize and resign himself to that truth? Hardraada had made his rejection brutally clear on that last journey.

Well, if he had no father, no loyalty was due.

England offered him a place and status he had never been able to win in Normandy and was denied in Norway. He would reach out and pick the plum, and to devil with Hardraada.

He smiled recklessly as he looked up at the comet. He did not believe in signs, but the baron he was to become needed a coat of arms. Why not this blazing heavenly messenger that was filling all and sundry with fear and foreboding? The temerity of the upstart merchant-warrior flourishing such a banner would outrage William, King Harold of England, Hardraada, and possibly the Pope himself.

Yes, he would definitely claim the comet as his own.

Two

THE SETTING SUN glowered red in the west, but no more red than the blood staining Malik's tunic.

"I've done all I can." Father Bernard shook his head. "It is of no avail. I've stopped the blood, but the wound is too deep. He will die. I must go help the others."

"Stay!" Gage ordered harshly. "He's not dead yet. Help him."

Father Bernard looked around the battlefield and crossed himself. So many dead, so many maimed and wounded. It was hard to believe the Pope had sanctioned this terrible massacre. The Saxons had been slaughtered but so had many of William's troops, and now they expected him and his fellow priests to perform the miracle of healing what could not be healed. "I must go where I can be of help." He rose to his feet. "This man is dead."

"He breathes. There's a chance."

"I've wasted too much time as it is on this infidel while good, true Christians are in need."

Gage Dumont stood up and faced him. "Waste? This infidel is a better man than any Christian I know."

"Blasphemy. May God forgive you such—" Father

Bernard took a half-step back as he encountered the blazing blue eyes of Dumont. The man was almost incandescent with anger, and his face was the twisted visage of a demon from hell. He reached up his hand to cross himself but stopped in mid motion. Gage Dumont may have fought with the power of a legendary berserker this day, but he was only a man, not a devil. "It is a sin to make such a claim."

"It's a sin to let a man die when he could live." Gage drew his sword and pointed it at the priest. His tone was laden with cold ferocity. "He is not dead and you will not leave him to minister to anyone else until he is."

"What will you have me do? Even if you threaten to kill me, I cannot tell you I can heal this man. He's beyond help."

"I can heal him."

Gage whirled on the little crowd of prisoners standing under guard a short distance away. "Who spoke?"

"Lord Richard of Redfern." A tall, golden-haired man stepped eagerly forward and was immediately stopped by the guard. He called over the soldier's shoulder, "You want the man healed? Release me. It can be done."

"The man lies. No one can save the infidel," Father Bernard said.

Gage ignored him, his gaze raking the handsome features of the Saxon. "What makes you think you can cure him?"

"Not I. But my wife would have died on at least two occasions if not helped by a healer in my household."

"Traitor," spat out an older prisoner standing next to Richard of Redfern. "I did not send you the woman to be used to heal these Normans. I would die rather than give them aid."

"Because you are a fool, my lord Kells, " Richard

snarled. "King Harold is dead and we are beaten. You may have a taste for slavery, but I do not. We will never rise again unless we have something with which to barter." He called to Gage, "If you want your man to live, free me to go and fetch the healer. The woman is a slave and will be my gift to you."

"There is no time," Father Bernard said.

"My holding is but a scant hour's ride to the north," the Saxon said persuasively. "In two hours' time she can be at the man's side."

Gage studied Richard's face. "And what do you wish in return for this healer?"

"Only freedom," Richard said. "And the opportunity to serve you."

Gage hesitated and then said curtly, "You can have your freedom, but only a few hours hence you were killing my soldiers. I don't take enemies into my service." He turned to Captain LeFont, who was in charge of the prisoners. "Take the man and a company of soldiers to this Redfern and bring the woman back."

"You won't be sorry," Richard said as the captain cut his bonds. "As for the other, I'm sure I can prove how useful I can be."

"I care nothing for your usefulness. You'll not have the opportunity to do anything more useful than scramble for scraps with the hounds at my table if Malik dies." Gage turned to another soldier. "Put up my tent. We'll set up camp here."

Captain LeFont turned to him in surprise. "But I thought his grace wished to push on to London."

"Then he can do it without me. I'll join him later."

Father Bernard mournfully shook his head. "You will displease his grace for nothing. It will do no good. He cannot be saved."

Gage turned back to Malik so that the priest would not see the panic his words had sent coursing through him. "He *will* be saved."

. . .

"You broke . . . your promise." Malik's voice was a mere breath of sound in the twilight dimness of the tent. "You said . . . the barbarians would not kill me."

"Hush." Gage gently stroked back Malik's hair from his face. "Save your strength."

"When a man is dying, he should say . . . many things." Malik's eyes shut. "But I cannot think of . . . I was not . . . prepared."

"You're not going to die. I've sent for a healer."

He shook his head. "Too . . . late. A man knows when he is to die. Sad . . ."

Gage took both his hands and held tight. "Be silent. You're *not* going to die. Have you ever known me to break a promise?"

"This is not precisely . . ." He met Gage's eyes and smiled with an effort. "No, my friend, never . . ."

"Then help me."

His eyes closed. "I will try. It will be most interesting to see . . . how you keep this promise." He tried to laugh but managed only a cough. "And infinitely gratifying. Did we win the battle?"

"Yes. King Harold is dead and his barons slain or captured. We have England in our grasp."

"I knew . . . they could . . . never withstand my invincible sword."

"You were right."

"Did . . . William . . . knight you?"

"Yes. Will you be silent and rest?"

"Rest . . ."

Malik was still.

Fear leapt through Gage. Dead? He leaned forward and relief surged through him as he saw the slight rise and fall of Malik's chest. Not yet.

. . .

"Get up!"

The blanket was ripped off Brynn and she was jerked from her pallet.

"What!" Delmas cried from across the room. "Lord Richard, why are you—"

"Be silent!" Richard snarled. "I have need of your wife."

Brynn tensed with panic as she looked at him. Richard was breathing hard, his handsome face contorted, his brown eyes glittering wildly in the light of the candle held by the soldier behind him. "No!"

"You do not say no to me, wench." His hand tightened brutally around her wrist. "You do as I bid you."

She shook her head to clear it of sleep. He was still in armor and had clearly ridden straight from Harold's camp. It was unreasonable to think his need was of the flesh as she had first thought. "Is Lady Adwen worse?"

"I've not seen her." Richard grabbed her shawl and thrust it at her. "It is of no account. She is useless to me now."

"You are angry," Delmas asked. "How have we displeased you?"

Richard paid no attention to him. "Put on your shoes, woman. We have to reach the camp before the bastard dies."

"Camp?" She quickly put on her shoes and bound back her hair with a leather cord. "You are taking me to King Harold's camp?"

"Harold is dead. They're all dead. We're beaten." He grabbed her wrist again and pulled her toward the door. "But I will not remain a slave to these Normans. You will use your skills to heal the Saracen or I will cut your pretty throat."

"Saracen?" She did not understand any of this. It was the Normans who had defeated the English and yet Richard was raving about infidels. "I cannot leave Red-

fern. Your wife has been very ill since you left to join
Harold. She has the fever every night and I must—"

"You fool. Don't you realize everything has
changed? She does not matter. Everything is gone. I've
lost—" He broke off and started to pull her out of the
room.

"Wait! My bag of herbs." She had only time to
snatch the large leather pouch before he jerked her out
of the room, across the hall, and into the stable yard.

She received a confused impression of soldiers bearing brightly burning torches. Servants and shopkeepers
huddled in frightened groups against the walls. Horses
moved restlessly, their breath pluming in the cold air.

A soldier rode forward, mail armor gleaming cold
and bright in the torchlight. "This is the woman?"

Richard nodded. "Brynn. We can leave now, Captain LeFont."

Delmas came running out of the manor. His face
was white, his expression strained in the torchlight.
"But, Lord Richard, what of me? You cannot take her
away. She is my—"

"You presumptuous pig." Richard's hand lashed
out, knocking him to the dirt. "I will do what I wish."
He mounted his horse and pulled Brynn up on the horse
before him. "And take what I need. She serves me
now."

He spurred his horse into a gallop as the Norman
captain motioned the troop forward.

"I should not leave your wife," Brynn said with
desperation as the manor retreated in the distance. "She
could die without me."

"Then she will die. Forget her. From this day forward you will belong to the Norman."

"What Norman?"

"Lord Gage Dumont. He has an officer, a Saracen,
who has been wounded, and I've given my word that
you will cure him. You are my gift to him." He smiled

bitterly. "Though I doubt if that foreign savage will know gratitude."

"You cannot give me to him. I am not your slave."

"Your husband is my slave. What does that make you?"

"I am not—" She broke off with a low cry as his arms tightened painfully around her and his armor bit into her flesh.

"Listen well, Brynn of Falkhaar, you will heal this Saracen and serve the Norman as he demands." He whispered in her ear. "And, perhaps, if I gain his favor, I will persuade him to send you back to my puling wife. I've noted the affection you have for her. You would not want to see her die for lack of care?"

A surge of anger rushed through Brynn. He cared nothing for Adwen, but he was using her to force Brynn to his will. Adwen was a pawn and so was she. They all wanted to use her; Delmas and Lord Richard and now this . . . this Norman.

"Soon the manor will be deserted," Richard continued. "When they hear we've lost the battle and the Normans are overrunning the countryside, the servants will scatter like sheep. Who will care for Adwen?"

"Lord Kells will not let her die."

"Lord Kells is captive and will likely also become the slave of the Norman."

Her hopes sank at the words.

"So you see Adwen is your responsibility. Only you can help her."

She wanted to turn and strike him. Never had she felt more helpless or full of hate.

"Serve the Norman and I will find a way to send you back to Redfern. Prove unruly and I will forget Adwen exists." His arms loosened. "Do we understand each other?"

From their first meeting she had understood him

and his capacity for evil. She nodded jerkily. "I will serve the Norman . . . for now."

"For now," he repeated. "You never give in, do you?" He laughed harshly. "Interfering bitch. Do you know how often you've sent me away from the manor in a rage? You looked at me with those big eyes as if you were staring right through me, as if I were nothing. I wanted to crush you, rape you, stomp you into the ground. And you knew it, didn't you?"

"Yes."

"Well, you'd better not try your bold tricks on the Norman. You'll have no Lord Kells to protect you from him." He went on, savoring every word. "If you fail in healing the Saracen, he will use you as he sees fit, and, when he's finished, he will probably give you to his men. He's a hard man and as much a barbarian as that bastard, William, he serves."

She braced herself to ward off a surge of panic. She mustn't let him know how his words had affected her. He wanted to see fear in her, but she would not give him the satisfaction. "I'm sure there is little difference between Norman barbarians and Saxon savages. You are all the same."

He muttered a curse. "You will soon have ample opportunity to compare, wench."

The smell of blood and death reached out to her in the darkness even before they reached Hastings. She felt as if she were strangling, suffocating. She couldn't stand it. She started to struggle in Lord Richard's arms. "No!"

"What in Hades is wrong with you?" he growled.

"Death . . ."

"The Saracen will not die," Richard snarled.

"No, you don't understand. So much death . . ." She panted, trying to draw breath. "And I can do *nothing*."

"You will save the Saracen. Do you hear me?"

Why did he continue babbling about one man when she was drowning in the loss of thousands? Her body started to shake with sobs.

"What is wrong with her?" Captain LeFont urged his horse nearer. "I will not have her damaged. I would be as displeased as Lord Gage if she were unable to perform her duty, Saxon."

"Nothing is wrong," Richard said quickly. "A woman's weak vapors." He hissed in her ear. "Stop this wailing. The Norman must believe I've brought him a gift of worth. Will you—"

"His tent is just ahead." LeFont spurred toward a large tent glowing with light. He leapt from his horse and hurried toward the entrance. "It is Captain LeFont, my lord," he called. "Is he still alive? We hurried—"

"He's alive. Barely. Have you brought her?"

LeFont turned and snapped his fingers. "The woman, Saxon."

Richard dismounted and lifted Brynn to the ground. He said in a low voice, "Stop sniveling, or I swear I will give you cause to weep."

There was enough pain and sadness in this place to form a lake of tears, yet he thought her own pain would make a difference. Adwen. She must think of Adwen. She forced herself to close herself away from the waves of suffering and drew a deep, unsteady breath. No, Adwen was too far away. The Saracen. If she could concentrate on just one in need, she could sometimes block out the others.

"Where is she?" The Norman's voice again, rough, impatient.

Richard grabbed her bag of herbs, took her elbow, and shoved her forward into the tent. "Brynn of Falkhaar, as I promised. My gift . . . to please you in any manner you wish."

"You know what I wish." Gage Dumont rose to his feet and turned to face Brynn. Shock rippled through her. He was a giant of a man, towering well over six feet, with broad shoulders and muscle-corded calves and thighs. Richard was also a tall man, but he suddenly looked slight and ineffectual beside the Norman. Hair dark as night fell to Dumont's shoulders, framing high cheekbones and deep-set light eyes that exuded power and command. "Your former master says you're a healer." He pointed at the man on the pallet. "Cure him."

"I will try." She took her bag of herbs from Richard and moved toward the pallet. "What is his affliction?"

"A sword wound in the chest." His gaze narrowed on her face. "And you will not try. You will do it. He will not die. If he does, you will follow him to the grave."

The force of his will reached out, enveloping her in its power. A chill went through her as she realized Richard had threatened much the same and she had not been afraid. Gage Dumont was a very formidable man.

But when encountering formidable men she had learned to hide fear and meet threats with boldness. She looked directly into his eyes. "Do you intend to stand there, hurling foolish threats at me, or let me tend your man?"

A flicker of surprise crossed his face. "Not foolish. You'll learn I never make a threat lightly."

"Forgive her impertinence," Lord Richard said. "My wife has made a sort of pet of her and indulged her beyond her station."

"I see no sign she recognizes she has a station," Gage said. He turned and knelt by the pallet again. "And I will deal with her impertinence myself. You may go."

A ruddy flush colored Richard's cheeks at the cool dismissal, but he subdued his anger. "As you say, she's not entirely tamed. You may need my help."

"I've never needed help with a wench before. You gave her to me. Are you seeking to take back your gift?"

"No, but I would—"

"Go. I'm weary of looking at you."

"I'm a free man?"

Gage Dumont nodded, his attention still on Malik's pale face. "I'll tell LeFont to give you safe passage from this place back to Redfern. But don't become too comfortable there. William will be doling out your property with all the others when he has time to pay his debts."

Anger darkened Richard's expression before he forced a smile. "Perhaps by that time I will find a way to reclaim what is mine." He moved toward the tent entrance. "Don't worry, the woman will obey. I've taken measures to assure that she's quite eager to cure the Saracen."

Brynn felt a gust of cold wind as he lifted the flap and left the tent.

"You heard him," Gage said. "Heal him."

Brynn moved across the tent and knelt beside the Saracen. The flickering lantern light revealed a face of stunning comeliness. Beneath that dark beard the Saracen's features came close to perfection. And he was so young, not long past his twentieth year. She felt a terrible sadness. His body was slim and lithe and should have been brimming with strength. "What is his name?"

"You don't need his name to cure him."

"You will not tell me what I need or don't need. If you wish him to live, you will give me what I want," she said coldly. "Now, what is his name?"

He was silent a moment and then said, "Malik Kalar."

"Does he speak English?"

"He speaks English and French and Norwegian and four languages you Saxons have never even heard. Do you think because he is an infidel that he is an ignorant savage?"

"I don't care if he speaks the tongue of the angels." She carefully drew back the cover. "I only need him to understand me when I speak to him." She loosened his bandage. "And I am not a Saxon. I am Welsh."

"It is all the same."

"It is not the same. It will never be—" She broke off as she removed the bandage and the wound was revealed. "Dear God, you expect me to heal *this*? His chest has been carved like a roast at a banquet."

"It happened four hours ago and he's still alive. Malik has great strength. Help him and he will live."

"Sometimes it takes a long time to die."

He reached across Malik's body and his hands fastened on her shoulders. His eyes blazed into hers. "Those aren't the words I want to hear. *Heal* him."

His fingers were digging into her shoulders and she struggled to keep back a cry of pain. "If you break my bones, I can do nothing," she flared. "If you don't wish to know the truth, then leave this tent. He is dying. If I can save him, I will do so. But not because you command it."

He smiled unpleasantly. "Because your handsome Lord Richard commands it? You would do wise to obey me. He is no longer your master."

"He was never my master. No man is my master." She glared at him. "You are wasting time with this talk. You don't need to frighten me to have me wish to make this lad well. I cannot help myself. I am a healer. It is what I do. Now, call for hot water and clean linen for bandages."

He stared at her a moment and then his grasp loosened and fell away. "The priest cleaned the wound."

She had won. He was going to let her do her work. "Then I will clean it again. If the Saracen were to die, I will not be blamed for someone else's blunder. I've noticed that cleanliness is not necessarily a requirement for the priesthood." She shrugged off her shawl. "I'll need a fire just outside the tent and a small cooking pot to prepare my salves and medicines."

"He may die while you concoct your brews."

"Do you expect me to snap my fingers and make him well? I will cleanse the wound and then apply the salve I have on hand, but I will need much more." She added wearily, "If he lives through the night."

"He must not—" He turned away so that she could see only a shadowy profile. Haltingly, he said, "I'm not ungenerous. You'll be rewarded well if Malik lives."

Agony. For the first time since she had entered the tent she sensed an emotion other than anger and frustration behind that rock-hard exterior. He truly cared for this Saracen. "You would barter with me for a man's life?"

"Why not? We all begin bartering in the cradle." He turned his head and the hard, flintlike mask was back in place. "The older we grow, the more we want and the higher the price we're willing to pay." He jerked his head at the opening of the tent. "Go down that hill and look at the dead and maimed. That's the price Harold and William were willing to pay for this piece of Saxon earth."

She wished he had not reminded her of that battlefield. She had been trying to fight off the smothering sense of oppression since she had entered the tent. Now it came rushing back, almost overwhelming her. Blood. Pain. Death.

He muttered a curse. "What's wrong? Are you ill? You've turned white as snow."

"Nothing." She moistened her lips. "Just fetch me the linens. I must set to work."

He opened his mouth to speak and then changed his mind. He turned and left the tent.

She swayed, trying to fight back the tears and darkness. She must think only of the Saracen. No, he had a name. Malik. He was not his race, he was a person. She could do nothing for those thousands who had given their lives this day, but perhaps she could save this man.

"Malik," she whispered. "Do you hear me? I know you know I'm here. I'm Brynn of Falkhaar. I'm going to help you come back. I'll do everything I can, but you must help me too."

Not the slightest sign of response on that young, bearded face.

She had not really expected any reaction; he was too close to death. However, it was possible he had heard her. She never knew what could be heard or sensed beyond that deep veil of unawareness. She began to gently stroke the torn flesh around the wound. Dear heavens, his skin was so cold.

"What are you doing?"

She snatched her hands away and glanced guiltily over her shoulder at Gage Dumont standing in the entrance of the tent. She sat back on her heels and said quickly, "I was probing to see if there was foreign matter still in the wound. It looks clean, but you'd be surprised how small bits of metal and cloth can hide in the—"

"You weren't probing." His gaze narrowed on her face. "You were petting him. I didn't bring you here to stroke and cosset him. I could have gotten one of the camp whores to do that. God knows, he's had nearly all of them in his bed at one time or another."

She looked at him in astonishment and relief as she realized he thought she had been drawn by the Saracen's extraordinary good looks. "If I stroked him, it was in pity, not in lust. I would have to be twisted, indeed, to desire a man so close to death." She changed the subject. "Where is my hot water?"

"Coming." He crossed the room and knelt beside Malik. "LeFont is bringing it." He looked down at Malik and whispered, "*Merde*, he's scarcely breathing."

"As long as he breathes at all, there is a chance." She braced herself. He was not going to like what she was going to say. They never liked it and he was more dominant and interfering than most. "I want you to leave me alone with him."

He didn't look at her. "No."

"You will get in my way."

"He may die. He is my friend and I will not leave him alone in that final moment."

"You will leave me alone with him." She tried to inject hardness into her tone. "Or I will do nothing."

He lifted those ice-blue eyes to her face, and again fear went through her. "What did you say?"

She moistened her dry lips. "You heard me. I will not have your interference or questions. You must leave me alone with him."

"Must?" He echoed silkily. "I have no liking for that word."

"Must," she repeated. Sweet Mary, he looked as if he were going to strike her down. Well, she had been struck before and survived. It was unreasonable to fear a blow from this stranger. She met his gaze with a boldness she did not feel. "If you wish him to live. I will call you if I think the end grows near."

"I'm going to stay."

He was staring at her with anger and frustration, willing her to submission, and she had never encountered a stronger will. She felt her own determination wavering like a tree in the wind, but she must not give in. "Then you will stay and watch him die. For I will do nothing. Is that what you wish?"

His big hands opened and closed at his sides as his gaze fastened on her throat. She half expected him to reach over Malik's body and throttle her.

"*Damn* you." He rose to his feet and strode toward the tent entrance. "I'll give you until dawn alone with him." He paused and looked back over his shoulder. She barely kept herself from flinching at the menace in his expression. "I have no liking for being ordered about. I've spent my life endeavoring to make sure it will never happen. After Malik is well, I'll remember this."

He was gone.

She expelled a deep breath of relief. His presence in the tent had been like a storm cloud hovering over her. Now she could concentrate on trying to heal rather than defending herself.

A storm. Yes, that was an apt description of Gage Dumont. She had practically felt the turbulence and lightning flash around her while he had been in the tent. She had been surprised at the rush of power and exhilaration she had experienced when she had been forced to challenge the Norman, but it was foolish to seek out excitement when peace and serenity were clearly the most valuable of prizes. As a child she had been fascinated by storms, but that was long ago. She had suffered too much during these past three years to ever want more than the quiet forests of Gwynthal.

She reached out and touched Malik's temple. She could feel the faint pulse beneath her fingertips. "He's gone now," she whispered. "What a strange, upsetting friend you have, Malik. I think we'll be much better off without him. We'll just sit here and talk and presently I'll rub some of my special salve on that ugly wound. You don't really wish to stay where you are. It may seem peaceful and sweet, but there is still so much waiting for you here." She moved her hand to just above the wound. "Now, what shall we talk about? Not battles. They sicken me almost as much as they have hurt you. Shall I tell you about my Gwynthal? I'm going back there soon and I believe you would like it. It may be like the place you're at right now. No, it's much better." She settled herself more comfortably beside him. "The forests are cool and quiet and yet around every corner you find something wondrous . . . a night-blooming flower or a bird you've never seen before. Then you walk a little farther and you see a waterfall that cascades over rocks that sparkle in the sunlight. . . ."

The cold, crisp air that struck him as he left the tent did nothing to cool Gage's temper.

He felt like strangling the wench. He had been within a heartbeat of closing his hands on that soft throat and squeezing until she begged for mercy.

"She cast you out?" Lord Richard asked.

Gage impatiently glanced toward the campfire where Richard sat with his hands outstretched before the flames.

"I was afraid she would treat you rudely," Richard said. "She never permitted anyone in the chamber when she tended my wife. If she hadn't been a gift from my wife's father, I would have punished her for such behavior. Lord Kells was once the most powerful baron in the south of England, and I didn't want to offend him by damaging her. I should have—"

"What are you still doing here?" Gage asked roughly. He was irritated enough without having this handsome Judas hovering around him. "I thought you'd left the camp."

"I was only a short distance down the road and turned back. I thought I might be of help." Richard smiled. "It is not fitting to give a gift without making sure that it gives satisfaction."

"If this particular gift doesn't give satisfaction, you may wish you'd not come back." He added through set teeth, "I don't like not being present while she's treating him, and I will not be pleased if Malik dies at this slave's hands."

Richard's smile faded only a little. "That's why I returned. I have every confidence the woman will cure your friend but, if she doesn't, you—" He raised his hand as Gage's expression tightened. "On the slight

chance that God decides to take the Saracen, I wanted
to make sure that you were aware that the woman has
other skills."

"Skills?"

"The skill to comfort you in your sorrow in the
most desirable of ways. You've no doubt noticed how
winsome she is."

"No." He had been only vaguely aware of the physical presence of the woman. She was first and foremost
the healer, Malik's possible savior. He had to make an
effort to recall a more detailed image than a tall, slim
woman in a rough brown wool gown. He remembered
the eyes. Huge golden-brown eyes blazing at him, meeting his own with anger and pride. Fresh anger rushed
through him at the memory. "I noticed she's overbold
and without respect."

"It's her low Welsh blood. She means no harm."
Richard added quickly, "And boldness is not a bad thing
in a woman in the right circumstances. It makes her
easier to train in pleasuring." He smiled sensually, his
voice lowering. "She loves to touch and be touched.
She's tight as a glove and I've made sure she knows the
ways to keep a man from becoming bored in bed."

"And what was your ailing wife doing while you
gave the woman these lessons?"

Richard shrugged. "I did not take Brynn in the
same bed. A wife is for childbearing, but a woman like
Brynn is for play. I envy you. I shall miss her."

The man disgusted him. It was true women slaves
were often used for bed sport, but he found Richard's
callousness toward his wife repulsive. He reminded Gage
of Hassan, the head auctioneer of the slave market in
Constantinople. His voice was cold as he said, "I have
no desire to bed the slave. I want only her healing
skills."

"Oh, of course." Richard immediately backed away.

"I simply wanted to make sure you knew Brynn's full value."

And to try to ensure his own safety if Malik died at the woman's hands, Gage thought cynically. It was not a bad ploy; a woman's body was always valuable for barter. The Saxon had merely erred in thinking the bedding of a woman was high enough compensation for losing a friend. "You have told me. Now you can feel free to leave here."

"I thought I might stay and—" Richard stopped as he saw Gage's expression. He rose to his feet. "If you wish." He smiled again. "I'm sure that we will meet again, my lord."

Gage didn't answer as he settled himself before the fire. He was barely aware of the man leaving. His thoughts were once more on Malik lying near death in the tent.

And that damn woman who had dared to bar him from Malik's side.

The sun had barely cast the first pink shadows in the east when Gage entered the tent.

The woman was sitting by Malik and stiffened as she saw him. "What are you doing here?"

By the saints, she was wary. What the devil had she been doing to Malik? She had been with him all night, leaving his side only to hurry back and forth to the campfire for water and the preparation of her salves.

"It's dawn," he said harshly. "I promised you that you would have him to yourself only until the first light." He strode over to the pallet. "How is he?"

"Alive." She wearily ran her fingers through her hair. "Better, I think."

"Better? He looks the same to me." He studied Malik's face. "Did he wake?"

"No."

"Speak?"

"No."

"Then why do you say he's better?"

"I just . . . feel it."

He smiled sardonically. "Astonishing."

She shook her head. "I cannot explain." She shrugged at his skepticism. "I don't care if you believe me or not. It is true. He's growing stronger. He'll wake before sunset and I'll give him a strengthening broth." She yawned. "And now I intend to go to sleep." She settled down beside Malik. "I suggest you do the same. You look more haggard than he does. I have no time to tend two patients."

He frowned. "You can't sleep. He may need you."

"I have not slept in two nights. If he needs me, I'll be here beside him." She put her hand on Malik's chest above the wound as she nestled closer and closed her eyes. "He is healing. He has no need of either of us right now. Go away."

"Have you forgotten this is my tent?"

"Then lie down somewhere and be silent . . ."

The blasted woman was already asleep, he realized with frustration. He reached down to shake her awake and then stopped. Was there the faintest color in Malik's cheeks? He couldn't be sure, but his breathing seemed the slightest bit easier.

Christ. Tears stung his eyes as, for the first time since he had seen Malik struck down, he allowed himself to hope.

He stared eagerly at Malik, searching for some other sign.

Nothing.

He turned and spread a blanket on the ground across the tent and sat down. The woman might feel safe enough regarding Malik's condition to rest, but he did not. He would sit there and keep guard over Malik until she woke.

. . .

"Who . . ."

Brynn drowsily opened her lids at the whisper.

Dark eyes staring into her own only inches away.

She was immediately awake. The Saracen had come back!

"Who . . ." Malik whispered again.

"Brynn," she whispered. "I am Brynn of Falkhaar."

He frowned in puzzlement. "I know it is rude, but I do not . . . remember . . . our coming together."

"Shh. You must rest."

"He's awake?" Gage Dumont was suddenly towering over them like a huge, dark cloud.

"Gage?" Malik asked.

"Yes." Gage knelt beside him. "How do you feel?"

"Bruised. Pained." He tried to laugh. "And weak as an infant just out of the womb." His glance shifted back to Brynn. "And so I fear I did not give this lovely damsel a fitting ride. You are new, are . . . you not?"

"She's not a whore." Gage smiled. "And it grieves me to inform you that your wound rendered even you incapable."

"Impossible." He frowned. "Wound?" His brow cleared. "The battle."

Gage nodded. "The battle."

Brynn stared at him in amazement. His hard expression had softened miraculously, and he looked almost boyish. It was clear the kinship between the two men was both deep and long-standing and she felt a twinge of envy. It had been a long time since she had felt such a bond with another. "Stop talking. You will tire him." Brynn rose to her feet. "I'll go prepare the broth."

Once outside the tent, she moved quickly to the campfire and exchanged the pot of hot water she had kept simmering all night for another. Keep busy. Don't think of the death and pain that lie beyond this hill. While she had been with Malik she had been able to submerge the sorrow, but now it came back as strong as ever. No, not quite as strong. If she steeled herself, she could keep back the tears. Perhaps when Malik was stronger she could convince the Norman to move him from this dreadful place.

She glanced to the north, wondering how Adwen was faring. Surely Richard would not let her die since he believed he held a threat over Brynn only while his wife lived. She pressed her hands to her throbbing temples. It was hard to believe that only yesterday she was at Redfern, calmly going about her duties. A battle had been fought and suddenly everything in her life had changed. She had been torn away from all familiar surroundings and cast here in this brutal place with a Norman who called her his slave. What was going to happen to her?

Well, she would not stand there and whimper. This change of circumstance might not be as bad as it seemed. It might even be possible her opportunity to escape and return to Gwynthal would come sooner with the Norman. It was not as if she cared about Redfern.

But she did care about Adwen. She had fought to keep herself apart, but she felt a deep affection and pity for the girl. She knew she had to help her.

She wearily shook her head. She was too bewildered now to assess the situation and make plans. She must live from moment to moment until she saw her way clear.

Malik stared after Brynn in bemusement as she left the tent. "She does not hesitate to speak her mind, does she? I've never heard a woman order you about before. Who is she?"

Gage's lips twisted sardonically. "My slave."

Malik blinked. "Extraordinary. Has anyone imparted that information to her? Perhaps she is confused regarding the relationship. I would have sworn she thought you her slave."

"I intend to set that right quite soon." Gage straightened the cover over Malik. Christ, he was going to live. It was too good to be true. "You should not be talking."

"So she said." Malik's gaze was still on the tent entrance. "But I feel much stronger now and my curiosity is aroused."

"Heaven help us." Gage sighed and then answered, "She was the slave of Lord Richard of Redfern. We captured him during the battle and he bartered the woman for his freedom. He said she was a fine healer and it seems he told the truth. I would not have given a breath for your chances of living through the night."

"She saved me?"

"It would appear so."

"Ah, an angel at my side," Malik said. "I should have known when I saw her face. There is a radiance about her."

"Radiance?"

"Did you not see it? When she smiled it was—"

"She didn't smile."

"No?" Malik frowned, puzzled. "I was sure she smiled. I felt as warm as if the sunlight touched me."

"Fever."

"No." Malik's brow cleared. "Oh, well, it is of no matter. I will know when I see her again."

"Know what?"

"If cupid's arrow has struck me to the heart."

"Dear God. Not again."

"This is different."

It was always different for Malik, and Gage could already see trouble on the horizon. He said with precision, "She is *not* an angel. When not tending Lord Richard's wife, she plies her whore's tricks on her master. He assures me she is very well taught in that respect."

"Poor maid."

"That poor maid has a tongue sharp as a dagger."

"What other weapons does a slave have? Her tongue, her body . . ." He looked questioningly at Gage. "You are not usually this intolerant with those less fortunate than you. Why does this woman—"

"I told you not to let him talk." Brynn strode into the tent, a wooden bowl in her hands. "But I walk out of here for only a short time and I come back to find you chattering. Do you wish to undo all my work? I should never have left you alone with him."

"He said he felt stronger." Christ's blood, he was actually on the defensive with the wench.

"Of course he feels stronger. They always feel stronger than they are. We have to nurture that strength." She knelt beside Malik's pallet. Her voice changed, softened as she spoke to him. "Now, I'm going to feed you this broth and you must eat every bite. I know you have no hunger, but every morsel you eat will strengthen you. Do you understand?"

Malik nodded, his intent gaze fixed on her face. "I understand."

She began to carefully spoon the broth into his mouth.

Gage remained by the pallet for a few moments but began to feel completely unnecessary. The woman was ignoring him and Malik was totally absorbed in the broth and his angel. He rose to his feet and withdrew to his own pallet across the tent. He doubted if either knew he had gone.

He settled himself cross-legged on the pallet and watched the woman feed Malik.

Radiance? It must have been fever that had led Malik to use that word in referring to Brynn of Falkhaar. He could detect the fire of vitality, but her expression held no glow of human kindness. She was intent, almost stern, and he could sense the indomitable will of which he had been aware since she had walked into the tent.

However, now that he studied her, he could see the comeliness that Lord Richard had tried to use as a lure. Her pale brown hair, tied carelessly back from her face, was of a fine thickness and fell nearly to her waist, and the loose brown gown she wore clung to her full breasts and broad shoulders before skimming the lines of a slim, strong body. Her mouth was large but well formed, and her other features had a pleasing symmetry. Her skin was not the pale alabaster lauded by troubadours, but its gold-toned clarity was near luminous in the dimness of the tent. Perhaps that luminosity was the radiance Malik saw in her.

She must have sensed that he was assessing her, for she lifted her eyes from Malik's face and met his glance. It lasted only a moment before she focused once more on Malik, but an impression remained with him.

Defiance and . . . fear?

As Malik said, she had few weapons and her situation was extremely vulnerable.

If she did feel fear, she would not let him see it.

He felt an unreasonable surge of irritation as he realized he *wanted* her to fear him. It made no sense. Malik was right. He didn't make war on the helpless. Even though she had annoyed him, he should not feel this overwhelming urge to dominate and subdue.

Yet he did feel it, blast it. From the first time she had looked at him he had experienced that tingle of antagonism.

"There." She put down the bowl and gently wiped Malik's mouth with a cloth. "Now you must go back to sleep."

"I don't wish—" Malik broke off and then said wearily, "Perhaps . . . I am a little tired."

"Of course you are." She gently stroked his temple. "Your body has too much to do. It needs to rest."

"You'll be here when I wake?"

"I won't leave you." She settled down beside him

and put her hand over the wound. "See, we will sleep together."

"Only sleep? What a waste . . ." He touched her cheek with his index finger. "Radiance . . ." He closed his eyes and the next instant was deeply asleep.

But she was not asleep. Gage could feel her tension reach out to him across the room.

"Why are you staring at me?" she hissed.

"Because it pleases me. I find you . . . unusual."

She stiffened, and he was once again aware of the wariness of the woman. "There's nothing unusual about me, and I don't like people staring. Your friend is safe now. Have you no duties to attend?"

"None more important than Malik." He stretched out on his pallet, facing her. "And I'm tired too. You and Malik may have slept all day, but I didn't."

"That was your own fault. I told you he was getting better."

"I didn't trust you."

"I think you trust no one."

He smiled. "You're wrong. I trust Malik."

"Then it's good that he will live." Her face clouded. "It's a terrible thing not to be able to trust."

She was talking of herself, he realized. "Is there no one you trust?"

She started to shake her head and then stopped. "I trust Selbar."

"Who is—"

"Never mind." As if regretting revealing a weakness, she hurried on. "And it is very foolish of you not to trust in me when you clearly know nothing of healing yourself."

"I know enough not to give up when a fool of a priest tells me there is no hope."

"That is true. It is important never to give up hope." She closed her eyes. "Perhaps you are not so ignorant as I thought."

"Many thanks," he said ironically.

She did not answer, but he knew she was not drifting off to sleep. She was closing him away from her.

Anger and annoyance flared in him again. He was happy Malik was on the way to recovery, but something about both the situation and the woman chafed at him unbearably. Just the sight of her lying there with Malik made him want to reach out and—

What?

He did not know, but the impulse was both primitive and violent. It could be he merely felt helpless. It was his custom to shape events in the way he wished them to go, and now he could not do it.

Well, these circumstances would not last. Malik would heal and then Gage would once again be in control.

He closed his eyes and willed himself to sleep.

Selbar. Who in Hades was Selbar?

Three

"I BEG PARDON for disturbing you, my lord," Delmas said hesitantly. "I would talk with you about my wife."

Richard looked up from his goblet with a scowl. Christ, was his lot not bad enough without being approached by this whining rabbit? The slave had been hovering around him for the entire two days he had been back at Redfern. "Go away, or I will skewer you like a pig for roasting."

Delmas flinched but did not move from the doorway of the hall. "You must return her to me."

Richard took a drink of ale. "Must?" he repeated menacingly.

"It's not right to part husband and wife."

"Indeed?" Richard rose to his feet and moved a trifle unsteadily across the hall. He briefly regretted the amount of ale he had imbibed. It would impair his pleasure in punishing the impertinent swine. "You dare to tell me what I should do?"

"It is only . . ." Delmas moistened his lips. "No, my lord. Whatever you do is proper. I'm sure you thought giving her to the Norman was for the best. It is only . . ." He suddenly burst out, "I must have her back."

"A young wife is too full of juice and fire for a man of your years," Richard gibed. "She will be much more content with the Norman."

Delmas hesitated. "What of your lady? She may have need of her."

Richard's hand lashed out and knocked Delmas to the ground. "My lady is my concern and mine alone." God in heaven, he was weary of the reproachful looks these minions had given him since he had returned. Even Alice had dared protest when he had taken her away from serving Adwen to use in his bed. Well, he had lessoned that slut and would teach respect to this whining rat. "Mine!" He kicked him in the stomach. "Keep your mouth and your—"

"Forgive me, my lord." Delmas skittered across the floor out of reach. "I merely thought Brynn would serve you better here than with the Norman. If you believe her to be of more service . . ." He got to his feet and stood gazing at him with desperation as Richard started toward him again. Then, as if coming to a decision, he said, "I sought only to save the treasure for you. The Normans have taken enough from us."

"Treasure?" Richard stopped. "What treasure?"

"My wife knows where there is a great treasure trove."

"Liar."

"No, truly." He took a step back. "I have not been able to force her to tell me where it is, but you are far more skilled. Think, my lord, William will have knowledge only of Redfern and your present wealth. When you retrieve the treasure, you could secret it away from him and use it to barter back your former stature."

The slave was probably lying, but a few questions would not hurt. "Where is this treasure?"

"Gwynthal."

He did not recognize the name. "Wales?"

Delmas frowned uncertainly. "I don't think it is in Wales."

"You don't know?"

"I found Brynn in the small village of Kythe in Wales. As I said, I could not force her to tell me anything about Gwynthal."

"Then how do you know about it?"

"Everyone in the village knew of Gwynthal and the treasure. Her father boasted of it when he had too much ale. He was always mumbling something about an island."

"An island!" Richard snorted in disgust. "How can a woman find one island in a vast sea? Or am I supposed to sail aimlessly until I find this island?"

"When I found Brynn she was in the forest far away from Kythe on the road to the village of Selkirk. Selkirk is on the sea. Doesn't that suggest she must have knowledge of where this island is located?"

"Perhaps."

Encouraged by Richard's interest, he took a step closer and said eagerly, "Can't you see? We need Brynn back."

We. Did the fool actually think he would share such a treasure if it did exist? However, it could prove wise to continue to foster the belief. Delmas was not only familiar with this Welsh village but was Brynn's husband and might be able to influence the woman. He turned and went back to his chair. His step was a little steadier; the effect of the ale must be leaving him. Good. He would need a clear head to sift truth from myth.

Treasure. It seemed too easy a solution to his plight.

Yet didn't he deserve a stroke of good fortune after the way fate had ravaged him? A useless woman as his wife, a king who could not keep his lords' lands safe from those Normans. Yes, it was time Richard was given his due.

He sat down and stared with contempt at Delmas's eager expression. Disgusting creature. How low he had fallen to be forced to deal with this vermin. He leaned back and allowed himself a faint smile. "If what you say is true, then I agree we must try to retrieve your wife from the Norman."

"It is true. I swear it."

"Oaths have little value. You want her back."

Delmas hesitated and then reached into the pouch at his belt. "I have proof. She had this when I found her. It was on a chain she wore about her neck and she fought like a young wolverine when I took it from her."

The small, perfect ruby in Delmas's palm shone bright in the candlelight.

Richard carefully hid his sudden interest. "It is of no great size."

"But clear and of an excellent color. Where would a simple village girl get such a jewel?"

Richard took the jewel and held it closer to the candle flame. The ruby was quite perfect. "Where, indeed," he murmured. He leaned back in his chair. "But I must know a great deal more before I can judge whether it's because you lust after her body or this so-called treasure. Tell me more of your meeting with Brynn of Falkhaar and this Gwynthal."

"Where is Gwynthal?" Malik asked.

Brynn stiffened, stopped in mid motion of spreading salve around the wound. "What?"

"Gwynthal. That is where you were born, isn't it?"

"Yes." She took more salve from the pot. "But I don't remember telling you about it."

"She didn't tell you," Gage Dumont said from across the tent. "I would have remembered."

"Perhaps you weren't in the tent." Malik frowned, trying to remember.

"I've scarcely left you since that first night," Gage said.

It was true, Brynn thought. He had been a powerful, vigilant presence since the moment of Malik's awakening, watching her for any false step, encouraging Malik. At times she had felt the sheer force of his will alone was pulling Malik farther and farther from the darkness.

Malik was still perplexed. "Cool green forests, wonders around every bend . . ." he murmured.

Her own words when she had been trying to reach him that first night.

"That's right, isn't it, Brynn?" Malik asked.

"That's right." She smiled at him. "I told you about Gwynthal the night I first came. I didn't think you'd remember."

"I didn't know I did." Malik yawned. "It just came back to me."

"But you said Malik had not awakened during the night," Gage Dumont said softly. "Or didn't you tell me the truth?"

"I don't lie." She started bandaging the wound. "Sometimes I can reach deep just by talking. I try to remind those who are away how much there is waiting for them if they come back to us."

"Surely an odd thing to do," the Norman said.

She whirled on him. "I do what I have to do. If you can do better, heal him yourself."

Malik quickly intervened. "I think you are very clever. Gwynthal must be very beautiful. Any man would want to come back to such a place."

She relaxed as she glanced at him. "Yes, very beautiful. I've never seen such a lovely, peaceful place."

"Peaceful?" Gage's tone was mocking. "I didn't think there was such a place on this earth."

"Because you do not seek it. Like all warriors, you

would rather kill and maim. Gwynthal has always been at peace."

"I cannot believe that."

No, Gage Dumont was everything that was dark and violent and storm-ridden. He would not accept or understand a land like Gwynthal. Yet she did not see that darkness when he spoke to Malik, she realized suddenly. When he was with his friend it was as if a brilliant ray of sunlight pierced the clouds, enveloping, absorbing everything in its path. What would it be like to have that brilliance centered on one? It would probably be even more disconcerting than the darkness. "I did not ask you to believe me."

"If Gwynthal is such a wondrous place, I'm curious as to why you're here among the savages."

"That is not an intelligent question to ask a woman who you call your slave. I had no choice. I was brought here." She finished bandaging the wound. "There, it is looking much better, Malik. The healing is beginning."

"It itches," Malik said drowsily.

"A good sign, but don't scratch it." She rose to her feet. "Take a nap now while I go and heat water to wash you."

She left the tent and strode toward the campfire. She drew a deep breath of clean, cold air. She had not realized how tense she had been until she had escaped Gage Dumont's presence. Those ice-blue eyes were too cold and watchful; he saw too much.

"May I be of service, demoiselle?" She turned to see Paul LeFont approaching on horseback. She had seen him infrequently since that first night, but he had been polite, even kind on those occasions. She remembered how fierce and stern he had looked beneath the torches in the courtyard. Now, with no armor and no helmet covering his gray-streaked hair, he appeared much more approachable. He was past his thirtieth year, a tall, lean man whose body was likely as hard as his face and whose manner was cool, precise, and confident.

"I need water for washing," she said. "If you would be so kind as to have someone fetch it."

"It will be my pleasure." He turned his head and issued an order in French to someone across the camp. "I would do it myself, but I must don armor. I'm leaving at once to escort the prisoners to William's camp."

The prisoners. She had been so involved with healing that she had forgotten those unfortunate souls. "Lord Kells?"

"Yes, he is among them."

"What will happen to them?"

LeFont shrugged. "That is up to his grace, since Lord Gage says he has no use for them."

"Do you have a fondness for this Lord Kells?" Gage asked from behind her.

Her tension returned at the silky utterance. It was as if the Norman were always trying to capture her in some mischief. "He's Lady Adwen's father and the first Saxon lord I knew here in England."

Gage nodded dismissingly at LeFont, and the captain rode away. "You did not answer me."

"What do you wish me to say?" she said impatiently. "He was not unkind."

"And you were grateful?"

"When I was brought here I was scarcely more than a child and had known a freedom greater than you can dream. Do you think I would be grateful to have a yoke placed around my neck?"

"You were not born a slave? Then you must have been a captive of war." He smiled. "How strange, when your perfect Gwynthal has no wars."

"Why should it matter how I came to be here? I'm here and I'm healing your friend."

"Yes, you are." He sat down by the fire and stared into the flames. A ray of late afternoon sunlight fell upon him and she suddenly realized that his dark mane was not black but a vibrant deep red. Strange that except in sunlight it looked deepest ebony. He said, "But I find you a disturbing woman and it makes me uneasy that I know little about you. It's not safe."

He found her disturbing? She had never known a man who generated such disquiet in her. She experienced a queer breathlessness whenever he looked in her direction. "Malik is safe with me. I could not harm him even if I would."

His gaze narrowed on her face. "Why not?"

"I'm a healer," she said simply. "It would destroy me."

"I've known many healers on the battlefields where I've fought and none of them were destroyed when their charges died." He smiled cynically. "In fact, I've suspected some of them were bribed to help the process."

"Then they were not true healers."

"And it could never happen in Gwynthal."

"Never."

At her quiet answer, the mockery faded from his expression. "I'm tempted to believe you."

"Good. Then you will not have to stare at me as if you suspected any minute I would slit Malik's throat."

"Perhaps that's not the only reason I stare at you."

Something in his tone caused her to stiffen with wariness. "Of course it is. You trust no one and you thought me a danger to your friend."

"You have a leaf in your hair."

"What?"

He rose lithely to his feet and crossed the four paces separating them. He reached out and plucked the small leaf from her hair before lightly touching the tendrils at her temples. "Your hair's very thick, isn't it? It's like a bright silky web . . ."

The breathlessness had returned and with it a weakness in her knees. He was huge and powerful tow-

ering over her, and she gazed up at him in helpless fascination. She had not noticed the deep curve of his lower
lip. She had a sudden impulse to brush the pad of her
finger over it.

She stepped back hurriedly and glanced away.
"Web, indeed," she said brusquely. "It catches everything, that's why I keep it tied back." She glanced down
the hill. "I wonder where my water is? The captain
promised that he'd have a man bring it."

She could feel his intent glance on her averted
face, but when he spoke his tone was impassive. "Then
he'll be here soon. LeFont does not tolerate laxity."

"And neither do you," she said shrewdly.

"And neither do I," he agreed. "I have little patience for those who do not perform well."

"We are ready to leave, my lord," LeFont called
from across the camp. He was now at the head of a
column of men whose armor gleamed in the sunlight.

"Good journey," Gage said. "Give his grace my
good wishes and respect. I'll expect you back in three
days' time."

LeFont nodded and lifted his hand and motioned
the company forward. How sad that such a splendid
parade should be wasted on the making of war, Brynn
thought. It was a proud, bold sight—prancing horses,
mail-clad soldiers, pennants flying in the crisp breeze.

The pennants . . .

"You seem to find my captain of undue interest,"
Gage said with an edge to his voice.

"He is a fine-looking man," she said absently. "But
I was looking at the pennant. It's the first time I've
noticed it." She pointed to the red insignia blazoned on
the white background. "It is most unusual. I've seen
lions and stags and many other symbols, but never a ball
of fire."

"It's not a ball of fire, it's a comet."

"A comet!"

"Why not? It appeared in the sky last spring. I saw it, I wanted it, it was mine. Do you dislike it?"

"No. I think it beautiful." But she stared after the company of soldiers with trepidation. What kind of man was Gage Dumont to have chosen such a symbol? She had known no fear, but even the good monks had crossed themselves when they saw that comet. Yet Gage Dumont had made this supreme gesture of defiance. She felt a sudden desire to escape his presence. "I think I will go search for my water. It is taking far too long." She started quickly down the hill, her feet stumbling on the scraggly tussocks.

She could feel him watching her but he did not follow.

I saw it. I wanted it. It was mine. Arrogant words from an arrogant man. But she had an idea he was much more than he seemed. She glanced back at LeFont, who was now almost out of sight around the bend in the hill. She wished she had not noticed that pennant with its bold comet. It brought back memories of the night she had watched the comet streak across the heavens. The thought that somewhere that same night Gage Dumont had also been looking up at that comet gave her a sense of intimate bonding.

Bonding? Sweet Mary, even their response to the comet had been different. She had stared in wonder and delight. He had decided to take it for his own. There could never be a bonding between them.

Brynn opened her eyes at dawn three days later to see Gage Dumont staring at her across the tent. She should be accustomed to it, she thought drowsily. His gaze always seemed to be on her since that day he had plucked the leaf from her hair.

The pearl-gray rays streamed over him, highlighting the hollow beneath his high cheekbones and turning his ice-blue eyes to the glittering metallic shade found in fine daggers. He looked as if he were carved from granite, warrior-hard and without mercy.

She inhaled sharply, coming wide awake. Her hands slowly clenched into fists at her side. There was something different in the way he was staring at her. At first there had been antagonism and annoyance and then, lately, a kind of catlike watchfulness, as if he were trying to determine something regarding her. The antagonism and annoyance were still present, but whatever he had been trying to fathom had now been resolved.

I saw it. I wanted it. It was mine.

He might look carved from granite, but granite was cold and he did not make her feel cold. She could feel the heat sting her cheeks and a strange liquid weakness in her knees. Fear? No, it was not fear either.

Whatever it was, she must push it away. Push him away.

She closed her eyes and nestled closer to Malik.

She heard a sound that might have been a low curse and was acutely aware of the waves of displeasure Gage Dumont was emitting.

She did not open her eyes.

"You should not still be here," Malik told Gage. "LeFont says William has pushed on toward London. You should be with him, protecting your interests."

"I sent a token company of men," Gage said. "We'll join him when you're better."

"That may not be until spring. I cannot even sit up yet." He wrinkled his nose in disgust. "I cannot do anything. I eat and then go back to sleep like a babe."

Gage smiled. "I believe you're a bit impatient. It's been only four days since we thought you a dead man."

"I thought I was too." He glanced at the flap of the tent. "Where is she?"

"The woman? She's outside, boiling water. She had to prepare more salve for your wound."

"It must be a truly wonderful salve. I've never seen a wound heal so quickly."

"You just complained your recovery was taking too long," Gage teased. "Perhaps the woman is not completely without skill?"

"Brynn."

"What?"

"Her name is Brynn. You never refer to her by name, just 'the woman.'"

"What difference does it make?"

"Her name is Brynn," Malik repeated. "And it makes a difference."

"By heaven, I believe you're besotted with the wench."

"Besotted is not the word."

"You've decided that you've been struck by cupid's arrow again?"

He shook his head. "No, I thought that only because of the radiance."

Gage smiled sardonically. "And the radiance has faded?"

"It hasn't faded . . . it's just . . . I cannot think of her in intimate terms. It would be a presumption."

"It wasn't a presumption when you became enamored with the Duchess of Balmarin."

"That was different."

"You said that before. It most certainly is different. One woman is a duchess and the other a slave. The duchess was charming and civilized and your 'radiant' healer is prickly as a bramble bush, has a tongue like a scourge, and is the most difficult woman I've ever encountered."

"I like her," Malik said simply.

"You have strange tastes."

"I know." Malik beamed. "Why else would I

choose you as a friend? You are not known to be without briars yourself. I've decided that I was sent into this world to cast out demons."

"You were sent into this world to torment and exasperate." Gage looked away from him. "Do you want me to give you the woman?"

"No." Malik's gaze narrowed on his face. "That relieves you. Interesting."

"I'm sure I'm not to be spared learning what you mean by that remark."

"Of course not. Do I not share everything with you? I find it interesting that you are clearly trying to look on Brynn merely as a faceless woman and not a person and that you did not wish to relinquish her."

"Nonsense. I wouldn't offer to give her to you if I wanted to keep her."

"Unless you are in conflict regarding her. You value my humble life and she saved it. Perhaps giving her to me was your way of removing temptation from your path."

"You think I want to bed the wench?"

"I know you want to bed Brynn," Malik said softly. "I've had nothing to do but lie here for the last four days and watch you. I know you well, Gage. I could hardly mistake lust when I have seen it so often in you."

Gage shrugged. "I've been without a woman since we reached England and she has a fine body. It is a natural response."

"I'm the last one to give you argument. Lust is entirely natural; it is the anger that I find puzzling. Why do you resent wanting to bed her?"

"I don't resent—" He broke off and then said harshly, "Well, perhaps I do. Why is it important? Are you trying to keep me from using her?"

Malik shook his head. "I believe you should bed her and be done with it. You will be kinder to her once you've sated yourself, and I think she needs kindness."

"I'm surprised you're not asking me to free her."

"In a land ravaged by war? She is safer belonging to you. Perhaps later . . ." He yawned. "All of this chatter is making me tired. Go away. I think I'll take another nap. . . ."

Gage rose to his feet and moved toward the entrance of the tent.

Brynn was standing by the fire, briskly stirring a mixture in the cooking pot. He stood there, watching her.

Her arms were firm and strong as they moved in a circular motion. The rising steam made the hair at her temples curl riotously and the wool of her gown cling to her full breasts, delineating her nipples.

She loves to be touched.

Tight as a glove.

Bed her and be done with it.

He was hardening, readying to the point of pain. He was not even sure at what point he had become aware that he wanted her. That afternoon when he had touched her hair? Yes, he had wanted her then; his palm had tingled as it had touched that silky softness. But he had tried to dismiss it, to go back to that frustration and annoyance he had known before. He did not like wanting a woman with this desperate intensity, feeling that he had to have her.

Yet why did he keep fighting it? She posed no real danger to him. She was his property. Why didn't he just pick her up and carry her into that stand of trees and sate himself as Malik had advised him to do? She was no virgin who would faint at the touch of a man. She had been trained to please Richard of Redfern, and he'd wager that whoreson's tastes were as twisted as his morals. Rage instantly seared him at the vision the thought brought to mind. Jealousy, he wondered incredulously. Impossible. He had never been jealous of any woman.

"Have you nothing better to do than stand there,

gaping at me?" she asked without looking up from the brew she was stirring.

Irritation jabbed at him. Her words were always sweet and soft for Malik; even with LeFont she was polite. It was only Gage who received the rough edge of her tongue.

"What are you doing?" Gage grimaced as he saw her tear up leaves and drop them into the pot. "You're not going to rub that slop on Malik?"

"Every bit of it." Brynn stirred the mixture with renewed vigor. "And you need not watch me every minute of every day. Do you think I'm going to poison him?"

"No." He shrugged. "But he may think so when you force that on him."

"He knows I do only what's good for him." She glanced down at the pot. "Even if you doubt me."

"How can I doubt you?" Gage asked mockingly. "When Malik assures me you're either a saint or an angel?" He sat down on the ground and wrapped his arms about his knees. "It would be sacrilege and I would instantly be cast down into hell."

She snorted. "I would not think hell would hold any great terror for you."

"Does that mean you believe I'm an archdemon?"

"I didn't say that."

"But then, you don't say much of anything, do you? Except to order me about."

"I order you about only when it's necessary for Malik's well-being. You wanted him cured and I cannot do everything myself." She moistened her lips. "I want to move him from this place."

"He's not strong enough yet."

"I have no intention of moving him any great distance. Just a few miles." She gestured to the north. "Perhaps to the forest over there."

"Why?"

"It is best."

"For Malik?"

"No." She hesitated for a moment and then said reluctantly, "For me. This is a bad place. Can't you feel it?"

"Feel what?"

"If you cannot feel it, I can't explain. I just want to be gone from here." She paused and then whispered, "Please."

He looked at her in surprise. "This must mean a good deal to you. You're more given to commands than pleas."

She didn't answer.

"What if I give you what you wish?" He lowered his voice to silky softness. "Will you give me a gift in turn?"

"I've given you a gift. Malik is alive. Isn't that enough for you?"

"It should be."

"But it isn't?"

"Malik will tell you I don't know the meaning of enough. The prize just over the horizon is always the sweetest."

"So you reach out and take it," she said flatly.

"Or barter for it. I prefer the latter. It suits my merchant's soul. I suppose Malik has told you that I'm more trader than knight?"

"No, he said you were the son of a king and capable of being anything you want to be."

"Which obviously did not impress you."

"Why should it? It does not matter their station, men are all the same."

He smiled. "Certainly in some aspects. You didn't answer. Will you barter with me?"

"I have nothing with which to barter."

"You're a woman. A woman always has great bartering power."

She straightened her shoulders and turned to look directly at him. "You mean you wish me to be your whore."

His lips tightened. "Your words lack a certain delicacy."

"They do not lack truth." She looked down into the pot. "You wish me to part my limbs and let you rut like a beast of the forest. I wonder you even seek to bargain. You think me your slave. Isn't a slave to be used?"

"Yes," he said curtly. "A slave is to work and give pleasure. And you're right, I don't have to bargain with you. I can do what I wish."

"I'm glad that is clear." She stirred faster, harder. "Shall we go into the tent now? Or perhaps you wish to take me in front of all your soldiers? I'd be grateful if you'd have the kindness to let me finish preparing this salve that is making your friend well and healthy. But, if I seem unreasonable, you must only tell me and I will—"

"Be silent!" His teeth clenched, he added, "I've never met a woman with such a—"

"I'm only being humble and obliging. Isn't that what you want of me?"

"I want—" He stopped and then said thickly, "I'm not certain what I want . . . yet. When I do, I'll be sure you're made fully aware of it."

He turned and strode toward the tent. Suddenly, he halted and whirled to face her. "Who is Selbar?"

She stared at him in astonishment. "What?"

"You said you trusted this Selbar," he said harshly. "Who is he? Your lover?"

She shook her head.

"Who is he?"

She didn't answer.

"Tell me!"

"Why should I?" she asked fiercely. "You think you

own my body, but you don't own my mind. I'll tell you nothing."

He muttered a curse and disappeared into the tent.

Her hands were shaking, Brynn realized.

She had known this scene would come since that moment two nights before, but she had never dreamed she would be this frightened. She took a deep breath, steadied her grip on the ladle, and began to stir again.

She had deliberately taunted him to bring the response Delmas would have given. A blow would have diffused the Norman's anger and perhaps curbed his lust.

But Gage had not struck her nor had he used her body. He had contained his anger and walked away. Not a good thing. It meant only that what he was feeling would simmer and grow until she might not be able to control him.

He would enter her in that terrible way Delmas had done.

No, it would not be like Delmas. Delmas dwindled into nothingness compared to Gage Dumont. Just the thought of that huge body crouched over her own brought a strange tingling and sensitivity into her every limb. If the Norman used her, it would be like being overwhelmed by a giant wave and dashed against the rocks. She was not sure she could survive it.

She was being weak and foolish. Of course she could survive it. It would be only her body. He could not take anything away from her that was of any real importance.

Besides, she need not think of that just then. She had skirted the danger for the moment. She would face the next battle when it came.

"What is in that salve?" Malik wrinkled his nose as she spread the balm over his wound. "It smells to the heavens."

"Only boiled-down herbs and water." Brynn kept her gaze on the wound, carefully avoiding Gage's stare. Why did he not stop looking at her?

"What kind of herbs?"

"You wouldn't know them if I told you," she said evasively.

"I might. My countrymen are far more skilled in the art of medicine than the Franks, and I hardly think the English are more proficient."

To distract him, she said quickly, "You think this mixture is odorous? In dire cases the recipe calls for a substitute for the water."

"What kind of substitute?" Malik asked warily.

She tried to keep a smile from tugging at her lips. "Dog urine."

"Ugh." A sudden thought occurred to him. "My condition is not dire now, but it was a few days ago. Did you . . ."

"Urine is also highly regarded for cleaning out the bad humors from the inner body. A fourth of a cup mixed with meat broth is said to be absolutely necessary in such cases."

"Broth." Malik's eyes widened in alarm. "I couldn't have been that ill."

Brynn shook her head mournfully. "You almost died. What else could I do?"

Malik swallowed hard. "Nothing, I suppose."

He looked so stricken, she could not keep on with it. She threw back her head and laughed. "Be at ease. I didn't use it. I don't agree that dog urine is necessary to affect a cure."

"Thank God," Malik said fervently.

"There are other ingredients just as good." She waited and then asked, "Don't you want to know what I did use?"

"I don't think so."

She smiled. "Very wise."

"It is?" he asked, dismayed.

"Your body has been strained enough. I would not have you worrying about things you cannot change." She finished bandaging the wound. "There. That should hold through the night. I'll go and get your supper."

"I do not believe I'm hungry."

"Of course you are." She rose to her feet and a sudden smile lit her face as she looked down at him. "Rabbit stew and savory herbs and nothing else, I promise."

"I'll get it." Gage abruptly stood up and moved toward the entrance. "I'd hate to have you interrupt this intimate little chat."

She tensed as he brushed by her. In the exchange with Malik she had almost forgotten Gage's silent presence, but he would not allow himself to be forgotten. He was there, powerful, overwhelming. She said haltingly, "It's my duty. You need not bother."

"If I thought it was a bother, I wouldn't do it," he said harshly. "It's not my custom to do anything I don't wish to do." He stood there, looking at her with a scowl. "Besides, I need to talk to LeFont. We're moving camp at dawn."

Her eyes widened in shock.

"We're following William?" Malik asked.

"No, I'm weary of this place. We're going to set up camp in the forest a few miles distant."

"We are?" Brynn whispered, a brilliant smile lighting her face. "Truly?"

"I said it, didn't I? Why should I repeat myself?"

"No reason." Her tone was nearly lilting. "No reason at all."

He hesitated, still staring at her luminous expression before turning and striding out of the tent.

"I take it that it was your wish to leave this illustrious battleground," Malik said.

She nodded, still looking at the place Gage had occupied. "But I didn't think he'd do it. It's a good deal of trouble to move a camp, and I had no firm reason."

"Then why did you want to leave?"

"You wouldn't under—" She met his gaze. Perhaps he would understand. She had never met a more sensitive or gentle person than Malik. "It's a death place. It makes me sad."

He nodded slowly, studying her. "I think it makes you more than sad."

She had been right about the sensitivity. In fact, he saw too much. She changed the subject. "I don't know why he agreed to move. He's a hard man."

"I don't deny that truth. However, it may be that he wished to please you." He paused. "Such conduct is common in the mating ritual."

She felt heat rush to her cheeks. She had not realized Malik had perceived the sensuality in Gage's attitude. "A man does not care about a woman's pleasure when he mates," she said jerkily. "And I believe your fine Lord Gage has little liking for rituals. He impresses me as a rough man who would just as soon take a woman in a hayfield as a bed."

Malik shook his head. "You are wrong. You have seen only the warrior. You will learn that Gage is . . . much more."

"I have no desire to learn more."

"You may have no choice," Malik said gently. "He wants you."

"And that is all that matters? A man reaches out and takes because he lusts? What of what I want?" Her hands clenched into fists at her sides. "It's not fair."

"But have you not found that life is seldom fair?"

"Yes." She drew a deep breath and forced herself to relax. She knew that anger was futile and was surprised she had lost control. Her emotional responses seemed to be volatile and increasingly intense since she had been thrown into this situation. "That's why one must sometimes guide it in the right direction." She turned to face him. "You are not like him. Will you help me?"

"I will not help you escape. You are safer here with us." He grimaced. "And if you stay, I will wager you are in Gage's bed before the week's end."

"I cannot escape yet." She frowned. "There is a problem at Redfern . . ."

"Problem?"

She ignored the question as she rushed on. "Tell me what he wants."

He raised his brows. "If you are not a virgin, then you know what he wants."

The heat in her cheeks burned higher. "No, that's not what I meant. Women are not really important to a man except for that brief moment. I cannot fight him unless I know what he wants."

"And you intend to give it to him?"

"I have to know."

"He is my friend. I should not ally myself against him."

"I saved your life. You would have died without me."

"True." A mischievous smile lit his bearded face. "And a little conflict in the air always makes life more interesting."

She breathed a sigh of relief. "You will help me?"

"What does Gage want? He already has great wealth and is now a baron."

"I did not ask what he has, I asked what he wants. I have never met a man who didn't want more than he possessed."

"You may be as great a cynic as my friend Gage." He studied her. "No, perhaps not, I think you still want to believe in dreams."

"Dreams have nothing to do with this. What does he want?"

He thought about it. "He thinks he wants to be king."

"Thinks?"

"He was shunned by everyone in the village and then rejected by his father. When you are pressed into the dirt, it's natural to want to rise to a position where that can never happen again."

"But not all men aspire to a throne," she said dryly.

"Not all men can rule. Gage has always known his capabilities, which makes his situation all the more frustrating." He smiled quizzically. "Tell me, sweet healer, can you give a man a throne?"

"No, but I might . . ." She frowned. "Can he be trusted?"

"What?"

"Will he keep his word?"

Malik was staring at her, intrigued. "He can be trusted."

"You're sure?" she persisted.

"I have staked my life on it many times. Your presence here is only the latest proof," Malik said quietly. "I have never known him to break his promise."

The treasure? Even if she could convince the Norman to give her his promise, it would be a risk. Vows given to women always had less weight than those given to men. And what if he decided not to bargain with her at all and tried to wrest the information from her by force as Delmas had done?

She shivered as she thought of all that relentless power leveled at her. She did not want to enter the arena with Gage Dumont. Surely she could find another way to escape this situation.

"You're afraid," Malik said. "You need not be. If you go willingly to his bed, he will treat you gently." He smiled. "And it is not forever. Gage grows bored with women in a very short time. No matter how skilled you are, you will not hold him long."

Skilled? She knew practically nothing of bed skills, nor did she wish to learn. However, it was a relief to know that if she could not avoid him, her ordeal would be brief.

But she would avoid him. She was giving up the battle before it began. Gage Dumont seemed formidable only because she was so weary of fighting. He might be ruthless, but she did not sense the evil in him she saw in Richard. She must look on the Norman as an opportunity, not as a nemesis. "I will not hold him at all." She added haltingly, "I thank you. You have been kind."

"I am always kind. I learned long ago that kindness is the one gift one never regrets giving." He grimaced. "But I have to warn you, Gage does not always agree with me when the gift causes a great deal of trouble. He accepts but he does not understand."

"I am surprised at his acceptance."

"Because you know only the warrior," he said again. "He is also merchant, poet, musician . . . many things."

Well, she would soon become acquainted with the merchant if she decided to barter what she held dearest in this world.

"But, if you think me kind, you might do me a great favor." Malik turned mournful eyes at her. "Please?"

"What do you wish of me?"

"A promise. Regarding the future ingredients in my stew . . ."

She sat in the corner of the tent, combing her hair as she did every evening before she settled for the night.

Gage watched as Brynn raised her arm and the teeth of the comb bit into the thickness of her fair hair.

There was no more sensual sound in the world than the hiss of a comb through the silk of a woman's tresses, Gage thought.

Sensual and arousing.

Once he had her, the torment would be gone. She would be no more to him than the whores who followed the soldiers. He should have done as she challenged him that afternoon and carried her into the trees and had his way with her. Why the devil hadn't he?

She smiled at something Malik had said and then reached down to run the comb lightly through his dark beard.

Fury burst through Gage at the small intimacy. Goddammit, she was always *touching* him. He jumped to his feet and blew out the flame in the lantern hanging from the post, casting the tent into darkness. But it wasn't dark enough. He could still see the outline of Brynn's body hovering over Malik.

"She was not finished," Malik protested. "Why did you turn out the light?"

"It's time to go to sleep."

"Another few moments would not have mattered."

"It matters. We break camp at dawn. If she wished to dally all night, she should not have asked to move from this place."

"Brynn does not dally and a few minutes is not all—" Malik broke off as Brynn made a motion with her hand.

"It's not important," Brynn said. "You should have told me sooner that I was disturbing you."

Her voice coming from the darkness was smooth as honey but without its sweetness. No, it had the bite and strength of a fine ale. "You are not disturbing me."

She did disturb him. Everything about her unsettled him. The way she moved, the wariness of the glances she gave him from beneath her lashes that was at odds with the boldness of her speech, the scent of soap and herbs that clung to her . . .

"But you said that—"

"Go to sleep."

She hesitated and then slid down to lie beside Malik on his pallet.

"No!" Gage drew a deep breath and then tried to temper the harshness of his tone. "There's no reason for you to sleep with Malik. You said he was no longer in danger."

"There is reason. It's not time for me to leave him."

"Tell me, do you sleep with all the people you tend?"

"Yes."

"How pleasant for the males of the species."

Malik interjected, "Gage, let it—"

"Leave him."

"I will not."

Gage stiffened. "You disobey me?"

"Gage, I am flattered you think I am capable of proving a threat to this fair damsel, but I—"

"Be quiet, Malik."

"Yes, I disobey you," Brynn said fiercely. "I know what is best for him and I will not leave him until I feel it safe."

"And your cuddling close to him makes him safe?"

She did not speak for a moment, and when she did, the word seemed wrenched from her. "Yes."

"And what of your fine herbs and medicines? Would they not do as well?"

"I don't—it is not the same—why can you not—"

"You appear a trifle confused. Perhaps you're mistaking your own desires for Malik's needs."

"No." Her voice was shaking. "Don't you think I would give you this small thing if I could? You are doing me a service in leaving this place and I owe you gratitude. But I cannot—it's not safe for me to leave him at night yet."

"Why not?"

"Sometimes the dragons come."

"Dragons?"

"Not real beasts. I'm not sure they exist, but there are other dragons. Weakness and infection and . . ." Her voice lowered to a whisper. "And death. They wait until we are least expecting them and then they pounce."

"And you think you can keep these beasts at bay by touching Malik?"

"I didn't say that," Brynn said quickly, a note of panic in her voice. "I never said I could heal by touch."

"It sounded very much like it to me."

"That would make me a sorceress. I'm no sorceress. God is the only one who can heal."

"And yet Malik swears that his cure is almost miraculous."

"Leave her alone," Malik said.

"Why, when the discussion is becoming so interesting?" He tried to see her expression, but her face was only a pale blur in the moonlit darkness. "Tell me more about these dragons you battle."

She did not speak.

"Or perhaps you'd like to tell me what is in that mixture that healed Malik."

"Have you not been listening? He is not healed yet."

"But it is the salve that heals him."

"Of course it is the salve."

"Good. Then you won't mind leaving him and sleeping apart tonight."

"I can't—" She broke off and was silent again. She finally said, "I won't leave him. I cannot help what you think. If you wish to believe I'm a sorceress and cured him by magic, then believe it."

"Oh, I don't believe it. Magic does not exist." He paused. "But you believe it, don't you?"

"If I believed such blasphemy, the church would burn me."

"Not if you could perform miracles for their exclusive benefit," he said cynically. "But fail once, and I fear the stake will have you."

"I am not a sorceress. It is the salve." She added quickly, "And I sleep with your friend because he may wake in distress and need me. It is that simple."

"Surely that is reasonable, Gage," Malik said. "As she said, it is merely a simple desire to protect me from harm."

She was not telling the truth and, if she did believe she had magical powers, he could hardly blame her. Witches were either worshipped or despised but always feared. Fear could be a deadly enemy. "Not simple at all." He lay down on his pallet. "But very interesting. By all means, sleep with Malik . . . tonight."

She settled down again, but he could sense the wariness in her even across the distance separating them.

She should be wary. She had given him another weapon tonight. Not that he had needed it. She was a slave and he the master. Yet he was beginning to think that he would use every weapon at his command before they were done with each other.

"Shh," Malik whispered. "All will be well."

He was comforting her, Gage realized with annoyance. Once again Gage was the villain and Malik the gentle knight. Well, why not? It was nothing to him if she thought of Malik as friend and Gage as foe. He did not want her trust or goodwill. All he wanted was to part her thighs and lose himself in her. As he had already concluded, fear was an ally that seldom failed. Let her fear him if it would bring him what he wanted.

A movement in the darkness; she was drawing nearer to Malik.

He smothered the fierce surge of rage and forced himself to close his eyes and shut them out. Tomorrow he would take her and be done with it. Then he would not care if she slept again in Malik's arms.

Four

"IS HE ALL right?" Gage paused beside the wagon to look down with a frown at Malik. "How is he standing the journey?"

"Well," Malik said quickly. "I feel fine."

"Not fine," Brynn said. "He is tiring. I didn't think those woods were this far. They looked much closer. Only an hour or so distant."

"I am fine," Malik repeated with a smile. "Journeys always invigorate me."

"Perhaps we should have waited another day," Brynn murmured. "But he slept well and I thought—"

"We'll be there in an hour's time," Gage interrupted, and wheeled his horse away from the wagon.

Brynn grimaced as she watched him ride away. "He's angry with me."

"Yes."

"And rightly. I should have told him you weren't strong enough to travel."

"I'd wager his displeasure has little to do with the state of my health." He smiled faintly. "And everything to do with the fact that he did not sleep nearly as well as I did last night."

"You mean—" She stopped as she realized how stupid she had been. Lust. "Then he deserves to not feel well. I don't understand why men must always be guided by their nether parts. It would be a much more pleasant world if they would think occasionally, instead of feel."

He chuckled. "I realize we are abysmally primitive creatures compared to you sweet damsels. You must forgive us. I am sure God made us that way to guarantee his children would survive on this earth during these perilous times." His smile faded. "But this particular time is not as perilous for you as you believe."

She glanced away from him. "I don't know what you mean."

"You were very frightened last night. You did not sleep well either." When she did not answer, he asked, "Do you have magical powers?"

"Of course not."

He studied her. "You are still frightened. Why? You saved my life. I would never betray you."

"You think that now. It could be different later."

"Not for me. Trust in me, Brynn."

She glanced back at him. She could almost believe him. Dear God, she needed someone with whom to talk. She was so alone.

What was she thinking? After all the turmoil she had been through, had she learned nothing? She could trust no one. She smiled with an effort. "You heard Lord Gage. There is no magic in this world."

A flicker of disappointment crossed his face before he said lightly, "How disappointing. You realize I do not believe as Gage does. My people believe the world would be a dreary place without magic." He paused. "If you should decide that you do have these powers, you could have no better protector than Gage. He fears neither king nor Pope and would delight in defying them. You would be safe with him."

Her gaze went to Gage's broad, armored back. Safe?

She felt as if she could reach out and touch the wall of power and violence surrounding him. Yet what if all that power were used in her defense instead of against her? She was terribly weary of battling alone against odds that seemed insurmountable. If she could strike a bargain . . .

"He would be kinder to you than Lord Richard."

She glanced back at Malik. "That would be no great feat."

"Then give Gage what he wants and accept his protection."

He meant go meekly to the Norman's bed. She should not be disappointed in Malik. He truly wished her well, and it was the bartering tool all men expected women to use. He did not know she had another possible weapon. "Close your eyes and try to nap. You're talking too much."

He sighed. "Which means I'm expounding on a subject you do not wish to discuss."

"Talk has no value without the means to act." She was silent a moment, thinking. "Would he—is Lord Gage—"

"Is Gage what?"

"He talks of barter. If I could give him something else he valued very much, would he still demand—service."

"What do you have of such value?"

She ignored the question. "Would he?"

"Not as a rule." Then, as he saw her relief, he shook his head. "But the rule may not apply in your case. I have never seen him this eager for a woman."

So even if she struck a bargain that involved Gwynthal, she might still have to yield to the act she hated. Was it worth that horror to gain her freedom? She fought down the instinctive revulsion and tried to think clearly. It might not be worth bedding the Norman for her own benefit, but what of Adwen? Copulation for a life. She remembered a song sung by a traveling troubadour in the hall at Redfern wherein the wife of a great lord killed herself rather than submit to the embrace of his enemy. It had been loudly applauded by the assembly. Choosing death before dishonor was entirely fitting for a woman.

But it was men who chose what was fitting, and fairness had little to do with those decisions. Was it just that a young woman's life depended on Brynn's submission? She had kept her body from being used by Delmas, but her instincts as a healer would not permit her to let Adwen perish if yielding it became necessary.

"Now, what could you have of such value?" Malik murmured.

She shook her head. If the barter was struck, she had no doubt Gage would reveal everything to him, but habit was too strong for her to tell him herself.

"Secrets." Malik smiled. "What a delight you are proving to be. I love secrets."

Malik loved every facet of life. It was his most endearing quality. She found herself smiling in return. "Some secrets are not always pleasant."

"But always interesting, and you could have no ugly secrets."

Fire. Blood. Screams.

Running through the forest with the beasts in pursuit . . .

"Couldn't I?" She pulled the blanket higher around his shoulders and looked at Gage Dumont. He was a man of secrets and she would wager most of them were laden with intrigue and violence.

As if he felt her stare, he turned his head and glanced over his shoulder.

She inhaled sharply and instinctively tensed. She always felt as if he were physically touching her when those icy blue eyes met her own. She felt that sensation of liquid heat and weakness that was becoming maddeningly familiar. It was all very well to objectively weigh the value of submission, but could she do it?

Of course she could do it.

His gaze narrowed on her face, and she had the uncanny feeling he was reading her mind. She shut her lids quickly and then realized that the act was too revealing and opened them again and stared at him boldly.

He smiled and turned and spurred toward the woods.

They reached the forest a few miles distant from Hastings before noon. The camp was struck on a hill overlooking a pleasant little pond, and Malik gave a sigh of relief when he was comfortably settled on his pallet in the tent. "Ah, this is much better. I believe I have an aversion to wagons."

"I'm truly sorry," Brynn said. "I meant you no harm." He was a trifle pale and wan but not exhausted. She breathed a sigh of relief. A nap and food and any damage incurred would be fixed. "I'll fix you a cup of broth and then—"

"Broth?" His eyes widened in alarm. "I told you I was fine. I have suffered no harm from this journey. On second thought, I'm not really tired at all."

"But you said—" Then she understood and began to laugh. "I wouldn't do that to you."

"I am not sure I trust you. I think you would use any means to make me well." He waved his hand. "Go away and let me sleep. I don't have the energy to argue at present and I will have to show you later that I have lost no strength."

"You are not being—" He had already closed his eyes and she shook her head resignedly. It would do no harm to let him nap first and eat later. A long rest might be the best medicine for him. "As you wish."

He opened one suspicious eye. "Such meekness. Are you planning something?"

"Perhaps." He deserved a little worry for his lack of faith in her word. She smiled mischievously over her shoulder as she left the tent. "I will start your broth cooking."

She heard his groan.

"You appear pleased with yourself."

Her smile instantly disappeared when she saw Gage standing beside the small fire outside the tent. She had not seen him since that instance on the trail, but she had known this moment would come.

"How is Malik?" he asked.

"Better than I feared. I don't think the journey hurt him. But he's very tired; he's almost asleep already." She tried to tear her gaze away from his and failed. She felt . . . seared. "I need to talk with you."

"Talk?" he repeated softly. "That's not the need I saw in you a short time ago."

"You are mistaken."

"No, you are lying." His lips twisted. "I'm disappointed. I thought you above such subterfuge. Do you wish me to use force so that you may claim virtue later? It is all the same to me." He took a step toward her. "Just don't drag the play on too long. My patience is wearing thin. Come along."

She took a step back. "Malik. I—was going to make him some broth to eat when he woke."

"Later." His big hand encircled her wrist and he strode away from the tent, pulling her behind him. As they passed LeFont, he tossed out, "Keep an eye on Malik. We'll be down by the pond."

LeFont nodded and smiled. "I'll make sure you are not disturbed, my lord."

Her heart leapt as she stumbled after Gage. It was coming. LeFont knew it. Dear heaven, and she knew it. Think. She had to think. He was not a man driven entirely by lust. Merchant, musician, poet, Malik had said. King. He wanted to rule. A woman was nothing to a man when compared to such a prize. Her breath was coming in short pants as he jerked her into the trees.

He released her wrist and turned away from her. "Undress." He took off his cloak and spread it on the leaves carpeting the forest floor. "Be quick."

"No."

He whirled on her. "What ploy is this?"

She moistened her lips. "No ploy. I told you I wanted to talk."

"Is this a game your Lord Richard taught you?" He pushed her back against the oak tree. "I have no liking for such teasing."

"I don't know how to tease. I'm telling you the truth. I do not want this."

"The hell you don't." His palm reached out and covered her breast.

Her heart stopped and then began to pound wildly. She could feel the warmth and hardness through the thin layer of wool that separated his calloused hand from her breast, and it was causing a strange change in her body. The nipple was hardening, peaking, and her breast was swelling. She looked down in fascination at his huge hand cupping and squeezing her. She had a sudden desire to know how it would feel to have both his hands on her breasts.

"The hell you don't," he repeated, but the harshness was gone from his tone, leaving only silken sensuality. "I'm not a fool. You want it." His thumb and forefinger gently pinched her nipple.

A streak of fire surged through her. No, fire was pain and this was not pain. It was heavier, throbbing, wilder than anything she had ever felt before.

He bent his head and his mouth hovered over her breast while his hand lazily squeezed the other. His breath was warm and she could feel her nipple rise as if to meet him. "You see?" His tongue licked delicately at her nipple through the rough cloth. "You *are* teasing me. Now, take off that gown and let us enjoy each other."

She bit back a cry as she arched against the tree. She wanted him to strip the gown from her. She wanted to fall naked to the ground and open her thighs so that he could do with her as he would. Was this what Delmas and Lord Richard felt when they were rutting? she wondered hazily. She had not thought women could feel this animal need. It had no dignity . . .

She would not be an animal. She would not be a vessel for him to spend his lust. She would not be—

His teeth bit gently on the nipple he'd brought to full arousal.

She groaned and her hands reached up to touch his hair. Closer. She wanted him closer. She arched up toward his mouth, offering more.

"Yes," he muttered. His hands went around to cup her buttocks and bring her into the hollow of his hips. Arousal. Hard, unrelenting . . . "Spread your legs. That's right . . . Now let me—"

She must not—she would not be his whore. To bargain something of value was one thing, but she was giving herself to him freely. It was somehow much worse than—

She tore away from him. "No!"

He stared at her in astonishment. She had caught him off guard, she realized. He had thought he had bent her to his will. He shook the hair out of his eyes and said with dangerous softness, "Come here. I will not be played with."

Play? She could have laughed aloud if she had not felt so desperate. She was shaking in every limb and felt curiously incomplete. Dear heaven, she wanted to return to him, to let him . . . She shook her head. "Why will you not listen? I have to talk . . . we need to barter."

He went still and then a cynical smile touched his lips. "Forgive me. I thought since you belonged to me that the usual haggling was unnecessary. What's your price? What do you want for taking me between your legs?"

The crudity of the question jarred her, and she found the madness leaving her. She drew a deep breath and stood up straighter. "You don't understand."

"On the contrary, there's nothing I understand better than the barter. Come now, don't hesitate. I'm a very rich man and I prefer a willing wench."

"You could be richer. You could have the wealth that most men only dream about."

"You're very greedy. I assure you I'm rich enough to pay you handsomely for your favors."

"No, that's not what I mean." She gestured impatiently. "I don't want you to pay me. I want to pay you."

"I'm weary of this nonsense." He took a step nearer. "If you think anticipation will cause my lust to sharpen, you're wrong." His tone roughened. "By God, I could not want you more."

"It's not nonsense." She backed away again. "Malik says you would like to be king. I can give that to you."

His skeptical glance ran over her coarse brown gown. "Indeed? Are slaves ruling the world now? Or perhaps you intend to use sorcery to do it?"

She ignored the mockery. "I told you I was no sorceress, but I can give you what you want. Providing a crown can be bought."

"Oh, anything can be bought with the right exchange. However, the price of a throne is too high even for me."

"Then I know where there is a treasure that would buy a thousand thrones."

Slowly the mockery faded from his face. "I believe you mean it."

"Of course I mean it."

"Let me understand you. You wish to ransom your virtue and your freedom for this incredible treasure?"

She frowned. "Don't be foolish. Neither of those is yours to give. I would not barter Gwynthal for something that is only mine to yield or take."

"Gwynthal?"

"The place of my birth."

"And the cache for this splendid treasure?"

She nodded. "You have never seen a treasure so beautiful. Emeralds and rubies and bowls of gold . . ." She trailed off as she realized he was looking at her totally without expression. "You don't believe me. I can prove it to you."

"How?"

"Come with me to Redfern."

"And you will show me this treasure? I thought it was at this Gwynthal."

"It is, but I can show you at Redfern that it exists." He said nothing, and she asked, "Why do you hesitate? I'm giving you what you want."

"You have given me nothing." His eyes went over her, lingering on her breasts. "Nothing."

Heat moved through her again, and for a moment she felt as if she were once more pinned to that tree, his huge body rubbing against her. She lifted her chin. "I barter with a treasure beyond price and all you can talk about is coupling."

"Perhaps because it's all I can think about." His gaze lifted to her face. "What will you take for this treasure beyond price?"

He still did not believe her but, at least, he was no longer on the edge of reaching out and taking what he wanted. "I wish safe passage to Gwynthal and your protection on the journey. When we arrive there and you have the treasure, I wish you to go away and leave me at Gwynthal." She added caustically, "It is very little to ask for a throne."

"Very little." He smiled. "If there is a treasure. I admit I find it curious that a slave would not use the treasure herself to purchase her freedom, if not a throne."

"Come to Redfern and I will give you proof."

Instead of assenting, he asked, "Why do you want to go to Redfern so badly?"

"The proof is there."

He slowly shook his head. "That is not all, is it?"

She was tempted to tell him of Adwen, but it was possible he might suspect she was luring him to Redfern only for her sake. Actually, that was close to the truth. "It is all that concerns you."

His lips tightened. "But not all that concerns you. Could it be that you're yearning for that handsome Judas who was so eager to pander you?"

"The proof is there," she said again. "Malik will be well enough to travel in a week's time. Go to Redfern and you will have no need to curry favor with William for a paltry holding."

"I don't curry favor." He studied her and then said softly, "You *are* trying to play games with me. You expected that gibe to annoy me."

Dear heaven, he was clever. "Why should I do that?"

"To goad me to do what you wish."

"I'm giving you what you want," she said desperately. "Why will you not listen?"

"Because I don't believe in mythical treasures."

"Then you're a fool!"

Astonishment showed on his face. "By God, it's possible you actually think you could give me this treasure."

"Go to Redfern."

He shook his head. "William is already irritated because I stayed here when Malik was wounded. It would not be wise to delay joining him."

"You said you did not curry favor."

"I also don't make the mistake of defying a monarch when it will bring me nothing in return."

"I told you—"

"But you did not convince me. You may believe what you say, but you also think you can heal a man by sleeping with him." He suddenly smiled with infinite sensuality and held out his hand. "Come. Heal my affliction, Brynn of Falkhaar."

"No!" She suddenly lost her temper. "Why should I? You're a stupid, blind Norman who would rather rut than reach out and grasp what is important to him. You deserve to wallow in William's dust. Malik was wrong. You have the brains of an ox and would rather sink in the mud than—"

"Enough."

"It is not enough. You come here and ride over me as if I were nothing and then think I should lie down at your bidding and—"

"I said enough!" He was suddenly towering over her, his hand covering her mouth as he glared into her eyes. "I have treated you with more patience than you deserve. I can do with you as I wish. You *belong* to me."

She bit down on his palm, and when he withdrew it with a curse she said, "I belong to no one."

"Not even to your pretty Lord Richard?" His hand closed on her breast and there was no gentleness in his grasp, only possession. "Forget him. You will never see him or Redfern again."

Why did he persist in thinking she wanted to remember that beast? He was important only as a threat to Adwen. "I have to go to Redfern. It is—" She gave a low cry as his hand involuntarily tightened on her breast.

To her surprise, he gave a low exclamation and his hand moved away from her. "I didn't mean—I didn't realize—" He whirled away from her and said haltingly, "It is not my custom to brutalize women."

She continued to stare at him in surprise. He appeared genuinely upset that he had hurt her. Neither Delmas nor Lord Richard would have given a thought to her pain if it had gotten them what they wanted.

He turned back and glowered at her. "Though it is entirely your own fault. You would tempt a saint to violence."

"You bear no resemblance to a saint."

"You see? You have a tongue that would burn—" He stopped and was clearly trying to gather his composure. "I have no desire to hurt you."

"You do not think rape would hurt me?"

"Not if you didn't fight me."

"Is that all you want? A body to lie lax and lifeless while you spend yourself?"

"It is what most men would—" He broke off and then the words tumbled fiercely. "No, by God, I want you hot and willing. I want you to moan and shake when I enter you. I want you to move against me and let me have you any way I want you."

She was trembling now. "I cannot give you willingness. It will not happen."

"It almost did. It will again. Your Lord Richard was right; you do have a passionate nature." His lips twisted. "But it seems I must teach you to channel it only in my direction."

Passion? Was that hot, powerful compulsion really passion? Whatever it was, it was too strong and must be banished. "I don't want—"

"You do want it, but perhaps you want what waits for you at Redfern more." He paused. "Shall we barter, Brynn?"

"I've already tried to barter with you."

"But I don't think you were entirely honest and you couldn't prove good intent. That's always necessary in such a pact." He smiled. "There's a possibility you do have proof of this treasure at Redfern. There's also the possibility that you wish to draw me there for reasons of your own and will waste my time. To take the risk I must have compensation."

"A visit to Redfern will not take much time. It's only a short distance from here."

"Nevertheless, I must be compensated." He was silent a moment and then added, "In one week Malik will be able to travel. It's your decision whether we go to Redfern or follow William to London."

He turned and left her.

She stared after him, startled at the abruptness of his departure. The first foray was over and she had won. If delay could be called a victory.

Of course delay was a victory, she quickly assured herself. He had left to her the decision to come to him and had not totally discounted her offer of the treasure. He wanted willingness, and she had a week to convince him that she would never give him what he desired and he should accept the much greater prize beckoning from Gwynthal.

A week could be a long time.

A week was not that long, Gage thought as he strode back to the camp.

It was damn long. What in Hades had led him to walk away from her again? He was a fool and as soft as one of those mawkish fools the troubadours sang about. He could have had her. Even now he could be between her thighs, his hands squeezing those breasts that had felt so firm and warm through the cloth of her gown. He could be moving and hearing her cry out to him as her hands dug into—

Christ.

He was hurting; heavy and engorged. He stopped at the edge of the encampment and reached out to grasp the trunk of a tree with one hand. His fingers dug into the bark until a ripple of pain went through him. He welcomed it as a distraction from that other maddening ache.

She would come to him. She wanted to go back to this Redfern. He would not have to use force. She would come and let him have her. He had only to wait.

Wait?

God's blood, he was heavy and stiff as a stallion scenting a mare in season.

He could wait.

A week was not that long.

"I wish you would go away, Gage." Malik sighed. "Brynn tells me I must rest and keep a serene mind, and how can I do that with you prowling around the tent like a tiger about to pounce?"

"I'm not prowling." Gage stopped prowling, threw open the tent flap, and looked out into the darkness. "Where is she?"

"In the forest. She likes the forest."

"Does she?" In the past three days she had certainly spent enough time strolling through the underbrush. He was not sure if it was because, as Malik said, she liked the woods, or wanted to avoid him. Either way he didn't like it. "You should have told her not to go. LeFont tells me there are wild boars in these forests."

"I am sure you've already told her."

He had told her and she had ignored him. Not that her disregard of his wishes in this matter was exceptional. She had scarcely looked at him or spoken a word since that day by the pond. "You appear to have more influence on her than I do."

"She says she's safe in the forest." He paused. "I think she is more afraid of the human beast than the animal."

"The soldiers won't bother her. They know she's my property."

"I wasn't speaking of the soldiers."

Gage knew he wasn't, but he had chosen to misunderstand. It was clear Malik had no intention of letting him do so. "Say it."

"If she is so opposed to taking you to her bed, why not let her win the battle?"

"The hell I will," he said harshly.

"I knew that would be your response." Malik sighed again. "I just thought I would make the attempt."

Gage whirled to face him. "You said before that I should bed her as soon as possible. What changed your mind?"

"I have gotten to know her better. To many women, taking a man is an easy, joyous matter. For her it would not be so. She could not rise from your bed and walk away."

"You think I should send her back to Richard of Redfern's bed? By God, I will *not*. If she can become used to pleasuring that whoreson, she can take me. She's done with him. I won't send her to Redfern, nor will I pay heed to her pleas and take her there."

"Perhaps it's not Richard. Perhaps she spoke true about this treasure."

"And perhaps she didn't. How would a slave know of such a thing?"

"How does a slave know how to read and write? It's a skill not many noblemen in this benighted country possess."

He frowned. "She can read?"

Malik nodded. "And write."

"She told you this?"

"She mentioned it in passing."

"You seem to have her complete confidence. What else did she mention 'in passing'?"

"Nothing. She is wary as a frightened bird. She

would not have told me if it had not slipped out." He made a face. "And don't glare at me. I have no desire to stand between the two of you. It would be most uncomfortable."

"Then don't interfere."

"I must do what my heart wills," he said simply.

"You might try doing what your head wills," Gage said dryly. "It will save considerable lumps and bruises."

"Are you threatening him?" Gage turned to see Brynn standing in the entrance of the tent. She frowned as she came forward. "You would threaten a sick and helpless man?"

"Yes, come and protect me, Brynn." Malik's eyes gleamed with mischief from beneath half-lowered lids, and he held out a pleading hand. "I cannot defend myself from this barbarian."

Brynn studied his guileless expression and then grimaced. "You defend yourself very well," she said, kneeling beside him, "and deceit deserves a few lumps and bruises." In spite of the tart words, her hands were gentle as they pulled the cover closer to his throat.

A tiny scarlet maple leaf was caught in her golden-brown hair, and he remembered the rueful remark she had made about her thick hair being a net. Gage could smell the scent of earth and crisp autumn air that clung to her. Her skin glowed in the lantern light and the air seemed to vibrate with the vitality she exuded. He wanted to step closer and pull the leaf from her hair and then gently run his fingers through the bright thickness.

Gentleness. It was the first time he had wanted to touch her with tenderness, he realized. Usually his body was too ready and hurting for him to think of anything but the lust that racked him.

"You shouldn't have gone into the forest alone," he said gruffly.

She stiffened but didn't look at him. "I was quite safe."

Her wariness irritated him more than usual. "That's my decision to make." He added mockingly, "I won't have my property damaged."

Her hand clenched on Malik's cover, but she replied evenly, "As you can see, I'm not damaged." She turned away and ordered, "Blow out the lantern. Malik needs to sleep."

Malik made a motion to lift the cover for her to lie down beside him.

"No." She smiled down at him. "It's time for you to sleep alone." She took off her cloak and spread it a few yards distant on the ground. "I'll be here if you need me."

Gage was almost as surprised as Malik. "I take it the dragons have gone back into their caves?"

"Laugh if you like. I don't care. There is a time for all things. It was wrong to leave him before."

She was bristling at the expected mockery, and yet there was something touching and gallant in her defiance. He abruptly turned away, picked up one of his blankets, and tossed it to her. "I'm not laughing." He blew out the flame in the lantern. "For God's sake, go to sleep."

Five

THE NEXT AFTERNOON the sun was shining brightly, and Brynn arranged to have four of LeFont's soldiers carry Malik out to lie on a pallet outside the tent.

Malik blissfully lifted his face to the sun. "Good. I almost feel alive again."

Brynn smiled. "I thought you'd like it. We'll come out for a little while every day now. The sun is a great healer."

"No better than you." Malik smiled. "What a sweet, modest lady. You give credit to everything and everyone but yourself."

"I'd say that was a very safe course."

Brynn turned to see Gage coming toward them.

He continued. "And shows the lady is wise as well as modest."

The words were barbed, but the tone lacked Gage's customary mockery when he addressed her. It was almost . . . warm. He might have been speaking to Malik. It was the second time he had surprised her. Last night she had convinced herself that moment of gruff kindness had been a whim, but now he was looking at her as if—oh, she did not know. She was probably imag-

ining that sudden softness, and this yearning for a dream
to become reality was very dangerous.

She pulled her gaze away. "It doesn't take wisdom
to tell the truth. Clean air and the sunlight is—"

"Ho! Permission to approach!"

Brynn knew that voice. Dread chilled her as she
turned to watch Lord Richard ride up the hill. He was
smiling broadly and dressed in his best blue wool surcoat
with the ermine trim. The sunlight caused his hair to
gleam golden and he was altogether the most splendid
and pleasing-looking of gentlemen.

Gage stiffened beside her, and she thought she
heard him mutter a curse beneath his breath. He strode
forward and motioned for the soldier to permit Richard
to pass.

"Who is this?" Malik murmured.

"Lord Richard of Redfern," she said absently. Why
was he there? Did Adwen need her? No, he would not
have dressed in his best and made the journey for Adwen. He had some other purpose.

Malik gave a low whistle as he watched Richard
ride into the camp. "A very comely lad."

"Yes."

Gage shot her a glance over his shoulder and bit
out, "I might remind you that 'comely lad' tossed you to
me without a qualm."

She frowned. "I expected nothing else."

"Then you show a meekness to him you never
showed to me."

She remembered Richard's scathing words on the
ride to Hastings. "He does not think me meek."

Those words failed to please him as well. "Yes, he
told me you often displayed a skill that—" He broke off
with another curse and strode forward to meet Richard.

"You did not handle that well," Malik said disap-
provingly. "Gage is in a most delicate state at the moment. You should not have taunted him."

Her brow wrinkled in confusion. "I don't know what you're talking about. I didn't taunt him. I merely told the truth."

"Then perhaps it would be best not to speak of your former master at all. Gage does not like it."

She shook her head impatiently. She couldn't care less what Gage did or did not like at present. All that was important was to learn why Richard was there.

Gage stopped before Richard's horse and said curtly, "I thought we'd seen the last of you. What do you do here?"

Richard kept the smile firmly on his face. "I come with an invitation." His gaze wandered to where Brynn stood beside Malik's pallet. "Ah, Brynn, I see you've used your skills to full advantage. How is our wounded soldier?"

"He is better," she said reservedly.

"You're looking well." He smiled. "But then, you always look well to me."

"What invitation?" Gage asked.

"Redfern," Richard answered him. "I invite you to come to Redfern."

"Why?"

"I hope you will choose it as your boon from William."

Surprise flickered over Gage's face. "How generous," he said with irony. "You wish to give me your lands?"

Richard shrugged. "As you said, William is bound to give my property to one of his barons. I've assessed the situation and decided it would be better to deal with you."

"I don't have to deal with you at all. I can take the land and send you on your way."

"But why would you do that? I know everything about Redfern. You could have no better agent than me."

"Agent?" Gage's eyes narrowed. "You would go from master to agent?"

"As a start. I'm a practical man."

"I'd also judge you to be an ambitious man."

Richard's pleasant expression didn't change. "Of course, but one must begin somewhere."

"You're a Judas. Why should I take on an agent in whom I have no trust?"

"Judas was reputed to be a very clever man, and clever men are useful. Besides, Christ wanted to be betrayed. You would not tolerate it. You'd watch me every minute." He added persuasively, "Come to Redfern and see what I have to offer you. It's a fine, rich property, isn't it, Brynn?"

"Yes."

Gage didn't look at her. "Stay out of this, Brynn."

"Has she displeased you?" Richard asked. "Now that she has done her duty toward your man, perhaps you'd like to be rid of her. I'll be glad to take her back."

"No!" Brynn's eyes widened at the violence in Gage's tone. He recovered quickly and said curtly, "She has not displeased me. Find another slave. This one is mine."

Richard shrugged. "I merely sought to ease your burden. Will you come to Redfern?"

"I will think on it." He turned on his heel. "It's not likely."

"I wonder if I might—" Richard hesitated. "You understand I would not infringe on your rights or property, but may I speak to Brynn alone?"

"No, you may not," Gage said flatly.

Adwen? Brynn wondered in alarm.

Richard nodded resignedly. "I merely wished to give her news of Redfern, but, if it offends you, I would not think of—"

"It offends me." Gage strode up the hill toward Brynn and Malik. "Good day, Lord Richard."

"Good day." Richard turned his horse and began the descent down the hill.

"Wait!" Brynn ran after him. "Wait, I want to—"

"No!" Gage grabbed her wrist, bringing her to a halt. "You will not go to him."

"Let me go!" she said fiercely. "Didn't you hear him? He has news. I must—" She broke free and flew down the hill. "Wait!"

Richard reined in and turned with a smile. "Rebellious as ever. I didn't think you'd let him stop you." He glanced past her. "But I don't think we have much time. The Norman is stalking down that hill, looking like a thundercloud."

She didn't look back. "What of Adwen?"

"Ah, she's not good. She had another bout of fever two nights ago. She cried out for you, but you weren't there."

"Of course I wasn't there." She glared at him. "You brought me here."

"But that doesn't alter Adwen's dilemma. She needs you. You must come back to Redfern."

"I'm trying."

"Try harder," Richard said. "The Norman seems quite possessive of you. You must have given him a great deal of pleasure. Convince him to bring you back to Redfern."

"Who is taking care of Adwen? Alice?"

Richard shook his head. "Alice has other duties now."

"Then, who—"

"Get back to Malik." Gage's hand closed on her wrist and whirled her away from Richard. "Now!"

"I need to talk to—"

"We have had our discussion," Richard interrupted. "We mustn't anger Lord Gage. I hope to see you both at Redfern." He put spurs to his horse and cantered down the hill.

Brynn stared after him in an agony of concern. She did not need to ask what duties Alice was performing. Did that mean Richard had designated no one to care for Adwen's needs? Even he could not treat his wife with such indifference. Adwen's only desire was to please and be allowed to love. She remembered that night of the comet when Adwen had curled next to her and called her friend.

"Stop looking like that!" Gage said roughly. "He's gone and good riddance." He pulled her toward the camp. "You will never disobey me again. You will never run after that—good God, you're weeping."

She had not been aware of the tears running down her face. Tears were a weakness, and she must show no weakness to him. She had to run away and hide. Hide and think . . . Poor Adwen . . .

"Let me go!" She jerked away from him and tore down the path toward the dense stand of trees that bordered the forest.

The woods . . .

She would be safe there, as she had been those many years ago.

"Brynn!" Gage's call rang after her. "Come back here!"

She returned to camp close to midnight. It appeared deserted, she noticed dully. But she had never been abroad at this hour. Perhaps it was always this quiet.

"Thank God," Malik said in relief when she entered the tent. "Are you well?"

"Of course I'm well." She knelt beside him. "You should be asleep. How do you expect to heal if you don't rest?"

He chuckled. "How do you expect me to rest if I have to lie awake and worry about you? I would far rather have been out scouring the forest with Gage."

"He's looking for me?" She wearily ran her fingers through her hair. Of course he would go after her, she thought bitterly. She was property.

"Ever since you left and with most of the men in the company." He shook his head. "He is not going to be pleased at the trouble you have caused him."

"He didn't have to come after me."

"He would say you didn't have to run away." He clucked reprovingly. "You look as if you've been rolling in the leaves. Your face is smudged and you have twigs in your hair."

"I wouldn't run away. I still have my duty to you." She poured water from the pitcher into the wooden bowl. "Lord Richard brought troubling news. I had to think."

"I would say this Lord Richard seldom brings anything but trouble. You are well rid of him."

"I'm not rid of him." In those hours in the forest she had realized she would never be free of him as long as Adwen was in his power. It could not go on. She must do something to alter the situation. She splashed her face with the cold water and then wiped it with a clean, soft cloth. "Better?"

He nodded abstractedly. "Gage thought you might have gone to Redfern after that young stag."

"Why would I do that? He would only chase me down and bring me back." Her lips curved scornfully. "Fine lords don't allow their property to wander off."

"I'm glad you realize that."

"Oh, I realized many things while I was in the forest tonight." She blew out the lantern and lay down on her cloak. "It does not make them fair. Good night, Malik."

"You're just going to sleep?"

"Why not?" She pulled the blanket over her. "I'm very tired."

"While Gage is out beating the shrubbery in search of you?"

"It will do him good. I judge he has a great deal of energy he has not been able to expend of late."

There was a moment of silence and then a chuckle came from the darkness. "Oh, yes, a great deal of energy."

Gage did not return until the last hours of night.

He was towering over her, the lantern in his hand lighting the grimness of his expression.

He was very angry, she realized sleepily. Well, what was different about that? It seemed he was always angry or annoyed with her.

"I'd like to throttle you," he grated.

Violence and rage . . . and something else. She could not deal with any of it then. "Go to sleep," she murmured. "We will talk in the morning."

"Did it never occur you could have lost yourself in those woods, that there are beasts that could tear you apart?"

"I was safe."

"Alone in the woods, with no means to defend yourself?"

He didn't realize that none of that mattered. The forest always accepted and protected its own. "Safe . . ." She rolled over and closed her eyes. "We will talk in the morning."

"We will talk now. It's time you realized who is master and who is slave."

"Tomorrow . . ."

She could feel him looking at her, sensed the waves of frustration and explosive violence he was emitting. She half expected him to tear aside the blanket and jerk her to her feet, to shake her, to throw her to the ground and—

He turned away and strode toward his own pallet.

She had never seen him more fierce or dangerous. He had never been more angry with her.

Why had she not been afraid? It was as if some subtle change had taken place between them. Trust? Impossible. He certainly had no trust in her and should not; she had resolved to use every means possible to free herself and Adwen. How could she have trust in him when he wanted only to use her skills and her body, to *own* her? Yet in that first moment of waking, even though she had seen the threat, she had somehow felt safe. . . .

Nonsense. It had probably been numbness that had dulled her fear of the Norman. Nothing had changed. He was the enemy and must be treated with the same wariness as Delmas and Lord Richard.

No, he wasn't like them. Gage Dumont might be ruthless, but he would never connive and use the helpless as the means to an end. The swiftness with which she instinctively rejected the comparison startled her. She must not soften toward him now. She must use him as he wanted to use her. He was the enemy.

She did not wake until nearly noon the next day, and when she opened her eyes she saw Gage sitting a few feet away.

"May we talk now?" he asked grimly.

She came fully awake in the space of a heartbeat. She sat bolt upright and threw off the blanket. "Presently." She glanced around the tent. "Where is Malik?"

"Outside in the sunshine. The day is warm. It's almost like summer."

"I'll go fix his meal."

"LeFont has chosen a man to care for him. He doesn't need you." He paused. "What happened yesterday must not happen again. We *will* talk, Brynn."

"I'm not arguing with you." She grabbed her cloak and a scrap of soap and strode toward the tent entrance.

"But I feel filthy and half asleep. I'm going to the pond and wash. Come with me if you like."

She hoped he would refuse. She was not prepared for him yet.

"I most certainly shall."

The sun was as warm as Gage had said, and she noticed Malik contentedly dozing. She ran down the hill and into the forest. She knelt beside the pond and started to splash her face and then grimaced as she saw her reflection in the water. The scanty ablutions she had made the night before had scarcely scratched the surface. Her hair was matted with dirt and leaves and her face—

She tensed when she heard the crunch of Gage's boots on the dry leaves as he came behind her. She was not ready. Perhaps she could find a way to— No, she must stop this caviling. She had come to a decision yesterday and, if it was to be done, it must be done boldly and by her will, not his.

She stood up and faced him. "I will be with you as soon as this dirt is gone." She reached up and unfastened the leather tie that held back her hair. "I hate being dirty." Her hair fell about her shoulders and she ran her fingers through it. "I've noticed you have a similar dislike. It surprised me. According to rumor, Normans bathe only once a year."

"And Saxons have two heads and spit fire and brimstone. Only fools believe rumors. Now that we've finished with this discourse on cleanliness, will you tell me why you were so upset that you ran away and lost yourself in the forest?"

"I didn't lose myself."

"Don't be evasive. What did that bastard say to you? He was— What the devil are you doing?"

"Taking off my gown." She didn't look at him as she discarded the garment and then bent down to untie her shoes. "I told you I didn't like—" She strode naked into the pond until she was waist high. The water was icy but she didn't feel cold. Her flesh was burning. . . .

"Look at me," Gage commanded hoarsely.

She didn't want to look at him. She wanted to dive beneath the water and cool her flushed body. She forced herself to turn and meet his gaze.

She inhaled sharply and stood there, helplessly looking at him.

"Why?" he asked. "Why now?"

"It's necessary." She swallowed. "I must go to Redfern and you said you must be . . . compensated."

He stood staring at her, a flush mantling his cheeks, his nostrils flaring slightly.

She could not bear this. She turned away, dipped her head in the water, and feverishly began scrubbing her hair. "Though I'd think the chance of gaining a treasure would be compensation enough."

"Not nearly enough."

"Then you're as greedy as all men."

"Probably more greedy."

Brynn heard a splash. She braced herself and watched him stride naked toward her. Power. Muscular thighs and calves clove the water as if it were a battleground to be conquered. A black triangle of hair thatched his broad chest and encircled his—

She quickly jerked her gaze up to his face and at once wished she hadn't. His expression had changed, intensified, become almost blindly sensual. He stopped beside her.

"I am greedy," he said thickly, "and more full of lust than any man you've ever had. At times I've wanted to devour you, absorb you." He reached out and took the soap from her. "I still do." He soaped his hands and then tossed the soap to the bank. "Don't move."

She couldn't have moved if she had wished. She could only look up at him as he stepped closer. She felt caught, fascinated, unable to think.

His soapy hands closed on her breasts.

She jerked with shock and his grasp tightened. "No, not again," he muttered. "You don't leave me again."

"I wasn't . . . trying to get away."

"Good. Because it's not going to happen. Never again." His hands moved over her breasts, gently pinching the nipples. "Do you know how I felt in the forest last night expecting in a minute to find you lying dead on the trail?" He drew her into the shallows, where the water was only up to her calves. "Spread your legs." His soapy hands delved low and began to rub the lather into her.

She arched backward at the indescribable sensation that shot through her. "What . . . are you doing?"

"Easing you." Two fingers gently entered and began a rhythmic stroking. "I'm a big man. I don't want to hurt you."

How odd, she thought dazedly. Delmas had never cared if he hurt her as long as his own lust was sated.

Gage's other hand was still probing, his thumb rotating as he found . . .

"No!" she cried out and clutched at his shoulders.

He stopped. "I hurt you?"

The sensation was so intense, it had felt like pain, but now she realized that pressure had engendered not pain but a hot throbbing and a terrible emptiness. "I—don't think—so . . ."

"Good, for I can wait no longer." His big hands cupped her buttocks and he lifted her. "Wrap your legs around me."

"Why do you—"

He plunged deep!

She gave a low cry and clutched at him with thighs and hands as his hips bucked back and forth and his big palms held her sealed to him. She felt stretched, part of him. She had not known men took women in this fashion, she thought dazedly. Perhaps they didn't. Only a man of Gage's enormous strength could—

"Move," he said jerkily in her ear. "Come to me, give to me . . ."

She was already moving, giving him the rhythm he demanded. She wanted to be closer, she *had* to be closer.

He was wading ashore, holding her tight as she moved frantically against him. She had seen animals mating in the forest with this same urgency. She was not an animal. . . .

But she had to move, she had to give. . . .

She was on her back on the leaves on the bank and he was a massive form over her.

In. Out. Long. Short. The sky was a blur of blue beyond his shoulder, and with every sobbing breath she took in the rich scent of earth and pine and soap. The sound of dry leaves rustling beneath their bodies was as sensual as his harsh breathing in her ear. He was not content to take, making her give everything.

It was not fair, she thought wildly. He was absorbing her as he had said he wanted to do. She did not want to feel this.

"Give it to me!" His tone was guttural. "Don't fight me. You're holding back."

What did he want? She couldn't give more than she was.

She screamed as he proved her wrong. Her back arched upward as her body was racked by the release.

She lay there panting, shuddering as the incredible spasms tore through her.

"Yes, that's what I want." His smile was savage as he moved harder, faster. He stiffened and then groaned and fell forward over her body.

He had given her his seed, she realized. How strange she was feeling no revulsion. The need was gone but the peace that followed was like a warm, soothing balm. It had never been like this before. Her arms instinctively tightened about Gage's massive shoulders.

He lifted his head and looked down at her. A lock of dark hair was lying on his forehead and he was laboring with every breath. "*Sacrebleu*, what did you do to me?"

She didn't know what he meant. His words made no sense, when it was he who had instigated this incredible joining. "Nothing." Her voice was so faint, it was almost inaudible. Where was the boldness and authority she had hoped to retain in this situation?

"The hell you didn't." His arms tightened around her and he rolled over on his side, still keeping her joined to him. The action shocked her. Delmas had always taken his pleasure and then left her alone. She felt chained, possessed, as much a part of his big body as during the act itself.

"I . . . wish to leave you," she whispered.

"Why?"

"It is not . . . fitting."

He chuckled. "I disagree. Since you're so delightfully tight, it's a bit snug, but I fit very well."

Heat stung her cheeks. "And such low talk is not fitting either. Is this how Normans conduct their . . ." She trailed off, as she couldn't find the word for what had transpired between them. It was not coupling as she knew it.

He leaned down and ran his tongue over her nipple and then made a face. "You still taste of soap. I fear I did not rinse you thoroughly. Not surprising. I almost took you while you were waist-deep in water."

How would that have felt? The cool water and him hot and hard within her . . .

He nibbled at a suddenly taut nipple. "I see you like the idea. Shall we go back into the pond?"

Sweet heaven, her body was changing, readying. What was happening to her? "No!" Her hands clenched into fists at her sides so that she would not bring them up to his hair. "Let me go. You've been compensated enough."

He stiffened. "Have I?" He slowly lifted his head and looked down at her. "I don't think so. I'm a man who requires great quantities of compensation." He deliberately reached around and cupped her buttocks in his hands and drew her closer. "Thank you for reminding me that I needn't worry about overusing you. I admit for a moment I forgot what the terms of our arrangement were." His hands opened and closed on the soft flesh. "All of this compensation for Redfern. You must wish to go there very much."

"Yes."

"And tell me, did that handsome young wastrel tell you that you should convince me to bring you back to Redfern?" He spoke in an almost idle manner, but there was an underlying menace that filled her with uneasiness.

"That wasn't the reason I—"

"Ah, so he did." He gently pinched her buttock. "Such a clever fellow to use a woman to further his aims. You must have gotten very used to obeying his commands to be so willing to pleasure me." His silky tone hardened. "I hope you weren't disappointed. You clearly prefer golden boys who use you to whore for them."

She should not have felt this hurt when it was what she had wanted him to think. "Let me go."

"I told you, I'm not through yet." He suddenly turned on his back and lifted her on top of him. "You should be aware of that by now."

He was stirring within her, she realized with astonishment. "Again?"

"You appear surprised." He reached up to cup her breasts. "It appears Saxons have little to boast about in their virility."

"What are you doing? This position feels . . . most strange."

"It won't for long." He pulled her hair over her shoulders and wound it around her breasts. "Another first? Good. I know I should appreciate any little tricks you've learned but, for some reason, the idea of you in bed with another man displeases me."

"I know no tricks."

"Perhaps no obvious ones." His smile faded and his expression became grim. "But a woman's pleasure is stirring enough, and you have a definite appetite for the sport. So don't show me anything anyone has taught you." His hips bucked upward in rhythm with each word. "I want you to pretend you're as without knowledge as Eve in the garden."

It would be an easy task, she thought hazily as she gripped his shoulders. Lust was new to her. All of this was new—hunger, need, pleasure. She bit her lower lip as he began to lift her with each thrust, to send her toward that explosive release she had known before. It was strange that violent pleasure and sweet healing could come from the same act. Dear God, she was enjoying it too much. Surely only whores liked men to do these things to them.

It was only because it was Gage Dumont. A man of such power would naturally generate deep feelings. She had never been tempted to taste this pleasure with anyone else. When they parted she would regain her cool dislike of coupling. When he was gone . . .

The thought brought an odd, hurtful wrench that surprised and frightened her. She cared nothing for him, she assured herself quickly. She would use him as he used her and—

"Stop it!"

She looked down at him.

A fierce scowl twisted his face. "Think of me," he said roughly. "Only me, damn you."

"I wasn't—"

"You were." He thrust deep, quickening the rhythm. "But not anymore."

Her throat arched as wave after wave of pleasure washed over her.

It might be a carnal weakness, but she would be a fool to push away this pleasure when her reason for accepting the Norman was just and right.

She was not a fool.

They did not go back to camp until nearly dusk and the evening fires were being lit on the hillside.

Brynn frowned as sudden anxiety struck. "I should not have left him so long."

"Malik? I made sure he was well cared for."

"But it was my duty." And she had violated that duty, she thought with disgust. She had lingered all afternoon, coupling time after time like an animal in season. Why had she not protested? "I should have been with him."

"You said he was in no danger." A trace of impatience threaded Gage's tone. "And may I point out that I was the one who brought you here to heal him and I'm the one who defines your duties."

She glanced at him in surprise. "It's true you had me brought here but when you gave him to me, your part was over. You cannot tell me not to heal or what my duties are. Only I can decide what is necessary now." But today she had weighed Adwen's good in the balance and let her responsibility to Malik slide. Dear heaven, it was difficult to serve everyone's needs. "When do we leave for Redfern?"

She was aware of a slight stiffening in Gage's demeanor. "Soon."

"When?"

"Do you think I lied to you? I assure you, I always keep to the terms of my barter."

"I don't doubt you. When?"

He was silent and then said, "In two days' time, if Malik is well enough to travel."

"He'll be well enough. We'll go slowly."

Gage's lips twisted. "Where is all your concern for Malik's well-being? It appears to be fading away in your eagerness to reach Redfern."

"That's not true," she said fiercely. "But I must strike a balance."

"What kind of balance?"

Malik against Adwen. Her duty was to both, but she feared Adwen's need was now greater. But Gage did not know Adwen and was totally devoted to his friend. "You wouldn't understand."

He smiled bitterly. "Oh, I think I understand very well."

His tone was so bitter, she glanced at him. Light and darkness. Power and strength. The rays of the setting sun dyed his hair raven black and yet his blue eyes held a brilliant luminosity. His expression looked softer. She had once thought him almost ugly, his features too brutal. Yet, even then when she could see no beauty, she had been aware of that aura of power that drew everyone to him. Whenever she had been in his presence she had been forced to struggle to keep from staring at him. He was exerting that same fascination at this moment, but now that she knew the textures of him, it was worse. She not only wanted to keep on looking, she wanted to reach out and touch the harsh plane of his cheek and—

She tore her gaze away from him and her steps quickened as they reached the edge of the camp.

Malik had already been taken into the tent and rabbit stew was bubbling over the small fire. LeFont was talking to a young soldier and looked up with a smile as Gage and Brynn approached.

"How is Malik?" Gage asked.

"Doing well, my lord. He had a good day. Very

good. He felt well enough to indulge in a game of dice with me and a few of the others." He grimaced. "He now owns my saddle. Though he's graciously allowing me to use it until I can find the money to ransom it from him."

"You didn't tire him?" Brynn asked quickly.

LeFont shook his head. "We stopped as soon as he appeared weary. I would he had tired sooner. I might have ended the day a richer man."

She should not have been away so long. What these strong soldiers considered wearying was not reliable. Brynn hurried into the tent.

Malik looked up with wide grin. "Good evening, Brynn. I now own a saddle, a silver-mounted bridle, and enough gold to—"

"So I heard." His color was good, his dark eyes sparkling. He was probably overexcited, but perhaps the day of gambling had not done him any ill. He had reached the point when boredom dragged at the spirit, and that was not good for the body. She relaxed and smiled. "Perhaps tomorrow you can give LeFont a chance to win his saddle back." She knelt beside him. "But I think I must be here to make sure that you don't overdo."

His smile faded as he said, "That's not necessary. Not if Gage . . . requires you." He paused before asking, "You did not fight him?"

Heat scorched her cheeks. She had expected Malik to realize what had transpired between Gage and her, but did not expect to feel this awkward . . . this *owned*. Gage was not even in the tent, and yet it was as if he were still inside her body. "No."

"It went well? He did not harm you?"

"He didn't hurt me." She pushed aside the blanket and checked his bandage. "Did you expect him to?"

"No . . ." He shrugged. "He is not usually violent

with women, but with you . . . It has been most unusual. I am glad you decided to surrender."

"I didn't surrender," she said, stung. "We came to terms."

"Terms?"

"We start for Redfern in two days' time." She rose to her feet. "I'll get your supper."

"Brynn . . ." Malik shook his head. "I know that when you have little else in your life, the attentions of a handsome rascal like Richard of Redfern would seem attractive, but he is not worth this. Even if you go to Redfern, Gage will not permit you to return to his bed."

"Return to—" Suddenly several of Gage's obscure references to Richard began to become clear. "Richard told him that he had used me in that way?"

"With high praise for both your enthusiasm and your lewd skills." Malik added gently, "So you can see that he is not worthy of the affection you bear him."

She looked at him incredulously. "Affection?"

"No?" Malik's gaze narrowed on her face. "If you don't feel affection for him, why do you wish to return to Redfern?"

For an instant she was tempted to tell him of Adwen. Malik was kind and would understand.

But he would also feel obligated to tell Gage Dumont, and the Norman was a hard man. He might think she had dangled the treasure before him to draw him to Redfern only for Adwen's sake. Let Gage believe she was fool enough to adore that monster. At the moment he appeared to have some feeling of possession for her, and his warrior's instincts would lead him to march into Richard's lair to banish any threat.

"I did not say I felt no affection for Lord Richard." She left the tent and strode brusquely toward the fire where LeFont and Gage were still talking.

Gage glanced away from LeFont and raised his brows inquiringly.

"He's well," she said curtly. She added to LeFont as she filled a bowl from the steaming kettle, "And eager to see what other prizes he can win tomorrow. I think he has his eye on your horse, Captain."

LeFont groaned. "I'll be glad when he's back on his feet. Though by that time, I may also be on mine."

A smile tugged at her lips. "It's entirely possible."

The captain sketched a quick salute to Gage and strolled away.

She could feel Gage's eyes on her and felt a ripple of uneasiness. Every act, every word, seemed different now. She moved quickly toward the tent.

"Wait," Gage muttered.

She didn't look at him. "Malik is hungry."

"Have I suddenly grown two heads? Why don't you look at me?"

She forced herself to stare directly at him. Would she ever be able to behold him without remembering him crouched naked over her, the muscles of his stomach clenched as he moved frantically within her? She suddenly experienced a warm tingling between her thighs.

"Ah, that's better," he said softly. He reached out and touched her lips with his fingers. "Your mouth is swollen. I was too rough with you. I'll try to be gentler next time."

He had been rough. They had both been rough and desperate and insatiable. She had met his lust with a lust just as shameless, she thought with disgust. It was all very well to tell herself that it was all right to enjoy the act, but she must not be swept away and forget her purpose. She took a step back, turning her head to avoid his touch. "I didn't expect you to be gentle with me. You must do as you will."

The softness vanished from his expression. "And you submit meekly and spread your legs no matter how much you detest it." He reached out and grasped her shoulders. "Don't lie to me. You were no martyr. I have claw marks on my shoulders to prove it."

"I did not—" She stopped and wearily shook her head. She was dealing too much in deceit, and it was choking her. She would not lie in this. "I tried not to like it. I don't know why I did. I couldn't help myself." She added haltingly, "I think perhaps you are not as other men."

Surprise flickered in his expression. "And I know you're not as other women. I'm not accustomed to such honesty." His grasp loosened and then his hand fell away from her. "If it is honesty. It could be a ploy to flatter my self-love. It would be a clever move and you're a very clever woman."

"A woman must be clever or be used." She moved toward the tent entrance. "And I don't care what you believe."

"As long as you get what you want from me." He smiled sardonically. "You're very free with your words. What if I change my mind about going to Redfern?"

"You won't change your mind. Malik says you always keep your word." She glanced at him over her shoulder. "And I believe he speaks truly."

"A blow and then a stroking. I wonder your Lord Richard didn't throttle you before tossing you to me." He paused before adding, "But you're right, I wouldn't think of not paying a visit to Redfern. I can't wait to see what is worth such sacrifice."

She had angered him, not hurt him. She must not fool herself that she had the power to make him feel anything but lust and anger. She must not probe or try to understand or do anything that would draw her closer to him. He was a remarkable man, but a man who wanted a kingdom had no place in the simple life she wanted to live at Gwynthal. "You won't have to wait long. You said we could leave in two days."

Not waiting for an answer, she went into the tent.

She was aware of his moody gaze on her for the next hour while she fed Malik his stew, ate a little herself, and then gently washed his face. He was already asleep when she tucked the blanket around him and moved to spread her cloak on the ground.

"No, not there," Gage said. He patted his pallet. "Here."

She tensed and then forced herself to relax. "Would you shame me in front of your friend?"

"My friend is sleeping the slumber of the dead." He repeated with more emphasis, "Here."

She moved slowly across the tent. "Have you not . . . Was it not enough?"

He reached up and jerked her down beside him. He settled her spoon fashion, with her back to him, and then pulled the blanket over her. "For the time being." His hand cupped her breast. "But one never knows when one requires further compensation. I prefer you within reach. Go to sleep. I'll wake you when you're needed."

How was she to go to sleep when her heart was nearly jumping out of her breast? "I don't like this. It makes me uneasy."

"You'll become accustomed to it. I like it very much." His lips feathered her ear. "You knew I wanted to take you away from Malik since that first week. I wanted you in my bed, not his."

Yes, she knew he had wanted her, but she had not dreamed she would actually *want* to have him do the things he had done to her. How far she had come since the night Lord Richard had brought her there. Even now she was beginning to relax, her body yielding, softening, taking on the shape Gage wanted of her. It was warm, pleasant . . . and safe. How long it had been since she had felt safe? "I didn't know I would have to sleep with you."

"And now you do."

"I would rather sleep alone," she lied.

He didn't answer.

Minutes passed and finally the tenseness gradually flowed out of her. How easy and natural it was to be there with him. He was a man who would always make demands, but he was not demanding anything of her now.

"I have news to tell you, my lord. A rider has just come from his grace's camp."

It was LeFont's voice, Brynn realized sleepily, and he sounded hesitant, not confident. She opened her eyes to see him standing in the entrance of the tent, silhouetted against a pale gray sky. The news must not be good if he thought it necessary to wake Gage at this early hour.

Gage removed his arm from around her and sat up. She suddenly felt cold and alone. Strange, since she always slept alone except when healing . . .

"What news?" Gage asked curtly.

"Hardraada is dead."

Gage's body jerked as if struck by a blow. He did not speak for a moment. "You're sure?"

LeFont nodded. "William had the Saxon prisoners taken at Hastings questioned. Hardraada invaded England from the north only a short time before we landed on the south shore. Harold had just come back from defeating him at—"

"But you're sure Hardraada is dead?"

LeFont hesitated, and then said bluntly, "Quite sure. He received an arrow in the throat at Stamford Bridge."

Pain. Brynn gasped and cowered back away from Gage.

He was sitting very still, and his voice had been totally impassive, but the waves of agony streaming from him were bruising her, tearing her.

LeFont continued. "Magnus is now king of Norway."

"Gage, my friend." Malik's voice came deep and gentle from across the tent. "You knew it would come someday. Men like Hardraada do not die in bed."

"No. He would have wanted no other end." A note of bitter mockery suddenly entered his voice. "You need not treat me with such gentleness, Malik. He ceased being anything to me long ago. Don't expect me to mourn him." He threw aside the cover and rose to his feet. "My only regret is that he won't know that I've won a fine slice of this England he lost."

He strode out of the tent and was followed closely by LeFont.

Pain. Sorrow. Worse because it was hidden.

Brynn wrapped her arms around herself and rocked back and forth. What was happening to her?

"Brynn?" Malik asked.

She didn't want to go after him. She didn't want to be near that pain. She couldn't stand it. She had not felt another's pain with this intensity since her mother had died. Why expose herself when she probably couldn't help?

Pain. Even deeper now that the first shock was fading.

She threw off the blanket and jumped to her feet.

"Don't go, Brynn," Malik called after her as she moved toward the entrance. "He's better off alone. He won't let you help him."

"I can't leave him alone," she said shakily. "Do you think I want to go? It has to stop. I can't—"

She was outside the tent, her gaze searching.

Gage was stalking down the hill toward the forest. His back was rod straight and his pace swift, his eyes straight ahead.

"Wait!" She flew after him.

He didn't stop; he didn't behave as if he even heard her.

She reached him as he entered the forest and fell into step with him.

"Go back to Malik," Gage said shortly.

"No."

"I don't want you here."

"I don't want to be here." To keep pace, she took two steps for every one of his long strides. "Do you think I like running through the forest at first light? My feet are already wet with dew and I—"

"Then go back to camp."

"I can't do that."

"Why not?"

"You need me."

"How eager you're becoming. When I need you I'll spread your legs and make use of you. I have no such desire now."

She flinched at the cruelty of the words even though she knew he was blindly striking out. "Where are you going?"

"Nowhere. Anywhere. I have thinking to do."

"Then I will go also."

"You have a problem with hearing? *I don't want you here.*" He strode forward into the underbrush, his pace increasing until she was forced to a near run to keep up with him.

He paid no more attention to her than if she had been a hound scurrying at his heels.

The trek went on for a long time as gray skies became the delicate pink of dawn and then lightened to full brilliant sunlight.

She couldn't breathe and a pain was starting in her right side. Dear God, would he never stop?

As he reached a narrow ribbon of a stream, he whirled on her and bit out, "You're gasping like a horse about to founder, you stupid woman."

"I won't founder." She took a deep breath, grateful

for even a moment's respite. "I can keep on as long as you can."

He stared at her for a moment and then knelt by the stream and began splashing water in his face.

She sat down beside him, her hand clutching her side.

He scowled at her. "What's wrong?"

"Nothing. A stitch." She knelt, cupped her hands in the water, and lifted them to drink. "Your stride is longer than mine."

"Then you shouldn't have been so stubborn."

"I could do nothing else." She studied his expression; there was little to see. Everything was inside, dark and whirling and twisting. It must come out, but she did not know if she would be able to bear it. "There's too much pain in you."

"I'm not in pain." He gave her a mocking glance. "And what if I were? What could you do? Do you have a magical salve that heals the spirit as well as the body?"

"No."

"Then are you going to touch me and heal the hurt?"

"I cannot touch you."

"Why not?" He held out his arms, his eyes glinting with recklessness. "Come lie with me as you did Malik. Let us see what magic you can weave."

She edged away from him. Even the thought of joining with him sent a jolt of panic through her. "There is no magic in me." She looked down at his reflection in the rippling waters of the stream. His image was distorted, easier to accept than the reality. "Did you love Hardraada so much?"

He didn't answer.

The poison must come out. "I find it strange you hold him in affection when Malik says he refused to call you his son."

"I don't hold him in affection." He smiled bitterly.

"I held his throne in affection but he did not see fit to give it to me."

"I think it is more than the throne."

"Then you're a fool. Why should I love a man who banished me from his land?"

"He banished you? Why?"

"He saw too much of himself in me. He was afraid I'd reach out and take what he wouldn't give." He shrugged. "Perhaps he was right. Perhaps in time I would have thought of putting hemlock in his ale."

"You would never have done that."

"He thought I might."

"Then he was the fool. You would never harm anyone you loved." She lifted her gaze from the stream. "And you did love Hardraada."

"I told you I did not hold him—" He broke off and shrugged. "It could be I cared for him when I first knew him. I was only a young boy and he seemed . . . everything. He was probably the greatest warrior we will ever know and was always looking for new triumphs. Yet he also had a great joy in life."

"How did you come to know him?"

"I was sent to his court when I was two and ten." His lips twisted. "My grandfather was very ambitious. He put his daughter in Hardraada's path when he encountered him in Byzantium, hoping he would become besotted enough to marry her. It was a false hope, but Hardraada did give her his seed before he went back to Norway."

"And your grandfather sent you to Hardraada?"

"Why not? What better way for a merchant to raise himself in the world than to have a prince as a grandson?"

"And your mother?"

"My grandfather permitted her to move to Constantinople when I was weaned. She had done her duty and she found life in the village too difficult and full of shame as the mother of a bastard."

And how difficult had been the life of the bastard in that French village? Brynn wondered sadly. No mother, a grandfather who wished to use him only for gain, and a father who had treated him with careless affection as long as he posed no threat.

That halcyon period could not have lasted long. Gage would never hover in the background and always be a man with whom to be reckoned. She almost wished she could have seen Hardraada and the young Gage together. "When did he banish you?"

"I returned to Normandy several years ago."

He had left Hardraada to become a prince of merchants when denied his birthright. Gage would never accept defeat; he would keep trying to wrest a victory from it. "You were better off without Hardraada."

"Was I?" His lips thinned. "Who are you to judge? I believe Hardraada's throne would have fit me very well."

"I don't believe you wanted his throne."

"I needed nothing else from him." He glared at her. "Nothing."

He would never admit the need that had been there, but talking about his father had eased a little of the pain. She could feel the knot in her own chest loosening. "If you say it is true." She rose to her feet. "If you don't mind, I will go back to camp now."

She could sense his surprise at the sudden move. "I believe that's what I've been trying to get you to do since we left."

"I couldn't do it then. You're more at ease now." She started to turn away.

"Wait!" He reached out and took her hand.

Bitterness and pain, tears that would not be shed, loneliness and darkness.

She went rigid as the emotions rushed over her,

overwhelmed her. She desperately wanted to tug her hand away. Yet where would all that pain go if she did not accept it? "Please," she whispered, closing her eyes. "Please, no."

"What's wrong, dammit?"

"Your pain. I *feel* it. Please, don't make me feel it. Hurts . . ."

He released her hand.

The pain was gone but now he was alone. He must not be alone. She reached out and took his hand again. She whimpered as fresh pain lashed out at her.

"What in Hades is happening to you?" he asked harshly.

"I don't know. It's never been like this. . . ." She reached out blindly and took his other hand. More pain cascaded over her, but he must not be alone. Then, suddenly, she knew what had to be done. She stopped fighting the pain and joined with him, letting the sorrow overwhelm her.

Tears ran down her cheeks as she stepped closer and laid her head on his chest.

"Christ." He stood there, stiff and unyielding. "Stop it."

She shook her head.

"Why the devil are you crying?"

She whispered, "Because you won't. Because it has to go somewhere."

"You're a madwoman."

The tears fell without ceasing.

He stepped back and looked down into her face. "You're mad," he repeated. His forefinger went out and traced the trail of tears down one cheek. "This isn't good," he said thickly. "Stop it."

The tears were easing as he was easing. She took a deep, shaky breath and then swallowed. "I've stopped. I'll go now." She turned and moved swiftly down the trail. "I've done what I could."

"Wait!"

She glanced over her shoulder.

"We've come a long way from the camp," he said haltingly. "Will you be able to find the path back?"

He was worried about her. Warmth rippled through her, and she smiled. "I grew up in forests. I could never get lost."

Gage did not return all day and was not at the camp when they turned out the lamp near midnight.

Brynn was still awake when Gage slipped beneath the cover and drew her into his arms.

Dull ache, sorrow, resignation. Not pleasant but bearable.

"If you start crying again, I'll beat you," he whispered in her ear. "I hate a weeping woman."

"I won't weep."

"I don't understand you." His tone was baffled.

"I know."

"And I don't believe you can heal by touch or know what I'm feeling."

"Then don't believe it."

"And don't think a few tears shed for my sake will soften my resolve. I have no need of them."

"I rejoice for you. Now I have need of sleep." She closed her eyes. "Good night."

She heard him mutter something and then one big arm drew her back against his body. Bonding. Her heart sank as she realized that sense of joining was still there. She had prayed that it would have gone when his pain was less sharp. It made no sense. It was as if the lust that had united them had torn aside a veil she could never replace. Well, she must give it time.

"Brynn."

"Yes."

"I don't need your tears." He paused and then said, "But I thank you for shedding them."

The gruff words were infinitely moving. She wanted to reach out and stroke him, take him to her. She must not. She must rebuild the barriers that had been so bewilderingly torn asunder.

"No thanks are required," she said reservedly. "It is my duty to help you."

His arms remained around her, but she was aware of withdrawal. Good. Keep away. Don't come near. Don't ever come that close again.

"I'm happy you realize where your duty lies," Gage said, mocking her. "Be sure you continue to do so when we reach Redfern."

S i x

"IT'S ALL MADE of wood," Gage said in disgust when they neared the timbered walls surrounding Redfern Hall. "Is this your fine Redfern?"

"Of course it's made of wood." Brynn didn't glance up as she straightened the cover over Malik and then settled herself more comfortably in the wagon. "What did you expect? Feathers?"

"In Normandy it's the custom to build castles of stone," Malik said.

"Well, it's not the custom in England. I've never seen a stone castle here."

"Then William will have had no trouble on his march to London." Gage shook his head. "It's a wonder that England has not been invaded a thousand times over." He kicked his horse and waved the company forward.

The high timbered gates were thrown open when they were within hailing distance, and Lord Richard rode to meet them, a broad smile on his face. "Welcome, my lord, how happy I am that you thought better of accepting my invitation. I hope it means you're considering Redfern?"

"Not necessarily."

"I'm sure you'll change your mind. Redfern is all that is desirable." His glance shifted to Brynn. "I hope you're in good health, Brynn?"

Byrnn frowned in puzzlement. What was he about? His tone was extremely courteous; he sounded just as she had heard him address the honored ladies in his hall. "Good enough."

"Are we to be kept waiting while you exchange pleasantries?" Gage asked.

"Certainly not. I've had my own chamber prepared for your lordship." Richard turned his horse and rode within the gates. "After you've rested, perhaps you'd honor me at my table. As soon as we caught sight of you, I set the servants to cooking a fine feast."

"I'm hardly in need of rest. It was only a two-hour journey from the woods where we were camped."

"Forgive me, I forgot what stalwart warriors you Normans are."

"Brynn!"

She turned to see Delmas hurrying toward her across the courtyard. A wave of revulsion went through her as she saw the almost desperate eagerness of his expression. He thought because she had returned he could make use of her again. She had been away from him so long, she had forgotten that sickening feeling of helplessness.

"What is it? What's wrong?" Gage's eyes were narrowed on her face.

"Nothing. It is only my husband."

Malik gave a low whistle.

"Husband?" Gage asked with deadly softness.

"Yes."

"Only?" Gage repeated. "May I ask why you didn't mention this . . . husband."

"Why should I? What difference would it have made?"

Delmas had drawn close to Gage and glanced up at him eagerly. "Greetings, my lord. Welcome to Redfern."

Gage ignored him. "What difference would it have made?" he echoed. "Why none, of course."

Delmas took a step nearer. "I would not offend you, my lord, but I wonder if you could do without Brynn for a short time? It has been long since we were together and I would—" He broke off as he met the Norman's gaze. He took a step back, his eyes widening.

Gage was going to kill him, Brynn realized. Delmas was within an inch of death.

"No!" She did not even realize she had slid out of the wagon until she was standing between Gage and Delmas. She pushed Delmas toward the stable and quickly started after him.

"Brynn!" Gage's voice was low, but a shiver went through her. "Come back here."

She didn't stop, her pace quickening until she was almost running. "I'll join you in a short time. I must talk to Delmas now."

"Come back here!"

She didn't stop. "Soon."

For a moment she thought he would follow her. She felt his gaze on her back until she disappeared into the stable. She halted just inside the door, her heart beating painfully hard.

"Whore!" Delmas's palm cracked against her cheek. "He would have slaughtered me and it's all your fault."

Anger flared through her. Why had she interfered? Delmas deserved to die. She should have stifled the impulse to save him and let Gage rid her of this burden.

Delmas raised his hand again.

"No," she said coldly. "You will never strike me again."

Delmas hesitated and then decided to bluff. "I will do as I like. You are my wife. Nothing has changed."

"Everything has changed." It was true, she knew suddenly. Delmas could neither help nor harm her. She had been beneath his yoke for so long that the idea was strange to her.

"Because you're the Norman's whore? I'll petition the church to make him return you to me. We said holy vows."

"I made no vow."

He ignored her protest. "Even the Normans will not flaunt the edicts of the Pope."

"All of England is in turmoil. Do you think the church will pay heed to the whining of one slave?"

"Lord Richard will help me," Delmas said. "He won't permit this Norman to have you."

She went still. "What have you told Lord Richard?"

He looked away from her. "I told him what I needed to tell him. I had to bring you back here."

"Gwynthal? You told him about Gwynthal?"

He nodded jerkily.

Brynn drew her cloak closer about her as a shiver ran through her. She had not imagined Delmas would ever tell anyone of the treasure. He must have been desperate indeed to trust Richard with that knowledge. "You're a fool. He will kill you."

"No, he needs me. We need each other." Delmas paused and then smiled craftily. "But, it's true, he's a brutal man. He will not treat you as gently as I have."

Gently? She stared at him incredulously.

"We could run away from Redfern tonight," Delmas murmured. "You need have nothing to do with Lord Richard or the Norman. We could go back to Gwynthal and you could give me—"

"No." Even now he could not believe he could no longer use her. He sickened her; she could bear no more. "I can't go anywhere. How is Lady Adwen?"

He shrugged. "Well, I suppose."

"What do you mean? Don't you know?"

He frowned. "She is no longer of importance to us. You will rue your decision not to go with me. Lord Richard is—"

She turned toward the door. "I'm going to the manor to see Adwen."

"She is no longer at the manor."

She stopped and turned. "What?"

"Lord Richard said—" He broke off. "She offended him. He wanted her out of his sight."

"She *offended* him?" Her hands slowly clenched into fists. "Where is she?"

He nodded at the small room at the back of the stable.

She couldn't believe it. It was the same room where she had fled to see the comet and was little larger than a horse's stall. She gave a low exclamation, strode toward the door, and threw it open.

A small, still figure was curled beneath a faded blanket on a cot under the window.

Too still.

She moved swiftly across the room. "Adwen!"

Sweet heaven, what had he done to her? Her eyes were sunken and smudged with dark circles, her lips swollen and cracked, her hair lank and lifeless.

Brynn sat down on the cot and gathered Adwen's hands in her own. They were as cold and inert as the rest of her. "Adwen, wake up."

Adwen stirred and opened her eyes. She whispered, "Brynn?"

Relief surged through her. "Yes."

"I . . . didn't think you were coming back. He said you were—" The words faded and it was a moment before she could speak again. "I felt so alone."

Brynn blinked back the tears. "You shouldn't have believed him." She pulled the cover higher around Adwen's shoulders. The blanket was thin; it could not possibly have offered much warmth. A flare of anger went through her as she looked around the room. Dirt covered the bed and the one small window. Cobwebs hung from the timbers of the ceiling, and a foul odor issued from the bucket beside the small cot. "You should not believe anything he says to you."

Adwen's eyes closed. "I know."

Brynn looked at her, startled. The Adwen she knew would never have doubted her beloved Richard.

"He wants me to die, you know. . . ."

"Did he tell you this?"

"No." Her eyes wearily opened. "But I am not stupid. He would never have put me out here with no attendant if he had not wanted to be rid of me. I couldn't believe it. . . ." Her voice strengthened with sudden ferocity. "I will not die. He should not have done this. No one should have the right to discard a woman as if she were nothing. It's not fair. I won't let him. It's not—"

"Hush." Adwen was getting too excited, and Brynn was afraid that fragile strength would snap. "You won't die. I won't let you."

"No, I won't die. I swore on my hope of heaven I wouldn't." Adwen's eyes brimmed with tears. "But I'm glad you're here, Brynn. It will be easier now. I felt so alone when Richard told me my father had died. . . ."

"He told you that? Lord Kells isn't dead. He was only taken prisoner."

"You're certain?"

"He's been taken to Duke William's camp. I'm not sure what fate awaits him, but it won't be death."

"So he lied in that also. So cruel. He wanted to take all hope away from me. . . ." Her eyes closed again. "Would it be all right if I go back to sleep? I think it strengthens me. I have to fight . . ."

"Yes, go back to sleep." She squeezed Adwen's hands affectionately and stood up. "Let me fight now."

"No, it has to be me."

Brynn stood looking down at her. She had changed. She appeared even more fragile and ill than she had since those first days Brynn had come to Redfern, and yet she glimpsed a strength she had never before seen in her. It was like catching the gleam of a sword lying beneath cloudy waters.

"We'll do it together," Brynn said gently.

"Together . . . yes." The next moment Adwen drifted off to sleep.

"Leave her," Delmas said from behind Brynn.

She glanced over her shoulder to see him frowning at her from the doorway. "As everyone else has done? How could you have known she was here and not helped her?"

He shifted uncomfortably. "Lord Richard said she was to be left alone."

"To die in this filthy hovel?"

"It was not my fault. I only obeyed his orders." He took a step into the room. "As you must do. He is master here."

"A master who obeys Lord Gage's slightest command."

He smiled slyly. "Not for long."

She was immediately suspicious. "What do you mean?"

"Do you think he would truly offer Redfern to Lord Gage? He only wanted you returned to Redfern." His smile became even more crafty. "It is possible an accident may befall the Norman."

She stared at him, startled. "He would murder him after inviting him beneath his roof as a guest?" It was against all the rules of Saxon hospitality. Surely even Richard would not commit such a breach of honor.

"I didn't say that," he said quickly.

But it was true. Why was she even surprised when

he had put his own wife out here to perish from cold and neglect?

"But it would be wise of you to curb your unruly ways and tell us what we need to know," Delmas said. "Why must you be so stubborn?"

"Adwen must be taken from this place." She turned and moved toward the door. "Carry her."

"You give *me* orders?"

"Carry her," she repeated. "Or I will go to Lord Gage and tell him you're conspiring with Lord Richard to harm him."

He blanched, obviously recalling that terrifying moment in the courtyard. "You would not."

No, she would not do it, but he need not know that. "Carry her."

He reluctantly moved across the room toward the cot. "Lord Richard will not be pleased." He lifted Adwen's frail form. Adwen stirred but did not waken. "With either of us."

Brynn paid no attention as she strode out of the stable and into the sunshine. Gage had vanished from the courtyard, but LeFont was still there, giving orders for the dispersal and accommodation of his men. She marched up to him. "I must see Lord Gage. Where is he?"

"He's also very eager to see you," LeFont murmured as he glanced curiously at Delmas and Adwen. "He told me to go after you and bring you to him. I'm glad you spared me the task." He nodded at the manor. "I believe Lord Richard said he had ordered a bath for my lord."

"And where have they put Malik?"

LeFont shrugged. "He said the South Chamber."

Adwen's chamber. She gestured to Delmas to follow her, then entered the manor and made her way through the hall, up the stairs, and down the corridor toward Adwen's former room.

Malik occupied the wide bed and warningly shook

his head at Brynn after she threw open the door. "I am well and comfortable. Go to Gage before his anger has time to build."

She ignored him and entered. "Presently. I'm here to make you less comfortable. Slide over on the bed."

"Why?" He saw Delmas with his burden. "Ah, you've brought me a woman to warm my nights? How kind of you. And I was beginning to think you had no compassion for my needs. You must truly think I'm getting better."

"She's not for you. I only need a safe place to put her until I can make arrangements for her. Move over."

Malik sighed. "I take it you have a new charge to heal?"

"Not new. This is Lord Richard's wife, Adwen. You are resting in her bed."

He slid over to the far side as Delmas placed Adwen on the bed. His gaze raked Adwen's pale face. "Poor lady. She looks very bad. What is her ailment?"

"Fever, exhaustion, and neglect. She has lost four babes in five years and Lord Richard saw fit to banish her to a dirty little room in the stable and abandon her." She settled Adwen more comfortably on the pillows before turning to Delmas. "Tell them to bring hot water and clean linens. Where is Alice?"

"She can no longer serve her. She has other duties now," Delmas said.

"Why can—" She stopped. She had forgotten that Richard had taken Alice to his bed. Well, he would have to give her up. Adwen might need more care than Brynn could give her, and Alice may not have been perfect, but she had never neglected Adwen. "Go get her."

Delmas shook his head.

"Then I will get her myself."

"Poor little demoiselle. I will care for her," Malik said softly.

"You?" Brynn lifted her brows. "You cannot even care for yourself yet."

"Then we will care for each other." His expression was meltingly tender as he looked at Adwen's still face. "I think she needs me."

"Alice will do as well."

Malik's jaw set obstinately. "She needs me."

She had neither the time nor energy to argue with him at the moment. "Have it your own way. I'll find Alice and she can tend to both your needs."

Malik's expression changed. "Go to Gage, Brynn. Do not delay any longer." He stared pointedly at Delmas. "And I would not take him with you."

"No, no, I must be about Lord Richard's duties." Delmas moistened his lips as he backed toward the door. "I've wasted too much time already."

The door slammed behind him.

Malik shook his head. "He has no more courage than a cockroach. Gage will crush him and splatter his remains on the dirt of the stable yard."

"A man should not be killed because he has no courage."

"You'd be wise not to defend him to Gage. It will only bring the cockroach's demise that much sooner." He waved his hand, his eyes going back to Adwen. "Run along to him. I will watch her until you return."

Brynn hesitated and then moved toward the door. She had no desire to confront Gage immediately, but it must be done. Malik was probably right; a delay would only make the situation worse.

So this is how it came, Malik thought wonderingly. One moment a man was alone, and the next he was given a gift beyond price to treasure for the rest of his days. Adwen was as beautiful and frail as the crystal bell his mother had given him when he had left his village. What beast would try to destroy anything so lovely?

Her eyes opened and looked into his own. She stiffened with terror.

"Shh, do not be afraid," he said quickly. "Brynn will return soon. I am Malik. I would never harm you."

"Stranger . . ."

"Not for long." He smiled gently. "We were not meant to be strangers. Can you not feel it?"

She continued to stare at him with those huge eyes, the tenseness gradually leaving her. She sighed and closed her lids again.

She was accepting him. Malik felt as if she had given him a gift. "Ah, you trust me?"

"No," she whispered. "Never . . ."

"Because I am a stranger?"

"No."

He went rigid. "Because I am a heathen Saracen?"

"No."

"Then why?"

"I cannot trust you." She yawned and turned over onto her side, her back to him. "You are far too comely. . . ."

Brynn threw open the door to Richard's chamber and strode into the room. Gage was immersed in the huge wooden tub, wreathed in steam and the scent of soap and herbs. Alice was kneeling behind him, scrubbing his back.

Brynn stopped just inside the room, her eyes on Alice. It seemed Richard had given Gage not only his chamber but his leman. The intimacy of the picture the two made was affecting her strangely, igniting an irritation that held elements of both anger and pain.

"Don't stop there," Gage said silkily. "Come closer."

By the saints, he was angry. She could feel the waves of rage rush toward her. She braced herself and moved forward to stand before the tub. "I came as soon as I could."

"I realize you had other 'duties' to perform. You've been away from your husband for a long time."

"Yes," she said absently, watching Alice's hands move around Gage's body and begin to scrub his broad chest. The maid's hands were as plump and well shaped as the rest of her and her movements seemed unnecessarily sensual. She tore her gaze away and back to Gage's face. It was without expression, but she sensed the anger had deepened. His body had turned rigid, and his eyes . . . She looked back at Alice. "Leave us. I need you to go to Lady Adwen."

Alice's hands stopped in mid motion. "I cannot."

"You will. She needs you. Wash her and make her comfortable. I've taken her to her former chamber."

Alice's eyes widened in alarm. "You should not have done that. Lord Richard will be very angry."

"Then he will be angry. Go to her."

Tears filled Alice's eyes. "I cannot. Do you not think I wanted to help the poor lady? He will not have it."

The idea of disobeying Richard clearly scared the woman out of her wits. "Did he not tell you that you were to obey Lord Gage in every way?"

Alice nodded, a flush mounting to her cheeks.

Brynn turned back to Gage. "Tell her to do it."

"And what if I want her here?"

"You don't want her here. You want only to curse and bite at me."

He stared at her and then motioned impatiently for Alice to go. "Go tend this . . ." He searched for the name. "Lady Adwen."

Alice jumped to her feet and rushed around the tub toward the door. As she passed Brynn, she whispered, "I truly did not wish her harm. He would not—I had to do as he wished."

Perhaps the woman was speaking truly and it was not avarice but weakness that had driven her. At any rate, it would do no good to berate her. "Then make amends by treating her with care and gentleness."

"I will. I will. I promise you." Alice hurried from the room.

"Which leaves me with no servant to cleanse me," Gage said softly. "It appears you'll have to take her place."

"I have no objection to the service," she replied, taking Alice's place. "You know it is only custom. If Adwen was well enough, she would cleanse you herself."

"Would she? I don't recall you mentioning Lady Adwen. Though I should not be surprised when you also forgot to mention a husband."

"Lord Richard told you that I was brought to Redfern to tend his wife."

"But you did not tell me about her. Not one word. What a secretive woman you are, Brynn of Falkhaar." He leaned back in the tub. "Take off your gown and climb into the tub."

She went still. "Why?"

"You have an odor about you I don't like. I wish it gone."

Perhaps the foul smell of that stable sickroom still clung to her. "I'll wash later."

"Now," he said with emphasis.

She stood up, pulled the gown over her head, and dropped it on the rush-strewn floor, then slipped out of her shoes. "It could not be so offensive, or I would smell it myself."

"Perhaps I'm more sensitive to it. Get in the tub."

"There is no room."

He gestured to his lap. "I'll make room."

She hesitated and then surrendered. He would not be dissuaded and she would do better to save her energy for the more important battles that seemed to be cropping up all over the horizon. She slowly climbed into the tub. The water was very warm, almost hot as she sank beneath the surface and settled on his lap.

"That's right." He arranged her legs on either side of his brawny thighs. "Now, that's not uncomfortable, is it?"

"No." It was a lie. This helpless position made her as uneasy as the silk-coated menace in his voice.

He reached around her with the cloth and began scrubbing her back with a circular motion.

"What are you doing? You told me to cleanse you."

"Soon. You're very tense. Why?"

"You know why. You're angry. It is surely a natural response."

He pressed her head into the hollow of his shoulder and lifted her hair. "Do you know that your hair feels like no other woman's? Thick and silky . . . and alive. If I touched only this mane in the darkness, I would know it was you." He began to scrub the nape of her neck. "Your muscles here are tied into knots. Do you fear me, Brynn?"

"No." The word was muffled.

His arms suddenly contracted around her. "Then you should. I want to *break* you."

"I've found it's a common impulse for a man to want to destroy a woman."

"Not for me. It never happened to me before I encountered you." He was silent a moment and then asked softly, "Did he take you?"

"Delmas?"

"Who else? Unless you have another husband crawling around this damnable place."

"No, of course not."

"Then, tell me pray, did he throw you down on the ground when you reached that stable and take you?" Each word was spaced with careful, lethal precision.

"No."

A little of the tension ebbed from him. "I will not have you lie to me in this."

"I don't lie."

"You didn't tell me about him. Omission can also be deception."

She was abruptly tired of his questions and accusation. "I didn't tell you about him because he didn't matter. I had enough to worry about without bringing up subjects that didn't concern you."

"You take your holy vows lightly." He paused. "It's just as well. I believe I'll rid you of this husband who you say does not concern me."

"No!"

Gage pounced. "So he does matter? You have a fondness for him?"

"I detest him, but I will not have him slain. I will not have that sin on my shoulders."

He bent down and kissed the hollow where her shoulder met her neck. "They're very lovely shoulders and you will have nothing to do with it. I assure you, I will hardly notice one more sin staining my soul."

"You will not do it." She started to struggle. "Do you hear me? I will not have it."

"Be still." He effortlessly quelled her movements. "Don't move. I don't want to hurt you too."

Violence again. "Why?" she asked wildly. "He has done nothing to offend you."

"Hasn't he?" He suddenly pushed her away and his eyes blazed down at her. "It offends me that the fool thinks you belong to him because a priest murmured a few words over you. It offends me that he has used your body as I have and that he *knows* you. It offends me that he exists." His hands tightened on her arms. "Oh, yes, he has greatly offended me."

"So you would kill him to rid yourself of the sight of him?"

"Why not?" He smiled recklessly. "I'll sweep him

out of your life as I would have washed his touch from your body."

He meant it. "It would be a sin," she whispered. "Life is a great gift. It should never be stolen away. I have no affection for Delmas, but I couldn't bear to be the cause of his death." Tears were suddenly rising to her eyes. "I heal. I don't destroy. It would be . . . I could not bear it."

"Stop weeping," he said roughly.

The tears continued to fall.

"It also offends me that you weep for him."

"I'm not weeping for him."

"Then stop it. Why do you always weep?"

"Do you think I wouldn't stop if I could? Look to yourself. I have wept more in the weeks I've known you than in all the years before."

"Damnation." He scowled. "Stop crying and I won't touch the vermin . . . now." He cradled her face in his big hands. "But you will not see him or talk to him. He will not touch you. You will not even mention his name or I'll slit him from loin to throat." His mouth covered her own, his tongue pushing deep in the moist cavity to toy and play with a wild urgency he had never shown her. It was as if he were starved and could not get enough. He lifted his head and said fiercely, "You belong to me. No one else. Only to me."

He was reaching between them, parting her thighs, adjusting their positions.

She cried out as he plunged deeper. "Only to me." He held her hips, sealing himself within her. He was breathing harshly as his hands opened and closed on the softness of her flesh. "I wanted to kill you when I saw you meekly follow him into the stable. I've been sitting here thinking of all the things he was doing to you."

"I told you—" Fullness. Warm, hard, rigidity. She could scarcely speak. "He—did nothing."

"I believe you. Which is the reason he may live a

little longer." He lifted her and then brought her with painstaking slowness down on the length of him. Again. Again. Again.

It was too slow. She was gasping, her hands reaching out blindly to him. "Gage . . . it is . . ."

"Do you like the way I fit you?"

"Yes . . ." He was sealed to her again, and she contracted desperately, trying to keep him within her.

It was of no avail. He lifted her again and began the same slow, sensual journey. "Better than your pretty Lord Richard? Better than that worm of a husband?"

"I did not like—" She bit her lower lip as the controlled friction sent a bolt of heat through her. "Much better. It is not the same. . . ."

"Then forget them." He crushed her in his arms and then reached down to cup her buttocks. "They're out of your life." He began bucking upward with frantic force as his hands moved her to a joint rhythm.

Warm, smooth water flowing over her.

Gage's solid heat within her.

She heard little helpless cries issuing from her throat as the fiery tension built.

"Yes," he whispered. "Moan. Cry out. Let me hear you."

She could do nothing else. Everything within her was rising, exploding, and must be freed.

It *was* free, releasing with such power that she could only gasp and hold on to him as if he were her only anchor.

He was still moving, muttering in her hair, "You see, mine. Mine . . ."

"No."

A great shudder rippled through him as he gave her his seed. His grasp involuntarily tightened around her. She knew he did not mean to hurt her, but she would have bruises tomorrow.

He leaned back in the tub, his eyes closed, his

breath coming harshly. "Stubborn . . ." He suddenly
rose to his feet and lifted her out of the tub.

The movement startled her. "What—"

He was striding across the room toward the bed.
"I'm weary of coupling with you everywhere but on a
bed. . . ."

"We're still wet," she protested.

"We'll dry and I promise you'll not be allowed to
rest long enough to grow cold." He laid her down and
his huge body followed, covering her. His hand slid between her thighs.

"You cannot want me again so soon."

Two fingers sank deep. "No, I want you to want me.
I want you to want and be appeased and want again."
His tongue caressed her ear as he began to leisurely
stroke her. "And sometime before this afternoon is over,
you will say you belong to me."

"No . . ." she said desperately. "I will not."

"Yes." He lowered his head and his warm tongue
lightly caressed her nipple. "Oh, yes, Brynn, you will."

"I did not mean it." Brynn stared out the window
at the setting sun. "It was not true."

He pulled the cover over her breasts and then
pushed her head into the hollow of his shoulder. "It was
true. You were most convincing."

Heat stung her cheeks. "It was you. You would not
let me—you made me do it."

"Didn't you receive pleasure?"

"Yes, but you . . . it was not true."

His hand possessively caressed her breast beneath
the cover. "I won't argue with you."

Because he considered himself the victor. She
should never have said those words. During those moments of madness she had felt part of him, magically
completed, but she should have resisted that confession.
Even though she had now regained her senses, that it

had happened made her feel vulnerable. It was dangerous to feel so close to someone when she must always stand apart.

"Who is Selbar?"

"What?"

"You said Selbar was the only one you trusted. I want to know about him."

She didn't want him to know about Selbar. Selbar was part of Gwynthal, part of what she was, and must be guarded against any invader.

When she didn't answer, Gage muttered a curse and then asked, "Did your father give you to Delmas in marriage?"

She tensed despite the quietness of his words. They were not layered with that possessive rage that had been there before when he had spoken of her husband. "No, my father left my mother and me when I was little more than a child."

"Why?"

"My mother was like me and he could not bear it."

"Like you?"

"She was a healer."

"I can see how his life would be in constant turmoil if your mother insisted on sleeping with all the men she healed."

"It was not—there was more."

"What?"

She did not answer.

To her surprise, he did not pursue the subject. "Then it was your mother who gave you to Delmas?"

"No."

"A male relative?"

"No."

He stiffened, and his tone was once more laden with soft menace. "He was your choice?"

"He was *not* my choice. I had no choice. I was forced to wed Delmas."

"Who forced you?"

She didn't answer.

"I *will* know, Brynn."

She could not tell him everything, but perhaps he would be satisfied with what little was safe to reveal. "Delmas forced me to wed him."

"How?"

"Delmas was slave to Lord Kells and when Lord Kells came to Kythe to visit his brother, Lord Giles, he brought Delmas with him." She closed her eyes. "After it happened, Delmas found me in Kythe forest. He told me later that he had searched for two days to find me."

"After what happened?"

She had known she must say the words, but they still came hoarsely. "After they burned my mother."

He went still. "Lord Giles?"

"No, the villagers. Lord Giles had no animosity toward my mother. She had healed many of his household. It was the villagers who feared her. They called her witch and blamed her for every wickedness that occurred in Kythe. She was not a witch. She was good and God-fearing." She swallowed. "She wanted only to help them, as was her duty."

"And they burned her for it." He asked thickly, "Did you see it?"

"Yes, they made me watch. I was going to the same fate on that stake the next day." *Flames. Screams. Helpless agony.* "It took a long time for her to die.

"They locked me in our cottage and Bilwak, the cobbler, stood guard outside. Sometime during the night, the guard was lured away and the door unlocked. I thought it might be Lord Giles, but Delmas told me it was his doing. I ran and hid for three days in the forest. I was trying to reach the coast and sail to Gwynthal, but Delmas caught me. He had heard rumors of the treasure and wanted it for himself. He thought I could give it to him." Her hands dug into the sheet. "He was a slave and knew there was only one way he could bind me to him so that he would have time to find out what he wanted to know. He put me in chains and took me to Father Jerome, the priest at the castle. He had told him he wanted to wed me and take me to England to save me from the villagers. The priest had met my mother and knew she was no sorceress." She added bitterly, "Like most men, he listened only to another man. He decided that I could have no better protector than Delmas and would not hear my protests. He said the words over us."

"Fool."

"He meant it kindly."

"Then save me from the kindness of fools."

She had felt the same at the time, but it was long ago.

"You never told him of the treasure?"

"No, he gave up trying to force me after a time. I had proved I had other value in Lord Kells's household. He had hopes of winning his freedom through my healing."

"How did he try to force you?" he asked slowly.

"How do men usually try to enforce their will?" She could feel the menace in him growing and said quickly, "I am free of him now. He can do nothing to harm me."

"You aren't free of him. Not yet."

The words sounded foreboding and sent a chill through her. She hastened to change the subject. "Lady Adwen needs great care, but she is better than I hoped. Malik seems very pleased with having a companion—"

"How did he hurt you?"

He was like a dog with a bone and she was suddenly angry at the inquisition. Her life was fraught with problems and she was tired of wondering and worrying how he would respond to the most casual word. "I will answer no more questions. It is in the past. What difference does it make?"

He was silent a moment, gazing out at the setting sun. "As God is my witness, I don't know." He suddenly rose to his feet and strode to the window. The scarlet light framed his powerful naked body and cast a fiery areolae about his loosened hair.

His hair was lit by the flames.

He will come.

The words of Adwen's dream suddenly returned to her.

But it was not midnight and Gage had no intention of destroying Redfern. She had seen too many strange and miraculous happenings to discount the possibility of Adwen's dream being a true vision, but he could not be the one. He was a man of violent emotions, but he would never deal in wanton destruction.

"Why are you looking at me like that?

He had turned once again to face her.

The words tumbled out before she could restrain them. "I was thinking that you're not a destroyer."

"Am I not?" He moved slowly toward the bed. "It is the duty of a soldier to destroy."

"But you . . . Malik says you are more than a warrior."

"Malik always thinks the best of everyone." He towered over her. With the light behind him she could not see his expression, but his voice was darkly brooding. "I give you warning, I can be very like my father, and there was no more bloodthirsty man on this earth than Hardraada."

She felt a chill go through her. "Then you should battle against such a heritage."

"Oh, I do. I learned early that bloodletting must be guided by the mind and not by passion. I've not killed a man in anger since I was a boy following my father on his raids." His hand came out and caressed her hair. "It disturbs me that I would have sliced your husband's throat without a qualm. It shows my temper is not as controlled as I believed."

She moistened her lips. "If it disturbs you, then you must know it's wrong."

"So the priests say. In truth, I've always agreed with them." His hand moved down to caress her throat. "I've always thought David a fool to be so obsessed."

"David?"

"King David, who saw Bathsheba and sent her husband to die in battle."

"You're right. He was a fool to give up his soul for a woman."

"Then why do I want to do it? I'm not a fool."

The very casualness of his tone made her heart leap with fear. It was as if he had already admitted the decision was inevitable. "You're not thinking reasonably. I'm no Bathsheba. You have no true affection for me. You've said Delmas's presence will make no difference, that you'll still couple with me, use me."

"I didn't tell the truth. It does make a difference. While he exists I cannot—" He stopped and shook his head. "We will not talk of him. Keep your husband out of my sight, and he may live."

Heaven knows, she wanted to escape any further mention of Delmas. Gage's violent response had frightened her. She swung her feet to the floor and tried to make her tone light. "I've told you I will avoid him, but he belongs to Lord Richard. You'll have to tell him that seeing Delmas about the hall doesn't please you." She picked up her gown and slipped it over her head. "I'm sure he'll accommodate you in any way he can."

He frowned. "Where are you going?"

"I must go see if Adwen and Malik are well and then find a place to sleep."

"You'll sleep here." His lips twisted as he gestured to the bed. "You should be accustomed to Lord Richard's bed."

"I've never been in this chamber before today." She bent down and put on her shoes. "And I've never coupled with that snake's spawn."

She wasn't looking at him but sensed his sudden alertness. "No? He said you—"

"Then he's a liar as well as a snake." She put on her other shoe. "And you were foolish to believe him."

"But you knew I believed him, didn't you?" His tone was edged. "And you let me continue. Why?"

She moved toward the door. "I had to get to Redfern. I wasn't sure you believed in the treasure and you're a warrior with a warrior's instinct to conquer."

"So you used me."

"As you used me."

"I'd be curious to know why you were so desperate to reach here."

"Adwen." She glanced over her shoulder. "It was always Adwen. She needed me."

"You could have told me," he said roughly. "I'm not so vile as to let a woman die for lack of care."

"I couldn't take the chance."

An undefinable emotion flickered across his face. "No, considering the lack of gentleness with which I've treated you, I suppose you were right not to trust in my benevolent nature."

For some reason she felt the need to reassure him. "You've not been unkind. Gentleness does not come easily to some men."

He smiled curiously. "Particularly when there is a battle both within and without." He paused. "And I assume there is no treasure?"

"Of course there is treasure. I don't lie."

"And where is this proof you said was here at Redfern?"

"Delmas has it. He took it away from me the night before we wed." She opened the door. "But if you don't want to see him, I don't see how you can get it from him."

"I will wait." He smiled sardonically. "For my temper to cool."

She had seen little sign of that occurring. "You don't need Delmas. If you agree to free me, I will lead you to the treasure." She frowned. "But we will have to wait until Adwen is able to travel. I will not leave her here to be abused."

"*If* I decide to go on this journey, I'll make sure Lady Adwen is protected." He suddenly frowned. "Go and see to them, but I want you to return and sit by my side in the hall tonight."

She looked at him, startled. "I cannot. A slave does not sit at the high table."

"She does if her master wishes it." His gaze moved over her. "And borrow a gown from Lady Adwen. I weary of seeing you in those rags."

"I should not leave—"

"If you don't come, I'll come after you. Do you want your Lady Adwen to be distressed when I drag you from the chamber?"

"It makes no sense," she said, exasperated. "Why do you wish this?"

"It should be enough for you that I do." He turned, facing away from her. "And I have every intention of satisfying my wishes. I'll see you in the hall."

Seven

"WHERE IS ALICE?" Brynn asked Malik as she entered Adwen's chamber. "I told her to come and tend to your needs."

"I sent her to fetch broth for Lady Adwen," Malik said. "I did not want to chance you giving her one of your concoctions."

"How is she?" Brynn studied Adwen's face as she approached the bed. She appeared much better now that her hair and skin glowed with cleanliness. "Did she wake at all?"

"Twice," Malik said. "Once just after you left and once when Alice was bathing her." He made a face. "She made Alice put a curtain between us so that I could not behold her."

"I see no curtain."

Malik grinned. "I jerked it down after she went back to sleep. I refuse to be denied such bounty. It is bad enough being confined to this bed. Surely I deserve a small reward."

"Not if it's wrested from Adwen. She's had too much taken from her already."

Malik's grin vanished. "Poor lady. It is a cruel world that could do this to one so helpless."

Brynn had a fleeting memory of Adwen's surprisingly fierce outburst in the stable. "Perhaps she's not as helpless as you might think." She went around the bed and checked Malik's bandage; it had been changed. Obviously Alice had been speaking truly when she said she would work hard to make amends. "The world is seldom kind, but it was her lord and husband who did this to her."

"Then her lord and husband should be sent to burn in Hades," Malik said pleasantly. "And I will be delighted to assist him there at the earliest opportunity." His glance shifted to Brynn. "If Gage does not cheat me of the pleasure before I am able to rise from this bed. It could happen if he thinks you still have a fondness for Richard."

"I never had a fondness for that beast." She looked back at Adwen. "How could I?"

Malik nodded, understanding at once. "I thought it odd. It was the lady and not the master who drew you here?"

She nodded. "I thought she needed me."

"It is clear she did need you."

She shook her head doubtfully as she remembered that impression of strength in Adwen. "Maybe." She went to the carved oak chest that was under the window and opened the lid. "I must go to sup in the hall tonight. I will return as soon as I can."

He shook his head. "Gage will want you in his bed."

"Then he must do without what he wants. I have duties to perform."

Malik frowned in concern. "No, Brynn, I saw Gage's face when you ran after Delmas today. You walk a very fine line if you wish to keep your husband alive."

Fear leapt within her. "Do you truly think he would kill a man for so little reason?"

"I saw his face," Malik repeated.

"I don't understand how men can take life and walk away. Don't they know how it darkens their souls?" she said with exasperation as she rummaged through the gowns in the chest to find one that might fit. "I don't understand *him*."

"At present I don't believe he understands himself either," he said quietly. "Which makes the situation more dangerous. From the time Gage was a boy, Hardraada took him on his raids, trained him in blood and violence, taught him to take what he wanted and let nothing stand in his way. In later years Gage learned other ways, but it would not take much to send him back to Hardraada's teachings."

Piracy and blood and the huge shadow of Hardraada cast over Gage's horizon.

"Do not return to this room tonight, Brynn. Soothe him. Give him what he needs." Malik smiled. "I don't think that task is proving too unpleasant for you."

Not unpleasant but perhaps more dangerous than he knew. Every time she coupled with Gage, the bonding became stronger, the emptiness of separation more intense. She was beginning to wonder how long it would be before she no longer felt complete without him. She chose a gown the color of dark red wine from the chest, closed the lid, and walked quickly toward the anteroom. "Send Alice to the hall to get me if Adwen worsens."

"Don't worry. I will care for her."

There was such gentleness in his voice that she glanced over her shoulder. He was looking at Adwen with protective tenderness, and she felt a pang of wistfulness. How wonderful it would be to be able to relinquish all burdens and nestle in the shelter of someone else's strength. What was she thinking? She was not a nestler and she would quickly grow impatient of anyone who tried to make her one.

But perhaps it would not be so bad for a little while. . . .

"See that you do," she said gruffly as she disappeared into the anteroom.

A fire burned bright in the huge hearth, where a wild pig was being slowly rotated on the spit. A young boy sat nearby, strumming his stringed instrument. Booming laughter issued from the high table.

Brynn stopped uncertainly in the arched doorway of the hall. What should she do now? She had no place here. Lord Richard had evidently invited all his vassals and their ladies to the feast. She recognized only a few of them; Edmund of Danworth and his wife, Joan. White haired Cyril Montbor and his son, Herbert of Kenmal.

"Come," Lord Richard called when he saw her. He stood up at the long table on the dais and held out his hand. "I have never seen you look more winsome." A brilliant smile lit his face. "Sit by my side, Brynn."

A sudden silence fell over the table. They were all staring at her. The men with curiosity, their ladies with haughty antagonism.

"She sits with me," Gage said from behind her. He took her elbow and urged her forward across the rush-strewn floor toward the dais. His touch was warm and comforting, and she felt a little of her uneasiness leave her.

"I want to leave," she whispered. "I don't belong here."

"Of course you belong here," he said roughly in a low voice. "You are wiser than any man in this hall and more lovely than any woman." He glanced down at her. "Particularly in that gown. I . . . thank you for wearing it."

She looked at him in surprise. The words had come awkwardly and she could not remember him ever commenting on her appearance. "It doesn't fit." She looked down at the tight bodice. "Adwen is much smaller than me."

"On the contrary." His gaze went to the bodice. "I ardently admire the fit of that gown. But, if you like, I will send a messenger back to my ship at Pevence Bay for material to have others made for you."

"Materials?"

"Silk from Byzantium, laces from Damascus." He smiled mockingly. "Like the money-pinching merchant I am, I never go anywhere without goods for barter."

"I don't need silks. I'm content with my own woolen gown. I would not have borrowed Adwen's if you had not insisted."

"I know." His lips tightened as he helped her up the two steps to the dais. "Because you're the most stubborn and willful woman in all this benighted country. Would it be too—"

"I've had a feast prepared that will rival anything you've tasted in Normandy." Richard gracefully gestured toward the high-backed chairs next to him. "You will see how diligently I'm trying to please you."

Gage glanced around the hall. "You've evidently done one thing to please me. Where did you send him?"

"It is of no importance." Richard waved airily. "But be assured you'll be spared his presence for your entire stay here. I would have sent Delmas away before your arrival if I'd known how tender were the feelings of Normans. I fear we Saxons are a much more insensitive lot. Delmas was always very obliging when it—"

"He is gone. We will not speak of him." Gage seated Brynn on his left side before taking the chair beside Richard. "You can bring him back in a few days' time, after we've left."

"Only a few days? I hoped for a longer stay." Richard motioned for the serving to begin. "Oh, well, perhaps we can change your mind. Redfern is such a pleasant place." He leaned forward and spoke to Brynn. "You must take him around the countryside and show him what a fine property this would be for him."

"I won't have time." She met Richard's gaze. "Adwen is not well and must be cared for."

His bland expression didn't alter. "Yes, Delmas told me you had moved her back to her former quarters. It was not well done. She is infectious, you know. I was forced to move her to the stable to protect us all from disease."

She stared at him in disbelief. "She's only suffering from the same fever she had before."

"Really? But we did not know that, did we? You were not here to tell us."

Her hand tightened on the goblet. She wanted to throw it at him.

Richard turned to Gage. "Brynn has a great fondness for my poor wife. She will not admit that Adwen was not meant for this earth." He sighed. "I fear the angels may take her at any time."

"No!" Brynn took a deep breath and then said, "I realize Adwen is an inconvenience to you, but she will not die."

"Inconvenience? How could that sweet lady be an inconvenience?" He lifted his goblet to her. "Though I admit that my taste runs to more spirited women. Naturally, a man wants a woman who can sit by his side and match his strength with her own."

Lies. Richard had no desire for any quality but submission in a woman. First, a subtle threat and then flattery. What was he about?

"Eat." Gage deliberately leaned forward, blocking her view of Richard. He tore off a small piece of meat from the portion on his trencher and handed it to her. "I agree with Lord Richard. We must nourish your strength." His voice lowered to sensual intimacy. "You will soon have need of it."

Heat flamed to her cheeks as she met his gaze. Nothing could be more clear than his inference. He had staked his claim before everyone in the hall. She could see by the lewd smiles on the faces of the men at the table that even now they were imagining her in the Norman's bed.

Richard laughed and lifted his goblet again. "Well said. How I envy you." He drank deep before adding, "And regret the day I was forced to give up such a prize. A slave such as Brynn does not come along every day."

Slave. Property. Owned. They were all looking at her, and she suddenly felt suffocated. "I find I'm no longer hungry." She jumped to her feet. "I must get back to Adwen."

"Brynn." Gage's voice was low but warning.

She ignored him and ran from the room.

He caught up with her before she reached the staircase. His hand grasped her arm. "Brynn!"

"I will not go back," she said fiercely. "You cannot make me. Find someone else to shame." She tried to free herself. "But you did not succeed. I was not ashamed. It is you and the others who should be ashamed to keep human beings beneath your yoke. I will not—"

"By God, will you be silent and listen?" He grasped her shoulders and shook her. "I didn't mean to shame you. It was never my intention— He was looking at you as if—and I was angry. . . . It just happened."

"And that makes all well? Of course it happened. You bring your slave to sit at your side at the table. You display me before your officers and Richard's vassals. I'm surprised you did not have me stripped naked before them."

"I did not display you," he said harshly. "And you've learned nothing if you think I'd let anyone see you unclothed but me." His hands tightened on her. "I meant to show you honor. I wanted to show them they must treat you with respect, that you were more than a slave."

"But I'm not more than a slave to you. You have proved that to everyone at Redfern. Slave and whore." She looked up at him. "And you will prove it again when you take me back to your chamber. They will chuckle and sneer and talk among themselves about all the things you are doing to my body. You know it and I know it."

"I don't know it."

"You do know it and you don't care."

He glared down at her. "Damn you. I'm not perfect. Sometimes I grow angry and my tongue runs away with me." He whirled and stalked back toward the hall. "But if I didn't care, I would have throttled you by now."

She called tauntingly after him, "Shall I wait for you in your chamber, my lord?"

"Not if you value your life. Go to Malik and that woman. Perhaps they'll be safe from your poison."

She stared after him in astonishment as he entered the hall. She had not thought he would let her go back to Malik and Adwen. It was a most unusual thing for him to do.

But then, his entire behavior tonight had been unusual. It had ranged from tentativeness to moody jealousy and then, at the end, perhaps . . . regret?

Had he really meant to attempt to raise her to a place of honor to shelter her from calumny? She felt her anger ebbing away as she considered the possibility. He had said it, and he was not a man who lied.

She felt a tiny bud of warmth unfold within her as she turned and started up the steps. He had tried to protect her.

She should not be this content. After all, he had

lost his temper and probably made things worse for her. He had not behaved in the gentle, knightly way in which Malik would have offered his protection. He had been rough and abrupt and unkind. She should ignore his intentions and think only of his deplorable actions.

Yet he had tried to protect her. . . .

A single candle burned in Adwen's chamber, and Alice was curled beside the flickering flames in the hearth. Brynn put her finger to her lips as the servant scrambled to her feet. She glanced at the man and woman on the bed who appeared to be slumbering. "All is well?" she whispered.

Alice nodded. "He was in some discomfort, so I gave him the same sleeping draught you taught me to make for Lady Adwen. Lady Adwen has been sleeping since you left."

"Good. You may go to your own bed. I will stay with them now."

"You will? I thought—" Alice broke off.

Alice had thought what everyone at Redfern thought, that she would occupy the Norman's bed. "Go to your rest. I will watch them."

Alice still hesitated.

"What is it?" Brynn asked impatiently.

"Could I stay here? I will be no bother. I will just curl here by the fire."

"Why would you—" Brynn stopped as she understood. Alice was safe here. "You believe Lord Richard will be displeased that you're helping Lady Adwen?"

Alice nodded. "He hurts me when he's angry." She shivered. "He always hurts me, but more then. If I leave here, he will find me and take me back to his bed."

"If you hate it so much, then you should have run away."

"Where can I run?" She bit her lower lip before she said, "I am with child."

Brynn felt a jolt of shock, mixed with anger. "Does he know?"

"Yes. I'm in my third month."

"And he sent you to Lord Gage for him to use?"

"I have barely started to round, and Lord Richard said I was still comelier than any woman at Redfern. He wanted to please Lord Gage and was not sure the Norman was still enamored with you."

Brynn felt sick with disgust.

"May I stay?" Alice asked again.

Brynn nodded toward the cot she had ordered brought in for herself and set against the far wall. "Sleep there."

"No, I will be fine here by the fire."

"Take the cot. I'm strong and healthy and not three months gone with child. I will have another cot brought in tomorrow." When Alice didn't move, she said sharply, "Now!"

Alice hurried toward the cot.

Adwen's chamber was large, but it would soon be filled to overflowing, Brynn thought wearily. She knew she should not have spoken harshly to Alice, but she had suddenly been overwhelmed by the realization that here was still another of Richard's victims she could not leave behind at his mercy. How was she to free herself and return to Gwynthal if she must worry about these poor women's safety? Well, it must be done, but she would dismiss it from her mind that night.

Had she heard something? She turned sharply toward the bed but could see no movement. She swiftly crossed the room. Malik was clearly deep in sleep, so the sound must have come from Adwen. Yet Adwen lay perfectly still. . . .

Adwen's eyes were open and glittering with tears. "Brynn . . ."

Dear God, could this night bring any more turmoil? "You heard?" she whispered as she sat down on the bed and gathered Adwen's hands in hers. "Don't weep. Everything will be fine."

"I tried so hard to have a child for him."

"I know. It was not meant to be."

"He hurt me too. But coupling is always painful, isn't it?"

Gage stroking her, entering her, lifting her. "Not always."

Adwen's gaze flew to Brynn's face. "The Norman does not hurt you when he beds you?"

"You know about the Norman?"

"Richard told me when he returned from Hastings that your duties would not only be healing. I prayed for you." Her hands opened and closed on the sheet. "And then, when I became ill again, I prayed for myself. I knew only God could save me. Richard wants me dead. He's always wanted me dead, but I would not admit it. I could not believe anyone could be so cruel. I wanted only to do what I had been taught was my duty. It was not my fault I could not have a child. In spite of what he said, it was not my fault." Her gaze went to Alice on the cot. "Poor woman, I don't envy her. A babe is such a wondrous thing, but I would rather die than give birth to his child now."

"That is not kind. A child is innocent of guilt."

"I know, but the child would be as beautiful as Richard, and I could not help but remember my foolishness. I remember when I first came to Redfern, I thought I had never seen a more handsome man. He was so full of smiles and graceful ways. He dazzled me."

"You were only a child."

"It is more than that. It is a weakness in me that I worship beauty. Even as the years passed, I could not see beyond his comeliness. I didn't think God would make a creature so beautiful and give him a black heart." Her lips twisted. "Remember when I told you how lucky I was that I didn't have a husband like Delmas? How stupid you must have thought me."

"I never thought you stupid," she said gently.

"Then you may be even more foolish than I." Adwen smiled. "But I will not remain stupid. I can learn and my will is not weak. I would have died in that stable if I had not been determined to keep alive. I want to live, Brynn. I want to be well. Will you help me?"

Brynn smiled. "That's why I came back."

Adwen's hand tightened on Brynn's. "I know it's not fair of me. You have your own troubles. What of Delmas?"

"Lord Richard has sent Delmas away."

"Why?"

Brynn looked away. "Lord Gage didn't want him here."

"Alice said the Norman was enamored of you. Is it true?"

"No, he is enamored of what lies between my legs."

"But you said he was gentle with you."

As gentle as a storm, as tender as a white-hot blaze. Her mind could not resist going back to that afternoon of coupling. "I didn't say he was gentle."

"You *like* it," Adwen said, her eyes widening in shock. "You like lying with the Norman. I thought he had given you no choice."

"He did not."

"But you enjoy him." Her brow wrinkled with worry. "Is that not wrong? You have a husband. It is a sin."

"Is it not a sin to have a husband who forces you to marriage? I said no vows."

"No vows are required from a woman."

"They are in Gwynthal."

"Then it must have very strange laws."

"Just laws." She patted Adwen's hand. "Don't be concerned. I sleep with the Norman because I must. It will not be for long and I'm sure God will forgive my body for betraying me."

"No one could help but forgive you anything, Brynn. It is you who must forgive me for questioning you. How do I know what is sin and what is not? Everything is changing, isn't it?"

"Be still. No forgiveness is necessary on either side. Are we not friends? Now go to sleep."

"Brynn . . ." Adwen hesitated. "Are all these foreigners so glorious to behold?"

"What?"

"Well, the Norman clearly pleases you and—"

"I did not say he—"

Adwen gestured impatiently. "His appearance does please you."

Sleek massive shoulders, eyes the blue of the northern sea. "Yes," she said cautiously.

"And this one." She gestured to the sleeping Malik. "He is even more beautiful than my husband. Richard told me that the Normans were all hairy brutes with buck teeth who seldom bathed. If the Normans are all so comely, it must be difficult to see beyond the surface to the evil."

"Malik is not Norman, he is Saracen and he's not evil. His heart is as good as his face."

Adwen doubtfully shook her head. "I thought that of Richard. It is too hard to tell what is behind a handsome face."

"Well, Normans are like Saxons. Some are comely, some are ugly. You need not worry about being overwhelmed." She stood up and got a blanket from the linen chest. "And you need not worry about anything tonight."

Adwen's gaze again went to Alice. "Poor woman," she whispered. "Life is not fair to women. There should be something we can do. . . ."

· · ·

"Good day." Gage strode brusquely into Adwen's chamber. "How are you, Malik?"

"Better all the time." He indicated Adwen. "May I present Lady Adwen? This is my friend, Lord Gage Dumont."

"Lord Gage," Adwen murmured. She studied him for a moment and then smiled and held out her hand. "Thank you for coming to Redfern."

Gage moved forward, took her hand, and gracefully bowed over it. "If I had known such a beautiful lady was hidden here, I would have urged William to invade England much sooner."

Brynn stared at him in astonishment. His manners were polished, his smile almost gentle. This was a Gage she had never seen. She caught Malik's knowing glance and remembered what he had told her.

He is many men—poet, merchant, warrior. You have seen only the warrior.

But it seemed Adwen was permitted to see another side of him. She should feel happy, not annoyed, she told herself. Adwen needed all the gentleness she could garner.

"You are very kind, but I have no beauty." Adwen raised her hand to the black circles beneath her eyes. "I feel as without color as an unlit candle."

"Then we must light the candle." Gage smiled. "Trust in Brynn. She seems to be very good at the task."

"I do trust her." Adwen reached out and took Brynn's hand. "Always." She looked up at him. "But she often sees what is practical and not what is proper. It is not fitting I occupy a bed with any man." She gestured to Malik across the bed. "I must be moved from this bed."

Malik sighed. "I knew it could not last. Do you wish to see me sicken and die of melancholy?"

"I must be moved," she repeated firmly. She pointed to the cot across the room where Alice had slept the previous night. "Perhaps another cot could be brought in and you could put me there."

"I assure you that Malik is too ill to behave with anything but the utmost gallantry." His lips twitching, Gage added, "Though in a few weeks your concern might have foundation."

Adwen's jaw squared. "I must be moved." She imperiously held out her arms. "Please."

"As you like." Gage scooped her up, carried her across the room, and set her with great care on the cot.

"No!" Malik protested. "If anyone is to be moved, it should be me. It is her right to stay here. This is her bed, her chamber."

"I have no rights." Adwen's lips curved bitterly. "My lord husband has made that clear. This cot is sheltered from wind and cold and much more comfortable than the one he sent me to in the stable."

Malik muttered a curse. "I will take the cot. Bring her back and move me, Gage."

"I will stay where I am," Adwen said firmly. "It is my choice to move. I have received no great wound. You must occupy the bed."

Malik said, "And what kind of man would I be to permit such a thing? Gage, you must—"

"I will do nothing." Gage looked with amusement from one belligerent face to another. "Not until the quarrel is settled between you. I refuse to spend my day transferring bodies about. Lady Adwen is light as a feather, but you're no mean weight." He turned to Brynn. "Get your cloak."

She looked at him in surprise. "Why?"

"We're going to ride out and see the property. You're going to show me the glories of Redfern. Did you not hear Lord Richard's instructions?"

"I don't obey Lord Richard."

He met her stare. "Then come because I ask it."

He was trying to tell her something. She could not tear her eyes away. "And if I refuse?"

"Then I will go alone."

He was asking, not demanding. The pleasure the knowledge brought was too sweet, and she instinctively shied away from it. "I must stay here and—"

An accident might befall the Norman.

Fear soared through her as she remembered Delmas's words. "You would be foolish to wander about an enemy countryside by yourself. Take Captain LeFont."

"I think not. It's never a good idea to let a defeated enemy believe you fear him." He started to turn away. "If you refuse to honor me with your company today, I'll try again tomorrow."

An arrow launched from hiding. An attack by Richard's minions as he rode through the forest. He might be dead tomorrow.

"No!" She whirled away and snatched up her cloak. "I'll go with you. I'll meet you in the courtyard. I must go fetch Alice from the kitchens to watch Adwen and Malik."

"It's not so bad a property as I first thought when I saw that crude dwelling," Gage said. "At least, the fields appear rich and well tended." His gaze wandered to the forest to the north. "How is the game?"

"Lord Richard and his vassals seem to find plenty to hunt." Brynn quickly glanced over her shoulder at the farmer, who had stopped to watch their progress. His regard was curious, not threatening, she realized with relief.

She turned back to see Gage's eyes narrowed on her face. "It's you who appear hunted," he said softly. "Are you expecting someone to follow us?"

She forced a smile. "Why should I?" she said, then changed the subject. "The wild pig that was served in the hall last night was no doubt killed in that forest. Lord Richard often brings down big game."

"He's a good hunter, then?"

"Yes. Very good." She could still feel Gage's stare but studiously avoided it. "He enjoys the kill." She again glanced over her shoulder. The farmer had gone back to his harvesting. "Are you ready to go back to the manor?"

"No, I believe we'll go and see if the hunting in that forest is as plentiful as you claim."

"No!"

He pounced on her immediate objection. "Why not? You like the woods. What's different about this one?"

"It's too far."

He raised his brows. "A quarter mile away?"

He was not going to give up. She searched wildly for a diversion. "Would you like to see where I grow herbs for my salves?"

"Is it in the forest?"

She nodded. "Just on this edge." No one knew about her little bower. If she could keep him there until dusk, perhaps he would not venture deeper into the forest. "It's a very pleasant place."

Gage motioned her to precede him. "Then by all means let's go there."

The small glade was completely enclosed by a thick tangle of shrubbery, and they had to force their way through. As usual, her spirits lifted as the scent of rosemary, thyme, and mint drifted to her. Her place. As close to Gwynthal as she could make it. She glanced eagerly over her shoulder. "This is my garden. Isn't it beautiful?"

"Beautiful," he echoed, looking at her. He got down from his horse and lifted her off the mare. "But a little out of the way for a garden. Wouldn't Lord Richard allow you a patch of land nearer the manor?"

"I didn't ask. I explained that I could find the proper herbs only in the woods."

"And no one knows about this place?"

"No." She added without thinking, "It's quite safe."

"Safe?" He turned to look at her.

"I meant that my garden is safe from being trampled by forest creatures," she said quickly. "They don't like the prickliness of the holly bushes."

"I don't think that's what you meant," Gage said. "What do you fear in this forest that you didn't in the one at Hastings?"

"Nothing. What could I fear?"

His expression hardened. "Tell me."

She was silent.

"Shall I go deeper into the woods and find out for myself?"

"No!" She would have to tell him. "Lord Richard is not to be trusted. He may try to do you harm."

"Indeed? How do you know?"

"Delmas told me." She saw the expected reaction and blurted out, "You see, you take the knowledge that Lord Richard may try to kill you quite calmly, but I make mention of Delmas and you grow angry. It makes no sense."

"I gather that Delmas didn't confide Lord Richard's plans so that you could give me warning?"

She didn't answer.

"So he was privy to Lord Richard's plans. I find it strange that he would confide such a plot to a slave. Now, why would he do that?"

She said reluctantly, "Delmas was desperate for help to get me back and told him of the treasure."

"Ah, your husband was desperate for your return."

"Because of the treasure. He cares nothing for me." Her hands clenched into fists at her sides. "Delmas is no worse than Lord Richard. Why accept one and hate the other?"

"It must be a grievous fault in my character." He turned and walked toward the brook. "Actually, I'm glad your husband is plotting my death. It will make it easier to remove him. Not that it would have been hard before."

"Lord Richard is the one to blame. Delmas only does his bidding." His expression didn't change and she spat out in frustration, "I wish I had not told you. Now you will think only of death and vengeance. I should never have warned you."

"Why did you warn me?" He took a step closer. "If I had been killed, it would have been one less enemy to plague you."

She hurriedly glanced away. "Better you than Delmas and Lord Richard."

"I'm not flattered by the comparison." He lifted her chin and forced her to stare into his eyes. "Look at me. Am I truly the enemy, Brynn?"

"You keep me from Gwynthal. You call me your slave. How can you be anything else but my enemy?"

"If you were not my slave, would you leave me?"

"Yes."

"Then you will remain my slave." He turned away, sat down, and took off his boots. "But if it makes you easier, I am not the trusting fool you think me. I would have to be a madman to believe Richard of Redfern would tamely hand his birthright over to me. I had LeFont take a company of men to search this forest and the surrounding countryside for malcontents yesterday after we arrived. He's making a similar search today."

Her eyes widened. "Why didn't you tell me?"

"Why? It is what I would have done in any enemy land." He took off his mail and tunic and lay down on the moss beside the creek. He closed his eyes. "But now that I know you have my interests at heart, I feel no hesitation about letting you guard me."

No one appeared less in need of protection. Nudity should have made him look vulnerable, but it did not. He was all bronze and ebony, a huge, gleaming cat sunning himself after the hunt . . . or before the hunt.

"What are you doing?"

He didn't open his eyes. "I think it clear. I had a disturbed night and feel the need for a nap. Wake me before dusk."

She stared at him uncertainly. "And what do you wish me to do while you sleep?"

"Do whatever you would do if I weren't here." He yawned. "This is your place, not mine."

Of course it was her place. Why was she so hesitant? She knew the answer. He had only to enter into a place and it became subtly his own. She was not sure she would ever be able to come back here without seeing his big body lying on that mossy bank.

Well, her sleep had also been disturbed, but she was wide awake and there was plenty to do. She had been gone too long. She knelt and began to pluck the weeds from the beds. The scents were heady, the birds singing, the sun warm, and the peace she always felt when she was here began to flow over her.

It was a long time later, when the rays of the sun had grown long over the glade, that she became aware he was watching her.

She glanced over her shoulder and smiled. "It's almost time to go."

"Soon." He stretched lazily before rising to his feet and moving across the glade toward her. "What are you doing?"

"Pulling weeds. They're trying to choke the life from my plants."

"And you're fighting them off." He knelt on the

other side of the row and began to pull at the intruding sprigs. "Do your plants have their own dragons for you to battle against too?"

"Of course. Where there is life, there is always death trying to take it away. If I didn't fight it, I would become part of it and I would hate myself."

"And it was your mother who taught you about herbs?"

She nodded. "From the time I was out of swaddling clothes I always knew that I must prepare myself to be a healer, to fight the dragons." She looked at him gravely. "She told me that there are many kinds of warriors in the world and the best kind are the ones who give life, not take it away."

"I wouldn't know about such benevolent warriors. I've known only the other kind." His lips twisted. "The ones like myself."

"But you could change."

"Only if the world changed." He reached out to pull another weed. "I could not tolerate life beneath a conqueror's heel. Look at you. You're a slave. What's your reward for fighting your dragons?"

"The battle itself," she said simply.

He glanced up and paused in mid motion. "Radiance . . ." he murmured.

"What?"

"Nothing. Just something Malik said about you." He plucked the weed and reached for another. "Before he decided it would be a presumption to become enamored of you."

She chuckled. "Presumption? I didn't think Malik had knowledge of the word. You are strange companions. Where did you meet?"

"Byzantium." He smiled. "He ran a sword through my arm."

"What?"

"My caravan was attacked in the desert by Saracen

bandits as I was returning to Normandy. Malik was leading them."

She frowned. "I cannot believe Malik a thief."

"He was an excellent thief. He and his men stole every scrap of goods, horses, and wagons in the caravan and rode away. Two days later he returned with horses and enough water to see us out of the desert." He grinned. "He also bandaged my arm and gave me a lecture on fighting men who are obviously of superior skill."

"A thief . . ."

"His village thought him a hero. They had suffered three years of drought and there was thirst and starvation until Malik took matters into his own hands. Tell me, would you choose virtue or life in the same circumstances?"

She answered without hesitation. "Life."

"I thought as much. So did Malik. No one loves life as much as he does. Except, perhaps, you." He looked around the glade. "He would like your garden."

"Yes." She impulsively took his hand and placed it on the sun-warmed earth. "There is so much life here. It's all around us. Can you feel it?"

"Yes." He turned his hand over and closed it around hers. "I've never felt more alive."

She inhaled sharply as she met his gaze. She had never felt more alive either. It was as if his life force were flowing into her, making her stronger, bringing her to the crest where earth met sky. She smiled luminously as she returned his clasp. "That is good."

"I want you," he said thickly. "I want to be inside you. I want to *feel* how alive you are. Here. Now."

She felt a tiny flicker of disappointment. "As you like."

He muttered a curse as he dropped her hands. "I said I wanted it. I didn't say I would force you to it." He got to his feet and moved toward the bank. "You don't understand."

"No, I don't." She watched him in bewilderment as he donned his clothes and then strode toward the horses.

"Come along," he said. "It's time we got back."

She stood up and moved toward the mare. "If you would explain, I might—"

"Don't expect me to explain it to you when I don't understand myself. We're alone here. I don't have to worry about you scourging me for bringing shame down upon you." He tossed her onto the mare's back and mounted his own horse. "And God knows, I don't believe in the code of knightly behavior preached at William's court. I've always found that it's seldom used when it isn't convenient." He put spurs to his stallion. "Dammit, and it is most certainly *not* convenient."

He was in a rage of frustration and more storm ridden than she had ever seen him.

Still, Brynn found herself smiling joyously as she followed him back to Redfern.

Lord Richard met them in the courtyard. "I hope you found my Redfern as beautiful as I do, my lord. If you had told me you were riding out, I would have come with you." He stepped forward and lifted Brynn down from her horse. "But I'm sure Brynn proved a most felicitous companion."

She quickly disengaged herself and stepped back. "I must get back to Malik and Adwen." She met Gage's eyes. "I trust you will not require me in the hall tonight?"

"No." He grimaced. "I believe we'll dispense with your company. It appears to be too upsetting for proper digestion."

She smiled. "I've noticed it a common practice for a man to blame every discomfort on a woman." She turned and started up the steps. "Look to yourself, my lord."

He chuckled and called after her. "I'll endeavor to do so." He paused. "If you will honor me with your presence tomorrow for another ride through the countryside."

The last words were spoken with the formality he might have shown a great lady. She stopped on the steps and turned back to scan his face for signs of mockery. She found none. "It will be my pleasure, my lord." She started up the stairs again.

"I'll go with you." Lord Richard hurried after her. "I've not paid a visit to my poor lady today."

What mischief was he planning now? She stopped and turned to face him. "She is too ill for visitors."

"But surely not for a husband? A husband is not a visitor."

"Brynn?" Gage asked softly.

She cast him a swift glance. He wanted her to give him cause to violence. In Gage's present uncertain temper it would not be wise to light any spark. She said curtly to Richard, "Come along, then." She moved down the hall. "But you cannot stay long."

"I will not stay at all. I have no desire to see my pale rag of a wife. I wished only an opportunity to talk to you. The Norman seems to be always at your heels." He added crudely, "Or in your body. The servants told me yesterday that they heard you grunting and screaming like the peasant you are after you banished Alice from his chamber."

She flinched at the words. She had not thought he could hurt her, but she felt suddenly besmirched. "Say what you have to say."

"The treasure. It has to be mine," he whispered. "Ours. Why should the Norman have it?"

"Delmas told me he had told you about Gwynthal.

I never told him there was a treasure. How do you know he didn't lie about it?"

"He would not dare lie to me. He has no courage." Richard smiled. "And he's not overly clever. He actually thought I'd share the treasure with him, which only proves his stupidity. I don't need him if I have you."

"But you don't have me."

"Not at the moment, but I've always been good at ridding myself of obstacles." He paused. "You can have no life with the Norman. He will only use you and then discard you. While I might even be willing to wed you."

She said coldly, "You have a wife."

"But the thread of her existence is so very fragile. If you were not so soft of heart, you could snap it yourself. However, I will see to it myself in time."

She felt her stomach churn. "You are truly a demon."

"No, just a man who knows what he wants. I was not destined to remain in the mud, groveling at the feet of other men." He stared down at her. "The Norman knows what he wants too. I doubt if he would cavil at ridding himself of an encumbrance."

"You're wrong. He's not like you," she said fiercely.

"Shall I call Delmas back and watch to discover if he is?"

"No!"

"You see?" he asked with satisfaction. "There is little to choose between the Norman and me. I would rid myself of a wife and he would rid you of a husband. You should be complimented. You must be as pleasing as Delilah if you can lure a man to his death."

Death. A wave of panic washed over her. "He is not like you," she repeated. "He wouldn't do it."

"You know he would," Richard said. "I look forward to partaking of your skills. I've grown weary of meek, mewling women who give a man no challenge. Yes, I think a marriage is not totally out of the question." He gave her a meaningful look. "Think well, Brynn. Join with me. Don't destroy yourself."

She shook her head.

"No?" His expression changed only slightly, but she received an impression of ugly menace. "Then I must change your mind. What a pity. I had hoped you would not make my task difficult."

Before she could reply, he turned on his heel and walked away.

Eight

"DON'T PULL THAT!" Brynn said sharply. "That's not a weed, it's rosemary."

"Sorry," Gage said meekly. "It all looks the same to me."

"I know. If it's green, it's a weed. If I didn't watch you, I'd have no herbs left in my garden."

"Not true. I've been growing quite skilled of late."

She snorted but did not answer.

"What use do you make of rosemary?" he asked idly.

"Headaches and nervous disorders. I also make salves for joint pain and bruises."

He pointed to a low-growing bush with glossy leaves. "And this one?"

"That's thyme. It's used for women's problems. Also, the oil cleanses wounds." She slanted him a glance from beneath her lashes. "And eases swollen testicles."

"Ah, clearly an herb of infinite worth. Be sure you keep a vast quantity on hand."

Brynn chuckled. "The first frost is late this year, but it's bound to come soon. Next time we come here I must pick enough herbs to replenish my medicine pouch. I've used almost all I had tending Malik and Adwen."

"I don't think they'll need your medicines much longer," Gage said as he pulled another weed. "The last time I visited them, they seemed much better."

"They are better." She smiled with contentment. Every day Adwen and Malik were gaining in strength and being thrown together in proximity seemed to be good for both of them. Malik had forgotten his boredom in his concern for Adwen, while Adwen was developing a tart playfulness Brynn had never thought possible in her gentle friend. "Now I use only the occasional sleeping draught. But when they're cured, someone else will need my herbs. There's always a need."

"So you're never without them?"

"Are you ever without your sword?"

He chuckled. "Seldom. And never when I go forth to battle dragons."

"Very prudent."

"I'm growing to like this task." He pulled another weed. "Perhaps I should abandon trade and turn farmer."

"I cannot see you tilling the soil for any length of time." Brynn looked up in amusement. "You're much too impatient."

"That charge is false." He added softly, "I believe I've given you nothing but patience of late."

She went still as the sudden sensuality of his tone took her off guard. It was the first time in the past two weeks he had allowed her a glimpse of the Gage she had first met at Hastings. During the days in between, he had treated her with the same half-whimsical half-humorous manner he displayed toward Malik.

He saw her response and added roughly, "It could not last forever, you know. I am no monk, Brynn."

"That has come to my attention." She lowered her

eyes to the work beneath her hands. "You wish me to return to your bed and be your whore?"

He muttered a curse. "You will not be my whore. I will hold you in honor and I'll make sure no other man gives you insult."

"To my face. What of the sneers behind my back? What of any children I bear you? You're a bastard yourself. Would you have your children treated as you were?"

"No!" He drew a deep breath. "I'm not my father. I'll make sure they are treated with fairness and not be made to feel shame."

"Until you grow tired of me and decide that you wish another woman."

"That will not happen."

"How do I know? Women are always used for barter, and no one is more skilled at a bargain than you. Malik says you're not constant and grow bored easily."

"What do you want of me, damn you? What he says was true in the past, but I've never felt for any woman what I feel for you."

And she had never felt the mixture of bonding, pain, and joy she had experienced when in his presence. But surely that was not love; it was too raw and earthy. Even during these last sunlit days she had been aware of strife and conflict beneath the surface. It would always be so with Gage Dumont, and that life was completely at odds with the peace she wanted. "I want you to let me go. I want no part of your world. All I want is to return to Gwynthal."

"I've not recently noticed your discontentment at being here."

"I am now." Her hands moved quickly, feverishly, almost ripping the weeds from the ground. That's what she must do with this dark temptation she experienced whenever she was near him, she thought desperately. Tear it out, banish it before it grew to dominate her entire life. "I wish to go home. Adwen is much stronger and Malik is able to walk and even sit up in a chair. There's no reason to linger here."

"We will start for Gwynthal when—" He paused before correcting himself—"*if* I decide to do so."

Her gaze flew to his face. "But there's no reason not to go. What of the treasure? Do you not—"

"I'm not sure there is a treasure."

She should have been aware he was still skeptical, but she had allowed herself to hope. "Why won't you believe me?" She added bitterly, "Delmas and Lord Richard have no trouble."

"Because they want to believe in it."

"And you don't?"

"I want it, if it exists. But at present I have another goal in mind." He stared down into her eyes. "I have offered you all I can. You know I cannot wed you. If I could, I would do it."

She stared at him in astonishment. "You would?"

He frowned. "Of course I would. Have I not made that clear?"

"No."

His breath released in a low exclamation of exasperation. "God's blood, I treat you with courtesy, I never touch you except in service, I let you keep that maddening silence on all things concerning your past. Is that the conduct of a man with a woman toward whom he has no permanent attachment?"

Bittersweet happiness surged through her as she gazed helplessly up at him. "It would not seem so."

"I have never—I have true feeling for you, Brynn of Falkhaar. You have strength and humor and an honesty I have never before found in a woman." His voice lowered to velvet persuasion. "And I believe you do not find me displeasing."

He was storm and sunlight, earth and sky. Always changing, never the same. "No, you are not . . . displeasing."

"Then come and live with me and let me care for you. I promise I will wed you when your vermin of a husband is dead." He saw her go rigid, and his lips twisted. "No, I have no plans to kill him. I've learned enough about you to realize that would be the quickest way to lose you." He paused. "But I don't always act with reason, so it would be wise of you to accept my offer."

"I cannot," she whispered.

"Why not?" he asked harshly.

Disappointment flickered in his expression. He was always so armored that the emotion must have gone deep for him not to be able to keep it from her. Would his deepest emotions always hurt her like this? This pain was not as intense as when his father had died, but it was still a throbbing ache. She wanted to reach out and touch him, heal him, take away the grimness from his lips and make him smile.

"Don't just look at me. Talk to me. Why?"

She must not touch him. She didn't want to know if the pain was greater than she thought. "Gwynthal. I must have Gwynthal and you would not belong there."

He smiled mockingly. "You don't think I'm worthy to be part of your precious home?"

Peace and storm. Eternal beauty and constant change. "It's not a question of worth." She tried to put it into words. "You're not the same. You couldn't stay at Gwynthal and not change it into what you wanted to make it." She added simply, "And that I could not bear."

His expression did not change. "So it's not a husband but a place I must battle. Very well."

"Why can't you see it's not possible?"

"It's entirely possible and it *will* happen." He stood up and lifted her to her feet. His hand grasped her wrist as he moved toward the horses. "And quite soon. As you say, I'm an impatient man." He lifted her onto her mare and stood, looking up at her. "You want me. Take me. I don't want a slave. Come to me willingly, Brynn."

She shook her head.

The softness vanished from his expression and he smiled recklessly. "It's not a good choice. Let's hope you will change your mind."

A carved teak chest was delivered by LeFont to Adwen's chamber before dusk that day.

He smiled at Brynn as he set the chest down. "A gift from my lord. It just arrived from Hastings. He said to tell you that he hopes the gown fits." He grimaced. "He sent my men combing the countryside for women capable of fashioning the material into a gown. It will please him if you wear it when you sit with him in the hall tonight."

She frowned as she looked down at the chest. So she was once more to brave the scorn of the hall. Was this Gage's way to show her what her lot would be if she was not under his protection?

LeFont said, "My lord said I was to wait until you opened the chest. He wants to make sure you're pleased."

"Open it, Brynn," Adwen said eagerly. "I want to see your gift."

Adwen was like a child in her delight, and Brynn couldn't disappoint her. She slowly opened the lid.

Shimmering silk the brilliant blue of the noon sky seemed to reach out at her with a glowing life of its own. She gasped when she touched it. The fabric was as cool and soft as the wings of a butterfly.

"Let me see," Adwen said.

Brynn lifted the gown and held it high.

"Beautiful." Adwen eyes were wide with enchantment. "I've never seen anything so lovely."

"It is silk from Byzantium," Malik said. "Gage traded four horses for that chest of materials."

"Why are you just standing there?" Adwen asked Brynn. "Go and put it on."

She didn't want to put it on. This gown was different from the one she had borrowed from Adwen. This was a gown from Gage's world, and she had the strange feeling that if she wore it, she would become part of that world. "It would suit you far better, Adwen."

"Lord Gage said that you were to wear it, demoiselle." LeFont's tone was polite, but there was an underlying command. "And that I was to return at evenfall to escort you to the hall." He bowed politely. "May I tell him you're pleased with his gift?"

"Of course she is pleased," Adwen said. "Who would not be pleased with such a gift? It is a gown a queen would be proud to wear."

"Demoiselle?" LeFont asked.

She shrugged wearily. "It is a fine gown."

LeFont bowed and quickly left the room.

"What's wrong, Brynn?" Adwen asked, frowning. "Don't you like it?"

"Yes." There was no use troubling Adwen over the true meaning behind the gift. She would not understand there could be anything but kindness behind such a lavish present. She doubted if Adwen had received a gift from Richard since her wedding day. "As you said, it's a gown for a queen."

"And you will look a queen in it," Malik said gently.

She glanced at him. Gage had spent many hours with Malik during the last week. Had he told him of his plans for her? If he had not, she would be surprised if Malik had not guessed.

"I am no queen," she said as she moved toward the anteroom. "I will only look myself, a brown wren dressed in peacock plumage."

· · ·

"Splendid," LeFont said as he took her hand and led her down the dimly lit hall. "My lord will be pleased."

She did not answer. She did not feel splendid. She was tense and stiff and angry at her own helplessness. What did Gage think to prove with this ploy? She knew what she must face when she entered that hall that night. They might hide their scorn to please the invader, but she would know it was there. No amount of silk or display of riches could—

What was that?

She stopped as she caught a scurry of movement from the corner of her eye.

"Demoiselle?" Lefont asked.

A shadow sidled around the distant corner, out the door, and was gone.

An icy chill shuddered through her.

She knew that shadow.

"What is it?" LeFont's hand went to the hilt of his sword. "Shall I—"

"No, it is nothing. Wait here!" She tore down the hall.

"Demoiselle!"

He was following her but she paid no attention. She dashed out the door; the air was cold, piercing the silk of her gown.

Where was he?

The door to the stable was open.

She flew across the courtyard and into the stable. "Delmas!"

He whirled to face her, his eyes glittering wildly in the lantern light. "What do you wish of me, bitch?"

She quickly glanced over her shoulder. LeFont had not yet reached the courtyard. "Come with me." She slammed the stable door shut and hurried past the stalls to the tiny room in the back. She closed the door and leaned against it, her breath coming in gasps. "Why did you come back? You have to leave here at once."

"You would like that, wouldn't you?" he snarled. "You in your fine gown and your bastard of a protector. You want me to go away and forget all I've worked for these years. You want to give it all to *him*. Lord Richard cast me out to live in that hovel across the moors, but do you think I haven't been watching you these weeks? I've seen you ride about and smile and laugh with that Norman dog. Well, it's come to an end. I will have what is mine. I will go to the Norman and tell him—"

"No!"

"Don't say no to me!" She could see the spittle at the corners of his mouth. "You're all against me! Even Lord Richard thinks to abandon me. I won't permit it. I will go to your Norman lover and demand—"

"Delmas, you're not thinking clearly." She crossed her arms over her chest to still their trembling. "You must not go near the Norman."

His hand cracked against her cheek with all his power. She careened back to the wall.

"Whore!" He stepped closer and hit her again.

"Cheat!" His fist hit her mouth, breaking the skin.

He was a madman, she realized dizzily; this frustration and rage must have been simmering for the past fortnight, robbing him of both reason and fear. "Listen to me, Delmas. Don't go to the Norman. He will hurt you."

"And you have such tender concern for me," he jeered.

"I don't want you dead."

"You lie."

It was no lie. She would not be able to bear it if she was the cause of any death. She would never be able to look at Gage without seeing her own blame. "Go away. We won't be here much longer. You'll be safe if you—"

His fist crashed into her stomach. She sank to the floor.

She couldn't breathe; her fingernails dug into the floorboards as she struggled to get her breath.

"It's all your fault," Delmas said as his fingers threaded through her hair and lifted her face. "I could have been a man of importance. It's your fault, yours and that Norman—"

She had a wild impulse to fight him or cry out for help. LeFont was nearby and might hear her. But if she fought her way free or LeFont came, Gage would know. . . .

She suddenly realized what she must do. She had to divert Delmas's anger from Gage. Violence had always been a release for Delmas. If he expended his rage on her, perhaps he would not seek out Gage, perhaps she could convince him to go away and hide again.

"I've never seen you so meek," Delmas sneered. "How well that whoreson has tamed you."

She didn't feel meek. She wanted to struggle and strike out at him. No, she must be strong. She might be able to win a minor victory now, but she would lose the battle if he went to Gage and Gage killed him.

Blood. Blood was spattering the floorboards in front of her from her cut lip, she realized dazedly. Dear heaven, she herself would have to hide from Gage until these wounds healed. She braced herself. Get it over.

"You'll never be anything but a slave, licking the boots of better men," she said coldly.

His foot lashed out, striking her shoulder. She bit her lower lip to keep from screaming out. Smother the anger. Taunt him. Accept the violence. Let him release all that fury on her. It was the only way to protect all of them from the unthinkable.

"Hurting me won't stop my words. You will never have the treasure of Gwynthal. You are not man enough to—"

"Witch! Harlot! Thief!" He punctuated each word with a kick.

Pain. She could stand it. She had borne far worse in those first days after they had wed. "Thief? You're the one who seeks to steal from me. You're the thief and—"

Darkness.

He had smashed her head down to the floor, she realized dimly. How much was enough to divert his rage? She must not let him kill her. . . . Her body was strong and so was her will. She would not let him defeat her. It would take more than a few blows to take away her life.

"Halt, monsieur." The words were spoken with icy precision. "Or I will take great delight in robbing you of your head."

LeFont. She struggled to open her eyes and saw LeFont standing in the doorway, a drawn sword in his hand, his expression as deadly as his tone.

"She is my wife. This is none of your concern," Delmas hissed.

"I beg to disagree. She is my lord's property and therefore very much my concern." He motioned with the sword. "Stand back from her."

"No," she whispered, her gaze shifting to Delmas's face. The punishment she had taken had not been enough, she realized in despair. He was afraid, but his rage was still a danger. "Leave us, Captain."

LeFont shook his head. "I cannot, demoiselle." He motioned with his sword, and Delmas reluctantly released her and stepped aside. "But I will let your husband leave unharmed." He added grimly, "For the moment. You are hurt and I cannot attend to both of you. Besides, my lord will no doubt wish to dispose of him himself."

Delmas's face twisted, but she couldn't determine whether it was with anger or terror. He gave a low exclamation and stalked past LeFont and out of the room.

The dizziness was overwhelming, and she closed her eyes. "You came too soon," she whispered.

"If I had come later, you might be dead," LeFont said bluntly. "Why did you not cry out?"

"Too soon . . ."

"My lord will not think so." He lifted her and carried her out of the stable. "He gave me orders to escort you safely to the hall. I'm not pleased you made me disobey. You should not have run away."

The cold night air was beginning to sweep away the darkness. "Let me down. Where are you taking me?"

"To my lord Gage."

"The hall?" She started to struggle. "I won't go. I have to—"

"Not to the hall. To my lord's chamber." He looked down at her. "I fear you are no longer presentable." He grimaced. "There is blood all over you. I will go fetch Lord Gage and bring him to you."

She reached up and touched her mouth. She had known her lip was split, but she had not realized there were other open wounds. "Much blood?"

"You look much as Malik did after the Saxon struck him down." LeFont entered the hall and started up the steps.

Seeing Malik hurt had thrown Gage into a terrible rage. LeFont's intervention was going to bring about the result she had most feared. She must find a way to keep that from happening, hide herself until she healed. "No, he must not see me." She started to struggle again. "Put me down, Captain. I will not—"

"What is this?" Gage was standing at the bottom of the stairs, looking up at them, Lord Richard directly behind him. He stiffened as he saw her. "Mother of God!" He took the steps two at a time. "What happened to her?" he demanded of Lefont.

"Nothing," she said quickly. She cursed the stupid

answer that had tumbled from her lips. Why could she not think clearly?

"I regret I did not come soon enough to—" LeFont stopped as Gage made a violent gesture. He shrugged. "It was demoiselle's husband, my lord."

Gage went still. "Her husband?"

She closed her eyes to shut out his expression.

Gage's voice was very controlled. "I'll take her." His arms closed around her as LeFont relinquished his grasp. "Go and get hot water and bandages. Then go to Lady Adwen's chamber and get Brynn's bag of herbs and salves. She will have need of them."

Lord Richard offered eagerly, "Permit me to be of help. I'll go to my wife's chamber and fetch the medicine. I cannot tell you how distressed I am that Delmas returned. I did warn him that he must not—"

"Get it!" Gage said.

Brynn opened her eyes as Richard hurried past them up the stairs and down the corridor. He did not look distressed, she thought dully; he reminded her of a sly, golden-furred cat who had just been fed.

Gage started up the steps.

"I have no need of salves," Brynn whispered. "I'm not badly hurt. I'm sure it looks worse than it is."

"Be silent," he said through his teeth.

"I will not be silent. What will you do? Beat me?"

"No." He looked down at her, his eyes shining wetly. "God, no."

"But you're angry enough to lash out in any direction. That is how Delmas felt. You should not blame him for feeling the same as you do now. It's not reasonable."

"I *do* blame him." His eyes blazed down at her. "By God, I do blame him. And no amount of reasoning is going to make me feel different."

It was no use arguing with him now. She would try

later once the first shock had passed. Besides, she was feeling so very tired. . . .

When Brynn next opened her eyes, she was vaguely aware she was unclothed beneath the cover and was surrounded by the minty scent of salve. Gage was sitting on a stool beside the bed, staring down at the floor, hands linked tensely, black hair shining blood-red in the candlelight. Blood . . .

"Gage . . ."

His head lifted, the motion swift and wolflike. "It will never happen again," he said without inflection. "No one will ever hurt you again. Not while I live."

"I was not hurt. Well, perhaps a little. But it was—"

"Your index finger may be broken; it looks as if it was stomped upon. Your lower lip is split. Your face and body have terrible bruises." He enumerated the injuries with no emotion. "Did he kick you?"

She didn't answer.

"He kicked you as if you were a dog who had displeased him," Gage said. "LeFont said he thought he would have killed you."

"He was wrong."

"He also said you told him he had come too soon and wanted him to go away. Why, Brynn?"

"I did not want—there was no need for him to interfere."

"No need?" He stood up, crossed the room, and brought back a hand mirror. He held it before her face. "No need?"

She cast one look at her swollen, bruised face and pushed the mirror aside. "It's not as bad as it looks. In a few days you will never know—"

"I'll know." The words were a deadly monotone. "I'll remember every bruise, every blow that was struck. I'll know."

She moistened her lips. "It is over. You must not—Where are you going?"

He glanced over his shoulder. "Where do you think I'm going?"

"No." She jumped from the bed and ran after him. "You will not seek him out."

"Go back and lie down."

She stood in front of the door. "I won't let you go," she said fiercely. "You are as bad as he is. All you can think about is blood and vengeance. Do you think I could not have fought him? It was my choice to let this happen. I did it for my own reasons, and I will not have you interfere."

"What reasons?"

"It is of no moment."

"What reasons?"

He was relentless; she knew he would not give up until he got the answer. "He needed a release for his passions. He would have done harm."

"And you were the release?" He shook his head incredulously. "You let him do this to you to keep him from causing harm to others?"

"I was not afraid of him. I was afraid *for* him. He was threatening to come to you and I knew you'd welcome the opportunity to—" She stopped.

"Kill him? Oh, yes." He lifted her out of the way and opened the door. "I most certainly would. How kind of him to give me the perfect excuse."

"You cannot do it. It cannot happen. These bruises are nothing. I'm a healer and a healer cannot cause death," she said desperately, her voice trembling. "I beg you, don't kill him, Gage."

He started past her.

"No!" She had to break through that hard wall that was hiding so much anger. It was the only way to save every one of them. She lifted her hand and slapped his face with all her strength.

His head jerked back with the force of the blow. Her stomach churned as she saw the red handprint appear on his dark cheek. It was she who had done this act of violence.

He stood quite still. His rock-hard expression did not change. Why would he not break? She swallowed and braced herself against the revulsion she knew would come.

She slapped him again.

He looked down at her, his blue eyes cold as the sea. "I am not your husband. I do not release my anger on helpless women." His face betrayed no different emotion. "It will never happen again." The door swung shut.

Panic soared through her as she heard the key turn in the lock. He was going in search of Delmas and taking no chance of her interfering.

Her gown . . . Where was her gown?

She caught a glimpse of shimmering blue beside the bed and moved toward it. Her knees were weak and she was shaking. She snatched up the soiled and torn gown and pulled it over her head.

Shoes? There they were, tossed on the other side of the bed.

It took her a moment to rid herself of enough of the dizziness to bend down and put on the shoes. Hurry. Ignore the weakness. She must be quick. . . .

She went to the window and threw open the shutters.

It was too far down. . . . She could not give up. Perhaps she could tie a few of the linens together and—

A key was turning in the lock!

She whirled toward the door.

Lord Richard stood in the doorway. "Come, you must hurry."

"What are you doing here?" she asked warily.

He frowned. "Do you wish to stand and argue, or

do you wish to save Delmas from the Norman?" He stepped to one side. "I saw him following Delmas to the stable. You don't have much time."

The door was open; she would sort out Lord Richard's motives later. She darted across the room and out into the corridor.

Richard followed her as she ran down the stairs. "I told you it would happen. Did you think you could tame that barbarian? I'm told he is just like his father when the blood lust is upon him."

"Be quiet." She did not want to hear it. It brought back the vision of Gage standing before her, his face hard and totally without mercy. She flew out the front door and across the courtyard.

A scream!

"No!" She threw open the stable door.

Blood everywhere. On the wall. On the straw on the floor.

On Gage.

He stood with a pitchfork in his blood-soaked hands. Delmas was suspended on the other end of the pitchfork, the prongs piercing through his body. As she watched, Gage released the pitchfork and her husband fell to the floor. Delmas whimpered, his hands clawing at the prongs still protruding from his chest. His gaze fixed balefully on Gage. "You did it. You—did—it all. All your . . ." A violent shudder racked his body.

Death.

She reeled back against the wall. She was suffocating. Too late to heal. Delmas was dead. And Gage had murdered him. No, Brynn was the murderer. It was her fault.

"Brynn!" Gage was turning toward her, his hand outstretched.

Blood on his hands. Blood on her hands.

"No," she whispered, backing away. "No . . ."

She whirled and ran out of the stable. She made it

only halfway across the courtyard before her stomach heaved and she threw up its contents.

"Poor Brynn." Richard's hand was beneath her elbow. "But I did warn you that there was little to choose between the Norman and me." He gently tucked a strand of hair behind her ear. "Except I think you'll find any association with Gage Dumont fraught with bitter memories now. Wouldn't it be better to accept my protection?"

"Take your hands off her," Gage said softly from behind them.

She turned and looked at him. Powerful. Deadly. Savage. At this moment Richard was in as much peril as Delmas had been. More death. No, she could not bear it.

She tore away from Richard's grasp and ran up the step and into the manor.

Escape. She must get away. She must hide and try to heal.

Adwen's eyes widened in shock as Brynn darted into the chamber and slammed the door. "Dear God," she murmured, staring at Brynn's bruised face. "Richard said you had need of salves, but we had no idea that Delmas had done—" Her jaw set angrily. "He is an evil man, Brynn. He should be punished."

"I think perhaps he has been." Malik was studying Brynn's expression. "Gage would not stand for this. How bad, Brynn?"

"Dead." She swallowed to ease the nausea assaulting her again. "Pitchfork."

"Ah, you saw it?"

"Yes." She would always see it. The sight would be there before her for an eternity. She moved over to the hearth to the basket containing her belongings. "I have to leave. I cannot stay here. . . ." She took a clay pot from her medicine pouch and set it on the hearth. "You don't need me anymore at all, Malik. You'll be sitting a horse within a week, but you must not overdo it the first few days. I look to you to care for Adwen. If the fever comes back, have Alice make her a draught from the powder in that jar. I don't think it will. She is healthier than I've ever seen her. I truly think she is—"

"Where are you going?" Adwen interrupted. "You are not well yourself. I won't have you going off alone. It's not safe."

"Don't worry, I'll be safe." She had no time for further assurances. She was surprised Gage was not there already. She would have to slip out the back door to avoid any chance of encountering him. She snatched up her medicine pouch and her other belongings and headed toward the door. "God keep you both."

"Ah, Brynn, I thought you would be leaving us after such a tragic happening."

Brynn froze in the act of opening the gate.

Richard stepped out of the shadows beside the high gate. "I was waiting for you. I don't suppose I can persuade you to stay?"

"No."

"I could call the guard, you know. I've noticed the Norman's men are very eager to please him, and they know how he values his slave."

She turned to confront him. "Then do it."

He smiled. "I was but teasing you. It would not be to my advantage to betray you. I have no wish to bring you to the Norman's bed again. On the contrary, it's my most earnest desire to separate you. I want you for myself."

"You want the *treasure* for yourself," she corrected.

"Ah, the treasure . . . Are you ready to join forces and lead me to it?"

"No, and there's no way you can follow me."

"How will you prevent me? Magic?" He shook his

head. "Delmas may have believed such nonsense, but I don't."

She felt a chill as she realized that Delmas had revealed even that dangerous secret. "Not magic. I'll travel through the forests. I know them well."

"But I'm no novice in the forest. I'm an excellent hunter, remember?" He tilted his head appraisingly. "I believe you would be very interesting quarry. According to Delmas, you have experience as prey."

"Yes." The muscles of her stomach tightened as she remembered those days of running and hiding in the forest after her mother's death. Richard would take as much malicious enjoyment as those other hunters. "But I know the way far better than you," she said boldly. "So if you wish to stop me, do it now."

He considered her words and then smiled again. "I would never force you to stay against your will. Go forth, sweet Brynn, perhaps we will meet again." He turned and walked away.

She drew her cloak closer about her as she watched him saunter across the courtyard. He had surrendered too easily and his smile was too sweet and glowing. Would he follow her? Well, she had no time to linger and wonder. She was far more worried about Gage's discovering her than about Richard's unusual behavior.

She slipped through the gates and hurried out into the waiting darkness.

Nine

"WHERE'S BRYNN?" GAGE asked from the doorway to Adwen's chamber. "Has she been here?"

"A full quarter of an hour ago," Malik said. "I'd wager she's outside the gates and already on her way to Gwynthal. What kept you?"

Gage muttered an imprecation. "Our fine Lord Richard. He told me Brynn had told him she was going to the kitchens to talk to Alice about your care after she was gone."

Malik lifted his brows. "And you believed him?"

"It seemed reasonable at the time. I wasn't thinking clearly."

"Evidently," Malik said. "But no harm done. Since she will be on foot and you on horseback, you should have no trouble overtaking her."

Gage had a sudden thought. "Did she take her herb pouch?"

"Of course. You know she would never leave without it."

Gage remembered Brynn's remark in the garden about the necessity of replenishing the herbs in her pouch. He had little doubt her destination would be

Gwynthal, and it wasn't reasonable for her to take a long journey without her precious medicines. "Then I'll have her back here tonight."

"Before you go after her, I'd wash my hands. Don't you think she's seen enough blood this night?"

Gage went to the washstand and poured water into the wooden bowl. "Yes, she has." He looked down as the water turned pink when he dipped his hands into it. "I'll never forget her face when she—" Christ, there was no sense in dwelling on what could not be changed. He turned away, grabbed a linen, and wiped his hands. "I should be back soon. I'll leave LeFont here at Redfern to protect you and care for your needs."

"She wants to go home," Adwen said suddenly. "Let her go to Gwynthal."

Gage turned to look at her.

"Delmas was a wicked man," she said, "and I don't think it was an evil deed to kill him. But you have hurt Brynn in doing it. She needs to go home and heal."

"I won't let her leave me," he said harshly.

"Then take her there yourself. Brynn has given to all of us. Give to her now."

"I'm not known for my generosity." His lips twisted bitterly as he moved toward the door. "I'm far better at taking than giving. Brynn will attest to that fact."

He had found her.

Brynn stiffened as she saw Gage stalking toward her across the glade. The moonlight polished his hair to a bright ebony and lit his bold features with merciless clarity. She should never have come here, she thought in despair. She had hoped he wouldn't remember that idle remark about the herbs, but Gage remembered everything. She quickly stuffed the last leaves in her pouch and sprang to her feet. "You should not have followed me. Go away."

"No." He stopped before her. "You're never going

to be rid of me, Brynn. Not if you run to the ends of this earth."

"I cannot . . ." Her voice vibrated with pain. "I cannot even look at you without hurting, without seeing—" She stopped, unable to continue.

"Delmas speared like a frog?" Gage asked bluntly. "Then you'll have to forget it."

"Forget it?" She would see that scene in the stable for the rest of her life.

"Just as I'll have to forget how I felt when I saw what Delmas had done to you. It should be easier for you. You were guiltless and he deserved to die."

"My fault," she said dully.

"You had nothing to do with it."

She shook her head. "Bathsheba."

He gave an exclamation under his breath. "You are *not* Bathsheba and you bear no blame for anything that happened tonight."

She shook her head again.

He reached out and gripped her shoulders. He stared down at her, his features tight and harsh in the moonlight. "Would you believe me if I told you I did not kill that cockroach?"

Hope leapt within her and then instantly died as she remembered what she had seen. "No."

His lips twisted. "I didn't think so. You have little trust in me. Then I will not bother to say it." He turned away. "And you'll have to accept what happened and go on. Come along, we'll go back to Redfern."

"I won't go back there. I'm going to Gwynthal."

"Yes, you're going to Gwynthal." He strode toward his horse. "But not like this, alone in the night. We'll go back and make proper preparations for the journey."

She wasn't sure she understood. In that hideous moment in the stable it had seemed that the entire world had changed, that she was completely alone again. It was difficult to imagine a circumstance that included Gage. "You're taking me to Gwynthal?" she whispered.

He smiled sardonically. "Why are you surprised? Didn't you promise me a great treasure?"

She nodded.

"Then why shouldn't I accept what you offered me? It seemed you wish to cheat me of everything else."

"But you didn't believe me."

"I didn't disbelieve you. It's my nature to doubt what I cannot see." He mounted his horse. "And sometimes doubt what I do. Someone with as little trust as you should understand."

"There has never been trust between us." And now there could never be, she thought with aching sadness. She had never realized how close to him she had grown. How near to faith, how near to—

She cut the thought short, but it lay burning in her mind like a brand.

Dear God, no, she had not loved him. She would *not* love him.

"You don't have to look at me with such horror," he said roughly. "I don't have a pitchfork in my hands now."

He had killed Delmas. If she loved Gage, her crime would even be worse than she had imagined. She would always wonder if she had tried hard enough to prevent Delmas's death. It was only passion. It was not love.

He held out his hand to pull her up on his stallion. "Come, I grow weary of being stared at as if I were one of your dragons. I'll take you back to the manor and let you hide from me with Adwen and Malik."

Sweet Mary, how she wanted to reach out and take his hand, touch him, accept comfort, accept passion. She could not understand it. How could she feel like this when she could still see him dripping with blood? She put her hand behind her so that she would not be tempted and stepped back. "You need not bother. I'll walk."

He muttered a curse and jumped from the horse. He grasped her by the waist and tossed her on the horse's back. "I'll be the one to walk, if you can't bear to touch me." He grasped the reins and started leading the horse from the glade. "But, by God, you *will* touch me. I'll give you time to come to terms but I—Christ, I hope I can give you time."

"I'll never come to terms with it," she said unevenly. "Never."

"It will be better for you if you do, but regardless, you'll have to accept it," he said grimly. "For you will never leave me, Brynn."

They saw the red glare lighting the sky before they crested the hill overlooking Redfern.

Brynn's first thought was that the comet had returned, and then she dismissed it at once. This light was no pure stream but a malignant mouth stretched wide, as if it wanted to devour the night sky. "What is it?"

"Fire." Gage's pace quickened as he half led, half pulled the horse the last few yards up the hill.

"Are you sure?"

"I'm a disgusting barbarian, remember? You won't be surprised that I burnt any number of towns and villages while I was raiding with Hardraada." He added bitterly, "Oh, yes, I know well what that glare means, though I didn't set this one."

"I didn't say you—" Brynn broke off, staring in horror as they reached the top of the hill.

Redfern was engulfed in flames!

The roof of the hall was ablaze, and several of the outbuildings had also caught fire. It would be only a matter of time before the outer walls and gates became barriers of living fire.

"God's blood," Gage muttered.

"Adwen. Malik," she whispered. "We have to—"

She got no chance to finish the sentence. Gage leapt on the horse behind her and kicked the animal into a gallop.

The wind tore at Brynn's hair as they sped down the hill and through the gates.

Screams.

People stumbling dazedly about the courtyard.

The crash of burning timbers as they fell to the ground.

"My lord," LeFont shouted to Gage across the courtyard.

Brynn turned to see the captain and his soldiers trying to beat out the flames leaping from the hall to the chapel.

"We had no chance," LeFont called. "It happened so fast we could not—"

"Malik?" Gage asked.

LeFont shook his head. "The front hall caught first. We couldn't get through the flames."

"The devil you couldn't." Gage reined in his horse and jumped to the ground.

Brynn slipped from the saddle and followed him as he ran across the courtyard toward the hall.

The entrance to the hall was no more. Flames. Flames everywhere.

"Stay here," Gage shouted to Brynn.

How could she stay when Malik and Adwen were in that inferno? She had to find a way to get to them. "The rear door!" She ran to the left, narrowly dodging a falling timber as it crashed to the ground. "We can—"

Gage was already ahead of her, skirting the burning wreckage of the hall and dashing down the passageway between the chapel and the hall itself.

She saw him momentarily falter.

"Tend to her," he shouted over his shoulder.

Tend to whom? she wondered in confusion. Then

she saw the huddled form, half sprawled, half leaning against the wall of the chapel.

Alice!

She knelt quickly beside her and realized with relief that the woman was still alive. She examined her quickly. Alice was not burned, but a deep cut scored her temple and she appeared to be in a deep faint. What should she do? Alice needed care, but Adwen most certainly was in peril.

"Captain!" She darted back and motioned for LeFont to come and pointed to Alice. Then she retraced her steps, following Gage's path to the rear of the hall.

By the time she reached the open door, he had already gone inside. Great plumes of black smoke billowed out, but she could see no flames. She stepped inside and her lungs were immediately assaulted by the searing smoke.

Kythe. The stake. Screams.

No, that was long ago. She had been unable to help her mother, but she had a chance to save Malik and Adwen. She covered her mouth, trying not to breathe as she moved down the corridor toward the stairs leading to the bedchambers.

"Out!" Gage shouted, emerging from the dense smoke. "This roof won't last long."

He was carrying Adwen in his arms, her face buried in his chest.

"Malik?" she gasped.

Then she saw Malik stumbling behind Gage. She moved quickly forward, slid her arms around his waist, and put his arm around her shoulders. "Lean on me."

"Out, Brynn!" Gage insisted. "Now!"

Did he think she wanted to stay in this inferno? Her lungs were on fire. "Get out yourself." Bearing a good portion of Malik's weight forced her to move slowly, and when she reached the entrance it was to meet Gage as he was reentering the hall. He pushed her out into the open air and took Malik himself, half lifting him down the steps and away from the burning building.

Sparks!

Crashing timbers!

A tremendous blast of heat!

Brynn looked over her shoulder. The entrance through which they had just passed was now completely obliterated by a wall of flame.

"Brynn." Adwen's gaze was fixed in horror on the burning wreckage. "How terrible . . ."

"Yes." Brynn inhaled great gulps of air as she knelt beside Adwen. "How do you feel?"

"We couldn't get out." Adwen began coughing. "Malik tried, but we couldn't get out to—" She bent double, struggling to get her breath.

Malik fell to his knees beside Adwen. "Easy, *chérie*, do not talk. We will have you out of here in a moment. Gage has gone to get the horses."

"Can you walk a short distance more, Malik?" Gage had reappeared beside them. "LeFont has the horses at the gate, but they'll go mad if we bring them this close to the flames."

"I can walk." Malik slowly got to his feet. "What is this inferno to a hero such as me?"

Adwen made a sound suspiciously like a snort.

Malik gave her a pained glance. "I would have rescued you. Gage did not give me the opportunity."

"Were you going to fly through a locked door?" Adwen asked caustically.

Malik flinched. "I would have found a way."

Gage lifted Adwen in his arms. "Then find a way to get to the front gate before the rest of Redfern goes up in flames." He turned to Brynn. "I know you're almost as hurt as Malik, but can you help him?"

Hurt? For an instant Brynn was confused. So much had happened that she had almost forgotten the bruises and cuts she had received earlier in the evening. It seemed a long time ago. "Of course I can help him." She rose to her feet and put Malik's arm about her shoulders again. "Come, Malik. Only a little farther and we'll be out of this."

"Such humiliation," he muttered.

"Oh, be silent," Adwen said tartly. "Would you rather have the beard burnt off your handsome face?"

He brightened. "You think me handsome?"

She sighed in exasperation and closed her eyes as Gage bore her away.

Malik's limping gait suddenly took on a slight strut. "She does think me handsome."

Astonished, Brynn pointed out, "Malik, we've barely escaped with our lives."

"Well, one must always strive to claim joy in every adversity."

At present Brynn could see no joy in this tragic morass, but she was glad someone could. "Well, don't be too joyful. Adwen has a great fear of comely men."

His face fell. "Ah, that is too bad. But I think you're right. I remember . . ." Malik trailed off, his eyes on Adwen, who was now being lifted to LeFont's horse. "Where is Lord Richard?"

Brynn looked around the confusion in the stable yard. "I don't know. I haven't seen him." She suddenly looked at the burning hall. "Could he be—"

"No, he's not in there." Malik lips tightened grimly. "I'd place a wager he was safely away before the hall was completely aflame."

"What do you mean?"

"Mount! Ride for the hill and set up camp." Gage was beside them, leading two horses. He hoisted Malik on one of them and slapped the horse's hindquarters, sending it galloping through the gates. He turned and reached for Brynn. "You too."

"No." She backed away, taking in the sight of panicky men and women in the stable yard. "I can't leave here. I may be needed."

"Not here. I've ordered my soldiers to herd everyone out of Redfern and up to the camp on the hill. We'll stay until it is completely deserted." His hands encircled her waist and he lifted her to the horse. "That's all that's possible for anyone to do. In a few hours there will be nothing left. Redfern is gone."

She stared dazedly at the blazing hall where she had spent these last years. He was right. Soon there would be only ashes.

"Go." Gage slapped the mare's rear and sent it after Malik's.

Could you fly through a locked door?

Adwen's words suddenly came back to Brynn as she passed through the burning gates. At the time Brynn had been too absorbed by the danger to realize the impact of the words.

Locked door?

Brynn was too busy to question Adwen regarding her words until over two hours later. A constant flow of people streamed through Redfern's gates and up the hill to the camp. Some had burns from trying to fight the blaze, some were merely stunned and confused at losing all their meager belongings. It was difficult to realize which injury was the deeper, but both had to be tended. In spite of her protests, Malik insisted on moving from wounded to wounded with her, bathing away the dirt, holding bandages for Brynn to tie. Sometimes he just sat and spoke gently to them, offering understanding and comfort.

Brynn visited Alice's pallet several times during those hours, but she did not wake. Not a good sign. She washed the woman's temple once again, then turned and walked toward the huge rock at the edge of the hill against which Adwen was leaning, a blanket wrapped around her shoulders.

"How is Alice?" Adwen asked.

"I don't know. I wish she'd wake." She sat down beside Adwen. "Are you chilled? Do you need another blanket?"

"No." Adwen stared at the conflagration below. She had the same stunned expression on her face as the others who had escaped the inferno. "It's gone," she whispered. "I feel very strange. It's as if I were seeing everything I was burning away."

Brynn knew what she meant. She, too, had a sense of a part of her life coming to an end. She had never been content here, but it was a terrible way to escape from Redfern. Fire and death. She shuddered when she realized that Delmas was down there in that stable being devoured by those flames.

But she could not think of that now. Too many people were in need, and Adwen was one of them. "I'm sorry we had no time to save anything," she said gently.

"I'm not," Adwen said. "This is the only thing I would have regretted leaving behind." She opened her hand to reveal an exquisite silver rosary that Brynn recognized. It had belonged to Adwen's mother, who had given it to Adwen on the night before her death. Adwen was sure it was an amulet and it had never left her side during her long illness. "The rest is of no importance." She smiled. "In truth, being without possessions makes me feel . . . free."

"Free?"

"My bridal gifts from Richard. My dowry to him. All the sad memories of those years when I could not leave that room. All the doubts and guilt . . ." She expelled a deep breath. "All gone."

"I hope so," Brynn said. "But memories don't burn as readily as timber. They seem to go on and then they come back."

"Well, they're gone now and I'll worry about them returning later." Adwen shivered. "I thought I was going to die, Brynn. It was very strange. I became enraged. Remember when I used to accept death? Not now. Suddenly I was filled with a terrible anger and strength. I think I knew the anger Samson must have experienced when he destroyed the temple. If Gage hadn't come, I felt as if I could have broken down the door myself."

The locked door. "Did he have to break it down? Was it truly locked?"

"Oh, yes, it was locked." Her lips tightened. "Malik and I were both awake and heard the key turn in the lock. After you left, I was upset, and Alice went to the kitchen to prepare a soothing draught to help me sleep. I heard someone at the door and thought it was Alice returning. It was not."

"Who?"

"Richard. I didn't see him, but who else could it have been? Who else would want me dead? I heard the key in the lock and a short time later I smelled smoke."

"It's not reasonable." Brynn's brow furrowed in puzzlement. "Why would he burn down his heritage just to kill you?"

"It's not his heritage. Not any longer. He knew the Normans would soon take it and Redfern never meant anything to him but as a path to power." Her lips curved bitterly. "No more than I did. Why not burn us both and start anew? A rich Norman widow would suit him splendidly."

"If he has no heritage, no Norman would give his kin to him."

"But he is so comely and can be as sweet as the flowers in the spring. He would find a way."

I might wed you.

Lord Richard's words suddenly came back to Brynn. Could it be he had sought to clear the way not to a rich Norman widow but to Brynn herself? After Delmas's death he had known that Brynn was desperate and had seen her leave Redfern. What if he had not learned Gage had followed her? Burning down the hall could have served the dual purpose of ridding him of a wife and the invader who might get in his way. It was possible he could have decided to set events in motion with one stroke of the torch.

Adwen turned to her in sudden alarm. "I'm being foolish. I'm not free, am I? He's still alive."

"I believe he is."

"Then why has he not come forward? It's not like him not to put on a brave show and try to prove black is white."

Brynn looked down at the burning ruins. "It would be difficult to convince anyone that this wickedness is heaven sent. Dear God, all those poor people . . . Winter is coming and they have no roof over their heads."

"He doesn't care about them. In his world there is only Richard, and his strength and cleverness have always gotten him everything he's wanted. I was his only failure. It's no wonder he wants to see me dead."

"I won't let him hurt you, Adwen."

"No, *I* won't let him hurt me," she said with sudden fierceness. "I must not depend on anyone else. I'll be as strong and clever as he is."

"You're already clever, and you'll be strong as well when you're better."

"I have no time to be ill. Do you think he'll stop because he failed in his purpose this time? He'll keep trying until he gets what he wants. I must be ready when he comes for me."

Brynn smiled. The glimmer of strength she had noticed in her friend since she had returned to Redfern was no longer nebulous but shining clear. "I'm sure you will be, Adwen."

Adwen looked back at Redfern and whispered,

"Life is precious, isn't it, Brynn? He tried to take it from me. He tried to take it from all of us."

"Life is very precious."

"You're angry at Gage for taking Delmas's life. I know it was a sin, but I wonder. . . . It seems that some lives are more precious than others." Adwen spoke slowly, as if trying to work things out. "He was very cruel to you. If Delmas had lived, would he not have caused you and others more misery?"

"Perhaps."

"Then, why do you—"

"Because now he has no chance to be anything else. Who knows what Delmas was like when he was a child or what events twisted him to be the man he was? Perhaps some miraculous change would have taken place in him if he had lived."

Adwen frowned doubtfully. "You believe this?"

"No." She sighed. "I cannot think of miracles and Delmas at the same time. But I'm a healer and I cannot permit myself to judge who should live and who should die. Sometimes miracles occur when you least expect them."

"Well, I don't believe he would have changed, and I'm glad he can no longer hurt you." She added emphatically, "I believe God would not waste his time with such a brute, and neither should any of us."

Brynn was slightly taken aback at such a fierce reaction from gentle, loving Adwen. Brynn felt as if she could see her changing and evolving before her eyes. "God must not have felt him a waste when he brought him into this world."

"God also brought poisonous snakes into the world, but he didn't mean them to slither around and bother the rest of us. Delmas should have stayed with the other snakes."

"I . . . see."

"But you don't agree." Adwen shook her head. "In

many ways you are much wiser than I, but I think in others you lack reason." She wearily leaned against the rock. "I don't know. I will have to think about it. It's very difficult to form opinions when all my life I've only accepted what everyone has told me was truth. It makes me doubt every—Look! There they are!"

Brynn's gaze followed Adwen's, and relief surged through her. Gage, LeFont, and the company of soldiers were riding up the hill. They evidently had decided they could be of no more help and were returning. She had not allowed herself to admit how worried she had been about Gage during these past hours.

Dear God, Gage looked like a demon fresh from Hades. His face was smoke-blackened, but though his hair was soot-coated, in the glare of the flames it still glinted with its own fire.

"He's coming," Adwen murmured, her eyes on Gage. "My dream. The fire. It was him. . . ."

Adwen had made the same connection Brynn had reached on Gage's first day at Redfern. "Perhaps. It doesn't have to mean anything. It could be mere chance."

"It does mean something. It's exactly as I saw it. You believe in miracles. Why do you deny them when they come to you?"

"Lord Gage is not a miracle."

"He saved me. He saved Malik." She gestured to the people on the hillside. "He saved all of them. He seems a miracle to me."

He had begun to seem a miracle to her also, Brynn thought wistfully. A miracle that had unfolded with such infinite slowness, she had not realized what she held in her hands until it had been tarnished and then dashed to the ground.

"He's not a miracle," she repeated, and turned away. "I've lingered too long here. I must go see to Alice."

"No, let me." Adwen threw off the blanket and struggled to he feet. "You have too much to do."

"Sit down. You can barely stand."

"I won't have to stand to watch over Alice. I must no longer pamper myself. Malik is not well either, and he's helping." Adwen moved with halting steps toward Alice's pallet. She smiled at Brynn over her shoulder. "Be at ease. I know nothing of healing, but I know all about childbearing. If she as much as twitches, I will call you."

Brynn frowned worriedly as she watched her walk away. Adwen's will was strong but her body was still weak. She was not so sure how much strain she could endure.

"How are you?"

She stiffened when she saw Gage on his horse a few yards away.

"Well enough." She studied him and felt a surge of sympathy as she saw that even the smoke could not mask the lines of weariness marking his face. "Better than you. At least I've had a chance to wash the soot from my face."

"I regret that I offend you."

"You don't offend me. Adwen says you're a miracle. How can a miracle offend?"

"A miracle?" He smiled sardonically. "I'm sure you told her how mistaken she was."

"Yes, but she didn't agree with me. Adwen is becoming very stubborn." She averted her glance. "We are not too bad here. There are four men with painful burns, but Alice is the only one I'm worried about. Her head is cut and I'm afraid inhaling the smoke may have done harm. She is with child."

"Lord Richard's?"

"Yes."

"What a delightful fellow. He was the one who struck her down and left her to burn."

"You know this?"

"LeFont said one of his men saw Alice following Richard, pleading with him. He turned and hit her and she fell against the wall."

"Adwen says she believes he was the one who set the fire."

"He did. He set the hall ablaze first and the stable burst into flames only minutes after he rode out of it and through the gates. There's no doubt he meant to burn all of Redfern." He turned his horse and nudged him forward. "I'm leaving a company of soldiers here for your protection, but don't stray from camp."

She went still. "Leaving? Where are you going?"

"After Lady Adwen's dear husband. He can't have gone far."

Fear tore through her. She had thought him safe, and now he was riding again into danger. "You won't find him. He knows the countryside too well."

"One of LeFont's men is an excellent tracker. We have a good chance of—"

"You *don't* have a chance," Brynn said fiercely. "What if the fire is only a ploy to rob you of shelter and lure you into the open? What if he's gathering his vassals and planning to lie in wait to murder you?"

His eyes narrowed. "And what do you care if he does? Surely a murderer's punishment should be murder itself."

"Don't you see? The violence goes on and on. It never stops."

"And if I kill Lord Richard, will that be your fault too?"

"Yes, for I brought you here."

He muttered a curse beneath his breath. "You must have a talk with God someday. You evidently think you bear a common responsibility for all of mankind." He nudged his horse forward. "*If* I killed your husband, it was my doing and mine alone. If I kill Lord Richard, it will be my responsibility. My will, my act. You have nothing to do with it." He lifted his hand. "LeFont!"

He galloped down the hill with LeFont and the soldiers following.

T e n

"YOU ARE ALIVE," Alice whispered. "I thought you dead, my lady."

"Ah, you're awake." Adwen smiled down at her. "Brynn will be pleased. She was worried about you. I'll call her."

"No!" Alice's hand reached out to stop her. "Wait, please. I would talk to you."

"Not now. You've been hurt and must rest."

"I tried to stop him," Alice said hoarsely. "He had a torch and I knew . . . I saw him lock the door and I ran after him. I've sinned against you, but I would never—"

"Hush." Adwen's fingers pressed against the other woman's mouth. "You have not sinned against me."

"I have fornicated with your husband. I bear his child."

"I know. I heard you tell Brynn."

"You did? But you said nothing."

"Because there was nothing to say. It is you who have been sinned against."

Alice shook her head. "I confessed to the priest

and he said that the sin was mine, that I had tempted Lord Richard."

"Did he?" Adwen's lips tightened. "And the good father told me that my sin was that I was not a dutiful and submissive wife, or God would grant me a child. It seems that women are the root of all iniquity in this world and men innocent as the Virgin Mary."

"The priest told you that?" Alice shook her head. "It is not true. No one could have been kinder or more docile than you."

"Docile." Adwen tasted the sound of it. "It is a pale, weak word. . . . I have no liking for it." She squeezed Alice's hand. "And I think we have both been too docile in the past."

"It is the way of women."

"It is the way men tell women that they should be." Adwen's gaze went to Brynn across the camp. "Brynn is not docile. Perhaps we should learn from her."

"You do believe me?" Alice asked. "It was never my wish to—"

"I believe you." Adwen gently stroked the hair back from Alice's face. "You've always been kind to me, Alice. Why should I think you meant me harm?"

"The child . . ." Alice rushed on, "I don't know why God gave me this child and denied you. It will only be a burden to me, and you wanted it so."

"Yes, I did want a babe." That was the only clear truth in her life at Redfern. It would take time to sort out the other truths from lies, but the bearing of a child had not been only duty. When she had been with child, she had been filled with wonder and joy, and when they were taken from her there had been darkness. "A child is a wondrous gift."

"Perhaps if you are the lady of a great lord." For the first time a note of bitterness threaded Alice's voice. "Not if you're a servant with neither a husband nor means to provide. Then a babe is only a shameful burden."

Adwen was feeling shame herself. She had been thinking of her own sorrow, her problems, and this woman was beset by a far worse fate. It was a cruel world for a woman who broke the rules set by Church and man even when forced to do so. "The shame is not yours, it is Richard's," Adwen said. "And as for a burden . . . yes, a babe is always a burden." But, unlike Alice, it would have been a burden Adwen would have accepted with joy even if it were accompanied by shame.

Adwen looked down at the burning Redfern. "But I'm no more a great lady than you. I have no husband, no father, no home. Perhaps you are even better off than me. As a child I was taught to run a household, but you have knowledge of how to earn your bread. Such knowledge can be a great treasure. I envy you."

Alice was looking at her doubtfully.

"Truly," Adwen said. "Will you share your knowledge with me? I have nothing to give you in return. I don't even know if I will be quick or slow. I think when I first came to Richard I was not too stupid, but he did not want me to think." He had wanted nothing but submission and her body, she thought bitterly, and she had given until he had drained her. "I might even be more of a burden than a babe."

"Oh, no," Alice said eagerly. "It will be my pleasure to help you, my lady."

"You must call me Adwen, and it will also be my pleasure to help you." Adwen smiled. "When I find a way."

Alice looked abashed. "Adwen?"

"I told you I was no longer a great lady." Adwen rose to her feet. "I'm only a woman like you, and we must take care of each other. Now, close your eyes and rest. I'll go and get Brynn. She will want to see how well you are doing."

Alice obediently closed her eyes.

So meek. Adwen felt a burst of anger as she started across the camp. Alice had always been timid and meek and had been cruelly used. Was it the fate of all gentle human beings to be so abused?

"You are disturbed," Malik said as he appeared at her side. "You should not have chosen to care for Alice. I would have done it."

"Why shouldn't I have—" At first she had been so absorbed, his meaning was not clear. Then she understood and all the anger stored within her was set free. "You think my feelings are too tender, my soul too sensitive to wait upon my husband's leman?"

"I did not say—"

"You meant it." She did not look at him as she strode away. "You're like all men, you think we're weak and without strength. Well, it is you who *make* us weak and rob us of our strength. You use our bodies and dull our minds. You think it right to beat us and make us serve you, to give us children and then desert us."

"I am truly a wicked fellow," Malik said solemnly. "And clearly grievously forgetful. I do not even remember giving you a child. What did we name it?"

She glared at him. "You know I didn't mean—" She broke off as she saw his bland expression. Incredibly, she suddenly felt a smile tugging at her lips. "Beelzebub."

"It was a boy?"

"A demon, as any babe of yours would be." Her smile disappeared. "You see, you think so lightly of us that you pay no heed to my words."

"When they apply to me, I will give them every concern. But you are not talking to me; you are talking to your husband." He smiled gently. "So, instead, I will ignore this venom you are spewing and try to make you smile again. Perhaps, if I am fortunate, you will even laugh. You need to laugh, Adwen. Laughter is good."

When he smiled he was more beautiful than any man she had ever seen. His face lit with warmth and it was like watching a sunrise. She stared helplessly for an instant before she forced her glance away. "Laughter is for the jesters in the hall."

"Shall I be your jester, Adwen? Shall I serve and delight you? I can, you know."

She looked back at him and instantly wished she had not. Sunrise again. Her pace quickened as she approached Brynn, and she looked straight ahead. "I want nothing from you. I want nothing from any man."

"I like the idea of a boy, but Beelzebub is not a good name. We will call him Malik, after me."

A boy as beautiful as this man. She felt a sudden pang of sorrow. Not for her. Never for her.

"What is wrong? What did I say?"

"Nothing."

He reached out and stopped her. "It is not nothing when I cause you pain. It is everything."

"I am barren," she said haltingly. "I cannot bear children."

"With your husband. If there is fault, perhaps it is with him." He puffed out his chest. "Now, since I have no faults . . ."

"What are you saying? The fault is always with the woman."

"In my country we do not believe that is always true."

"You don't understand." She broke free and backed away from him, her voice hoarse with pain. "They die. They're mine for a while and then they die."

"I do understand." His voice was soft as he held out his hand to her. "Come to me. Let me be your friend. Let me share your sorrow."

She wanted to take his hand. He was not like

Richard, who had blamed her and made her ashamed of her body. Her husband had never shared her sorrow when she had lost the babes, never even visited her until she was well enough to try again.

Yet even if she found she could trust Malik, he would only try to take away this new freedom she had been granted with Redfern's destruction. The comfort he offered would come at too high a price.

She turned and almost ran the remaining short distance to where Brynn was standing on the side of the hill.

"Alice is awake," she said breathlessly.

Brynn started to smile and then stopped as she saw Adwen's expression. "What's wrong? Doesn't she have her senses?"

"She seems very clear."

Brynn looked over her shoulder. "Is Malik—"

"I told Alice you'd come to her," she interrupted. "But when you're finished, call me and I'll go and sleep beside her." She frowned. "You should sleep yourself. Alice isn't the only one who bears wounds."

"When I'm finished here." Her attention shifted to the trail down which Gage Dumont had disappeared a few hours before. "It's been a long time, hasn't it? They should be back soon."

She was worried about the Norman, Adwen realized. Poor Brynn, so much inner conflict and pain. Just when her own way was becoming clear to her, Brynn's path was beset with obstacles. "They went after Richard?"

Brynn nodded as she continued to scan the trail.

"You won't make them come sooner by staring down that hill," she said gently.

Brynn turned away. "I know. I'm being very foolish." She started across the camp toward Alice's pallet.

Malik was already kneeling beside Alice, Adwen saw. She couldn't hear his words, but she suddenly heard

Alice chuckle. It didn't surprise her. The impudent scamp could probably make a dying woman laugh.

As if he felt Adwen's gaze on him, he looked up and met her eyes. He smiled brilliantly and his expression was filled with understanding and a little wistfulness that was near irresistible. He wanted her to come to him.

Too high a price, she reminded herself desperately. Much too high.

Gage did not return to the camp until just before dawn.

Safe! Relief surged through Brynn as she saw him. Even in the half-darkness no one could mistake Gage's giant silhouette. Brynn watched the riders trot up the hill; no pennants flying this night. The company looked as weary as Brynn felt.

Brynn walked forward to meet them at the edge of the camp.

Gage's stallion reared as she stepped out of the bushes, but he was weary too and Gage quickly had him under control. Not so his temper.

"Haven't you been to sleep?" he asked roughly. "How much do you think you can stand?"

"As much as you." She braced herself, afraid to ask the question.

She didn't have to. Gage shook his head and said, "We didn't find him. So you may go to your rest with a clear mind. No blood has been spilled to taint you." He turned to LeFont. "Have the men get a few hours rest and then go back to Redfern and see what you can salvage. Blankets, food, anything." He glanced back at the smoldering, blackened ruins. "God knows, it won't be much."

"And what do we do with them?" LeFont asked.

"We try to make these people as comfortable as we can while you rebuild their homes."

"Build?" LeFont recoiled in horror. "I am a soldier. I do not build."

"Then it should give you reason to find craftsmen who can do the task for you," Gage said. "Quickly. I want dwellings here before the first snow. Stone dwellings and the castle will also be stone. As strong and impenetrable as Bellerieve."

"Why are you doing this?" Brynn asked in bewilderment. "Are you going to accept Redfern from William as your own?"

"Perhaps. It's close enough to the sea for trade. The ground is fertile."

"Perhaps? You're expending a great deal of effort and money if you aren't certain."

"Then I'll have to have my coffers replenished, won't I?" He turned to LeFont again. "If you can find craftsmen and workers within the week, I'll put Gillaume in charge of the building and you can accompany us on our journey."

LeFont did not even ask their destination. He was too relieved to be rid of the ignominy of relinquishing his sword. "I'll find them. If I have to send back to Normandy, I assure you that you'll have your craftsmen." He dismounted and motioned the other soldiers to follow suit. "Four hours rest. No more."

Brynn watched the men disperse. "This is most strange. Why?"

Gage dismounted. "I don't like random destruction. It offends me. There's destruction in war, but it's done with a purpose in mind."

"Tell that to the innocents who get in the way of your purpose."

"There are few innocents left in the world." He wearily rubbed the back of his neck. "I'll not make excuses for myself. I do what has to be done to live and prosper in this world." His gaze searched among the sleeping bodies. "Where is Malik?"

"Over there." Brynn gestured to a pallet beneath the tree. "He's exhausted. He and Adwen insisted on helping me."

"But he had the good sense to lie down and go to sleep when his strength ran out." His tone roughened. "For God's sake, go and rest."

"I will." She ran her fingers through her hair. "I was only waiting for you to return."

"To see if I brought you Richard's head?"

"No, I wanted . . ." She was too tired to hide and protect herself. "I wanted to make sure you were safe."

He went still. "You did?"

"Of course I did. Do you think me so hard that I would wish that monster to live and you die?"

"I don't know what to think of you. I've never met a woman who would cast off a man for saving her life."

"I wasn't in danger."

"Delmas nearly killed you," he said savagely. "The next time he might have done it."

"It was wrong." She swallowed. "I will not be Bathsheba. I will not live with you with that sin on my soul."

"The hell you won't!" His eyes blazed down at her. "I won't be cast off, Brynn. I will have your body. I'll worry about your soul later." He was silent, struggling for control. "We will leave for Gwynthal in two weeks. I give you that much time to heal, mourn your pig of a husband, and prepare yourself to come back to my bed."

"You are too generous, my lord."

"Yes, I am." He turned and strode away from her.

She would not do it. She must fight him. If she allowed herself to fall once again under that sensual spell, she did not know if she would have the strength to walk away from him when they reached Gwynthal. He knew her body so well, how to please it, how to make it crave and burn. Sweet Mary, even the memory was making her breasts swell. She must forget him, block the thought of him away from her.

She turned and walked to the pallet she had prepared for herself beside Alice. Think of Alice. Poor Alice, who would bear Richard of Redfern's child.

Brynn could have a child. If she went again to Gage's bed, within a year she might bear his child. The idea brought no revulsion, only a melting, aching tenderness. Gage's child . . .

She should feel fear and despair at the thought of bearing a bastard. Not joy. Not love.

Love.

Dear God, save her. Let it not be true.

She did not want to love this warrior, who was so foreign to everything she believed. She did not want to accept the truth that because she had loved and yielded, a man had died.

But it had happened.

And she did love Gage Dumont with all her being.

She was not even surprised. How long had she been fighting the knowledge that was now here before her? It did not change anything except make the sorrow more intense. She could not have Gage. To take him into her body and her heart would be to reward herself for an act that she must not condone.

Gage's child . . .

Perhaps she could not have Gage, but what of his child? Something of him could be her own. Surely she could be granted this boon?

But could she bear to leave him after the child was born?

The answer was a swift and violent no, and she felt tears sting her eyes. No, she could not have even this gift. After they reached Gwynthal she must leave him and make the cut clean and final.

"We must talk," Gage said as he dropped down beside her before the fire. "Rather, you must talk."

"About what?" Brynn asked warily. It was the first

time he had approached her during the past ten days. They had both gone their separate ways: she caring for the refugees and helping to erect shelter here on the hillside, he supervising the start of the rebuilding of Redfern down in the valley below.

"Tell me about Gwynthal."

"I've told you about Gwynthal."

"Not enough. I have no intention of starting a journey to a land that could be beset with enemies without my knowing more about it." He paused. "And if there is true reason for the journey besides your desire to go home."

"You still think I lied to you?"

"No, but I need you to tell me. You were not entirely honest with me regarding your reasons for coming to Redfern." He stared into the flames. "You've led a hard life. I wouldn't blame you for saying anything that would rid you of your enemies. I won't be angry or condemn you. If you wish so desperately to go to your Gwynthal, I will take you there. Treasure or no."

Warmth flooded through her as she looked at him. She did not want to feel this softness. She wished he would be hard, unfair. It was difficult to keep armor in place when he displayed such generosity. "I didn't lie. There is a treasure."

"Where did it come from?"

"Plunder. War." She smiled sadly. "Where do most great treasures come from? I'll not be sad to see it gone from Gwynthal."

"Whose plunder?"

"Hevald's. He was a great warrior who lived many centuries ago. He came from Wales but fought and won many battles from the Saxons here in England. He was much renowned and many legends and tales were told about him. But he grew weary of battle and blood and decided to renounce all he had been before. He took his beautiful new bride, his officers and wagons filled with gold and jewels, and returned to the land of his birth."

"Gwynthal?"

"No, Kythe in Wales. But Kythe was also torn by war and dissent. So he left Kythe and traveled farther west to the sea. He stayed at the village of Selkirk for four months while he built a ship. Then he and his followers set sail, seeking a place to settle in peace." She added simply, "He found Gwynthal. An island without war because it had no people."

"And how far away is this island?"

"Two days by ship after we leave Selkirk."

"So close?" He raised his brows. "And yet this treasure has remained undiscovered for centuries?"

"Gwynthal is guarded by high cliffs. From the sea there appears no way to dock a ship near it."

"But you know a way?"

"Of course, it's where I was born."

"Then why didn't you stay there?"

"My father was not content in Gwynthal. He said it was too serene." Her lips curved bitterly. "He was like you. He found life without conflict like meat without salt."

He did not answer the challenge. "But you said he left your mother and you."

"Not before she followed him to Kythe." She was silent a moment before she blurted out, "What could he expect of her? He knew when he wed her she was not like those other women. She was a healer. She had to give to them. In Gwynthal it was accepted, but in Kythe . . ."

"They called her a witch."

"Not at first. They merely thought her odd and unwomanly. Then, over the years, it changed. She was too strong, too strong for them, too strong for my father. I think it was when they saw my father desert her that they truly began to fear her." She closed her eyes, shutting away the memories. "I don't want to talk anymore. Is it enough?"

"Yes." She thought she sensed him reaching out to her but felt no touch. "Answer one more question. Who on Gwynthal will I have to fight for this treasure?"

"No one." She opened her eyes and swallowed to ease the dryness in her throat. "No one knew of the treasure but my mother. She was descended from Hevald's chief adviser, Bentar, who was given the task of hiding the treasure when they reached Gwynthal. When Hevald died he gave his treasure to Bentar and since then the knowledge of the hiding place was passed on from eldest child to eldest child in the family."

"And she told you of its whereabouts?"

Brynn nodded. "And gave me her ruby talisman to wear around my neck. I was wearing it when Delmas found me in the forest. He took it from me."

"And I'd wager Richard took it from him."

"Perhaps. There's been no sign of him?"

"No."

"He will follow us, won't he?" she whispered. "He's waiting somewhere, watching us . . . I can feel it."

"I hope he does follow us."

So he could kill him. She shivered and drew her cloak closer about her. "I do not. I don't want him near us."

"Because he'll taint your beautiful Gwynthal?"

Let him believe that if he wished, she thought. Let him believe she cared more for a place than for him. Don't let him realize that every time he appeared on her horizon, Gwynthal appeared to be fading farther and farther in the distance. "He has no place at Gwynthal."

His lips curved in a bitter smile. "Another intruder to be cast out of your Eden?" He made a motion with one hand as she opened her lips to reply. "Oh, I agree he has no place there, but he does have a place in hell and I shall endeavor to send him there." His glance shifted back to the fire. "We leave for your Gwynthal at dawn the day after tomorrow."

She was finally going home. It was difficult to believe. "Truly?"

"Providing you're sure you remember the way to your Gwynthal. I have no doubt I could find a guide to this Wales, but after that we'll be at a loss."

"You need not find a guide. I remember every tree, every turn of the road of the journey."

He raised his brows. "It was a long time ago."

"It's the way home," she said simply. "When Delmas brought me here I knew I'd find a way to go back."

"But you had no idea you'd be so unfortunate as to be in the company of a lowly Norman." He paused. "You should know I have no intention of giving you your freedom once we reach there. No one ever said I wasn't greedy. I want the treasure and I want you. I intend to have you both."

"You may have the treasure, but when we reach Gwynthal I'll take my freedom and you won't be able to stop me."

"We will see." He rose to his feet and stood looking down at her before he said, "But we are *not* alike."

"What?"

"I'm not like your father. Like him, I may grow bored without a challenge but that is our only similarity. No matter what you did, I would stand firm. I would never leave you." His low voice rang with intensity. "I would fight in your cause. I would let no man, woman, or creature on this earth hurt you. I would battle all your dragons, Brynn of Falkhaar."

Before she could reply, he had turned and walked away. It was just as well, she thought dazedly; she did not know how any woman should respond to such a declaration.

Shut it away. Don't think of those impassioned words.

Easy to say. Impossible to do.

I would battle all your dragons, Brynn of Falkhaar.

The day of their departure dawned clear and cold but no colder than Gage's expression when he saw the wagon. He rode across the camp to where Brynn and Malik were stowing blankets and food in the wagon's bed.

"What is this? Unload this wagon. We're taking only mounts and pack horses."

"We'll need the wagon."

"Wagons break down, their wheels get stuck in mud and snow. I want to travel fast."

"We've waited this long." She placed another folded blanket in the wagon. "A few days longer on the journey won't matter."

"It will be more than a few days if it starts to snow. Tell her, Malik."

"Snow is bad," Malik agreed obediently. "But I agree with Brynn, we need this wagon."

Gage cast him an exasperated glance. "Unpack it."

"I said we take it." Her jaw set as she turned to face him. "Adwen is much stronger, but she cannot ride long distances yet. She will need to rest in the wagon when she tires."

"Adwen!"

"The wagon will bear little weight most of the time and be able to travel quickly. Don't you think it better to have Adwen in the wagon and still be on the move than have to stop and wait for her to rest?"

"She can't come with us," Gage said. "She's just risen from a sickbed."

"I won't leave Adwen behind," Brynn said flatly. "You needn't worry. I will care for her if she falls ill again."

"Adwen and the entire world," Gage muttered.

"Richard hasn't been captured. He tried to kill her once. He could try again if he finds her helpless and unprotected."

"I'll set a guard over her."

Brynn shook her head.

"Then we'll take her to a nunnery and have the good sisters look after her."

"No!" Malik said quickly. "No nunnery."

Brynn felt a fleeting amusement at the panic in his voice before returning to the serious subject at hand. "Do you think that a holy sanctuary would stop Richard? He would burn it to the ground as he did Redfern." When Gage's expression still did not soften, she added, "Or he might take her hostage. He knows I have affection for her. He could use her to make me abandon you and join with him."

A wry smile broke the sternness of his face. "And I don't have to ask if you would do it."

"No, you don't," she said brusquely. "Not when you weigh gold against a life. We will take her."

Gage hesitated and then he nodded curtly. "We'll take her. But she must keep up."

"I will help her," Malik said. "Do not worry, Gage. All will be well."

"I hope you're right." Gage stared inquiringly at Brynn. "Content?"

"Not entirely." She braced herself. "Alice is coming too."

"What!"

Brynn said quickly, "I know she is with child, but she is only four months gone and she's very strong. She told me her mother worked in the fields until the moment of her birth."

"Then let her mother care for her until the babe is born."

"Her father will not accept a child of shame into

his house. She has no place to go. I want to take her to Gwynthal."

"And I suppose they will accept her there?"

She nodded. "They are more just to women than in other places."

"You said you were only a child of nine when you left there and you were very unhappy in Kythe. How can you be certain your memory isn't playing you false? That you aren't remembering Gwynthal as you wish to remember it?"

Her eyes widened with sudden uneasiness. She had never questioned her memories of Gwynthal. Gwynthal had always been home, the perfect place, the haven. She shook her head vehemently. "My mother told me— It could not be—I remember it too clearly. The peace and the silences . . ." She whirled on her heel. "Why are we wasting time? Let us be on our way. We're going to take Alice and that's the end of it."

She expected him to argue with her. Gage was not one to accept two such defeats tamely.

"Very well," he said slowly. "Take your Alice."

She glanced over her shoulder and the uneasiness returned as she saw his expression. Pity?

No, she must have been mistaken, for now his face was as impassive as usual. He turned his horse and started toward the head of the column. "I suppose I should be glad you don't plan on bringing along all of Redfern."

"I'm slowing you down," Adwen said as she settled herself on the pile of blankets in the bed of the wagon. "Forgive me, Brynn, I thought I'd be stronger than this."

"You can't expect to be as strong as the rest of us." Brynn tucked a fur rug around Adwen's shoulders to close out the chill. It had been growing steadily colder all day and there was a damp bite to the air. She hoped the snow would hold off until they reached shelter.

"And you're growing stronger every day. When we started out you could ride for only a few hours before you had to lie down. Yesterday you didn't have to use the wagon until noon and today it's three hours later. Soon you won't have to use it at all."

Adwen made a face. "Lord Gage will be happy when that is true."

"Why? Has he said anything to you?"

"No, he's been very tolerant, but I can see he's impatient with the delay."

"It's his nature to be impatient. Ignore him."

Adwen gazed at her speculatively. "As you are doing?"

"I don't ignore him." She avoided Adwen's eyes as she tucked the blanket over her feet. "I answer when he speaks to me."

"But nothing else. I'm sure he doesn't like it. He's been looking quite fierce of late."

"I can't help what he does or does not like." She could not care if Gage was displeased with her. She had to keep him away, to block out all intimacy, or he would invade every part of her.

"It would do no harm to be kinder to him." When Brynn looked at her in surprise, she added, "As he was kind to all those poor souls at Redfern. It's not many men who would take the trouble to rebuild what he had not destroyed. It was an act of mercy."

"I assure you he has little mercy."

Adwen frowned, troubled. "I think you're unfair to him."

"And I think you should save your strength and not worry about Lord Gage." She patted Adwen's hand and started backing out of the wagon bed. "Keep covered, there's no sun at all in these dense woods. It should be dark soon and we'll be able to stop for the day."

Malik was standing by Brynn's horse a short distance away and lifted her to the saddle. "How is she?" he asked in a low voice.

"Just tired. She's standing the trip much better than I thought she would."

"She has a great spirit." His lips tightened. "Or it would have been broken many years ago." He mounted his own horse but did not nudge him forward. "She grieves, you know."

"Over Lord Richard? You're wrong, she wouldn't—"

"Not for that villain. She grieves for the babes she lost."

Brynn frowned. "She doesn't talk about them. They died before she came to term. She never saw them, Malik."

"She still grieves. I think it is because she was never given a chance to grieve when they were taken from her. She tries not to think about them, but I think they are always with her. I wish I could give her ease." Then he smiled with an effort. "But she does not trust me. Can you imagine a woman with so little judgment, she cannot see what a noble man I am?"

"No, I can't imagine," Brynn said gently.

"Brynn!" Gage called from the head of the column.

"He wishes to start," Malik said. "You go on ahead. I will stay here and ride beside the wagon and talk to Adwen. Sometimes I can make her smile."

He made them all smile. This journey would have seemed much longer if it hadn't been for Malik's droll remarks. But Gage was not smiling at the moment, she noticed. He had turned his horse and was riding back toward her. She kicked her horse into a trot, which quickly brought her alongside him. "She's settled. We can move now."

"Thank you," he said caustically. "But from now on I'll decide when we stop."

Brynn immediately bristled. "Adwen's been very good. She needed this rest."

"We could have waited until we were through these woods and in the open."

"Why would that have—" Then she understood. She glanced apprehensively at the thick shrubbery and overhanging trees bordering the trail. "Lord Richard? Has he been seen?"

"No, but a moving target is much less easy to attack."

"A man alone?"

"We don't know he's alone. He may have gathered followers from the countryside eager to attack the enemy when we're weakest."

"You've reason to be displeased with me," she said haltingly. "I thought only of Adwen's well-being. From now on I'll ask your opinion before I order the wagon driver to stop."

"What astonishing kindness," Gage said. "And if you don't agree with my opinion?"

"Then I'll do as I think best." She suddenly flared, "And you don't have to be unkind. Adwen is doing the best she can. We're making quite good time. We should be in Kythe by next week and reach the coast a day later."

"Did she say I was unkind?"

"No, but she realizes you're impatient with her."

"I'm not impatient with her. I think she's been very brave. I've seen her reeling in the saddle before she would give in and let you call a halt." He met her gaze. "It's you I'm impatient with."

She should have ridden away and not engaged in conflict with him. It had brought about the result she most wanted to avoid. She moistened her lips. "I've given no cause for impatience."

"The devil you haven't. I'm weary of you avoiding

me and answering me curtly. It's time it came to an end."

She stiffened. "In what manner?"

"Why, in the most pleasant manner for both of us." His smile was tiger-bright. "Tonight you will come to me and share my blankets as you did at Hastings."

"I will not."

"Would you rather I forced you? I will, you know. Think how that would distress Adwen."

"You wouldn't force me."

"I'll do anything it takes to break down this wall you've built around yourself," he said softly, his ice-blue eyes clear and without mercy. "Hardraada taught me to be very skilled at breaking down walls and destroying citadels, Brynn. You don't want me to demonstrate how skillful."

"I'd fight you and you would not—" She broke off as she realized arguing with him would do no good. This was the warrior she had first come to know at Hastings; ruthless, relentless, storm-driven. Words would not bend him to her will. Dear God, what would influence him?

"Nothing," he said as if reading her mind. "You'd be wise not to battle me in this, Brynn." He nudged his horse ahead of her and his words floated back to her as he regained the head of the column. "If you feel the need to prove your strength, find a conflict you can win."

They stopped at twilight at the edge of the wood and set up camp, close enough to the trees for shelter but with a clear view of the terrain on the other three sides. Though the clouds remained heavy and dark on the horizon, the snow failed to materialize. However, the moist chill made the campfires blessedly welcome. Gage ignored Brynn as he supervised the building of these fires, saw to his horse, and sent out soldiers to form a protective ring around the camp. Then he settled in front of the largest fire with Malik, speaking in a low voice and apparently oblivious of everyone but his friend.

But he was not oblivious, Brynn thought, seated across from him. He was not looking at her, but she sensed he knew every move she made. Perhaps it was her imagination, she told herself. Perhaps he had changed his mind and—

"You're very quiet, Brynn." Adwen delicately licked her fingers as she finished eating her second piece of roasted rabbit. "And you ate little. Are you tired?"

"No."

"I am." Adwen smiled. "But I cannot get enough to eat, so it must be a good tired. I remember I had no appetite at all when I was ill before."

Brynn glanced at Adwen's rosy cheeks and bright eyes and felt a deep surge of gratitude. This was the way Adwen should look, the way Brynn had feared she would never look. "Yes, it's a good tired. You're sleeping well?"

"Like the dead." Adwen covered a yawn. "I can hardly wait to finish eating before going to my blankets." She stared dreamily into the fire. "Journeys are strange, aren't they, Brynn."

"Strange?"

"Don't you feel it? It's like that wonderful time between sleeping and waking. Almost like a dream. We need not make plans or face consequences that have plagued us in the past. We have only to drift from one place to the other."

"I don't consider the pace Gage has set 'drifting,'" Brynn said dryly. Then she smiled. "But I'm glad you feel it is so. You've been anchored in heavy water too long."

"So have you." Adwen drew up her legs and laid her chin on her knees. "But you don't allow yourself to drift, Brynn. Even on this journey you hurry around, tending to my needs, making sure Alice is well. I saw you bandaging LeFont's hand yesterday."

"He cut it on a branch. Cuts should be attended to at once or they become a danger."

"And no one else could do it?"

"Why should they? I'm the healer."

Adwen laughed and shook her head. "Someday you will be crushed to the ground with all the burdens you take upon yourself."

Brynn felt a flicker of surprise at the statement, which was so similar to the ones Gage had made. She smiled. "Nonsense. I have strong shoulders."

"And we all lean on them." Adwen mused, "I wonder what you would do if we didn't have to do that any longer. Would you take wing and fly away like a butterfly?"

Brynn snorted derisively. "Do I look like a butterfly?"

Adwen shook her head. "You're more like a lovely falcon, all gold and russet, with strong wings to shelter and soar."

Brynn felt her cheeks heat with embarrassment. "You must be more weary than I thought. Your judgment is definitely clouded. You'd best go to your pallet."

Adwen yawned again. "I won't argue." She rose to her feet and started toward the wagon under which three pallets had been placed for Brynn, Adwen, and Alice to protect them from the elements. "But you might stop all that sheltering for a while and soar a little. Are you coming?"

"No, she's not," Gage said quietly from across the fire.

Adwen stopped in surprise.

Brynn inhaled sharply.

Gage stood up and moved to his own pallet a little distance from the fire. He lay down and then lifted the blanket as if in invitation. "Brynn."

She tensed and sat still, looking at him. She could feel Malik's watchful, and Adwen's bewildered, stares fixed upon her.

She could refuse him. He might not force the issue.

She was fooling herself. Of course he would force it. Gage always did what he said he would do.

I will fight all your dragons, Brynn of Falkhaar.

Why had those words suddenly come flying back to her? He was fighting her, not her enemies.

Adwen took a protective step closer to Brynn. "Perhaps she does not want—" She looked from Brynn to Gage and back again. "Brynn?"

If Brynn refused him, Adwen would feel she had to intervene. This newfound contentment would be shattered. It was clever of Gage to realize how desperately Brynn wanted that serenity to continue.

She rose to her feet and strode toward Gage. "Go to your sleep, Adwen." She lay down beside Gage, jerked the blanket from his grasp, and tucked it around herself. "I'll see you in the morning."

Adwen hesitated. "Are you sure that is what you want?"

• "I'm sure." Brynn closed her eyes and was immediately assaulted by the scent of leather and musk that always clung to Gage. "Go to sleep."

She heard Adwen moving slowly away.

"Go take your pallet and set it by the wagon, Malik," Gage said. "Adwen may need protection if Richard decides it's time to take a hostage."

"I doubt that's the reason you want me gone," Malik said ruefully.

"No, but the reason is sound."

And the one ploy that Malik would find irresistible, Brynn thought. He would let the world crumble, if it meant Adwen remaining safe. Only seconds later she heard Malik's departure.

The muscles of her stomach knotted.

"Be at ease," Gage said roughly. "You're so taut, it's like lying next to a log."

But a log has no feelings, no senses. "I don't want to be here."

"Yes, you do." His arm slid around her beneath the blanket. "And if your conscience would allow you to be honest about it, you would admit it. This is where you belong."

"No," she whispered. "It's not true."

"Then why are you afraid to be here? Do you fear I'll use you?"

"Yes."

"Fear?" he prodded. "Is that what you really feel?" His hand cupped her breast. "Now? This minute?"

Her teeth bit into her lower lip as she realized her breast was swelling, peaking beneath his touch. "You know it's not. But it makes no difference that my flesh is weak. In my heart I don't wish to couple with you."

"In your heart you wish nothing else." His tongue plunged into her ear. "And, by God, before we reach Gwynthal, you'll tell me so."

Her body felt flushed, burning, her heart pounded painfully. "You would take me here, in full view of the others?"

"They're asleep." His hand lazily rubbed back and forth on her breast. "Or will be soon."

"They could wake."

"I doubt if you'd care by that time." His thumb and forefinger plucked at her nipple. "This gown does not please me. I think we'll have to be rid of it."

"I would"—a wave of heat spread through her as his fingers compressed and then tugged—"become—chilled."

"No, you wouldn't. You'll still have the blanket for cover and it's warm here by the fire." His hand slipped down between her thighs. "But we'll wait for a while if you like." His palm cupped and then rubbed back and forth. "Though it annoys me not to be able to touch your flesh down here. I remember this fleece was wondrously soft and yet had a delightful springiness as it brushed against me while I moved in and out of—"

"Be silent," she broke in desperately. "Such talk is most unseemly."

His hand slid up her skirt. "And it makes you wish to do unseemly things, doesn't it? Wouldn't you like to slip off your gown and ride me like you did by the pond that first day?" Then, as he felt the muscles of her stomach clench under his hand, he added, "Ah, I see you do. Let's see how much." His hand moved down and tested the moist heart of her. "Very much indeed." He lowered his lips to her ear. "It would be easy to close your eyes and let me do what I wish with you, wouldn't it? Then tomorrow you could tell yourself that I had forced you."

Her body was hot, aching. She arched upward with a little murmur of need.

"But I'm not going to let you be anything but honest with yourself and me. I'm not going to enter this lovely tight sheath. I'm not going to give you my seed until you ask it of me." He found the nub for which he was searching and began to slowly rotate it with his thumb.

She cried out as a searing jolt of need streaked through her. "Then why are you . . . doing this?" she panted. "It can bring you no satisfaction."

"Satisfaction?" he asked grimly. "It may kill me."

"Then let me go back to Adwen. I cannot stand this."

"You will stand it," he said fiercely. "I'll stroke your body until it feels strange without my touch. I'll give you pleasure and torment. I'll wake you in the night with my tongue or my fingers or my voice telling you all the ways I will have you when you ask it of me."

"Please . . . I can never ask it of you."

Two fingers slid deep within her. "Let us pray for the sake of both our sanity that you change your mind."

Shocking . . .

Sinful, she thought sleepily, it must be a dream. It could not be . . .

"Wider," Gage's voice, muffled against the heart of her. "Just a little wider, Brynn . . ."

Her limbs obeyed without her volition.

His tongue!

Her eyes flew open as his tongue firmed, teasing, tormenting the nub.

"Gage. No." She panted. "This is not—"

His mouth . . . hungry.

Teeth . . . nipping gently.

She convulsed, her own teeth biting into her lip as the dark madness overpowered her.

His hands grasped her hips, holding her in place as he took her response, stealing the release she could not deny him.

After it was over, she lay there, shuddering, trembling in every limb.

He moved up and lay beside her, settling his arm over her shoulders.

"This cannot be a good thing," she said shakily. "I have never heard of a man doing such a thing to a woman. And—"

"It's a very good thing," he interrupted. "It's not an uncommon way to pleasure a woman in Byzantium. I would have showed you the way of it before, but I was always too impatient to get inside you." He drew her closer. "Go to sleep."

"So you can wake me in such a manner again?"

"I told you how it would be. And your response was everything I could wish. I look forward to experimenting with other forms of pleasure." He began to stroke her breasts through the wool of her gown. "But this garment really does get in the way."

"I won't take it off." It was clearly no barrier, but she felt vulnerable enough without lying naked in his arms. "Don't ask me again."

He looked at her in surprise. "But of course I'll ask you again. I want it off."

"Wake, Brynn," Gage whispered. "Open your limbs."

Again? She felt the heat begin between her thighs as if on signal. She could not remember how many times he had awakened her that night. Once it had been with his mouth on her breast sucking strongly as his fingers brought her to pleasure.

And his mouth . . .

She stretched, seeking.

He chuckled. "Not this time. It's nearly dawn." A cool damp cloth was applied to the juncture of her thighs.

She opened her eyes. "What are you doing?"

"Soothing you. You have a long ride today, and I toyed with this lovely part of you most of the night in one fashion or the other. Are you sore?"

"No." She wanted his hands and mouth there again and not his "soothing" cloth.

He smoothed the curls with the cloth. "Your breasts?"

"No." Her breasts did ache a little. He had not been gentle, but had fed on her like a hungry child. At one time he had made her release with just that violent suction.

"Your breasts are very sensitive to touch." He said thickly, "They harden and swell like ripe fruit. I'd like to suck them when you are with child."

She lost her breath at the vision his words brought.

Her belly swollen with his child, Gage naked over her, his lips on her breast.

"You'd like that too," he said. "I'll have to see what I can do." He threw the cloth aside and handed her her gown. "Dress quickly. They'll be stirring soon."

When had she taken off her clothes? She vaguely remembered a moment of frantic need when any barrier between them seemed too much. Gage had wanted it gone, but there had been no triumph when he had gotten what he wished. Just his hands on her naked flesh, playing with her as if she were an exquisitely desirable toy.

She pulled the gown over her head and got to her knees, settling it in place. That was better. The coldness of the wool against her body was jarring her out of the sensual euphoria.

Gage's eyes narrowed on her face. "It will happen again tonight, you know. Tonight and every night. Your body will become so accustomed to it that you won't be able to do without me."

She was terribly afraid he might be right. Even now she felt full-bodied and sensual as never before. She didn't look at him as she started hurriedly across the camp. "I must go wake Adwen."

Eleven

"TAKE OFF THE gown," Gage said.

Brynn pulled the garment over her head and settled down with her back to him. After four days the act was commonplace now. She wondered if she would have been able to sleep at all without his hands on her naked body.

His big palms instantly cradled her breasts as he settled down beside her. Possession. Sometimes it started like this; no wild sensuality, only this comfortable sense of belonging.

"I want inside you," he said in her ear. "Will you take me?"

That was commonplace too; the request before the onslaught of seduction.

"No."

His grasp involuntarily tightened on her breasts. "My God, you're a stubborn woman. Why will you not—" He broke off and she could sense the effort for control. "This can't go on. You *want* me, damn you."

She did want him. The pleasure he gave her was wild and exotic, but there was no primeval joining, that searing bonding that made her feel totally complete. "It will go on." She paused. "Unless you choose to call a halt. I think this restraint is not natural for a man. It's you who are suffering, not I."

"Natural? No, by God, it's far from natural." He took his hands from her and rolled onto his back, looking up at the night sky. "What is right and natural for both of us is what you're denying us."

"You take everything else, why not that?"

"You know why. When you come to me, you must never walk away again."

"You know why that can never be."

"Because of the death of a man you detested?" He raised himself on one elbow and looked down at her. "I didn't kill Delmas."

She went still. "I saw you."

"You didn't see me kill him because I didn't do it."

The scene in the stable flooded back to her. "I did see."

"Have you ever known me to lie?"

"No." For an instant hope soared through her before the picture in the stable returned. "Not until now. You've always told me you believe only what you can see and touch. I *saw* you."

"But you've never thought as I do. You believe in faith and miracles." His voice was bitterly mocking. "Where is your faith now, Brynn?"

She was silent, the tears stinging her eyes.

He muttered a curse. "Perhaps you're right not to trust me. I probably would lie and cheat and murder for you. It was only fate that kept me from slaughtering your husband like the pig he was. I was even in a rage at being cheated of the pleasure."

The faintest hope was reborn. The bitter words were more convincing than any declaration.

I probably would lie and cheat and murder for you.

What was she thinking? He had also said those words with chilling conviction and he was very clever.

He could become the silk-voiced persuader, the merchant who could buy and sell anything in the flicker of an eyelash. She must not be blinded by what she wanted to see as truth. "You're right, I cannot trust your words."

He smiled sardonically. "I didn't think you would. That's why I didn't protest my innocence in the beginning. Cynic that I am, I don't know if I'd believe you in the same circumstances." His lips tightened. "But there is one difference in us. I would not abandon you. No matter what your sin, I'd claim it as my own."

"Our natures are not the same."

"We're more similar than you will let yourself believe. We're both honest, determined, and totally ruthless when it suits our purpose."

She looked at him in astonishment. "I'm not ruthless."

"You're more ruthless than any soldier in my acquaintance. You'd trample over half the world to save a life."

"That's not true."

"Oh, you'd be careful not to inflict any lasting wound, but you'd definitely trample all obstructions underfoot to protect the one you were healing."

"You're wrong. There are other ways."

"I'm not wrong. You don't know yourself. You say you must break with me because of guilt, but you're far too clear-seeing to blame yourself for Delmas's death." His voice was relentless, driving each word at her. "You may have grounds to think I'm to blame, but you refuse to give me the faith you would Adwen or Malik. Why is that?"

"I saw . . . the pitchfork."

"Faith, Brynn."

The tears were running down her cheeks. "I cannot—"

"Then it's not guilt, it's something else. You're using Delmas as a barrier between us. Why? You know I will wed you and treat you with honor."

"Bathsheba . . ."

"We are *one*. Why do you push me away?"

"We are not one."

"Do you think I would have fought you and for you if I hadn't been certain? God's blood, I have no desire to have a woman rule my life. The only way I can tolerate it is if I also rule yours. We will be one. We *are* one."

"I don't rule your life. You do what you please with me and everyone around you."

"Is that why I'm traveling to this unbreachable island to seek a treasure that no one has ever heard about?"

"You said you believed me."

"I want to believe you, but I'd go to Gwynthal anyway. Nothing could keep me away now."

"Why?"

"Because I think the answer is there."

"Answer?"

"To why you'll not admit what we both know is true."

She shook her head. "I've told you what waits for you at Gwynthal. You will find nothing else."

"No? We will see."

To her relief, he lay back down. Perhaps this tortuous passage was at an end. She was awhirl with the strange thoughts and doubts he had put into her head. She was not as he saw her. She was always honest with herself. Why would she continue to push Gage away when she had admitted to herself that she loved him?

Yet it was true that she would have given Malik or Adwen her faith no matter what the circumstances.

But Gage was different. Gage exuded a dark violence that neither of them possessed.

"I will never talk of this again. I'll never ask you for fairness or honesty," Gage said. "But I swear everything

I said to you tonight is truth." When she did not answer, he laughed without mirth. "And you say you're not hard. Let's test you, shall we? You said you thought I was the one suffering. You're right. Do you know the pain a man suffers when he wants and cannot spend?"

She did not know but she had suspected. He had tried to keep it from her, but once she had seen his face twist with agony, and there were times he had lain apart from her, his muscles knotted, his spine rigid.

"It's a torment you cannot imagine."

"Then don't put yourself in such a position."

"By denying me, you hurt me. Doesn't that offend your healer's instincts?"

"No." It was not the truth. The thought of Gage in physical pain was agonizing. "It's your own fault."

"No, it's yours. All you need do is yield to me and the pain will go away. I will be healed."

"I won't listen to you," she said desperately.

"But you will remember." He drew her into his arms. "Won't you, Brynn?"

Yes, she would remember. Even now the tautness of his muscles was being mirrored in her own body. She closed her eyes and willed herself to sleep.

A long silence fell between them before Gage said, "Brynn."

"I don't want to talk anymore."

"Kythe."

She was taken by surprise at the change of subject. "What?"

"When will we reach Kythe?"

"I'm not sure. Tomorrow or the next day. I don't remember very much about how long it took us between the Welsh border and Kythe."

"I find it curious you remembered everything else. You knew every stick and stone of the way here before we reached it."

She felt a sudden burst of rage. "Well, I don't re-

member how long it took us after we left Kythe. I'm not
perfect. You can't expect me to remember everything."

He was silent again. "We don't have to go to
Kythe. We could go direct to the sea."

"We need supplies, and Kythe is the only village
nearby. Why shouldn't we go?"

"Your mother."

She felt her chest tighten and the familiar coldness
of her hands. "That happened a long time ago."

"They also wanted to burn you," he reminded her
dryly.

She felt a surge of hope. Perhaps there was good
reason for them not to go. "You think there will be
danger?"

"No, I've no doubt we can handle any attack from
farmers and shopkeepers."

She was being foolish . . . and cowardly. "Then
we will go to Kythe."

"You're certain?"

"Of course I'm certain. As I said, it was a long time
ago." She closed her eyes. "Now I'm weary of speaking
of this nonsense. I want to go to sleep."

They reached the village of Kythe late the next
afternoon. It was an ordinary village of thatch-roofed
cottages in the shadow of Kythe Castle. Ordinary and
peaceful. No feeling. No memory.

*Screams. The crackle of flames. The smell—oh God,
the smell!*

"What is wrong?" Adwen whispered, her gaze on
Brynn's face. "You look as—"

"I can't stay here." Brynn felt as if she were
smothering.

"But Gage says we must get food and supplies from
the villagers."

"Then let him get them. I can't stay here." She
turned her mare and kicked it into a headlong gallop.

She heard Gage call her name, but she didn't stop until she was several miles outside the village. Then she slipped from her horse, staggered a few feet, and was violently sick.

Smoke. Screams.

"Christ." Gage's arm was around her waist, holding her steady as she heaved and heaved again.

When she was finally able to lift her head, she gasped, "I will not go back. I can't do—"

"No one is asking you to go back," Gage said roughly. "If you'd said anything about—I shouldn't have listened to you, but you acted as if you didn't mind, dammit."

"I wasn't sure . . . I didn't think about it." She staggered to lean against a tree. "I've never let myself think about it since that night."

"You know I wouldn't let any of the villagers harm you."

"I know . . ." She closed her eyes and leaned her head back against the trunk. "They've almost forgotten about it."

"What?"

"I *feel* it. So much evil and they hardly remember. Once in a while it comes back to them and they feel anger . . . satisfaction and pleasure." She was beginning to shake. "Pleasure!"

She was in his arms, her head pressed against his chest. "Hush."

"She was good. She wanted to help, to heal . . ."

"Shall I burn it down?"

She looked up at him, shocked. "What?"

"They burned her. Shall I burn the village to the ground?"

"You wouldn't . . ."

"Look at me. Would I do it?"

Warrior. Hard. Merciless. "Yes."

"They hurt you. Revenge can be honey-sweet." He

smiled with cold savagery. "Shall I let you light the torch?"

She shuddered. "No."

"Are you sure?"

She nodded jerkily. "Even if I could do it, she would not have wanted it. She wanted to help them."

He shook his head. "Then you're a fool to follow her example."

"Perhaps." She swallowed. She couldn't argue with him with that horror so close. It was hard to remember her mother's teachings when she could think only of the way she had died. "Can we leave this place?"

"As soon as Malik comes with the supplies. I told them to hurry. We should be miles away from here by nightfall."

"You can go back if you like. I don't need you."

"I'll stay." He stepped back. "Don't move. I'll get water and a cloth to cleanse you."

She didn't think she could move if she tried. Never in her life had she felt this limp and weak.

He was back in a moment, wiping her face as if she were a small child, and then he gave her water to wash her mouth.

"Better?" he asked.

"Yes." She was still shaking but was no longer ill. "I just want to be gone from here. I cannot stand . . . She was so good and they've forgotten that about her. . . ."

"Shhh." He sat down and drew her back into his arms, cradling her. "Tell me about her."

"That night? I can't—"

"Not that night. Tell me of *her*."

"Why?"

"Because I'll never forget. Tell me what to remember of her. What was her name?"

"Mairle."

"What did she look like? Was she fair like you?"

"No, she was dark. She had fine blue eyes. Deep blue, not like yours. She had a lovely smile. She smiled a lot . . . until my father left."

"Was she kind to you?"

"Oh, yes, she said we were like sisters as well as mother and daughter."

"Sisters?"

It was hard to explain. "We were equal because of the healing. It was as if we were alone in a circle that no one else could enter. She kept saying, 'Don't worry, Brynn. They can't come in but we can go out to them.'" Her hand clenched on his tunic. "But when she went out of the circle to help them, they killed her. She should never have done it. I told her. I could see how fearful they were becoming after she lay with Roark."

"Who was Roark?"

"The baker's son. He was only nine years old. He was climbing in a tree and had a terrible fall and I think his back was broken. He was dying. The herbs did no good; they only brought sleep. She knew she would have to lay hands on him."

"As you did with Malik?"

"Yes, as I did—" She stopped. What was she saying? The words had come tumbling out in a frantic release of feeling. She had already revealed too much while healing Malik, but she must never speak, never admit to this. Had she learned nothing from her mother's death? "No, it was the herbs. Touch brings only comfort. It's not—"

"Tell me," he urged hoarsely. "You need to let it out. Whatever it is has been festering within you all these years. Trust me. Don't you know by now that I'd never hurt you?"

He was right. The memories she had suppressed had been full of poison and fear, but she could not—

"Don't be afraid. It hurts me when you're afraid."

She didn't want to hurt him. She never wanted to

hurt Gage. . . . He held her gaze, and she saw only truth, the will to know and nothing to fear.

Yet she still couldn't look at him as she told him. She buried her head in his chest. "The herbs do much. Knowledge of their use does more." She paused and then said in a rush, "But the touch heals."

He was silent.

"Why am I telling you this? You don't believe in anything you cannot see."

"Because you need to tell me."

Yes, that was true and perhaps his disbelief only made the confidences safer. "It's not magic. I think it comes from God. I think he chooses certain people to give this gift and it must be used." Her voice was suddenly fierce. "It's *not* unnatural. No more than the gift of a beautiful voice or grace of movement. It's just not . . . usual."

"And people don't understand."

"No."

"When did you realize you had this 'gift'?"

"The year before we left Gwynthal. I wasn't frightened. My mother had told me that it was always passed from mother to eldest child and would probably come while I was still a child. She received the touch when she was only seven."

"Why should you have been frightened?"

"Because it came to me when I knew I had to heal Selbar."

He stiffened. "And am I finally to know who is this Selbar?"

"A wolf. I found him hurt in the forest, his shoulder and chest had been ripped open. He had been gored by a stag."

His eyes widened. "A wolf!" He started to laugh. "A wolf?"

"A beautiful wolf. He would have died if the healing hadn't come to me."

His laughter disappeared. "And you might have died while tending your 'beautiful' wolf."

"It was a gift and had to be used."

"I think your mother would have forgiven you for not using it in this case."

"But I would not have forgiven myself. Not after it came to me." She thought back, remembering that day in the forest. "It felt very strange. My hands began to tingle and then they felt almost hot, and when I put them on the wound I could feel Selbar's flesh begin to heat. I stayed with him all through the night, and in the morning I knew he would live."

"He might have lived without you."

"Yes, if God willed it. I don't say the gift works all the time. It's easier with children or people like Malik, who see clearer than the rest of us. But sometimes they won't come back. Sometimes they die. . . ."

"But the baker's son didn't die?"

"No, he lived and he healed. Four months later he was back climbing trees. At first they called it a miracle." She shut her eyes. "And then they called it something else."

"Witchcraft."

She shuddered at the word. "She was not a witch. I'm not a witch. It's a gift."

He was silent, holding her in blessed comfort.

"You still don't believe me, do you?"

"I wish I could. If it was within my power, I'd give you what you wish of me." He stroked her hair. "But I know you're not a witch and that you're kind and lovely and desire only the best. And I will fight to protect you and what you term your 'gift' until the day I die. Is that enough?"

It was not enough; it still left her alone in the circle. Yet it was still a gift without price. He had heard what she was and not shown the revulsion or fear she had seen on the faces of those others who had learned of the gift. He had said that no matter what she was, he would accept her. She experienced an easing, as if a burden had been lifted from her. "I cannot ask that of you. The gift is mine and so are the consequences."

"You're not asking; I'm telling you." He pressed her face into his shoulder. "Now, speak no more about it. Rest and drive everything from your mind until we can leave this place. How far are we from this fishing village?"

"Selkirk? A full day's journey. We should camp here tonight."

"And are you leading my men now? I say we go on as soon as they come with the supplies. I want to be gone from here. We'll travel all night and reach the village while it's still light and I can find a ship for which to barter."

He never traveled at night; everyone knew that it was far more dangerous for both animals and humans. He was doing it because she needed to be away from this place. Warmth flowered within her, and she closed her eyes and let it flow over her. Conflict would inevitably come again, but she would accept his strength and comfort and enjoy this moment now.

The day was cutting-cold and the wind stung viciously when they arrived at Selkirk at dawn the next day. The village looked smaller to Brynn. She had remembered it as a bustling, noisy town, but there were only twenty or so houses perched haphazardly along the rocky beach. It was too early in the day for there to be many people stirring in the streets, but she could see two small boats putting out to sea and four others being readied.

"What's wrong?" Gage asked. "Isn't this the place?"

"Yes." She couldn't be mistaken. "I just thought it was bigger."

"Everything is bigger to children." Gage turned to Malik. "I don't how long we'll have to be here. See if you can find a roof to shelter us for a change. It's damned cold along this shore."

"What are you going to do?" Malik asked.

"What I do best. Barter." He kicked his horse into a trot. "I want to catch those fishermen before they set sail and not dawdle here until they return at sunset."

Dawdle? Gage didn't know the meaning of the word, Brynn thought ruefully. He was always in motion, always restless. It only underscored the depth of his affection for Malik that he had been willing to suffer those weeks of inactivity when she had been fighting to save the Saracen.

"Come along," Malik said. "We'll get you women out of this sharp wind. Adwen looks blue with cold."

"Thank you," Adwen said with sarcasm. "But I'm not suffering. It's you who I've noticed shivering and quaking like a leaf in the wind."

He looked pained. "You always pay heed to the bad things. Did you notice what a fine seat I have on this steed? Or how keen my wit? No, just that I'm vulnerable to cold. We do not have these hideous north winds where I was born."

Adwen lowered her lashes to veil her eyes. "I'm glad you explained. Then I'll no longer condemn you for your softness."

"Softness?" Outraged, he said, "There's no softness in—"

"Adwen may not be cold, but I am," Brynn interrupted. The badinage between them always amused her, and she had been tempted to let it continue, but she was too tired. Both her emotional response to Kythe and the long journey here had drained her. "And I need sleep."

"At once," Malik said. He waved his arm at LeFont, and they started toward the village.

The villagers proved to be extremely suspicious and

not receptive to bargaining. It took the better part of an hour for Malik to accomplish his mission. He was scowling when he strode back to where he had left Brynn and Adwen. "Gage is not going to be pleased if the menfolk are as canny at bartering as their wives. I managed to get the use of only five of the houses and then at great price. I'm surprised they didn't take the beard from my face." He nodded at a small house facing the beach. "Quarters for you and Gage, Brynn." He turned to Adwen. "Alice and you will occupy the house next door and LeFont and the rest of the men will crowd into the remaining three houses."

"And where do you sleep?" Adwen asked.

"On your doorstep."

"What?"

"There's no other way to prove that I am no weakling." He struck a heroic pose. "I will curl up on your doorstep and face the cold while I protect you from all harm." He added morosely, "Even though I will probably suffer a grievous chill that will take me away from this earthly plane."

Adwen snorted. "I give you two hours on that doorstep."

"You will see." Malik drew his cloak closer about him and started toward LeFont. "Now go inside and warm yourself while I see to the business of settling everyone comfortably on this forlorn shore." He sighed. "Everyone but me."

Adwen stared after him with a frown. "Will he really do that?"

"It wouldn't surprise me," Brynn answered.

"Well, stop him," Adwen said. "He's been ill. It would not be good for him."

"He's not ill now. He's as strong as he ever was."

"It's still foolish. Tell him not to do it."

"Why don't you?"

"Because that's what he wants me to do. He wants

me to tell him I think he's strong as a bull and need not prove anything to me. Well, I won't do it."

"Why not?"

"Because he takes advantage of every— I just won't!" Adwen called Alice, who was talking to LeFont. "Alice, come, we have shelter." She looked defiantly at Malik. "And I'm sure there will be a warm, cozy fire."

"I'm sure also," Malik said mournfully.

Adwen muttered something beneath her breath and stalked toward the cottage.

"Is she angry?" Alice asked as she reached Brynn.

Brynn shrugged. "I have no idea." The relationship between Malik and Adwen was complex, and she was never sure from minute to minute what the two were feeling. "Why don't you ask her?"

"She probably won't tell me. She doesn't talk about Malik." A blast of wind buffeted them, and Alice shivered and hurried toward the cottage.

Alice's body was rounding more each day, Brynn noticed. She was glowing with health and the trip seemed to have invigorated rather than taxed her. More, Alice seemed to carry herself with a pride that had never been present during all those years when she had served Adwen. Now the two women were friends rather than servant and mistress, and both had benefitted from the change.

She glanced down at the beach, where Gage sat on an overturned fishing boat, talking to a little group of villagers gathered around him. He was gesturing, smiling a little as he sought to persuade and cajole. His hair shone jet black, not auburn, on this dreary day and blew wild and free in the wind. If it was cold here in the shelter afforded by the row of cottages, the wind must be knife-sharp down there by the water. When Gage came back he would be chilled to the bone and, if Malik was correct, that return would probably not be anytime soon.

Well, she could do nothing for Gage by standing there in the cold, worrying. She moved quickly toward the cottage Malik had designated.

Gage did not return from the beach until after darkness had fallen.

Brynn was standing on the hearth and looked up when he came in the door. "You look terrible. Close that door and come to the fire."

It was no lie. Gage's cheeks appeared chapped and there were lines of exhaustion engraved beside his mouth.

"Fire? What is that?" His lips curved mockingly as he crossed the room and held out his hands to the blaze. He closed his eyes as the heat struck him. "Ah, I remember now."

She unfastened his cloak and laid it on the chair. "Take off your armor."

"In a moment."

"Now. You're so tired, you look as if you could fall asleep at any moment. I don't want to have to pull and tug that heavy mail to get it off you, then."

"Shrew." He fumbled at the leather buckles. "My fingers feel as though they're made of wood."

"Stand still." She rose on tiptoe and unfastened the mail at his shoulders and then undid the other buckles. "Now take it off and the rest of your clothes, too, while I go have the water brought."

"Water?"

"For your bath. LeFont has had his soldiers heating water in readiness for the past hour."

He looked at her oddly. "How kind of LeFont. I've never known him to be so solicitous of my comfort before."

"When you're unclothed, get in there." She nodded at a shallow wooden barrel she had scrounged from the villagers. "It will probably smell of wine, but it's the only thing I could find to use. When I mentioned bathing, the women looked at me as if I were mad."

"Wine is better than the odor of fish I've been smelling all day."

She wrinkled her nose. "You seem to have acquired it," she said as she opened the door.

When she returned he was sitting in the small tub, frowning with annoyance. "Let's get this over," he said impatiently. "I'm stiff. I'm cold. And I have grave doubts of ever getting out of this tub. I think I'm stuck."

"We can always chop the wood away from around you." She motioned to the two soldiers following her, bearing steaming buckets of water.

Four buckets of hot water and a quarter hour later Gage leaned back in the tub with a sigh of contentment.

"Warmer?" Brynn soaped his broad back and then rinsed him.

"Yes. I was beginning to doubt if it would ever happen. By God, that wind was cold."

"You should be accustomed to cold. Isn't Norway a cold land?"

"Yes, but it's been a long time since I was in Norway. Byzantium is warm and Normandy's climate is not unpleasant. I wonder that Hevald decided to venture this far north when he was seeking his land of peace."

"Gwynthal isn't this chill. I told you, the interior of the island is sheltered by high cliffs." She rose to her feet. "I think you're as clean as I can get you in that little tub. Stand up and I'll dry you."

He groaned as he struggled to his feet and then stepped out of the tub. "Almost."

"Almost what?" she asked absently as she toweled him dry.

"You almost had to call LeFont with the hatchet."

"Well, it didn't happen." She draped the huge cloth about him. "And I was lucky to find a tub even this big. It's entirely your fault for growing so large."

"It's a family curse. Hardraada was over seven feet tall."

"Truly?" She had never seen a man of that size.

"Truly."

She shook her head. "Astonishing. Sit down on the hearth while I have the tub removed and then I'll give you some stew."

He settled on the hearth and leaned back against the stones. "May I ask why you're being so kind to me?"

"Because I'm rested and warm and you are not."

"You've never felt the need to equalize before."

"You make it very difficult to be kind to you. You always reach out to take before anyone has a chance to give." The wind whistled into the cottage as she opened the door and called for the soldiers. "Keep that towel about you."

She was frowning when she came back after the tub had been removed. "Malik is actually sitting on Adwen's doorstep."

"I know. I ran into him on my way here and he told me that was his intention."

"What foolishness. It's ice cold out there. Perhaps Adwen is right and I should tell him to go to shelter."

"Leave them alone. Malik wouldn't thank you for your interference."

He was probably right, Brynn thought. Malik usually knew what he was doing.

"My supper," Gage prompted her.

She crossed to the pot of stew bubbling over the flames. "Did you get the boats?"

"Only four." He took the wooden bowl and spoon she handed him. "And they're quite small. None of them will hold more than eight. That means we'll have to leave most of LeFont's men and all the horses here."

"You won't need an overlarge force on Gwynthal."

"I hope not." He finished the bowl of stew before

he said, "But nothing stays the same. Gwynthal may not be the peaceful haven you remember."

"It will be the same," she said quickly. "Gwynthal never changes. More stew?"

"No." He put his bowl on the hearth. "I have something to tell you."

She stiffened warily. "What?"

He threw aside the towel and rose to his feet. "Perhaps I should say I have something to show you." He crossed naked to his clothing piled on the chair and retrieved his leather pouch. "It seems we're not the first strangers to come here this autumn. A week ago they were visited by a young nobleman, fair of hair and comely of face."

"Richard?"

"He didn't give them his name." He opened the pouch. "But he wanted to go to an island north of here. He bought a boat from them together with the services of a young man to help sail it. He paid with this."

She looked down at the small ruby in his palm.

"Is it yours?" he asked.

"Yes. Delmas must have given it to Richard."

"I·thought as much." He gave the ruby to her. "The young man, Walter, gave it to his father to keep for him when he left the village. It seems he had the good sense not to trust anything so valuable on his person while accompanying Richard."

The jewel felt cool and alien against the flesh of her palm. She had worn it all the years of her childhood, but now it seemed as if it didn't belong to her. Any fondness she had felt for it had been tainted by Delmas's greed and Richard's malice. "This Walter might have led Richard to Gwynthal, but he wouldn't have been able to find a place to dock. It was folly for him to even try."

"If Richard did succeed, then we may be met with an unpleasant surprise when we arrive."

"He couldn't find a way," she said positively. She went to her leather pouch in a corner of the room and placed the ruby inside. She doubted if she would ever wear it again. "Gwynthal is safe from him." In spite of her assurances, Richard's appearance on the horizon filled her with unease. He had not been following, he had been ahead of them. It was disconcerting that he was doing the unexpected.

She gathered the blankets in the corner and brought them to the hearth. "These are our own. I aired them earlier this afternoon. The ones on the bed were dirty and I didn't trust them to be insect free." She spread out the blankets. "Do we leave tomorrow?"

"Yes, at first light."

"Then lie down and go to sleep." She took off her gown and settled down. "Why are you standing there? You know you're exhausted."

"Yes." He lay down on his blanket and rolled away from her. "Good night."

She stared at him in astonishment. There was no mistaking the pointed rejection. She curled into a ball, careful not to touch him. "Good night."

There was a silence in the room broken only by the hiss of the burning logs.

"Why?" he asked quietly.

It was what she wanted to ask him regarding his withdrawal from her.

"Why have you been kind to me tonight?" he asked.

"Why were you kind to me in Kythe?"

"Then it's gratitude?"

"Yes. No. Why must you ask for reasons? You were in need and I wanted to give to you." She paused and then said haltingly, "Why are you not holding me? Are you too weary?"

"I've never seen you the way you were at Kythe. I thought to give you time."

Kindness again. "When you hold me . . . I find it pleasant. I feel very much alone and a little frightened. If it would not be too much trouble . . ."

His arms were around her, heavy, warm, shielding. "It's no trouble," he said thickly.

She buried her face in his chest. "Thank you." The thatch of hair on his chest smelled vaguely of soap and the herbs she had tossed into the water. "I don't wish to disturb you."

"Then your wish is in vain. You always disturb me." His arms tightened around her. "Go to sleep. You'll need your rest. It will be an unpleasant voyage on that cold sea tomorrow."

"Yes . . ." Her arms tightened around him. She wanted to talk to him, draw closer to him, but she knew she must lie very still and let him go to sleep. Gage had not had any rest that day, but had suffered the cold and wind for her sake. "We'll both go to sleep. . . ."

She was drowsily aware of the crash of the surf against the rock-strewn shore and the wind's mournful howl. The sounds of desolation only intensified the pleasure of lying before a bright, warm fire, being held close in Gage's arms.

Malik was forced to hold on to his cape with both hands to keep the bitter wind from tearing it from his body.

"The fool is huddled there on the doorstep like a huge sack of barley," Adwen said in exasperation, peering out the window. "Tell him to go away, Alice."

"Tell him yourself. It's between the two of you." Alice yawned as she moved toward her pallet on the far side of the room. "I'm going to sleep. This baby and I both need our rest."

Alice had been Adwen's last hope of avoiding becoming involved in Malik's latest madness. Both Brynn and Alice had stepped aside and left it in her hands.

Well, she would not tell him, Adwen decided. Even if she bothered to try to sweep the idiot off her doorstep, she knew he would not go. She had realized the moment he had told her of his intention that there was more underlying it than the obvious. He was a man who believed in symbols, and if she allowed him to cross her doorstep . . .

He could stay out there all night. She had no desire to have another man in her life when she had not yet rid herself of the first. She now had a freedom and contentment she had never known before. Why would she want a jester who did not take anything seriously?

The wind whipped again and Malik seemed to grow smaller as he contracted to brace against its power. He buried his face in his cloak.

She had been outside only a short time that afternoon. She had been fervently grateful to get back inside the cottage. The weather had been miserable then, and it was much colder now.

We do not have these hideous north winds where I was born.

Well, let him go back to his Byzantium. He should not be among strangers anyway. Except for Gage Dumont, she had sensed he was very much alone. Why had he come to this country where he was regarded as an ignorant heathen? She herself had thought Saracens were ignorant until she had met Malik. Though she would never have admitted it to him, his wit and vast knowledge on all subjects had stunned her. She had found it was she who was ignorant. Since she had rarely been able to leave her sickroom during the years of her marriage, in desperation she had called upon the priest to educate her far beyond a woman's usual lot. To her great annoyance, Malik told her much of what she had learned was wrong and patiently corrected her at every turn.

Thunder.

Was it starting to rain? No, that was only the pounding surf, she realized in relief. Not that it would have made any difference. She would let him drown before she invited him to cross her threshold.

It *was* rain. Big drops falling on the doorstep, being driven like spikes against Malik's shivering body.

"Mother of God!" She took three steps and jerked open the door. "Get in here!"

Malik scrambled to his feet. "I thought you would never ask." He smiled happily. "I was sure I would have to stay out here until I took root. Though how anything could take root and flourish in this inhospitable weather I have no idea. It would be—"

"Be silent." She grasped his arm, pulled him into the cottage, and shut the door. "Alice is trying to sleep." She dragged him over to the fireplace. "I would not have given in, you know. It was the rain."

He nodded. "I should have expected the rain. When the cause is just, God always perseveres." He held out his hands to the blaze and sighed contentedly. "And provides."

She scowled at him. "Have you eaten?"

"Oh, yes, I knew I must fortify myself for the battle." He sat down on the hearth and gracefully crossed his legs. He was always graceful, every movement full of lithe strength and vitality. "Proceed."

"I'm not going to do battle with you. As soon as you've warmed yourself, you will leave."

"It will take a long time to warm myself. You left me for an eternity out in that raging wind."

"I had nothing to do with it."

"You know that is not true. I was out there suffering for your sake."

"Because I made a casual remark? I did but tease you and you did this foolish thing."

"It was not foolish." He gazed into the fire. "I have no respect for William's glorious knights, but they do have a custom that I do approve. When jousting in tournament they carry their lady's favor and dedicate their battle to her."

"What has that to do with anything?"

"My battle was with the wind and cold. I dedicate it to you." He turned and looked into her eyes. "Will you give me your favor?"

She felt a melting deep within her. How beautiful he was in the firelight. Beautiful and more. So much more. "I am still wed."

"That does not stop the ladies of William's court." He nodded ruefully. "But I understand it would seriously hinder you. Do not worry, I am a patient man and I believe that situation will soon be resolved."

She could not stop looking at him. Honor and kindness. Humor and passion. All waiting behind that beautiful mask of which she was so afraid.

"What else?" he asked. "Give me another wall to scale, Adwen."

"This is foolish," she said huskily. "I'm not a prize to be won. Take your sweet words and handsome face to a woman who will—"

"Ah, there it is," he interrupted. "Perhaps the steepest wall of all. You hate my face."

"I *don't* hate your face."

"I think you do. If it displeases you, then we must do something about it." He leaned forward, gingerly took a half-burned twig from the hearth, and lit it from the flames. "It is not the face itself but the comeliness, and that should be easy to fix. A burn on the cheek, perhaps one over the eyebrow . . ."

"What are you doing?" She watched in horror as he brought the flame close to his cheek.

"Scaling the battlements." He smiled as he touched the flame to his bearded cheek. "It's a difficult—"

"Fool!" She knocked the twig from his hand. "Madman! You would have actually done it."

"With great reluctance. I detest pain." He raised his brows. "It would be easier for me if you'd do it yourself."

"Me? You wish me to burn you?"

"I told you. My face offends you, therefore we must rid ourselves of the problem."

He would do it. Just as he had sat four hours out in that freezing cold. "You fool. You idiot. You—" Tears were running down her cheeks. "Don't you dare— Promise me you won't—"

"Shh . . . I take it you do not hate it that much?"

"Promise me."

His hand reached out and touched the path of her tears. "If you promise to look beyond the face to the man."

She nodded jerkily.

He gave a sigh of relief. "Ah, another wall scaled without a wound."

She couldn't say the same. She was not sure whether she had suffered a hurt or if an old wound had been opened to release its poison. All she knew was that she felt shaken and vulnerable as never before in her life. She had to retreat, to put up defenses. She wiped her cheeks on the backs of her hands and forced her tone to tartness. "You've not come out unscathed. Your beard is singed."

"I will shave it off tomorrow." He suddenly frowned. "But that may not be a good thing."

"Why not?"

"I have a confession to make."

"What?"

His eyes lit with mischief. "Without my beard I'm twice as handsome. A virtual Adonis. Men are so jealous, they wish to do battle, and women swoon as I pass.

The sun has been known to hide behind a cloud because of the radiance of my—"

"I cannot bear this," Adwen said, groaning.

"But you are laughing. That is good."

Her laughter faded. "I don't want to be a wife again. I did not find it pleasant."

"How could you have, wed to that foul vermin? I will have to strive to convince you it is not always so." He reached out and took her hand. "I will bring you joy, Adwen."

She could almost believe him. His touch was igniting waves of strange feeling throughout her body that filled her with uneasiness. The barriers must be built higher. She jerked her hand away. "Alice told me that the soldiers tell tales of the joy you bring to all women. I would not be one of many."

"You would not be one—" He stopped, searching for words. "I will not tell you that I sampled these women because I was in search of the perfect woman. It would not be fair to them when they brought me great joy. I *like* women. I find them glorious in body and far stronger and close to the divine than most of us poor males." He held up his hand when Adwen opened her lips to speak. "But, when I saw you, I knew that you were the woman who would complete me. What we will be together will be without equal." He held out his hand to her again. "And it will break my heart if you will not give me your favor, Adwen."

She could not take his hand. If she did, she would yield all she had fought for this night.

She must not take his hand. She would not give up her freedom.

She took his hand. "This means nothing," she whispered. "I will not lie with you. I make no promises."

His hand tightened around her own. "I do not ask either. We will just sit before the fire and hold hands and enjoy being part of each other. You will flow into me and I will flow into you. You will see how sweet it can be."

Closeness. Sweetness. A singing in the soul. A merging without merging.

"You see?" Malik asked.

"I have a question to ask," she said dreamily.

"Anything."

"Are you really twice as handsome without your beard?"

"No, I lied." He paused. "I'm four times more comely. That's why I grew the beard. I could not bear to cause such envy among—"

"Be silent." She was laughing again. "You're probably as ugly as sin. I've no doubt that beard masks a weak chin and your vanity is . . ." She trailed off as she realized in how many ways he had moved her this night. Humor and tears and this precious closeness she had never known.

It had been a mistake to let him in. Now there might be no turning back.

She closed her eyes and repeated desperately, "I make no promises."

But she could not bring herself to release his hand.

Twelve

GAGE!

Brynn's eyes flew open, her heart pounding with terror.

Blood. Gage. Death.

No!

Then, as she came fully awake, a shudder of relief went through her. A dream. Only a dream.

Gage was next to her in front of the fire, breathing deeply, evenly, his arms still in a loose embrace about her. She lay there, staring at him.

Gage staggering forward, the hilt of a dagger protruding from his back, falling . . .

Only a dream. Dreams did not always come true. Actually, only a few of her dreams had become reality. She had been worried about Richard when she had fallen asleep, and her fears had no doubt tricked her into that horrible nightmare.

But what if it were a true vision? What if Gage were destined to die in such a horrid manner?

The pain that tore through her was unbearable.

His eyes flew open as if she had called him. "Brynn?"

Her trembling hands reached out to touch his face. Firm, warm, and vibrant with life.

"What is it?" Gage asked.

She did not want to speak of it. It was only a dream. He wouldn't believe it had any portent anyway. Forget it. Bury it. "I didn't mean to wake you." Her fingers brushed his lips. "It was only a dream."

"More of a nightmare judging by the way you're shaking."

"Yes." She nestled closer to his warm, hard body. "But it's gone now."

"Is it?"

Not entirely, the chill still lingered. "Quite gone." She buried her face in the hollow of his shoulder. "And it won't come back."

He chuckled. "Because you will it so."

Hope leapt within her at his words. Destiny could be fought. She battled the dragons every time she healed an affliction, and she knew many would have died if she had not intervened. Even if the dream were a true vision, who was to say she could not change fate? "Yes, that's right. Because I will it so."

But what if she did not prevail? What if these moments were among the last they would spend together?

Silence except for the hiss and crackle of the burning logs.

"If you have need—I would not deny you," she said in a muffled voice.

He stiffened. "Need?"

She did not answer.

"Lust?" he asked. "I'm curious to know why, after refusing me for days, I'm to receive this splendid gift. What of guilt? Am I suddenly less a murderer? Have the angels come down to whisper to you of my innocence?"

"No." She was silent a moment and then blurted out, "Why do you ask questions? You want this, take it."

"Why?" he persisted. "What of your own guilt? Are you no longer Bathsheba?"

"I'm still guilty. That will always remain. Always." She swallowed. "Why are you arguing with me? You said that I must learn to accept what happened. I've done it, and that's the end of it."

"But why have you accepted it?" He pushed her away from him and lifted her chin on the arc of his finger. "Why now?"

Tears stung her eyes so that she could barely see. "It has come to me . . . that I have . . . a certain affection for you."

"What kind of affection?"

He would not relent, and she was weary of fighting him. "It is my belief . . . that I . . . love you."

His breath released explosively. "I believe you do too, and, by God, it's past time you admitted it. Now, what are we to do about it?"

"I've already told you what you can do about it."

"I'm to be allowed to spill my seed into your body? That's not good enough."

"It would have been good enough two nights ago."

"But that was before I realized what strides I've been making. Will you wed me?"

"No, I cannot."

"You can and will. You've said you've accepted my transgressions. Take the next step."

"You ask too much."

"No more than I give."

"It's easier for you. You have no—" She stopped, hesitating.

"Honor? Conscience?"

She shook her head. "You do have honor, but we look at things differently."

"Then teach me to view the world as you do." He smiled crookedly. "I don't promise to accept, but at least I'd understand."

He had understood about her mother, about the gift, but he would never view the world as she did. "I've told you what I offer you. Will you take it?"

He gazed at her for a long time. "No."

A ripple of shock went through her at the rejection. He had made sure she knew the pain he suffered from thwarted lust.

"You should be surprised. I'm surprised myself." He removed his arms and shifted away from her. "Good night, Brynn."

He turned his back on her.

"You're a very changeable man," she said, stung. "And clearly have no idea of what you wish."

He kept his back turned to her. "I know exactly what I wish, and I have no intention of sacrificing an entire caravan for a camel."

She frowned in puzzlement. "What is a camel?"

"A hump-backed creature I use for desert trading."

"And I am this camel?"

"There are similarities. You're equally stubborn and carry more burdens on your back than a dozen camels. I won't be one of them. You may have forgiven me, but not yourself."

"I don't need to forgive myself to give to you."

"But I need you to forgive yourself. For some odd reason, I find it necessary that you come to me with a whole heart." He added wearily, "Go back to sleep. Perhaps your dreams will be more pleasant this time."

The dream.

Fear rushed back to her. She wanted to reach out and touch him, take him into her, but he had made it impossible. She realized by this restraint he thought he could get her to yield more, but it filled her with desperation. She did not want him to withdraw from her at this crucial time. She wanted to give him whatever pleasure she could, take what she could. She did not want him to be alone.

Blood. Gage. Death.
It might not come true.
Pray God it would not.

"Are you sure this is your Gwynthal?" Adwen wrinkled her nose. "I see nothing pleasant about it. It looks to be a hard, cold place."

An eager smile lit Brynn's face at the sight of the sheer limestone cliffs. "It's not like that when you reach the interior. Once you get beyond the rocks and into the valley—" She stopped as she saw Adwen's skeptical expression. "You'll see."

"Let's hope we all will," Gage said, still rowing strongly against the rough waves. He glimpsed the three other boats behind their own. "Providing you'll kindly guide us beyond those rocks before we're all dashed to pieces."

Brynn pulled her glance away from the island. "To the north, around the headland. There's a cove . . ."

"I see no cove," Gage said.

"It's behind that huge black rock."

"Rock? It looks to be a cliff."

"There's a cove behind it. Swing to the east and then around the far end."

Everything was blessedly familiar. Even the sea gulls' scream was a song of welcome. She was home.

"Where's the village?" Gage asked.

Brynn pointed to a path leading from the beach straight up the hill. "It's right over that crest, but the castle is several miles distant."

"Castle?"

"Did you think Hevald would live in a hovel? He built a fine castle when he came here." The boat reached the shore and Brynn didn't wait for Gage to help her but jumped out onto the rocks. "You'll approve, I'm sure. It's a fine stone castle. He had no fear of invasion, but he wanted to make sure his home would withstand the years as well as the weather."

"And did it?"

"Of course it did." She frowned. "Though, when last I saw it, the years and neglect had taken their price. It's a sad place now."

"Sad?" Adwen asked.

Brynn shifted her shoulders uneasily. She did not want to think of that sadness or anything that was less than perfect about Gwynthal. "Perhaps it was only a child's fancy." She started up the rocky path she'd indicated. "Let's go to the village. I want you to see—"

"Come back," Gage called out. "There's no need to rush. We'll wait for the others."

He was wary of what he would find on Gwynthal, she realized as she retraced her steps. It was a legitimate fear, since Gwynthal was unknown to him.

But she was home.

Adwen stepped closer and took her hand. "I'm sorry I misspoke your Gwynthal, Brynn. I'm sure it's a fine and lovely place."

Brynn knew Adwen was not certain of any such thing but feared she might have hurt Brynn's feelings. "Why should I mind? Gwynthal has survived the centuries by appearing to be uninviting." She glanced at the other boats nearing the shore. "But I wish they would hurry. I can't wait to be on our way."

"Do you remember anyone living in the village?"

"Of course I do. We lived at Falkhaar and not the village, but I knew—" She stopped. Whom did she know? Her happy memories of Gwynthal were of running through the forests, learning herb lore from her mother, playing on the grounds of the castle. Everything else was vague and distorted. "I knew Father Thomas, the priest."

"Not a wide acquaintance," Gage said dryly. "Is the treasure near this village?"

She shook her head. "No, in the forest beyond the castle."

"Then let's push forward and retrieve it," Malik said as he jumped out of the second boat. "And get away from this chill shore."

"Are you still cold?" Adwen asked. "Perhaps you shouldn't have shaved off your beard."

"Ah, yes, I do miss it." Malik beamed at her. "Not only did it keep my face warm, but it hid my weak chin."

"True. Well, perhaps you can grow another one."

Brynn stared at both of them in bewilderment. Malik had no weak chin, and without his beard he was even more handsome. When he had appeared at the boats two days earlier, she had been stunned at the difference, but since he had commanded the second boat she had not had an opportunity to see Adwen's reaction to the change.

"If God wills," Malik said. He and Adwen exchanged another look and Brynn suddenly felt a pang of envy. A secret joke among lovers. She should have realized that a step had been taken. The tartness in Adwen had mellowed, Malik's concern eased.

The third boat was landing and LeFont stepped out, lifted Alice to the shore, and immediately began barking orders to the other soldiers in the boat regarding the unloading of the supplies.

"Is this the only landing place on the island?" Gage asked Brynn.

"Yes." She turned away from watching LeFont. "May we go now?"

"As soon as I give LeFont his orders," Gage said. "He's to stay here and guard the boats until we return."

"There are no thieves on Gwynthal."

"How do you know? You seem to have little acquaintance here."

"My mother told me."

"Your mother wouldn't have lied to you, but when you're away you sometimes don't remember things clearly." He met her gaze. "The guards stay here."

He was not speaking only of her mother. He was warning her that her own memories might not be true. "It's a waste of LeFont's time, but do as you wish."

"I will." He crossed the distance separating him from LeFont.

"But it's truly a waste," she muttered to his retreating back.

"Perhaps," Malik said. "But he may also be thinking of another danger."

"Richard? You think he might have followed us?"

"It is possible. He could have hidden down the coast from Selkirk waiting for us to arrive and then set sail when we did."

"We saw no sign of him on the way here."

"But we had fog for a good portion of the way. It's easy to hide in the fog."

"And when it cleared he could have stayed just far enough away to keep LeFont's sail in view," Adwen said matter-of-factly.

Adwen was not afraid and Brynn should not have been either. After all, Richard was only one man. Even if he found the way into the cove he would not be able to prevail against their numbers.

Gage.

Blood.

But she hadn't seen Richard in the dream. Only Gage and the dagger . . .

"Brynn." Alice was beside her, her voice thin and strained. "I would speak with you."

Brynn was immediately jarred back to the present. "Are you well? How did you stand the journey?"

"Fine. Captain LeFont and the other soldiers were very kind to me."

"It was a long trip, but you'll feel better once we start walking. I'm sure you feel cramped and—"

"I want to stay here," Alice interrupted. "I don't want to go with you."

Brynn frowned in puzzlement. "Why not?"

Alice flushed. "I'm weary of travel. Will you tell Lord Gage?"

"But you're with child. You may need me."

"I'm strong and healthy, and so is my child. I'm months from my term. I'll wait for you here."

"Don't you wish to meet the villagers? If you're to stay, you'll need to find a place to settle."

The flush grew deeper. "I may not choose to stay on Gwynthal."

Brynn's eyes widened in shock. "Why not? I thought we'd agreed that you'd settle here with your child. Once you become accustomed to it, you'll like it here. It's much more pleasant once you leave the coast and the people are kinder than at Redfern."

"I didn't agree. You just—I know you thought you were doing what was best for me, but I may not—" She stopped, looking thoroughly miserable. "Will you tell Lord Gage?"

"Of course," Brynn said. "If you truly wish it."

"Oh, I do. I do," Alice said fervently. "You don't need me, and I'll be of much more use here. I can cook for the soldiers and gather wood for fires. . . ." She was already hurrying back to the shore.

"Listen to her." Brynn shook her head. "We shouldn't leave her. She'll tire herself, waiting on all those men."

Adwen shook her head. "LeFont won't permit her to exhaust herself. Haven't you noticed how careful he is of her well-being?"

"LeFont?" Brynn asked, startled. "No."

"Then you're certainly blind." Adwen chuckled. "He treats her as if she's made of eggshells." She smiled indulgently as she watched Alice hurry toward the captain. "And she treats him as if he were a god from Olympus."

"Fortunate soul," Malik murmured. "Some men are given worship while others receive only abuse."

"She doesn't want to stay on Gwynthal because she has a fondness for the captain?" Adwen was right. She had been blind, Brynn thought, too involved in her own concerns to notice what was going on around her. Now she remembered the many times on the trail she had seen Alice and LeFont talking, laughing. "But she's bearing another man's child. What if he will not wed her?"

"I think he will." Malik added gently, "And if he does not, she must take the consequences of her acts. You cannot cure her woes as you would her body, Brynn."

"What kind of life will she lead as the wife of a soldier? She would be much safer if she stayed here."

"But perhaps not as happy. We do not all value peace as much as you do. Let her go to LeFont."

"You speak as if I were holding her captive. She can go where she wills. I want only what's best for her." Yet she did feel an odd sense of betrayal and loneliness. She had looked forward to having a friend there after the others left. She went to meet Gage, who was returning from speaking to LeFont. "I've been talking to Alice."

His eyes narrowed. "She told you about LeFont?"

Another surprise. "You knew too?"

"I knew they were spending a great deal of time together and LeFont was behaving in an unusual manner. There's usually a woman behind such conduct."

She forced a smile. "Well, then it won't surprise you that Alice wishes to remain here instead of going with us."

"He's a fine soldier and a good man, Brynn."

"Yes, he is." She changed the subject. "Will all the soldiers remain here?"

"I'll make that decision once we've met the villagers. Do most of the islanders live in the village?"

"Yes, but there are several farms between here and the castle."

"And are these farmers friendly?"

She tried to remember. She was beginning to realize what an isolated life she had led as a child. They had come to the village only on rare occasions and she had but a vague memory of staying the night at a farmer's house on the journey from Falkhaar. Friendly? They had been welcomed and accepted, but she could not recall. . . . "They won't attack us, if that's what you mean."

"That's what I mean. I don't want them to embrace us, just not kill us."

"I told you Gwynthal was a place of peace. It takes greed to breed discontent, and we've always been content."

"Even when they see us with packhorses bearing treasure?" He smiled cynically. "I think that would make anyone a trifle discontent with their own lot."

She shook her head. "What would they do with gold and jewels? It would have no value here; Gwynthal has its own barter system."

"They could sail away to the outer world, where it does have value." He paused. "As your father did."

"My father was not . . . he was not like the other men here." All of these questions were making her uneasy and tainting the joy of homecoming. She wanted to be done with them. "Are you coming, or are you going to linger forever?" She didn't wait for an answer but started up the trail. When she glanced over her shoulder, Gage was right behind her, followed closely by Malik and Adwen.

When they reached the top of the hill, she stopped and took in the sight below. Gwynthal.

Verdant dense forests; solitary and sensuous. Blue lakes. Rich, rolling farmland. This was the Gwynthal she remembered, the Gwynthal of a thousand dreams.

She turned and said eagerly, "See? Didn't I tell you? Isn't it beautiful?"

"Everything is still green here," Adwen murmured. "The leaves are only starting to fall. How extraordinary."

"The interior of the island is all valley. I think the cliffs protect us from most of the harsher weather. I can remember perhaps only one snow a year as a child." She pointed in the distance. "Look, you can see the towers of the castle from here."

Gray towers and battlements wreathed in mists, waiting for her.

I've come home, Hevald. I've come home.

"How long is the journey?" Malik asked.

"Two days." She indicated a forest beyond the castle. "And that's Falkhaar Forest."

"Where you grew up?"

She nodded as she stood, looking at the forest. "We had a small cottage near the castle. It's where we've always lived, since the days of Hevald. I wonder if it's still there. . . ."

"Why shouldn't it be?" Gage asked. "The weather is mild and without flaw and, if there are no robbers or sinners of any sort on your island, the cottage should be as you left it. Surely you don't have doubts?"

She lifted her chin at the faint mockery in his tone. "I have no doubts." She set out down the hill toward the village. "It was a slip of the tongue."

"Your village is very quiet," Adwen said as she paused to peer into the window of a shop. "I've seen only a few people and they ran into their houses and shut the door when they saw us."

"They're not used to outsiders. No one comes here." But she wasn't a stranger, Brynn thought. She belonged here and, unreasonable though it might be, the silent rejection hurt.

"And that's the way you all like it," Gage said. "Safety. Security. No visits from the outside world."

Brynn's jaw set. "That's the way we like it."

"My village was a little like this," Malik said. "But then the drought came and we had to go out into the world to save ourselves."

"There usually comes a time when you have to leave the womb and venture forth." Gage glanced at Brynn. "Or you become lazy and dull or die of sluggishness."

"They're not lazy or dull," Brynn said.

"Then why wasn't there a guard on the cove? Your Eden should have been protected from invaders."

"I told you, no one knows the way—"

"We did."

"Because I brought you." She glared at him. "I told you that you wouldn't understand, that you didn't belong. We need no guard to keep—"

"Who are you?"

She whirled to see a white-haired old man in the robes of a priest standing in the path before them. She felt a rush of relief; she knew that face.

She stepped forward. "Father Thomas?"

He ignored her. His faded blue eyes were wary as they fastened on Gage over her head. "What do you do here?"

"Don't you remember me? I'm Brynn of Falkhaar."

He shifted his attention to her. "Falkhaar?"

"You knew my mother, Mairle."

A flicker of emotion other than distrust crossed his

lined face. "She had the gift. She cheated us of it when she went away. Is she with you?"

"No, my mother died." She persisted. "I'm Brynn. Do you remember me? We visited you whenever we came to the village."

He stared at Gage once more and said accusingly, "He's a stranger. You should not have brought him. We don't like strangers here."

"He won't stay. I'm taking him to Falkhaar and then he'll leave the island."

Father Thomas shook his head. "You should not have brought him. He's not one of us." Then his glance encountered Malik and he stiffened at the sight of the Saracen's bronze skin. "This one either. Dark as Satan . . ."

"We are most certainly not one of you. Nor do we want to be," Gage said. "But I assure you Malik has satanic impulses only on occasion. The rest of the time he's fairly innocuous."

"Take them away," Father Thomas muttered, backing away. "Different. Wicked. They're different from us. . . ."

"They're not wicked." Brynn followed him. "Different doesn't have to be bad."

Father Thomas looked at her in astonishment. "Of course it does."

"It *doesn't*. Listen to me, I know these—" She was talking to air. Father Thomas was stalking away down the street.

"I believe we may have trouble obtaining horses and pack mules," Malik murmured. "Your one acquaintance doesn't appear to be overwelcoming, Brynn."

"He's an old man and his mind seems clouded," Brynn said defensively. "I'm sure the others will be more accommodating."

"If we can get them to come out of hiding or open the doors," Gage said dryly.

Adwen nodded. "Perhaps Brynn should try to go to them. She belongs here."

At the moment Brynn felt more of a stranger than any of them. If Father Thomas had not known her, then she could not expect recognition from anyone else. The priest had even spoken with resentment of her mother. Did the rest of the islanders feel the same? She straightened her shoulders and smiled with effort. "Yes, I belong here. You wait here and I'll go—"

"Take Brynn and Adwen to the edge of the village, Malik." Gage turned on his heel. "I'm accustomed to bartering with people who have no trust."

Brynn felt a rush of relief but felt bound to offer, "I'll go with you."

"I don't need you. Wait for me." The smile he gave her was surprisingly gentle. "I do better alone."

Malik watched him go up to the first cottage and knock on the door before turning away. "Come, we will do as Gage suggests. Perhaps we can find a place to make camp. He may get us the animals, but I doubt we'll be given lodging for the night."

It was not the homecoming Brynn had envisioned. Even the unfriendly folk at Selkirk had been persuaded to give them shelter.

"Don't be disappointed," Adwen whispered as she took Brynn's arm in comfort. "What does it matter that an old man thinks we're enemies? You said you didn't know any of these villagers anyway."

Brynn nodded brusquely as she started after Malik. Adwen was right, of course, she had merely voiced aloud Brynn's thoughts. She shouldn't be sad or uneasy because of this encounter. Everything would be fine once they reached Falkhaar.

Gage was able to obtain only four ancient horses and three small donkeys.

When he led the animals into the camp after dusk

that evening, Malik took one look at them and shook his head. "I am disappointed in you. Is this the man my people call the Prince of Barter? These creatures may fall dead before we reach the end of another day."

"They're not that bad," Gage said testily. "We don't need battle steeds or mounts capable of enduring vast distances."

"No, but we do need horses capable of putting one foot in front of another."

"Then go and make your own bargain," Gage said as he sat down before the fire and held out his hands. "But don't expect to be back by morning or be offered anything better."

"Unfriendly?" Malik asked.

"You were more friendly when you put your sword through my arm on our first meeting." Gage shrugged. "But they're no threat. I doubt if there's a weapon in the entire village. They stared at me as if I were a wolf looking for his dinner."

"It's a natural response," Brynn said quickly. "You have a fierce manner about you."

"Yes, I do." He grimaced. "And my manner would have gotten even fiercer if I'd stayed among those sheep much longer. I was tempted to trim their fleece every time they sidled away from me."

"They're not sheep."

"Close enough." He took the bowl Malik handed him, ladled out stew, and started to eat. "But not too meek not to try to best me in a bargain."

"I will stake these poor specimens where there is more grass," Malik said as he took the reins of the animals. "Who knows? It may be their last meal. Will you help me, Adwen?"

"You can't even lead a horse to grass without aid?" In spite of her scornful words, Adwen jumped to her feet and followed him.

"The people here aren't sheep," Brynn repeated. "They've just been trained to live in peace."

"By Hevald the magnificent."

"Why are you being so cruel?" She bit her lower lip. "You act as if you hate them."

He finished the stew before saying wearily, "Perhaps I do. Perhaps I want them to be without virtue because then they won't matter to you." He set the bowl down and stared into the fire. "A few of the villagers with whom I talked remembered your mother . . . and you."

"You asked about her?"

"Of course I asked them about her," he said roughly. "I could see how that old priest hurt you by his indifference."

"I wasn't hurt."

"The devil you weren't."

"I just don't understand why he would think she had cheated them. She loved them. Perhaps it is only Father Thomas who feels that way. Surely the others don't resent her."

Gage stared into the fire.

"Do they?" she whispered.

"No, of course not. It was only that crazy old man."

He wasn't telling the truth. Gage, who never lied, was lying now, hoping to save her from hurt.

"It isn't fair. Until she left, she gave her gift freely."

"Perhaps too freely. Maybe they grew to think it belonged to them because it was always there. You might learn a lesson from her mistake." He changed the subject. "Where in Falkhaar Forest is this treasure located?"

"There's a cave in the side of the cliff bordering the south side of the island. That's where the treasure is hidden."

"Providing it's still there." He paused. "Did your mother ever tell your father of the treasure?"

He thought her father might have come back and stolen the treasure, she realized. "No."

"Why not?"

"I don't think she trusted him."

"Yet she loved him enough to leave Gwynthal and follow him."

"I didn't say she didn't love him. She just didn't trust him. She was afraid he would bring strangers here to take the treasure and hurt Gwynthal."

"As you've done."

"But this is different. You'll go away and leave us alone. You would never hurt Gwynthal."

"How do you know?"

"You just wouldn't. You have honor."

"Good God, I believe you're saying you trust in me."

She stared into the flames. "I do—trust—you."

He muttered an imprecation beneath his breath. "At last. Wresting admissions from you is like wading through quicksand." He paused. "You trust me totally or with reservations?"

He wanted her to say she believed he had not killed Delmas. She could not do it. "I think you would not hurt anything I loved."

"With reservations. Well, it's better than nothing." He looked out into the darkness. "It's a day's journey to Hevald's castle?"

"Yes."

"And another day to the cave?"

She nodded.

"Then in less than a week's time we should be back at the ship with the treasure."

And then he would sail out of her life. The pain the thought brought was terrible in intensity.

"Oh, no, you won't rid yourself of me that easily." Gage's stare was fastened on her face. "We'll come to terms long before that."

It was odd how he seemed able to read her thoughts. Odd and a little frightening. He was coming closer with every day that passed. "I wanted to speak to you about the treasure. I want a portion of it to go to Adwen and a smaller one to Alice. The treasure will allow them some measure of independence."

"They may not need it."

He meant that both Adwen and Alice had found loving protectors. She experienced again that pang of loneliness. "I still want them to have it. The treasure is vast; you will hardly miss a tiny share."

"And nothing for Brynn?"

She shook her head. "I've never wanted riches. I won't need it. Will you promise me?"

"If you like. But riches for a woman sometimes brings more danger than safety."

"Because men prey on women and try to take their riches from them." Brynn had seen that among the noble families in England. "Then I'll require another promise from you. I wish you to defend Adwen and Alice from those who would take the treasure from them."

"Now, that's a promise fraught with trouble."

"Will you do it?"

"Yes, I'll do it." He smiled lopsidedly. "But I find it curious that a woman seeking only peace should be so determined to involve me in war."

"You involve yourself in war. If you must do battle, it should at least be in good cause."

He chuckled. "In the cause of those you care about."

"Yes." She lay down on the pallet and closed her eyes. "Come to bed. We must start early if we're to reach the castle before nightfall."

He was beside her, the blanket warm over them and his arms enfolding her. "Poor Brynn, it's been a difficult day for you."

It had been difficult. She had come expecting— She didn't know what she had expected, but it wasn't coldness or this feeling of not belonging. "It will be different at Falkhaar."

"I hope it will. I don't like you hurt." His lips feathered her brow. "And it makes me angry that there are no dragons, only sheep to fight."

"They're not—" She gave it up; she did not want to argue with him. In less than a week she would no longer have his arms around her. She nestled closer, her cheek in the hollow of his shoulder. "I expected too much. It will take time to become accustomed to Gwynthal again."

He didn't answer. It seemed he didn't wish to argue with her either. Maybe he recognized that this might be one of their last times together. Perhaps he was becoming resigned to her staying here after all. . . .

Gage!

Dagger!

Blood dripping on the grass, running into the veined leaves lying beneath the trees.

Brynn lunged upright, her breasts rising and falling with the effort to breathe.

"Another nightmare?" Gage asked drowsily without opening his eyes. "Go back to sleep." He pulled her down and cuddled her close.

Her heart was beating so hard, she was sure Adwen and Malik could hear it across the fire. "I will." She deliberately relaxed her taut muscles. She did not want Gage to come fully awake and ask questions.

The same dream.

No, not quite the same. Before she had seen only Gage and the dagger. This time she had seen the place. Trees. Grass. Leaves lying on the ground.

Blood on the leaves.

She shuddered and felt Gage's arms tighten about her.

She deliberately relaxed again. A nightmare. It didn't have to be true.

But this was only the second death dream she had had more than once.

Kythe. The flames.

There were grass and trees all around them, she realized in sudden panic. It could happen there, that night.

No, it had been daylight in the dream. She still had time. She could keep it from happening.

She must keep it from coming true. She would watch and guard and keep him from all harm. She would not let him be taken from her. She would not let the dragons have him.

"All right?" Gage murmured as if sensing her inner turmoil.

"Shh, everything is fine." Her arms tightened about him with fierce maternal strength. "I promise you, all will be well."

Thirteen

"MAY I ASK why you've been watching me as if you think I'm going to cut off your head and serve it to Malik for his supper?" Gage asked impatiently.

"Please," Malik protested. "I've been called a heathen but never a human-flesh eater."

Gage ignored him, his gaze fixed on Brynn. "Well?"

"I don't know what you mean," Brynn said haltingly. "I was not aware of staring at you. I think you must be imagining it."

"I wasn't imagining it. Since you woke this morning you've been—"

"Look!" With relief at the distraction, Brynn pointed at the towers that had suddenly come into view. "There's the castle! Is it not beautiful?"

Adwen's eyes widened. "It's truly wondrous. I've never seen such a fine castle."

Brynn turned to Gage. "Do you have any in Normandy so grand?"

"I've never seen one this large," Gage admitted. "My own Bellerieve looks tiny in comparison and even William's castle is smaller."

"Hevald needed a large castle. Once he arrived

here he made himself king and his captains and lieutenants knights." She kicked her mare, sending the horse cantering. "Come along, there's a fine moat to see. It's like—" She abruptly reined in as she realized her eagerness had almost played her false. She had been going to ride ahead and she must not let Gage out of her sight. She turned her horse and waited for them to catch up. "Hurry. You're very slow. Don't you want to see it?"

Gage was coolly speculative. "Why did you stop?"

"Why not? I've been here many times before. I grew up playing in the grand hall and the other chambers. After Selbar became my friend we played in the courtyard all the time. It's you who have never seen it." She turned to Adwen. "We can sleep under a roof tonight."

"Maybe." Gage clearly remained doubtful. "Your castle is nearly in ruins."

"It is not," she defended. "It's still as strong as ever. I didn't say it was in good repair."

"What happened here? Why isn't the castle occupied?"

"They're all gone." She rode over the drawbridge and through the gates. She had forgotten how desolate a sight was the deserted castle until she saw it through their eyes. Grass sprouted between the stones of the courtyard, and the second step leading to the front entrance was broken. Yet the decay did not bother her as much as the silence. "I told you it was a sad place."

"I think we'd better leave here and make camp in the forest," Gage said. "There's no telling what you might find in those halls."

Blood running into the veins of the green leaves on the ground.

"No!" Brynn slipped quickly from the mare's back. "I want to spend the night here at the castle. There's nothing harmful here."

Nothing as harmful as what might await them in the forest.

She turned to Adwen. "There's a covered well across the courtyard and the chimneys drew well at the time I left. We might even have baths."

"Baths," Adwen murmured wistfully.

"Surely it would do no harm to use the castle," Malik said to Gage. "We can triumph over a few rats and cockroaches."

Gage looked up at the dark windows of the towers. "If it's only cockroaches . . ." he murmured. "I have a strange feeling that—" He shrugged. "Foolishness. We will stay if it pleases you," he told Brynn.

"It pleases me," she said firmly.

"Good." Malik dismounted and lifted Adwen down from her horse. "Let's go find that well and make sure it's still free of pollution."

Brynn watched them stroll across the courtyard before turning back to Gage.

He was standing with head lifted as if he were listening to something, his expression curiously intent while he stared at the castle.

"They're here, aren't they?" she asked softly.

He looked at her. "Who?"

"Hevald and his bride and all his brave knights. I've always felt them here."

"Nonsense."

She shook her head. "Sometimes the spirits remain for one reason or another. That's why this is a sad place. It's not good to cling to earth instead of heaven." She smiled. "I thought you'd be able to feel them."

"Why?"

"Because you're a warrior, like Hevald. I can see you striding through these halls in your armor. . . ." She could imagine it clearly, his dark hair glowing red as he passed the tall arched windows on his way to the hall to join Hevald and the other knights. She could almost hear the clink of armor. . . . "There's nothing to fear. I think you'll feel at home here."

"And I think you're a little mad, Brynn of Falkhaar." But there was no mockery, only gentleness in his voice. He turned away and began to gather the horses' reins. "Go inside and see if you can find us a place to sleep that's not overrun by creatures. I'll take these animals into the forest and stake them out where there's plentiful grass."

The forest!

"I'll go with you," she said quickly as she snatched the donkeys' reins and followed him. "You may need help."

"I need no help."

She was already pulling the small donkeys toward the gates. "Of course you do. You cannot possibly tend to all these animals by yourself."

To her relief, he didn't argue but merely smiled teasingly. "Perhaps your spirits could give me aid."

"I think they're too absorbed in their own concerns to bother with ours."

"How selfish of them." He led the three horses across the drawbridge and into the forest. "And I was thinking your Hevald such a splendid fellow. You'd think he'd offer—what are you looking for?"

Brynn jerked her gaze from the surrounding shrubbery. "Why, grass for grazing. What else would I be looking for?"

Suspicion showed in his face. "That's what I'm asking."

She avoided his glance as she led the donkey to a grassy patch and tied him to a tree. "That should do splendidly. Can't you hurry? I want to get back and see if Malik has found the well still usable."

For an instant she thought he was going to pursue the matter, but then he turned away and started to unsaddle the horses. "What about wolves?"

"What?"

"Are the animals safe? You said there were wolves in this forest."

"It was much farther north where I found Selbar." Selbar. She felt a surge of warmth as she thought of the wolf. She would see him soon, perhaps even tomorrow. "Wolves don't range far when game is plentiful in their own territory. I've never seen one close to the castle."

"You think your wolf will still be alive?"

She had never considered anything else. "Of course, he was very young when I found him. He will be in his prime now."

"I don't imagine wolves often die of old age." He finished tying the leads to the trees. "And you said you knew him for only a short time before you left Gwynthal. If he's gone back to his pack, he may have forgotten you."

"I haven't forgotten him."

"He's only a beast, Brynn."

"I know." Yet he had been more than a beast to her. After she had healed him, he had been companion and playmate, a bulwark against the loneliness of being in the circle. "He won't have forgotten me."

"It could be dangerous to approach him."

"He'll come to me."

"With pack in tow?"

"I don't want to talk about Selbar. It will be fine."

"We have to talk about him." He turned to face her. "I won't see you hurt again."

"I told you, he won't attack me."

"But he may not remember you any more than that priest in the village did. Prepare yourself for it."

"You don't understand. Selbar will be different. He truly cared about me."

"I hope you're right."

"I'm right." She had to be right about Selbar. In many ways he was Gwynthal to her—wild and beautiful and part of her. She couldn't bear the thought of losing him. She turned and started back toward the castle. "You'll see."

He fell into step with her and said grimly, "I most certainly will. For I have no intention of letting your first encounter with your wolf be without me."

The water in the well was unpolluted, but they waited until they had swept and laid fires in the hall before they heated water for baths.

It was fully dark before they settled before the large fireplace to eat the bird Malik had brought down earlier in the day.

"This is truly a splendid castle," Adwen said. "I wonder that some of the villagers didn't come here to settle instead of staying along the coast." She finished her piece of meat and reached for another. "It's such a waste. You said that there is no member of Hevald's family living?"

Brynn shook her head. "His wife bore no children."

"How sad." Adwen added with a touch of bitterness, "He must have been very disappointed."

Brynn knew she was attributing to Hevald her own husband's response. "Yes, he wanted an heir for all this, but it was said he never blamed his bride. He loved her with his whole heart."

"Myth," Adwen scoffed. "Men always find fault with the woman where their issue is concerned. I'm sure your noble Hevald was the same."

"I don't agree," Malik said. "It's not entirely unlikely a man would find a woman more important than her issue."

Adwen met his gaze. "It's easy to say that when the circumstance is not your own. You might feel differently when other men display their fine, strong sons and you have none."

"I would not feel differently."

They were not talking of Hevald's barren wife, Brynn realized. The air seemed to vibrate with Adwen's pain. Even if there came a time when Richard no longer stood between them, Adwen's inability to bear a child might present an insurmountable problem to Malik's suit.

"Easy to say," Adwen repeated. She looked away from Malik and rose to her feet. "I'm weary. I think I'll go to my blankets now." She made a motion with her hand as Malik moved to accompany her. "No! Stay here."

Malik ignored her. "But I must protect you from the cockroaches."

"I can protect myself." She strode across the room to her pallet.

"Of course you can." Malik strolled after her. "Forgive me, it was only a ploy to save my pride. I am deathly afraid of cockroaches. I was hoping you would have the kindness to defend me."

"You lie." She lay down and pulled her blankets up around her. "You have no fear of anything on this earth."

"Oh, but I do." He settled himself on his pallet a few feet away from her. "Would you like me to tell you what I fear most?"

She quickly closed her eyes. "No," she whispered. "I don't want to know."

"Someday I will have to tell you anyway. For it is a very great fear and one only you can lay to rest." Malik stretched out before adding, "But for the time being I will let you address this smaller fear. Shall I give you my sword to vanquish the cockroaches? I fear my hand would shake too much."

"Fool," she said thickly.

"No?"

"No." She turned her back on him.

Brynn watched them from across the hall. The two

pallets were a few feet apart, they were not touching, and yet she had the odd feeling there was an invisible cocoon about Malik and Adwen, binding them together. Perhaps their troubles were not as bad as she had feared.

"Have you eaten enough?" Gage asked.

"Yes." Brynn wiped her lips and then her fingers. "I've had plenty. Are you done? There's something I want to show you."

His brows lifted as he rose lazily to his feet. "I hope it's not one of your spirits. I'm in no mood to deal with them this night."

Brynn stood up and moved toward the door of the hall. "I don't promise you won't feel their presence, but that's not what I wish to show you." She grabbed one of the torches they had lit and entered the dark hall. "It's a chamber . . . I used to come here as a child." She held the torch high as she climbed the stone steps and then traversed a long, dark hall. "It's my favorite place in the castle. I want you to see it." She wanted to share it with him. She had a frantic desire to share everything with him, to make sure he experienced everything that was hers to give before it was too late.

She would not think such gloomy thoughts. Nothing would happen to him. She would make sure no harm—

"Here it is." She threw open the wide, brass-studded door and stepped inside. "I think it must have been a council chamber."

He followed her. "Why?"

"The tapestries." She stared up at the faded tapestries that still occupied all four walls. Scenes of battle, scenes of jousting, one scene of a knight kneeling before a bearded ruler. "No gentle scenes of court life, no troubadours, no picking of the harvests. This is a warrior's chamber."

"Then I'm surprised you like it so much." He took

the torch from her and wandered around the chamber, looking at the tapestries. "Why?"

"Because this is what they were and what they gave up for peace. That's the glory of this chamber. Can't you see them here, gathered about a table, talking, laughing . . ."

"Can you?"

"Yes. Yes, I can." She walked over to stand beside him. "I can see it all."

"So can I," he murmured, studying the tapestry of Hevald knighting a young armored squire. "Extraordinary."

"I thought you would." She touched his arm. "It's not like the other rooms that are full of sadness. This one isn't sad at all."

"Why are the other rooms sad? What happened here?"

"They left him," she said simply. "He had put down his sword but his officers weren't ready. After the castle was built there was no challenge for them. They were bored without constant warfare and grew restless here on Gwynthal. One by one they drifted away until at last there was only Hevald and Bentar left. When they died the rest of the servants left the castle and moved to the village."

"Except Bentar's offspring."

She nodded. "They didn't want to leave the castle so they built a cottage not far away. I'll show you the cottage tomorrow." She took the torch from his hand, moved toward the fireplace across the room, knelt, and lit the wood. The flames sprang bright and warm, casting a glow over the large room. "But it never meant . . . this is a special place. I wanted to share it with you."

"I see you did. This room has been freshly swept and you must have laid that fire this afternoon."

Of course he would notice those details. There was

not a good deal Gage did not notice. "I didn't have time to do very much." She made a face as she glanced at the broken remains of the oak council table and chairs she had pushed to the corner of the room. "I suppose I should have gotten rid of those years ago, but it's part of the room, part of what I feel when I come here." She turned to look at him. "I was afraid you wouldn't be able to—" She stopped, inhaling sharply.

The firelight had thrown Gage's giant shadow on the tapestry, transposing it directly over the figure of Hevald as he stood knighting the young squire. For an instant it appeared that Hevald had come to life, that the two were joined.

"What's wrong?" Gage asked, moving toward her.

She watched the shadow move out of the tapestry and smiled. "Nothing. A trick of the firelight."

Gage and Hevald, she thought. Of course. She marveled she had not realized it before.

Gage stopped before her and stared down at her. "I'm not sure I like this Hevald."

"Why not?"

"Because you like him too much."

She laughed with genuine amusement. "It's true. I have a great and special feeling for him but, given time, I believe you'll understand. He was much like you."

Gage shook his head. "I cannot see myself building a fortress to peace. I'd probably be like Hevald's knights and become bored and wander away." He glanced over his shoulder at the tapestry as he placed the torch in the holder beside the fireplace. "I'd wager he became bored himself. If he hadn't been so stubborn, I've no doubt he would have abandoned this castle and left Gwynthal."

"He would not have gone back to war. He was weary and sickened by it all."

"No." He stared thoughtfully at Hevald's face in the tapestry. "But life offers adventures to a man other than chopping off heads."

She smiled. "Perhaps he should have become a prince of merchants."

"Possibly." His glance shifted back to her and he smiled in return. "But that takes a skill and patience I'm not sure Hevald possessed. There aren't many men as extraordinary as myself."

Her smile became a chuckle. "You sound like Malik."

His smile faded. "No, Malik has considerably more patience than I do." He knelt beside her and gazed intently into her eyes. "Why did you wish to share this with me, Brynn?"

The moment had come. She had not thought she would feel this shy and uncertain. She moistened her lips. "It's a special place."

"Yes." He waited.

"I want you to know—I cannot tell you I don't believe what I saw—" She reached out and nervously grasped his hands. "But if it did happen—if you killed Delmas. I wish to—" She closed her eyes. "I accept it."

He went still. "What do you accept?"

"I accept that if I have to live with guilt for the rest of my life, I will do so." She leaned forward, laid her head on his chest, and whispered, "For I cannot live without you."

"Thank God." His hands cradled her nape and he rocked her back and forth. "I thought it would never come."

"And I will pray God frees you of all guilt. It was my fault that it happened at all. You were innocent of—"

"Hush. I've not been innocent since the day I went with Hardraada on my first raid." He brushed his lips on her temple. "But it would be much easier for you if you'd trust me in this."

"I'd like you to— Will you—" She turned her lips so that they pressed the strong cord of his neck. "I want to belong to you tonight. Here. In this place. Please do not refuse me."

He pushed her away from him and looked down into her face. His voice was uneven. "I don't think I'm capable of it."

She stood up. "Undress." She moved to the shadows by the hearth and retrieved the blanket she had put in readiness. She spread it before the fire and then pulled her gown over her head and tossed it aside.

She turned to look at him.

Naked, powerful, ready. She started to tremble as he walked toward her.

It was like watching a storm approaching, knowing it could ravage you, destroy you, and yet fill you with exhilaration and excitement. She took an eager step forward, then another.

He made a low exclamation and lifted her, thrust into her in that savage, animal way he had taken her that first day.

She cried out, her head falling back as she was filled with him.

He froze, his chest lifting and falling with his labored breathing. Holding her close, joined to him. He slowly lowered his head and his lips covered hers.

Golden tenderness. Scarlet savagery. Only Gage could ever combine the two.

He lifted his head and his eyes were shining wetly. "I—have true—I—love—oh, what the devil!" He sank to his knees on the blanket, thrusting wildly, deeply.

She lay on the floor, looking up at him. His hair was a black-red tangle as it fell about his shoulders. His nostrils flared as he moved deep and strong within her.

She lunged upward, trying to take more of him. "Gage . . ."

Muted tapestries behind him whispering their dreams of faded glory. Firelight and flame. Hevald over her, in her, his shadow dominating her, pleasuring her.

No, not Hevald this time. Gage, alive, moving, loving. One. Same. Joined.

Forever.

"I would like you to say it, please." Brynn sat up and leaned on one elbow, looking down at him. "Just once."

"Say what?"

"All of it. Not just a broken remnant."

Gage smiled sheepishly. "Oh, very well. Though it's not easy for me." He kissed the creamy swell next to her nipple. "You have magnificent breasts. I adore them."

"I am not my breasts. I'm Brynn of Falkhaar."

"I beg to disagree. You are these magnificent breasts and this lovely body." His hand brushed the curls surrounding her womanhood. "And this place of pleasure." He pulled her down on top of him and rocked her back and forth. "How I do love that place of pleasure."

"You may not enter there again unless I hear other words from you."

"Oh, you want to hear that you are my lady and my wife? That I hold you in honor and that I respect your mind and heart as well as your body?" His voice was muffled in her hair. "It is a solemn declaration. I don't know if you deserve it after all you've made me undergo."

"I deserve it."

He chuckled. "So you do." His laughter faded and he said gruffly, "I . . . love you, Brynn of Falkhaar."

She felt tears sting her eyes and her arms tightened about him. "That did not seem too difficult."

"More than you know." He rolled her over onto her back and looked down at her. "And now I need words from you. When do we wed?"

She stiffened. "We will talk of that later."

"Now."

"I said I didn't wish to—" She looked up at him urgently. "Please. Don't spoil this night."

He muttered a nearly inaudible curse. "You cannot live without me but you will not wed me? What madness is this?"

She didn't answer.

"This doesn't please me," he said with precision. "You bring me here. You use me. You make me—"

"I didn't use you. I just wanted—why won't you let it alone? Why must you ask more?"

"Because I have the deplorable fault of wanting things clear instead of muddied." He paused, taking a moment to study her face. "You've been behaving most peculiarly all day. You watch me like a vulture about to pounce and then you persuade me to couple with you."

"You needed little persuasion."

"True. I wanted to believe all was well and that I could take what I wanted. But all is not well, is it?"

"We'll talk after you have the treasure." Her jaw set with determination. "I don't want to think of—"

"Wedding? Children?" He paused. "Leaving Gwynthal?"

Leaving Gwynthal. She had not even let herself consider that possible ramification if she wed Gage. She had not even considered marriage. She had wanted only to join with him, give to him, take from him. She had wanted to snatch a perfect moment before—

The chill returned as she recalled the dream. "No!" She pulled him down and held him close. "Don't talk," she murmured desperately. "Please, don't talk. Not yet. Not now."

He was stiff and resisting and then, suddenly he relaxed and held her close. "Very well. Not now. I suppose I've won enough for one night." He added grimly, "But soon. By God, very, very soon, Brynn."

•   •   •

The cottage was in even worse disrepair than the castle. A tree had fallen on the thatched roof, leaving a large hole, and her mother's herb garden was a only a tangle of vines and weeds.

"Well, we won't spend the night here," Gage said dryly as he stood in the doorway and looked up at the blue sky clearly visible through the hole. "How close are we to this treasure cave?"

"Not far. Perhaps a few hours. But I'll need daylight to find it."

Malik gazed at the sun appraisingly. "Well, we don't have more than an hour before sunset. We'd best camp and set out in the morning." He turned his horse. "Is there a brook nearby, Brynn?"

"About a mile into the forest." A night in the forest, a night of danger. She turned back to the cottage and said quickly, "Why don't we stay here? I'm weary, aren't you? It wouldn't take long to sweep away the debris. We did it at the castle. At least it would afford us a little shelter."

"There's a very large tree in your cottage." Adwen made a face. "And I don't think I want to find out what's nesting in those branches." She kicked her mare into a trot and guided her back to the trail. She called over her shoulder, "I don't fear cockroaches, but I'm sure I heard something slither."

"It's only a cottage, Brynn," Gage said. "Your mother's no longer here. She chose to leave this place. It's not good for you to stay."

He thought the reason she didn't want to leave was that she wanted to cling to memories of her mother and feared it would bring sadness. She did feel sad, but it was a sweet sadness. She glanced at the herb garden where she had spent so many happy mornings trailing behind her mother. She felt no lingering spirits here as she had at the castle. Her mother had been taken cruelly, but her purpose in life had been fulfilled. She had been given a gift and had used it selflessly and unstintingly. She whispered, "You're right, she's not here."

He took her arm and led her toward her horse. Waves of support and comfort flowed gently over her as he lifted her to the saddle. "I know you're tired. We'll stop soon. You said this brook was only a mile?"

She was suddenly jerked back to the peril that had caused her to protest leaving the cottage. She had an idea this mile was going to seem an eternity. "Yes." There was no use protesting or trying to change their minds. She could only wait and watch and try to make sure no harm came to him. "You go on ahead. I'll follow you."

His brows rose in surprise. "The trail is wide enough for two."

But she wouldn't be able to watch him as closely if he were beside her. "I want to be by myself."

He shrugged and kicked his horse into a trot. "Keep close."

"I will." She had no intention of falling far behind. She had to be near enough to intercede in case of attack. "I'll keep very close."

Someone was watching.

They had gone only a quarter mile into the forest when Brynn felt a chill run through her. Her gaze frantically searched the thick underbrush on either side of the trail. Nothing. No sign of anyone.

But how would she know if there were a thousand enemies lurking behind that veil of heavy shrubbery?

Her hand tightened on the reins. Perhaps it was her imagination. Perhaps her fears were playing tricks on her.

God in heaven, it was *not* imagination. Someone was there. She was as certain of that presence as of Gage ahead of her on the trail.

Her palms were clammy and she was shaking. Why

didn't Gage sense the danger as she did? Where were his warrior's instincts? He seemed totally unaware. Perhaps that was how it happened. A moment of distraction and then a dagger thrust from out of—

"Gage!"

He glanced inquiringly over his shoulder.

What could she say to a man who believed only what he saw? I had a death dream? I have a feeling that there is danger here? He would never believe her.

"Come on!" She kicked the mare into a gallop that brought her even with Gage. "I'm weary of this pace," she said, then her hand came sharply down on his stallion's hind quarters.

"What the—" Gage cast her a startled glance as his horse broke into a dead run, snorting and plunging forward.

She followed him, keeping beside him as they passed Malik and Adwen.

"Brynn, is something—" Malik started.

There was a curve in the trail ahead. What if Richard was there waiting for Gage?

She whipped the mare into more speed and rounded the curve ahead of Gage.

No one was there. Richard was not standing in the trail waiting for Gage.

But the eyes were still upon them. Keeping pace, running as they were running.

Stalking. Watching. *There.*

She reined up by the brook, panting, her chest rising and falling.

"What was that about?" Gage asked as he fought the stallion to a standstill before dismounting. "You nearly ran Malik and Adwen off the trail."

"The mare was thirsty." She slipped from the saddle and led the mare to water. "I wanted to get here."

"Obviously," Malik said dryly as he and Adwen

reined in beside the brook. "We truly were not going to drink all the water in the brook before you got here."

"I know." The sense of being watched was gone, she realized with relief. He had not followed them. She glanced at the long rays of the sun filtering through the trees. It would be dark soon and they would be safe. If it was going to happen, it would be in daylight. "We'd better set up camp before it gets any darker."

"I'll go gather wood." Gage started toward the shrubbery to the left of the trail.

"No!" She pushed past him. "I'll do it. Take care of the stallion. He's still upset."

"So am I," he murmured as he watched her disappear into the forest. "And getting more uneasy every minute."

"Are you going to tell me about it?" Gage asked as he settled down in his blankets that night.

She had known the question would come. She had been aware of his grim demeanor since they had arrived at the brook. She was surprised he had asked her nothing during the meal preparations or when they were eating. "Tell you about what?"

"Whatever is disturbing you."

"Nothing is disturbing me."

Gage made a rude noise. "The devil, it isn't. It's better now than when we were on the trail, but you're still stiff as a lance."

"It's been a strange time for me . . . the castle, the cottage . . ."

"Is that any reason for you to be afraid?"

"I'm not afraid." She lay down beside him and closed her eyes. "Good night."

She thought he would pursue the matter, but he only made an exasperated exclamation and enfolded her in his arms.

Darkness surrounded them, and he was safe in the dark. She must wake before daylight broke that safety.

If she slept at all. At that moment she felt as if she would never sleep again.

"I'll be glad to be gone from this damned island," Gage said roughly. "I don't like what it's doing to you."

It wasn't the island, it was the evil they had brought there. The evil she had brought—Richard and his greed for riches. If Gage was killed, it would be her doing.

"It's not Gwynthal."

"Oh, no, how could it be the fault of so perfect a place?"

"It's not—good night."

He muttered something inaudible and tightened his grasp around her.

Stay away, she prayed. Let him keep safe. Make the dream only a dream.

He was there again.

She woke in the middle of the night in a panic, the fear tightening her chest worse than if the dream had come.

Because *he* had come.

She could feel him staring at them, lurking out of sight.

How long had he been there before she had roused?

She lay there, frozen. It was agony not doing anything; she wanted to run screaming into the shrubbery after him.

Why not? she wondered desperately. Why shouldn't she go after him? It was better than waiting for him to attack. Better than seeing Gage killed.

Killed. She felt sick at the thought. She could not bear it.

Slowly, carefully, she shifted Gage's arm from her body and sat up.

A stirring. Something had changed out there in the darkness. . . . The stare was still as intent, but now it was wary.

Let him be wary, she thought fiercely. She rose to her feet and moved silently from the circle cast by the dying fire and into the forest.

Where was he?

She closed her eyes, trying to sense the direction.

Her lids flew open.

He was coming!

She could feel him moving through the under-brush—swift, deadly.

Then she saw his eyes.

Yellow, wild, glittering in the moonlight.

Yellow?

"Selbar?" she whispered.

Relief made her almost dizzy. She reached out and grabbed the trunk of the tree next to her. Not Richard. Selbar. As the wolf padded forward out of the under-brush, she could not mistake the long scar that sliced across his shoulder and chest.

She smiled and stepped forward. "You've come to greet me?" she crooned. "Come, boy, let us see—"

"Don't move!" Gage said from behind her. "Stop where you are, Brynn."

It was the wolf that stopped. Selbar snarled low in his throat and crouched, preparing to spring.

"Go back," Brynn said, taking another step for-ward. "He won't hurt me. Come, boy, come and—"

What was wrong with Selbar? He was staring at her without recognition, his lips curled back in a snarl.

Gage ran forward and thrust himself between Brynn and the wolf. "Don't move," he said again. He lifted his sword.

What was he doing? "Put it down. Don't hurt him!"

Selbar hesitated, still snarling. The next instant he was gone, as silent as he had come.

Disappointment surged through her. "You shouldn't have interfered. Selbar wouldn't have hurt me."

"For God's sake, are you too blind to see that he was stalking you? He would have sprung and ripped your throat out in another minute."

She shook her head. "He wouldn't have—" She stopped as she remembered that menacing stare the wolf had given her. Selbar had not known her, she realized in desolation. He might have even killed her as Gage had said. "He didn't remember me."

"You're shaking. Come back to the fire."

She let him lead her through the forest. She felt dull, dazed. "I don't understand. He treated me as if I were an enemy. I was never his enemy. There was a bond . . . I loved him."

"I know you did." He pushed her gently to her blanket and wrapped another covering about her shoulders. "He's a beast of the forest. You can't expect him to have a memory as long as yours."

He had said that before, she recalled. She had argued with him but he had spoken truth. "I thought everything would be the same here. I was sure he would be the same."

He sat down beside her and pulled her close. "How did you know he was out there?"

"I felt him. He was following us."

"Then you must have had an idea he would be a threat to you or you would never have taken my knife."

"Knife?" She looked at him in bewilderment and then followed his gaze to her hand.

She stiffened in shock. Her hand was clenched around the bone handle of Gage's huge dagger.

"I don't remember taking it," she whispered.

"It's a good thing you did. You roused me slipping it

out of the sheath. Not very good protection in dealing with a wolf."

But deadly when dealing with a man. One downward stroke and the knife would quench out a life. Why had she taken it if not to kill Richard? She remembered the ferocity she had felt when she had slipped into the forest. Would she really have taken a life to protect Gage? God help her, she was desperately afraid she would.

The dagger dropped from her hand to the ground and she buried her face in Gage's chest.

"It will pass, Brynn," he whispered. "Nothing stays the same. Perhaps he did recognize you, if he was following. It could be I startled him and he acted on instinct."

Nothing stays the same.

Selbar might have killed her.

She might have given up everything she believed to protect Gage.

She did not understand any of this, she thought wearily. She wanted a world where everything was clear and uncomplicated, a place where all hurts could be healed and souls were steadfast and unchanging. She had thought Gwynthal was such a world.

It was not.

Fourteen

"THIS IS YOUR cave?" Gage peered into the dark opening of the grotto. "You didn't tell me we'd have to swim to reach your treasure."

"Bentar didn't want to make it too easy to find. Otherwise someone would have stumbled across it a hundred times over." Brynn dismounted and tied the mare to a tree beside the cave. "And you won't have to swim. There's a boat tied at a mooring several hundred yards inside the cave."

"If the rope hasn't rotted away," Malik said as he lifted Adwen to the ground.

Brynn had not considered that possibility. "It was a very strong rope. I remember my mother changing it right before we left Gwynthal."

"Then we may have a chance of avoiding building our own boat." Gage moved toward the opening. "Is the mooring on this side of the spring?"

"Yes, but let me go first. There's a ledge that borders the spring, but the cave curves like a snake and this first stretch is almost totally without light." She entered the cave and pressed back against the wall. Darkness, cool moisture, the rushing sound of the water only inches away. It was all so familiar. How many times she had come here with her mother. "Be careful; the ledge is slippery."

"How deep is the water here?" Adwen asked uneasily.

"Not very deep. Ten, twelve feet."

"Deep enough to drown," Adwen said as she edged farther along the ledge. "I don't swim."

"I will protect you," Malik said.

"You swim?"

"No, but I will allow you to tread on my shoulders while I walk on the bottom of this abyss. I will even warn you when I am about to drown so that you may try to save yourself. What bravery, what sacrifice. Could anyone do more?"

"Yes, they could refrain from chattering nonsense and distracting me from the task of keeping my footing."

"Sorry," Malik said meekly.

"The mooring is just ahead around the curve," Brynn said. "It will be lighter once we reach it. There are several openings in the roof of the cave that allow the sunlight in."

"Good," Gage muttered. "I don't like not knowing what's ahead of me."

Characteristic, Brynn thought. She had never been uneasy here, just accepted the darkness. Gage, however, was fighting it, seeking to change it.

She rounded the curve, and suddenly the darkness was leavened. Falling on the water was a ray of light which streamed from a narrow crack in the roof of the cave.

The boat was still there, tied to the iron pole driven into the ledge, jouncing gently on the water. She breathed a sigh of relief and her pace instinctively quickened.

"Be careful," Gage snapped.

"You be careful. I know this cave." She jumped

into the long boat and moved to the rear. "My mother brought me here many times. There's nothing to fear."

"Why would she bring you here? To make sure no one had stolen the treasure?"

"No, she wanted me to play with it."

Adwen frowned in puzzlement. "Why?"

"So that I would place no special value upon it. It was a toy, a pretty toy, but when it became overfamiliar, it meant nothing to me. I was a healer and she wanted to make certain that nothing would ever blind me to that truth."

"She sounds like a very wise woman," Malik said as he picked up the oar, dipped it into the water, and guided the boat away from the mooring.

"Yes, she was very wise." But that wisdom had not prevented her from giving her love to a man who was not as wise. Nor from risking her life for a child she had barely known. "About some things." She looked at Gage in the front of the boat, rowing strongly, cleanly. Her own heart was no wiser than her mother's. Last night she might have killed for this man; today she was giving him her heritage.

She had forgotten how eerie and mystical this journey was through the grotto. The boat glided almost silently on dark green waters, encountered a brilliant pool of sunlight that lit the shadow figures in the boat with blinding clarity, and then slid back into darkness again. It was like journeying through life or perhaps . . . eternity, she thought dreamily.

"How far, Brynn?" Gage asked.

She roused herself and looked around. "Just around the next curve. You'll find the ledge widens and there's a mooring. . . ."

She was the last to leave the boat after it was tied to the mooring. She supposed she had been as eager as they the first time her mother had brought her to see the treasure. The toy was old now. "There's a break in the wall of the cave." She gestured. "You'll find the treasure there."

She heard Adwen's excited exclamation before she entered the alcove.

Gage was standing frozen, his gaze on the dozens of chests overflowing with pearls and jewels. "My God." Then he murmured, "I should have bargained for more packhorses."

"You can always make two trips."

"Pretty . . ." Adwen reached out and touched a golden plate.

Brynn felt a surge of warmth as she saw Adwen's expression. No greed. Just the same awe Brynn had known as a child when confronted with all this beauty. Adwen had been a wife before her childhood had really ended. She had never been permitted the joys other children knew.

Brynn sat down on the ground beside a chest in the corner. "I like this one, Adwen." She pulled out a long gold chain with square red jewels. "I always played with this necklace when my mother brought me here."

Adwen sat down beside her. "Rubies?"

Brynn slipped the necklace over Adwen's head. "I don't know. They're very large. Does it matter?"

Adwen shook her head as she reached into the chest and pulled out another gold rope laced with amethysts and pearls. "This would be pretty on you." She placed it around Brynn's neck and tilted her head appraisingly. "Perhaps not. The pearls are too pale for you—" She got on her knees and started rummaging through the chest. "Emeralds!" She held up a necklace in triumph. "Green. I always think of you when I see trees and grass. . . ."

"So do I," Gage said. Brynn glanced at him, expecting to see impatience. He shook his head indulgently. "Toys."

Malik moved toward the small chest nearest the door. "This one first?"

Gage glanced at the chest. "Why not?" He turned and moved across the chamber.

"Do you wish us to help you?" Brynn asked.

Gage shook his head. "We'll go faster alone. There will be more room in the boat. You stay and play."

She immediately turned back to the chest. "There's a diadem with lovely blue stones somewhere in here, Adwen. I used to pretend I was queen of the fairies and I'd plucked a piece of the sky to make my crown. . . ."

"We're ready to go," Gage said. "If you can tear yourself away."

"But you've taken barely a fourth of all that's here." Brynn said as she stood up. "Don't you want any more?"

Gage smiled. "You should know better. I want it all. It's my nature."

"Then why?"

"It's all the pack animals can carry." He helped Adwen to her feet. "And, as you promised, enough to buy a kingdom if I choose. Even I should be satisfied." He added, "Temporarily. As you said, we can always come back."

"Yes." Brynn took off the diadem and carelessly threw it into the chest.

"Don't you want to take it?" Gage asked.

Brynn shook her head. "Why? I'm done with it."

"Are you?"

He was smiling so curiously that Brynn asked, "What are you thinking?"

"That your mother succeeded admirably." He turned to Adwen. "And you? Do you wish anything?"

"Not among these. They're Brynn's." Adwen moved toward the boat. "But I'll accept the gift of the small share Brynn says you've offered me. I'm not fool enough to think I can make my way penniless and alone in this world."

"While Brynn believes she doesn't need anybody or anything," Gage murmured as he helped Adwen and then Brynn into the boat. "How refreshing to encounter a touch of reality in this place."

Brynn could have told him she knew she needed him and that she had been deluged by reality since the moment she had set foot on Gwynthal. She had been thrown into constant confusion and heartache, but now it was almost over. Gage had his treasure. What did she have?

She had Gwynthal, of course. She had the prize she had yearned to possess since she had been torn away from the island as a child.

But if she took Gwynthal, she could not have Gage. He would never stay on Gwynthal. The thought brought a wave of pain so intense, she instinctively blocked it. She did not have to think of decisions or leavetakings now. She still had time.

"I suppose you know these poor old beasts won't be able to make it back to the boats, Gage," Malik said as they came out of the cave into the sunlight a short time later. "Even if we go slowly, the burden is too great."

"Then we'll stay at the castle and you can go back and bring LeFont and the rest to help." Gage lifted Brynn to the saddle. "And you can try your powers of persuasion on those kindly villagers to make them yield us a fine, strong wagon."

Malik snorted. "I do not think that likely." He shot a sly glance at Adwen. "I have noted of late that my powers of persuasion have not been the greatest."

"I have noted that too," she said calmly. "But then, some people respond more to vain boasts and blustering than others."

Brynn barely heard them. Her eyes were fixed on the forest through which they must pass to reach the castle. "How slowly do we have to go? It took us nearly two days to reach here."

"Another day perhaps," Gage said. "If we start now, before sunset."

"Then let's go." Brynn kicked her horse into a trot. Three days to reach the castle, three days to reach safety. Once they reached Hevald's stronghold, all would be well. When LeFont arrived, Gage would be surrounded by his soldiers. Surely no harm could come to him then.

Not once they reached the castle.

They were a day's journey from the castle when Brynn again felt the eyes upon her.

She was standing by a narrow brook, watering the mare, when suddenly, out of nowhere, she knew he was there.

But who was there? she wondered in frustration. Was Selbar stalking her again? Or was the enemy more deadly?

She lifted her head, trying desperately to see through the thick foliage.

"It's time to go, Brynn," Adwen said. She arched her back, trying to stretch the cramped muscles. "I'll be glad to get to the castle. I believe this slow pace is more tiring than one that's speedier, don't you?"

"What?" she asked abstractedly. It might be Selbar. It had been near there when she had first sensed him stalking her. "Oh, yes, I grow very impatient. I want to *be* there."

And have Gage safe behind high walls, she thought desperately.

They were only a few hours from the castle when they stopped again to water the animals.

"Can't we go on?" Brynn asked. "We're so close."

"Not if we want these donkeys to survive." Gage

loosened the packs on one of the animal's backs. "They need the rest as well as the water."

But *he* was there, watching them, as he had been all afternoon.

She edged closer to Gage. He was frowning, saying something in a low tone to Malik.

Malik shrugged and then nodded.

Gage turned to Brynn and thrust the stallion's reins into her hand. "Will you water my horse? I want to check the saddlebag on that donkey." He strode toward the donkey that was standing a few yards away.

Brynn watched him start to shift the saddlebag before leading the stallion toward the stream where Malik was standing with Adwen.

Malik turned to her with a smile. "Almost there. You will have to promise to care for Adwen tonight after I leave you at the castle. She assures me she has no fear of cockroaches, but I do not believe her."

"You're going to start off tonight to get LeFont?" Brynn asked. "Why not wait for daylight?"

"Gage is impatient." Malik raised his brows. "Which I am sure you know full well." He stepped in back of her and placed his hand on the stallion's saddle. "He wants to be—"

Had she heard something in the bushes? She whirled around and stood on tiptoe to look over Malik's shoulder.

Gage was gone!

Brynn dropped the stallion's reins and pushed Malik aside. "Gage!"

"Easy." Malik put his hand on her arm. "He will be back soon."

"Where did he go?"

"He went after the wolf. He caught a glimpse of him in the underbrush two hours ago."

Relief surged through her. Not Richard after all. "He actually saw Selbar?"

Malik nodded. "And you did also, didn't you? Gage noticed how disturbed you were." He grimaced. "We all saw how upset you've been today. It would have been difficult not to be aware of it. He told me to keep you busy while he got rid of the wolf. He didn't want you to try to go after him again tonight yourself after we slept."

Fear tore through her. "What do you mean, get rid of him?"

"Not kill him," Malik said quickly. "He merely wanted to frighten him away."

But what if Selbar attacked Gage? One of them would die. "He shouldn't have done it. In what direction was he going?"

Malik shook his head. "I will not tell you. Gage wants no interference in this."

"He won't hurt the wolf, Brynn," Adwen said. "Trust him."

"And shall I trust Selbar too?" Brynn asked. She pushed Malik aside and ran toward the shrubbery beside the donkey, where she had last glimpsed Gage. The branches whipped her arms and body as she pushed aside the underbrush. It had been only a few moments; he couldn't have gone far.

But Selbar might have been waiting for—

Pain!

She staggered and would have fallen as agony overwhelmed her. She opened her mouth in a silent scream.

Gage!

Selbar, no, no, no . . .

Wrong direction. She was going in the wrong direction. The pain was over there. No, it was everywhere.

Blind. Dark.

She stumbled . . . somewhere, following instinct alone.

Pain again!

She bent double . . . her back.

No, Gage's back . . . Gage's pain!

Ahead . . . just ahead.

"Well, how delightful. You've come to me. I was afraid I'd have to lure you into my web," Lord Richard said.

Gage lay crumpled at his feet, a dagger in his back. Not Selbar. Richard . . .

Gage hurt, Gage dying . . . Blood flowing on the leaves.

Richard reached down and pulled the dagger out of Gage's body.

Blinding agony shot through her. It was a moment before she could hear what Richard was saying.

"In truth I didn't expect to dispose of the Norman so easily. He was so intent on stalking some game of his own that he didn't hear me slip up behind him." He bent and wiped the dagger on the grass. "But he was a strong brute. I had to stab him twice, and I don't think he's dead yet."

Not yet. But close, so close.

"Don't you want to help him?" Richard asked softly. "I doubt if you can heal him, but you could try." He crooked his finger to motion her nearer. "Come heal him, Brynn."

If she came closer, he would kill her. If she didn't come closer, Gage would surely die.

Malik. Malik would almost certainly have followed her. If she could keep Richard at bay for only a little while . . .

She started slowly toward Gage. I'm coming. Don't die, please don't die. . . . "You followed us from Selkirk?"

"Of course. We landed after dark the same day you arrived."

Oh, God, he was bleeding, the blood trickling . . .
 Malik, where are you?

"I didn't know you were behind us," she said dully.

"I kept a good distance between us. I chose to track

rather than follow you. One man alone stands little chance against two warriors like Dumont and the Saracen."

"You couldn't get your vassals to come with you?"

He shook his head. "They were afraid. Fools. They couldn't see that the future held nothing under William."

Gage was scarcely breathing. Had the dagger struck his lungs? "Take the treasure and leave us alone. We don't want it."

"You may not want it, but I'd wager the Saracen is a different matter. I think he'd object strenuously to losing such a prize." He glanced down at Gage. "And he values the Norman. When he finds out I've killed him, I'd have to look over my shoulder for the rest of my life. No, my plan is best. Wait, pick you off one at a time, and then I'll have no problems."

"What makes you think Malik won't go after you at once?"

"If he does, then I'll have him." He smiled. "We both know what a fine hunter I am."

"You'd kill Adwen too?"

"Adwen bears me no love these days. I need no witnesses to damage me in the sight of William and his court when I take my place among them. Yes, she will have to go too." A peevish frown marred his handsome face. "You're moving very slowly. Are you seeking to trick me?"

"No!"

"I think you are." His hand tightened on the knife hilt. "Should I pierce the Norman again?"

Panic soared through her. "Why? You said you'd struck a fatal blow."

"But he's not dead yet. Or perhaps he is. Come and see."

He was growing impatient. She could not wait for

Malik. She would have to deal with him herself. "I'm coming."

"Not fast enough." He stooped over Gage, dagger lifted.

"Wait!" She ran the last few yards and fell to her knees beside Gage.

"Better." Richard straightened and looked down at her. "This is how I've always wanted you. On your knees before me. It's a pity I won't be able to take the time to enjoy it."

When he brought down the knife, he would be off balance for an instant. Her only chance was to lunge upward and strike him in the stomach with her head. Perhaps if she knocked the breath out of him she would have a chance to grab the dagger. Sweet Mary, a struggle would take time, and Gage had so little time. She glared up at him. "What are you waiting for? Do it!"

"What sacrifice. How unfortunate the Norman will never know how devoted you were to him." His grip changed on the dagger as he prepared for the thrust.

She murmured a prayer and braced herself to spring.

The dagger rose. "I'm glad you're looking at me. Stabbing the Norman in the back was most unsatisfactory. It wasn't as if—"

He screamed and fell forward!

Malik?

Gray fur, yellow eyes, white teeth, sunk into the back of Richard's neck.

Selbar!

"God!" Richard was cursing, the knife in his hand flailing wildly as he sought a target.

But Selbar was behind him, snarling, shaking him by the neck as if he were a rabbit.

Then the wolf released him for a moment and Richard rolled over, faced him, and lashed out with the dagger.

Brynn acted instinctively, lunging forward and deflecting the blade to one side.

"Bitch!" Richard's hand lashed out, knocking her to the ground.

A snarl, a streak of gray and white leaping over her.

Richard's scream became a gurgle as Selbar's teeth tore out his throat.

Brynn watched in sick horror as the wolf brought him down to the ground.

Blood. Agony. Death. Over almost before it had begun. Selbar backed away from Richard's body and then whirled on her.

Wild eyes, bloody mouth, bared teeth.

Then he was gone, loping into the forest.

She shook her head dazedly. Everything had happened so fast that it was difficult to comprehend.

But she could comprehend the fact that Richard was lying dead. Had it come too late for Gage?

No, there was still life.

She crawled the few feet separating her from Gage and cradled him in her arms. "I'm here. I'm here, Gage." She rocked him back and forth in an agony of tenderness, her hands searching for the wounds on his back.

Two, very close together. Very deep.

"You can't leave me. Do you hear me? You have to stay."

"Brynn?" She looked up to see Malik at her side, breathing hard, looking down at her. "How bad?"

"Bad." The tears were running down her face. "He's dying, Malik."

He went pale, but his stricken expression lasted only an instant. "Then you will have to stop it. Just as you did for me."

"I may not—it's different."

"How?"

"I cannot stand apart. I *feel* his hurt. It's like being

wounded myself," she whispered. "It's never been like
this before. I don't know if I can control it."

"Christ. Is there nothing you can do?"

She wasn't sure—it was like stumbling in the darkness. Gage was spiraling so deep, she wasn't certain she
could reach him.

Yet she *had* to reach him.

Malik knelt beside her, his face strained. "What
can I do? Do you need your herb bag?"

Herbs? She gazed at him incredulously.

"He cannot die," Malik said hoarsely. "There has
to be something. . . ."

"I cannot reach him." She held him desperately
closer. He was drawing farther and farther away with
every passing moment. "Don't you understand? I cannot
reach him."

"I won't believe you will let him die," Malik said
roughly. "Think."

She could not think. The pain was too overwhelming. Gage's pain . . . Her pain . . . One.

One. She had been one with Gage before, she remembered suddenly. The night his father had died. She
had touched him, joined with him, and his pain had
eased with the sharing.

But that had been emotional, not physical healing.
To yield herself totally to a joining with a dying
man . . .

"What is it?" Malik asked.

"I cannot stand apart . . . but if I can become one
with him . . . I might be able to reach him and make
him let me heal."

"I do not know what you mean."

She had no time to explain it any clearer. This was
her only hope. She lay down on the grass and wrapped
her arms around Gage, her palms carefully covering
both wounds. No heat. No tingle that denoted healing.

No pain. It was the latter that frightened her, for it was a sign that he was slipping away.

"Brynn?"

"I'm going to sleep," she said, fading into the darkness. It would not be sleep, but she did not know how else to describe the journey into that shadowy realm. "You mustn't touch us until I wake."

"Let me take you to the castle. It will be night soon. I cannot leave you and Gage lying here in the forest."

"You must not touch us," she repeated fiercely. She closed her eyes. "Not until I wake."

"How long . . ."

Perhaps never. If she succeeded in linking with Gage, there was every chance he would take her with him if he was swallowed up in that darkness. "However long it takes."

She could sense Malik's distress, but she deliberately shut it out as she surrendered herself to the spiraling blackness surrounding Gage.

I'm coming, beloved. Wait for me.

"They're so terribly still," Adwen whispered, as she stared at the two rigid figures wrapped together a short distance away. "Are you sure they're still alive?"

Malik nodded as he reached out and stirred the wood in the fire. "They live."

"It's been hours." Adwen's nails bit into her palms. "I hate this waiting. I want to do something."

"We have done all we can."

"We've built a fire for warmth and thrown a blanket over them," she said impatiently. "There has to be something more."

"If there is, Brynn is doing it." He glanced up from the fire. "You are beset by guilt, but Gage's wound was no fault of yours. Richard was not pursuing a wife, he was after the treasure."

"I know." One part of her knew this truth, but Richard had trained her too well in guilt over the years. The woman was always to blame. "It is just . . . I love Brynn. If she had not come to Redfern when I was ill, if she had not helped me . . ."

"If the comet had not appeared in the heavens and stiffened William's determination. If I had not let the Saxons wound me." He smiled sadly. "You see, we can go on forever allotting blame. Accept it as fate, Adwen."

"If I accept it as fate, then I'm helpless. I've been helpless too long." She paused. "Do you think we should return Richard's body to England for burial?"

"No, I have no intention of digging up that vermin."

She glanced at the forest where Malik had dragged Richard's remains and buried him before he had gone to get her. "Then should we get that priest from the village to move him to consecrated ground?"

"And have them start a wolf hunt that might kill Selbar?" Malik shook his head. "I choose the wolf over your husband's eternal soul. He has far more worth."

She did not argue. Richard had damaged too many people in her life and might take even more toll this night.

She looked again at Brynn and Gage, locked together, still as marble. Yet not really immobile, Adwen realized suddenly. She could sense vibration, intense turmoil, swirling beneath the surface.

"What's happening, Malik?" she whispered, startled.

Malik could sense that struggle also. "I think she's fighting the dragons. May God be with her."

He would not listen to her, Brynn realized in despair.

She had not expected it to be like this. She had not expected the joining to include remembrance.

Poignant memories from the boy Gage, lonely, defiant, unwilling to admit to any weakness.

Hardraada, Father, accept me. I can be anything you need.

Towns burning, blood, rape. It sickens me. Is it enough? Accept me.

Rejection. Hurt. Weariness. Then I will go my own way. I do not need you.

Byzantium. Too alien. Learn it. It's no more alien than Hardraada's world.

Silk and cinnamon, dark-skinned slaves, barren desert, burning sunlight, camels . . . Malik.

The memories whirled, almost too fast to comprehend. She reached through them desperately, trying to catch hold, trying to make him understand.

Listen to me, Gage. I'm part of you; past, present . . . forever. Right now you're weak but I'm strong. You need that strength. Take it. Believe in me. Use me.

Dear God, listen to me!

"Your hands—are hot."

Gage's voice.

Brynn fought her way up out of the darkness and opened her eyes.

He was staring into her eyes. "Hot—take—them away."

She was suddenly aware that her palms covering his wounds were warm, tingling, healing.

Thank you, God.

"Brynn?"

"Shh." She spread her fingers, feeling the power course through her. "It is a good heat. Close your eyes and go back to sleep."

He shut his eyes and a moment later drifted away. Malik was suddenly there beside her, but he was a blur. She was only aware of Gage and the power she was channeling to him.

"Gage?" Malik said. "I have to know, Brynn."

"Better." She closed her eyes, concentrating. "Go away. I've no time for you now."

"Anything you say," Malik said huskily. "Whatever you want." She heard him walking away, muttering jubilantly, "Better! She said he's better, Adwen."

F i f t e e n

SHE WAS SITTING on the stone hearth, combing her hair.

Gage had always loved watching Brynn run the comb through that bright tangle. He had a fleeting memory of that night in the tent at Hastings when she had laughed and run the comb through Malik's beard. Now the firelight set the gold threads in her brown hair glowing with life and—

Firelight? Hearth?

He remembered only the forest and—pain, tearing pain in his back—

"Did the wolf—" God, his throat felt painfully dry and he was croaking like a frog. He tried again. "Selbar—"

She went still and then looked down at him with a luminous smile. "It's time you woke. It's been more than three weeks, and I need help. I cannot be expected to do everything myself." She reached over and poured water into a wooden goblet. "But you'll find it easier to speak if you drink. I've been wetting your lips and getting you to swallow a little water and broth, but your throat must still be very dry." She lifted his head and helped him swallow. "Better?"

He nodded, his gaze going around the room. The council chamber. He was lying on a pallet in the council chamber at the castle. "How did—"

"We brought you here as soon as I was sure it was safe to move you. I knew it was going to be a long time before you were fully healed and we couldn't stay in the forest. The weather had turned cold." She glanced at the tapestry in which Hevald was knighting the squire. "And I thought it was possible I might have a little help here."

But how had he been wounded, dammit? "Selbar?"

"It wasn't Selbar. It was Richard. He stabbed you in the back."

Christ, he should have been more alert. He had been so intent on tracking the wolf that he had let his guard down. "Stupid . . ."

"You're not stupid," she said fiercely. "You were trying to help me."

"Stupid."

"Stubborn," she substituted. "And unwilling to listen to anyone's opinion but your own. You should have learned your lesson at Svengard when you almost had your head severed from your shoulders for your obstinacy." She set the goblet down. "But why should I argue with you? You were certainly stupid to try to deceive me and run off to contend with Selbar yourself."

"Afraid . . . for . . . you."

"I know." She smiled. "As I was for you. But it was not Selbar we had to fear. He killed Richard and saved us both." She put her hand on his lips. "I'll tell you the rest later. It's time you slept now."

He would have no choice; that dark lethargy was creeping over him again. "Malik?"

"He's well. I sent him and LeFont back to Hastings."

"Hastings?"

"To get your ships and bring them here. A long journey by land would not have been good for you."

He frowned. "It will . . . take him too . . . long."

"No, it won't. He should be here by spring." She stroked his hair back from his face. "And you will not have gained full strength until then."

"Wrong . . ."

"I hope I am. You must prove it to me."

He was too weak to even argue, he realized with disgust. "I will . . . later."

"Do that." She pulled the blanket higher about him and rose to her feet. "But rest now while I go tell Adwen and Alice that you've finally deigned to wake and return to us."

He was drifting off to sleep when he remembered the words that had almost been lost to him in the other news she had given.

Svengard. He was sure he had not mentioned that boyhood debacle in Norway. How had she known. . . .

"Adwen! Alice! He's awake!" Brynn said as she ran into Adwen's bedchamber.

Adwen looked up from her loom. "Why are you so excited? You kept telling me that it was only a matter of time."

"But he took so long. Three weeks . . . I couldn't understand it. I *knew* he was gaining strength." The worry and excitement she had not allowed herself to show Gage was bursting from her. "I should have known he would take longer than usual. What a stubborn man." Brynn snatched her cloak from the hook on the wall. "I can't stay inside. Do you want to take a walk with me?"

"It's snowing outside."

"I don't care. I have to get out. The snow started only a few hours ago. Alice?"

"And skid on those slippery stones in the courtyard? I don't want to have this babe tonight." Alice smiled indulgently. "Go on. Take as long as you like. You haven't left his side since he was wounded. I'll look in on him for you."

"You won't need to do that. He's asleep and won't wake for hours. I won't be long." She left the chamber and ran down the stairs and out the front door. She stopped and took a deep breath. The air was cold and still, the thick drops of snow falling to the earth without a hint of wind. It was nearly twilight and it was a gray-and-white world; the stones of the courtyard were covered with a layer of snow.

Beautiful snow. Beautiful Gwynthal. Beautiful world.

He was awake and back with her again. She felt a surge of happiness so intense, she felt like dancing across the courtyard. Instead, she proceeded more cautiously as she strode toward the drawbridge; Alice was right, there might be ice beneath the snow.

She had almost reached the gate when she saw the prints in the snow.

She stopped, inhaling sharply. Four prints, clear and unmistakable.

Paw prints.

Selbar.

She moved slowly forward, her eyes on the snow, trying to read the wolf's movements. He had come only as far as a few yards inside the gate and then must have sat down in this spot to gaze on the castle. There was a flurry of disturbance in the snow as if he had leapt to his feet, turned, and run back toward the drawbridge. Had that been when he had seen her come out of the castle?

She moved slowly toward the drawbridge. He would not be there, she told herself. It had probably been some fleeting memory that had drawn him to the courtyard, where they had spent so many hours. She must not hope. He did not remember her. He did not trust her. He was probably already deep in the forest with his pack.

She stepped through the gate.

Selbar was standing at the end of the drawbridge, facing the castle, as if waiting for her.

She stopped, staring into those wild golden eyes.

Moments passed while the snow fell softly between them like a veil of years gone by.

"Thank you," she whispered.

Selbar tilted his head at the words. Did he only recognize her voice or did he somehow understand?

He turned and darted into the forest.

For an instant she felt a pang of regret. Then a warm ripple of contentment flowed over her. He had come back to her. She knew it could never be quite the same. Life had changed both of them, but the bond was still there.

Selbar was like Gwynthal, she realized suddenly. She had made the mistake of coming back to both expecting everything to be as it was when she had viewed it through a child's eyes. She must accept the changes in Gwynthal as she had in Selbar. Then, if she was fortunate, someday they would both be fully her own again.

During the next three days Gage did little but eat and sleep and eat again. It was common at this stage of healing, but Brynn was astonished at the strength and stamina he gained with every passing moment. She supposed she should not have been startled; Gage was recovering with the same relentless determination with which he usually confronted life. Gage might well prove her wrong and be fit before Malik returned in the spring.

On the third night after he had first awakened, she

was settling down beside him on his pallet when he asked, "How did you know about Svengard?"

For an instant she didn't know to what he was referring and then remembered the absent remark she had made. "You must have told me."

"I didn't tell you. I would remember. Richard's knife struck me in the back, not the head."

"Can we not speak of this later?"

"No. I need to know. Lately, I've been having very unsettling—I need to know."

"Unsettling what?"

"Tell me."

"You won't like it."

"Tell me."

She sat up again and sighed resignedly. "I couldn't reach you. I had to link with you."

He frowned. "Link? What is that?"

She shrugged helplessly. "I don't know. I've never done it before. I was feeling what you were feeling and it was getting in the way. I couldn't heal you. The only thing I could think to do was to give in to it and—" She stopped.

"What?"

"Be you," she whispered. "I had to be part of you. Only I didn't know—memories."

His eyes widened. "You're saying you—"

"I didn't want to do it. I know it was a terrible intrusion," she said frantically. "It was the only way—"

"You're right, it would be a damnable intrusion . . . if I believed it had happened." He paused. "Prove it to me."

"Svengard," she said. "You said that—"

"Not Svengard. Tell me about Delmas and the stable that night."

She should have known that would be his first thought. "You were angry. You wanted to kill him." She shuddered. "You intended to kill him. You knew he was in the stable. The door was half open and you heard him whimpering as you walked into the stable." She closed her eyes as the ugly memory came flooding back to her. "He was pinned to the wall by the pitchfork. He was begging to be let down. You were tempted to leave him there, but you knew he was dying. You took the end of the pitchfork and jerked it out of the wall. . . ."

"And if I didn't kill him, who did?"

"You suspected Richard. You think Delmas went to him in a rage and Richard killed him and then sought to arrange the aftermath to his own advantage."

"By God, you *do* know."

She opened her eyes and whispered. "I'm sorry I didn't trust you. It won't happen again. I know now you would never lie to me."

"Certainly no one could know me better," Gage said caustically. He looked away from her. "Christ!"

"I told you that you wouldn't like it." She added defensively, "It's not as if I had any desire to know your thoughts and memories. Some of them were very embarrassing."

His gaze shifted back to her face. "Such as?"

Heat flooded her cheeks. "The harlot at the house in Zenvar."

"Oh, my God."

"There was nothing godly about what happened there. I thought what you did with me was wicked, but that was truly sinful."

"Just . . . different." He suddenly started to laugh. "What a predicament. I can't believe it." He shook his head. "Or I wish I didn't believe it."

His anger was leaving him, she realized with relief. It had not been nearly as bad as she had feared. She suggested tentatively, "At least, it was a good thing I learned you had no guilt in Delmas's death."

"Yes."

"And you would have died if I hadn't done it."

"A persuasive argument." He scowled. "But no amount of persuasion is going to make me like this . . . this nakedness."

"I know." She paused. "So you will just have to accept it, as you told me I would have to accept Delmas's death. It took time, but I did it." She added softly, "Because I love you with all my heart."

His scowl disappeared and an instant later he smiled. "Come here," he said softly. "I can't come to you."

Joy surged through her as she lay down beside him and nestled close. "I was afraid you'd be much angrier."

"I would be, except for one circumstance."

"What circumstance?"

His lips brushed her cheek. "It seems I picked up a few memories of my own."

She stiffened. "What?"

"You've lived a most innocuous life compared to my own, but there are still a few things I don't think you'd want anyone to know."

"For instance?" she asked warily.

"Mostly feelings. What a lusty woman you are, Brynn." He chuckled. "For instance, about that incident in Zenvar. I'd wager your response was not so much shock as fascination."

"That's not true. I was most—" She stopped and then admitted reluctantly. "Envious."

"Envy is a terrible sin. When I gain more strength, we will have to remedy it."

"What other memories did you find— No, I won't ask. It's best we don't discuss this."

"Safer, at least."

"It's most disconcerting." She thought about it. "But I'm glad you shared this with me. I was feeling very guilty."

"That damnable burden of guilt again. We'll have to remedy that too. I refuse to have a camel for a wife."

"They truly are most strange-looking creatures." She added tartly, "And after seeing them through your eyes, I don't appreciate being compared to such an ugly beast."

He groaned.

"I'm sorry," she said quickly. "I didn't mean—I know I said we were not to speak of—"

"Shh." He drew her closer. "It is bound to happen."

"You truly believe me?"

"How could I help it?" he said gruffly. "I cannot say I believe in magic, but I believe in you. You are no witch." His lips brushed her temple. "But if there is magic in this world, it is you, Brynn."

She buried her face in his chest, fighting tears, unable to speak. She was no longer alone. She would never be alone again. He had stepped into the circle.

April 10, 1067
Gwynthal

"Brynn!" Gage called impatiently as he entered the hall. "Where in Hades are you?"

"Here!" Brynn marched down the steps. "Though why I should answer to such rudeness I don't—"

"They're here!" He lifted her by the waist and swung her around in a circle. "I saw LeFont coming down the trail. They're only a few miles away. Let's go meet them."

They were there. A wild mixture of emotions flooded Brynn. She had known this moment would come, had thought she was prepared for it. Now she wanted only to run and hide. She pulled away and forced a smile. "You go on. I'll run and tell Adwen and Alice."

He had started to leave but he stopped and whirled to face her. "What's wrong?"

She should have known he would sense her distress even in his own excitement. Since their joining he had become exquisitely sensitive to her every emotion. Yet how could she explain when she was so confused herself? "It's a new—everything will be different."

He searched her expression. "We should have talked about this before." He grabbed her wrist and pulled her up the stairs. "Come on."

"But you wished to go and meet—"

"I can wait." He pulled her down the corridor, into the council chamber, and slammed the door. "Now, tell me what's wrong."

She looked wistfully around the chamber. They had spent so many happy hours there this winter. Peaceful, lazy days, passionate, languid nights. All gone. Well, what had she expected? Even if Malik and LeFont had not arrived, this magical period would have soon ended. Of late, she had noticed Gage's restlessness increasing in pace with his return to health. He was not a man who would long linger in Eden. "I will miss this place when we go."

"So will I." He smiled. "Therefore, I think we must plan to return frequently."

Her eyes widened. "Truly?"

"Why are you so surprised? It's a shame to let a fine castle like this go uninhabited. Of course, we will have to set LeFont to making repairs."

"He won't be pleased with the task." She launched herself into his arms and buried her face in his chest. "I will go with you wherever you wish. We need not—I want you to be happy."

"Then don't try to make me miserable. You know I would not be content if you were yearning for this place." He cradled her face in his hands and looked down at her with a rueful smile. "You've made sure I feel at least a portion of what you feel on every subject."

"I did not mean to intrude. I couldn't help it." She lifted her chin. "Would you rather have died? I did what I had to do to bring you back." She lifted her chin. "And it's just as bad for me. Some of your memories aren't at all good, and now they're my memories. If I didn't force myself to stop and think, sometimes I would act in as barbaric a fashion as you."

"I cannot imagine that circumstance." He brushed his lips across her brow. "But I can see I must guard myself from your wrath."

"Very wise." She blinked back the tears and laid her head on his chest. "It's about time you learned you must be wary of me. It's fortunate for you that I love you."

"I cannot be all you want of me, Brynn," he said in a low voice. "I'm not like your Hevald, who was content to stay here forever. There will always be somewhere I want to see, something I want to do. If you'll be honest with yourself, you'll admit that you wouldn't be content with staying here either. You've been restless yourself of late."

"All my life I've wanted to return here," she protested. "Why should I have changed?"

"I can't answer that for you. You'll have to tell me."

She thought about it. "I have a gift and Gwynthal gives me few chances to use it. The villagers are very healthy and there are no wars here."

"True. It's not every day you'll run across a soldier who is stupid enough to get himself stabbed by an assassin in this peaceful garden."

"And I've been wondering if the reason my mother was willing to leave the island and follow my father was that she felt that same lack."

"It's possible." He stroked her hair. "No place is

perfect. There will always be something missing that we find somewhere else. But we have the good fortune to be complete in ourselves wherever we are."

Good fortune. Wonderful fortune. She laughed shakily. "Heavens, you're clever. It's not enough that you have me agreeing to leave Gwynthal, but now you'd have me believe it's my own idea."

His smile held a hint of mischief. "Why not? A good barter is one in which all sides believe they've won. I refuse to be wed to a martyr." He smile faded. "I want you to be happy, Brynn. What can I do to make it right with you? Would you like our first child to be born here on Gwynthal?"

She looked up at the tapestry, at Hevald, whose wife had never borne him a child. She smiled. "I think we would all like that very much indeed."

A short time later Gage, Brynn, Alice, and Adwen met the column of soldiers as they rode into the courtyard.

Malik was back! Bronze and smiling and handsome as a God. Adwen tried not to let her eagerness show in her expression.

Malik's broad smile lit his face as he caught sight of Gage. "You look well, my friend. Much more robust than when I left this place."

"What news of William?"

"He was crowned King of England on Christmas Day and has since been busily trying to give away all his new land to his followers. If you wish aught from him, I wouldn't linger long in the asking."

"I won't. I plan to set sail next week for England. That should give us ample time to gather provisions for the journey."

Malik turned to Adwen. "And how are you, my lady? In good health, I trust?"

"Good enough." Her voice was uneven and she tried to steady it. "And you?"

"I could not be better than I am at this moment." His expression lit with mischief. "Well, perhaps a little better, but we will go into that later."

She had to stop staring at him. "You grew your beard back."

"I decided to take pity on those less comely than myself."

Sweet heaven, she had missed him. There was no one like him. No one in the world as full of humor and whimsy and gentleness; no one as mad and certainly no one who made her feel the need to reach out and touch, hold. "I'm sure we all are grateful for your kindness."

"Oh, I was not speaking of you. You're almost as beautiful as I am."

She laughed. "I thank you. It makes me feel much—"

"Adwen, come quick!"

Adwen turned to see Brynn hurrying across the courtyard toward Alice, who was being supported by LeFont. The captain's face was even more pale than Alice's.

Adwen muttered an exclamation and started across the courtyard.

"What is it?" Malik asked.

"If you had brains as well as comeliness, you would know," Adwen tossed over her shoulder. "The excitement was too much for her. She's going to have her babe."

Alice's daughter was born the following afternoon, after a nightmare of labor. Several times Adwen thought Alice was going to die or lose the baby. She did neither, and the child came into the world big, healthy, and yelling lustily.

"Is she not beautiful?" Brynn asked softly as she

looked down at the infant cradled in Alice's arms. "It's always such a miracle. . . ."

"I think I . . . love . . . her," Alice said wonderingly as she touched the baby's cheek with a careful finger. "Isn't that strange? All the while I carried her I felt no affection. I thought after she was born I would have an actual dislike for her. I knew I had to do my duty by her, but I didn't think . . . I would care. "

"But that's part of the miracle," Brynn said. "Perhaps the best part."

"Yes." Alice smiled luminously before shifting her gaze to Adwen. "I wonder if . . . would you mind? I must have a name for her. I'd like to call her Adwen."

Adwen looked at her, stunned. "You wish to name her after me?"

"It's a lovely name and you're my friend. If you don't mind—" She stopped, her eagerness fading as a sudden thought occurred to her. "Unless you don't wish your husband's bastard to bear your name."

"Don't be ridiculous." Adwen blinked back the tears. "I was only surprised. I would be honored for your child to bear my name." She swallowed and quickly turned away. "And now I think I'll leave you to rest. I know you must be weary unto—"

She almost ran from the room. She stopped outside the door and leaned against the wall as the tears rained down her face. She should go back into the room; Brynn might need her. Not yet. In a moment she would be strong enough to—

"May I help?" Malik asked. He sat cross-legged on the floor, leaning back against the wall.

"How long have you been here?"

"Only since this morning. I thought you would be too busy to need me until after the babe was born. How is Alice?"

"Tired, happy." She swallowed. "Very happy. She's

going to name the child after me. Isn't that kind of her?"

"Very kind." He rose to his feet. "And it should not make you weep."

"It doesn't—it's only—the little girl is so beautiful." Adwen wiped her eyes on the backs of her hands. "It made me sad. I'm very selfish. I wanted the miracle to be mine."

Malik took her in his arms. "Perhaps someday there will be a miracle for you."

She shook her head. "Alice knows there's no chance of that happening. That's why she gave the child my name. She wanted me not to feel . . . it was very kind of her."

"You break my heart," he said hoarsely. "Marry me, Adwen. Let me try to give you miracles."

She felt a wild burst of pain and pushed him away from her. "I'm not that selfish. I would not saddle you with a barren woman."

"You are blind. How many times must I tell you that I would not blame—"

"You would!"

She had to get away. She turned and ran down the long hall toward the staircase.

"Adwen!"

He was following her, passing her. He stood on the top step, barring her path.

"Get out of my way!"

"Never again." He stared down into her eyes. "Listen to me. I would treasure your child above all things, but there are other miracles in this world. There is laughter and passion and growing old together. There is living day after day with a wife who will love and care for my needs as I will for hers. These are all miracles and I will not be cheated of them. You will marry me, Adwen."

"No."

"Yes."

"And what will you do if I refuse?" she said defiantly.

He tilted his head as if considering the matter. "Toss myself down these stairs?"

Her eyes widened as she looked at the stone floor thirty feet below. "What?"

"If you refuse, my life will be over. What else is left for me?"

"You jest."

"You thought I jested about posting myself on your doorstep at Selkirk."

And about scarring his face with the burning twig. "You would not do it," she whispered.

"Do you dare chance it?"

"No." The tears were suddenly falling again. "No, you madman. I will wed you." She flew into his arms and held him with all her strength. "But you must not regret it. Promise me that you won't regret it later."

"Of course I won't regret it." He held her with loving tenderness as he whispered, "You have my promise, Adwen. No regrets and every miracle imaginable."

"Possible," she amended.

He smiled. "You do not yet know your husband."

Epilogue

"I DON'T KNOW where to put the council table," Brynn said with a frown. "After we bring in the bed, there will be no room for it."

"Throw it out in the stable," Gage said. "It's just a heap of broken rubbish."

"Hevald doesn't think so." Brynn frowned at him. "And neither do I. Don't be disrespectful."

He bowed mockingly. "My apologies to both you and Hevald."

"I'll forgive you when you find a place for the table."

He sighed. "What about the bedchamber down the hall? If that won't be too distant for your Hevald."

"I guess it will have to do."

"You know this is nonsense, of course," Gage said. "There are many bedchambers in this castle. Why have the child in this chamber?"

"Because it is fitting." She turned to the two soldiers waiting patiently by the door. "Take those pieces to the bedchamber down the hall." She watched them remove the table and then stood before Hevald's tapestry. "And because I want to have your son here in this room."

"It may be a daughter." He moved across the room to stand behind her. He slid his arms around her, his hands gently caressing her swollen belly. "We won't know for another two months."

"It will be a son. I *feel* it." She smiled at him over her shoulder. "But would you be disappointed if it's a girl?"

He chuckled. "A dangerous question and one I'd be a fool to answer."

"Would you?"

"I would love her as I do her mother."

"Tell me."

He pretended to think. "Not if you let me teach her swordplay and archery and—"

"I will not!"

"I fear it will be necessary," he teased. "A man needs a strong ally by his side when he goes into battle."

Brynn's laughter faded. "Will you have to go into battle? Is William going to try to take Redfern away from Malik and Adwen?"

"There's always that possibility. He wasn't pleased when I gave Redfern to Malik. The idea of a Saracen holding such a rich plum was not at all popular with his barons."

"You had no use for it when you had Gwynthal and Bellerieve. William gave it to you and it was yours to do with as you wished."

"As long as I keep it mine."

"Adwen was wife of the Saxon who held title to it. Surely that means something."

"Nothing." He frowned. "I'd feel better if Malik and Adwen came back from the East and took possession. LeFont's presence there is a formidable deterrent, but the matter needs to be settled. Once the confrontation is over, we'll have no more trouble."

"He says the Eastern physicians know many things

that we do not," Brynn said. "He's searching for a miracle for Adwen."

"Pray God he finds it."

"I think he will. Happiness itself is a powerful medicine, and I've never seen Adwen so happy." Almost as happy as she was, Brynn thought. No, no one could approach that splendor. "After our babe is born, I'd like to go to them. I want to be with Adwen when she needs me."

"I believe you're beginning to like moving from place to place."

"It's possible." She had found William's court interesting, but she would not be able to bear it for long periods. Bellerieve, on the other hand, was almost as beautiful as Gwynthal, yet so steeped in worldliness that she would constantly be challenged to use her gift. "As long as I can return to Gwynthal."

"Are we not here?" His lips brushed her ear. "I keep my promises, Brynn."

"Yes, you do." She looked up at the tapestry. Was Hevald smiling at her? It was probably a trick of the light or imagination; the entire world seemed to be smiling these days. "I've been thinking. I think we should name our son after him."

"If it is a son."

"I told you he would be. Trust me. Would it be all right with you if we give him his name?"

"Hevald? If you like."

"No, not Hevald. It's too heavy and weighty a name. I've never really liked it. I thought we would call him Arthur."

"But I thought you wanted to name him after Hevald."

"He was known as Arthur when he was a warrior. I told you, he and his warriors shed all the trappings of their old life when they came here."

"Including their names?"

She nodded. "It was to be a new life."

He frowned thoughtfully. "I believe I've heard of this Arthur."

"Of course you have. I told you he was greatly renowned."

"But Britain is not the entire world. What of your ancestor, his chief adviser, Bentar? Did he also change his name?"

She looked at him in surprise. "Yes, of course. He was very loyal. He would do as Hevald wished."

"And what was his name before coming to Gwynthal?"

She leaned back against him, gazing dreamily up at the tapestry of those bygone days and feeling the stirring of new life within her. "Why, his name was Merlin."

An Afterword
from the Author

Arthur of Britain, truth or myth?

In the British Museum there's a bundle of documents dated either 499 or 519 (the date is disputed) in which an entry regarding the Battle of Badon tells of Arthur carrying the cross of Lord Jesus Christ on his shoulders for three days and three nights. Later in the mid-eighth century a Welsh monk, Nennius, compiled what is known as the *Historia Brittoman*; in it Arthur is spoken of as a leader of battles but not a king himself. He's referred to as Arthur the Soldier.

Documented proof may be very scanty regarding the existence of this mysterious warrior, but fables abound. From as early as 1170 the Prior of Tewkesbury wrote: "Who is there, I ask, who does not speak of Arthur the Briton, since he is but little less known to the people of Asia than to the Bretons, as we are informed by pilgrims who return from the Eastern lands?" Troubadours sang of him, storytellers embroidered and glorified his deeds. The legend grew and changed until it became a part of the fabric of our lives.

How many of those fables are based on truth may never be determined. We do know that Arthur was a man able to arouse a passion and imagination that spanned the fourteen centuries from the Dark Ages to our own time.

Now, to my own fable of the Midnight Warrior. Was Gwynthal Camelot? Or was it Avalon, the island of healing, where the monk Geoffrey of Monmouth claimed Arthur was taken to heal from a death wound? I leave the choice to you. Every fable should be open to interpretation, imagination . . . and dreams.

ABOUT THE AUTHOR

IRIS JOHANSEN has more than twenty-seven million copies of her books in print and is the *New York Times* bestselling author of *Stalemate, Killer Dreams, On the Run, Countdown, Blind Alley, Firestorm, Fatal Tide, Dead Aim,* and more. She lives near Atlanta, Georgia.

Coming Soon from Bantam Dell ...

Two sizzling romances from

Iris Johansen:

The richly seductive

LION'S BRIDE

available August 2008

and its never-before-published sequel

THE TREASURE

available December 2008

Read on for a sneak peek of

THE TREASURE ...

#1 *NEW YORK TIMES* BESTSELLING AUTHOR

IRIS JOHANSEN

THE *Treasure*

THE TREASURE
Coming from Bantam in December 2008

May 3, 1196
Fortress of Maysef
Nosairi Mountains
Syria

His power was waning, fading like that bloodred
sun setting behind the mountains.

Jabbar Al Nasim's fists clenched with fury as he
gazed out at the sun sinking on the horizon. It should
not be. It made no sense that he should be so afflicted.
Weakness was for those other fools, not for him.

Yet he had always known it would come. It had
even come for Sinan, the Old Man of the Mountain.
But he had always been stronger than the old man in
both mind and spirit. Sinan had bent before the yoke,
but Nasim had prepared for it.

Kadar.

"You sent for me, master?"

He turned to see Ali Balkir striding along the battlements toward him. The man's voice was soft, hesitant, and he could see the fear in his face. Nasim felt a jolt of fierce pleasure as he realized the captain had not detected any loss of power. Well, why should he? Nasim had always been master here, in spite of what outsiders thought. Sinan might have been the King of Assassins, feared by kings and warriors alike, but Nasim had been the one who had guided his footsteps. Everyone here at the fortress knew and groveled at his feet.

And they'd continue to grovel. He would not let this monstrous thing happen to him.

Balkir took a hurried step back as he saw Nasim's expression. "Perhaps I was mistaken. I beg your forgiveness for intrud—"

"No, stay. I have a task for you."

Balkir drew a relieved breath. "Another attack on the Frankish ships? Gladly. I brought you much gold from my last journey. I will bring you even more this—"

"Be silent. I wish you to return to Scotland where you left Kadar Ben Arnaud and the foreigners. You are to tell him nothing of what has transpired here. Do not mention me. Tell him only that Sinan is claiming his price. Bring him to me."

Balkir's eyes widened. "Sinan? But Sinan is—"

"Do you question me?"

"No, never." Balkir moistened his lips. "But what if he refuses?"

Balkir was terrified, Nasim realized, and not of failing him. Nasim had forgotten that Balkir was at the fortress at the time Kadar underwent his training; Balkir knew how adept Kadar was in all the dark arts. More adept than any man Nasim had ever known, and Kadar was only a boy of ten and four when he came to the mountain. How proud Sinan had been of him. What plans he had made for the two of them. He had never realized Nasim had plans of his own for Kadar.

All wasted when Kadar had left the dark path and rejected Sinan to live with the foreigners. What a fool the Old Man had been to let him go.

But it was not too late. What Sinan had lost, Nasim could reclaim.

If Kadar did not die as the others had died.

Well, if he died, he died. Kadar was only a man; it was the power that was important.

"He won't refuse," Nasim said. "He gave Sinan his word in exchange for the lives of the foreigners."

"What if he does?"

"You *are* questioning me," Nasim said with dangerous softness.

Balkir turned pale. "No, master. Of course he won't refuse. Not if you say he won't. I only—"

"Be gone." Nasim waved his hand. "Set sail at once."

Balkir nodded jerkily and backed away from him. "I will bring him. Whether or not he wishes to come I will force—"

The words cut off abruptly as Nasim turned his back on him. The man was only trying to gain respect in his eyes. He would have no more chance against Kadar if he tried to use force than he would against Nasim, and he probably knew it.

But he wouldn't have to use force. Kadar would come. Not only because of his promise but because he would know what would result if he didn't. Sinan had spared the lives of Lord Ware, his woman, Thea, and the child Selene and given them all a new life in Scotland. Nasim had permitted the foolishness because he had wanted to keep Kadar safe until it was time to use him.

But no one would be more aware than Kadar that the safety Sinan had given could always be taken away.

Kadar had shown a baffling softness toward his friend Lord Ware and a stranger bond with the child Selene. Such emotions were common on the bright path, but Nasim had taught Kadar better. It seemed fitting that he be caught in his master's noose because he'd ignored his teachings.

The fortress gate was opening and Balkir rode through it. He kicked his horse into a dead run down the mountain. He would be in Hafir in a few days and set sail as soon as he could stock his ship, the *Dark Star*.

Nasim turned back to the setting sun. It had descended almost below the horizon now, darkness was closing in. But it would return tomorrow, blasting all before it with its power.

And so would Nasim.

His gaze shifted north toward the sea. Kadar was across that sea in that cold land of Scotland, playing at being one of them, the fools, the bright ones. But it would be just a matter of months before he would be here. Nasim had waited five years. He could wait a little longer. Yet an odd eagerness was beginning to replace his rage and desperation. He wanted him here *now*.

He felt the power rising within him and he closed his eyes and sent the call forth.

"Kadar."

August 4, 1196

Montdhu, Scotland

"She's being very foolish." Thea frowned as she watched Selene across the great hall. "I don't like this, Ware."

"Neither does Kadar," Ware said cheerfully as he

took a sip of his wine. "I'm rather enjoying it. It's interesting to see our cool Kadar disconcerted."

"Will it also be interesting if Kadar decides to slaughter that poor man at whom she's smiling?" Thea asked tartly. "Or Lord Kenneth, who she partnered in the last country dance?"

"Yes." He smiled teasingly at her. "It's been far too peaceful here for the last few years. I could use a little diversion."

"Blood and war are not diversions except to warriors like you." Her frown deepened. "And I thought you very happy here at Montdhu. You did not complain."

He lifted her hand and kissed the palm. "How would I dare with such a termagant of a wife."

"Don't tease. Have you been unhappy?"

"Only when you robbed me of craftsmen for my castle so that you could have them build a ship for your silk trade."

"I needed that ship. What good is it to produce fine silks if you can't sell them? It wasn't sensible to—" She shook her head. "You know I was right, and you have your castle now. It's as fine and strong as you could want. Everyone at the feast tonight has told you they have never seen a more secure fortress."

His smile faded. "And we might well have need of our fortress soon."

She frowned. "Have you heard news from the Holy Land?"

He shook his head. "But we walk a fine line, Thea. We've been lucky to have these years to prepare."

Ware was still looking over his shoulder, Thea thought sadly. Well, who could blame him? They had fled the wrath of the Knights Templar to come to this land, and if the Knights found out that Ware was not dead, as they thought, they would be unrelenting in their persecution. Ware and Thea had almost been captured before their journey started. It had been Kadar who had bargained with Sinan, the head of the assassins, to lend them a ship to take them to Scotland. But that was the past, and Thea would not have Ware moody tonight when he had so much to celebrate.

"We're not lucky, we're intelligent. And the Knights Templar are foolish beyond belief if they think you would betray them. It makes me angry every time I think of it. Now drink your wine and enjoy this evening. We've made a new life and everything is fine."

He lifted his cup. "Then why are you letting the fact that your sister is smiling prettily at Lord Douglas upset you?"

"Because Kadar hasn't taken his eyes off her all evening." Her gaze returned to her sister. Selene's pale-gold silk gown made her dark red hair glow with hidden fires, and her green eyes shone with vitality—and recklessness. The little devil knew exactly what she was doing, Thea thought crossly. Selene was impulsive at times, but this was not such an occasion. Her every action tonight was meant to provoke Kadar. "And I didn't invite the entire countryside to see your splendid new castle so that she could expose them to mayhem."

"Tell her. Selene loves you. She won't want you unhappy."

"I will." She rose to her feet and strode down the hall toward the great hearth, before which Selene was holding court. Ware was right: Selene might be willful, but she had a tender heart. She would never intentionally hurt anyone she loved. All Thea had to do was confront her sister, express her distress, and the problem would be solved.

Maybe.

"Don't stop her, Thea."

She glanced over her shoulder to see Kadar behind her. He had been leaning against the far pillar only seconds ago, but she was accustomed to the swift silence of his movements.

"Stop her?" She smiled. "I don't know what you mean."

"And don't lie to me either." Kadar's lips tightened. "I'm a little too bad-tempered tonight to deal in pretense." He took her arm and led her toward the nearest corner of the hall. "And you've never done it well. You're burdened with a pure and honest soul."

"And I suppose you're the devil himself."

He smiled. "Only a disciple."

"Nonsense."

"Well, perhaps only half devil. I've never been able to convince you of my sinful character. You never wanted to see that side of me."

"You're kind and generous and our very dear friend."

"Oh, yes, which proves what good judgment you have."

"And arrogant, stubborn, and with no sense of humility."

He inclined his head. "But I've the virtue of patience, my lady, which should outweigh all my other vices."

"Stop mocking." She turned to face him. "You're angry with Selene."

"Am I?"

"You know you are. You've been watching her all evening."

"And you've been watching me." One side of his lips lifted in a half smile. "I was wondering whether you'd decide to attack me or Selene."

"I have no intention of attacking anyone." She stared directly into his eyes. "Do you?"

"Not at the moment. I've just told you how patient I am."

Relief surged through her. "She doesn't mean anything. She's just amusing herself."

"She means something." He glanced back toward

the hearth. "She means to torment and hurt me and drive me to the edge." His tone was without expression. "She does it very well, doesn't she?"

"It's your fault. Why don't you offer for her? You know Ware and I have wanted the two of you to wed for this past year. Selene is ten and seven. It's past time she had a husband."

"I'm flattered you'd consider a humble bastard like myself worthy of her."

"You are not flattered. You know your own worth."

"Of course, but the world would say it was a poor match. Selene is a lady of a fine house now."

"Only because you helped us escape from the Holy Land and start again. Selene was a slave in the House of Nicholas and only a child when you bought her freedom as a favor to me. She was destined to spend her life embroidering his splendid silks and being given to his customers for their pleasure. You saved her, Kadar. Do you think she would ever look at another man if you let her come close to you?"

"Don't interfere, Thea."

"I *will* interfere. You know better. She's worshipped you since she was a child of eleven."

"Worship? She's never worshipped me. She knows me too well." He smiled. "You may not believe in my devilish qualities, but she does. She's always known what I am. Just as I've always known what she is."

"She's a hardworking, honest, loving woman who needs a husband."

"She's more than that. She's extraordinary, the light in my darkness. And she's still not ready for me."

"Ready? Most women her age have children already."

"Most women haven't suffered as she suffered. It scarred her. I can wait until she heals."

"But can she?" Thea glanced toward the hearth again. Oh, God, Selene was no longer there.

"It's all right. She and Lord Douglas just left the hall and went out into the courtyard."

How had he known that? Sometimes it seemed Kadar had eyes in the back of his head.

"Kadar, don't—"

He bowed. "If you'll excuse me, I'll go and bring her back."

"Kadar, I *won't* have violence this night."

"Don't worry, I won't shed blood on the fine new rushes you put down on the floor." He moved toward the courtyard. "But the stones of the courtyard wash up quite nicely."

"Kadar!"

"Don't follow me, Thea." His voice was soft but inflexible. "Stay out of it. This is what she wants, what she's tried to goad me to all evening. Don't you realize that?"

Where was Kadar? Selene wondered impatiently. She had been out here a good five minutes and he still hadn't appeared. She didn't know how long she could keep Lord Douglas from taking her back to the hall. He was a boring, stodgy young man and had been shocked when she'd suggested going out to the courtyard. "It's a fine night. I do feel much better now that I've had a breath of air."

Lord Douglas looked uneasy. "Then perhaps we should go back inside. Lord Ware would not like us being out here alone. It's not fitting."

"In a moment." Where *was* he? She had felt his gaze on her all evening. He would have seen—

"The Saracen was watching us," Lord Douglas said. "I'm sure he will tell Lord Ware."

"Saracen?" Her gaze flew to his face. "What Saracen?"

"Kadar Ben Arnaud. Isn't he a Saracen? That's what they call him."

"Who are 'they'?"

He shrugged. "Everyone."

"Kadar's mother was Armenian, his father a Frank."

He nodded. "A Saracen."

She should be amused that he had put Kadar, who could never be labeled, in a tight little niche. She was not amused. She fiercely resented the faintly patronizing note in his voice. "Why not call him a Frank like his father? Why a Saracen?"

"He just seems . . . he's not like us."

No more than a panther was like a sheep or a glittering diamond like a moss-covered rock, she thought furiously. "Kadar belongs here. My sister and her husband regard him as a brother."

"Surely not." He looked a bit shocked. "Though I'm sure he's good at what he does. These Saracens are supposed to be fine seamen, and he does your silk trading, doesn't he?"

She wanted to slap him. "Kadar does more than captain our ship. He's a part of Montdhu. We're proud and fortunate to have him here."

"I didn't mean to make you—"

She lost track of what he was saying.

Kadar was coming.

She had known he would follow her, but Selene still smothered a leap of excitement as she caught sight of him in the doorway. He was moving slowly, deliberately, almost leisurely down the stairs. This was not good. That wasn't the response she wanted from him. She took a step closer to Lord Douglas and swayed. "I believe I still feel a little faint."

He instinctively put a hand on her shoulder to steady her. "Perhaps I should call the lady Thea."

"No, just stay—"

"Good evening, Lord Douglas." Kadar was coming toward them. "I believe it's a little cool out here for Selene. Why don't you go fetch her cloak?"

"We were just going in," Lord Douglas said quickly. "Lady Selene felt a little faint and we—"

"Faint?" Kadar's brows lifted as he paused beside them. "She appears quite robust to me."

He's not like us, Douglas had said.

No, he wasn't like any of these men who had come to honor Ware tonight. He was like no one Selene had ever met. Now, standing next to heavyset, red-faced Lord Douglas, the differences were glaringly apparent. Kadar's dark eyes dominated a bronze, comely face that could reflect both humor and intelligence. He was tall, his powerful body deceptively lean, with a grace and confidence the other man lacked. But the differences were not only on the surface. Kadar was as deep and unfathomable as the night sky, and it was no wonder these simple fools could not understand how exceptional he was.

"She was ill," Lord Douglas repeated.

"But I'm sure she feels better now." Kadar paused. "So you may remove your hand from her shoulder."

Selene felt a surge of fierce satisfaction. This was better. Kadar's tone was soft, but so was the growl of a tiger before it pounced.

Evidently Lord Douglas didn't miss the threat. He snatched his hand away as if burned. "She was afraid she would—"

"Selene is afraid of nothing." He smiled at Selene. "Though she should be."